WI

MW00877191

## Lee Wardlow

This book is a work of fiction. Names, characters, places and incidents are the product of the author's imagination or are used factiously. Any resemblance to actual events, locales, or persons living or dead is coincidental.

## Dedication

My Brother Ryan.  He's larger than life to me. I love you with all my heart.

## Chapter One

### Adam

September was cooler than it had been for some time. We were all in short sleeved knit shirts now but soon sweatshirts would be required even with the bonfire. We were having a barbeque for our friends at the farm. A pig roasted over a blazing fire on a pit that we had pulled out of the barn. It hadn't been used since Joey and I graduated from high school.

Joey had started Fall Quarter at school so there were times when Betsy was working that Joy and I were alone. With Pa dating Mandy we couldn't hide at the farm behind him like we once had. She was married to my best friend. Had been for nearly seven months now. I had to remind myself frequently that she was no longer mine even though I could see the temptation in her own eyes.

Joy finally caved and started medication after our conversation at the July 4th town celebration. Her words, *I love you Adam Moore. I probably always will* still taunted me especially when I was forced to be alone with her. Joy was the love of my life.

Betsy was the only thing that made life easier. She was loyal. She was strong. Betsy was beautiful with her long black hair and her big clear blue eyes. A man should get lost in those blue eyes of hers if someone else's green eyes weren't always getting in the way. I wasn't going to let Betsy down again though.

When I was so low after Joy turned me away only Pa and Betsy had picked me up. I knew Joy was hurting too. I could see it. It was killing me but I couldn't do anything about it. They both tried to convince me to talk to Joy to try to change her mind but I hadn't done anything then when I had the opportunity. Now she was married to Joey.

I knew what she was doing because I knew Joy. She wanted to be sure she didn't change her mind. She wasn't strong like she used to be. Since losing her mother and the baby Joy was shattered. Joy couldn't bear the thought of hurting Joey and Betsy.

Joy was so broken over losing our baby she wasn't thinking straight and I had let her go. Last July when she told me how bad she really was I wanted to take her in my arms and tell her it would be okay that I hadn't stopped loving her either and I would somehow make it better but I looked around us and saw Betsy then I saw Joey and I knew that I couldn't. I didn't have the right. I knew she wasn't mine anymore to comfort and console. I said the only thing I could. **I won't let you give up on yourself** and I let her know she wasn't taking away my happiness with Betsy by hurting herself. That had seemed to reach her in the dark hole that was consuming her.

Today Joy looked better. Her eyes although not filled with the sparkle that once had consumed her beautiful green eyes were not hollow and empty. She wasn't trying to hide behind sunglasses so we wouldn't see her pain. Pa was standing next to her with Mandy on his other side. He had an arm around each of them. They were laughing. Her laughter didn't quite reach her eyes but she was definitely doing better.

Joey was standing by the pig roasting on the spit. Always the life of the party. Beer in hand. Now he seemed to have some control over himself or he would be in the doghouse with Joy. I was where I usually was. Off by myself sitting in a lawn chair watching all the mayhem. Taking it all in. I was quiet. Always had been. I learned by watching them. I saw a lot.

Joy walked over to the picnic table where Betsy was rearranging things, covering some dishes to keep flies out. Dusk was settling over the farm. The sky turning a brilliant dusky blue with streaks of orange and pink. I watched as Joy turned Betsy towards her. My two favorite girls were talking. Their heads were bent towards each other whispering conspiratorially. Betsy looked tired.

Betsy was wearing blue jeans today tight as usual, a white tee shirt and a black hoodie. Joy was wearing similar clothes. Their hair was pulled up in a ponytail. Neither wore much make-up if any at all. Joy rubbed her hands up and down Betsy's arms. I wondered what was going on that I didn't know.

Joy took Betsy's hand and they started walking away from everyone. After everything we had been through they were still the best of friends. I wasn't sure how that had happened but I was happy that they were.

"Where are you going ladies?" I called over my shoulder.

Joy turned her head towards me and winked. "For a walk Adam. To get some peace."

I wrinkled my brow. Something was definitely up.

**Joy**

I held Betsy's hand pulling her away from the party. We walked through the pastures. Nosy Adam always seeing more than he should asking where we were going. Betsy wanted to talk to me alone.

Like when we were little girls clinging to each other when something was wrong. Me hurt because my father had taken a belt to me or her hurt because no one at home paid attention to her.

Adam belonged to her now but I still hurt when I thought of them together. Like him, I buried the feelings I had for him deep inside me where the pain was only a distant ache not a crushing burn. It is what we had to do. It is what was necessary to survive. Had I made the right decision? My shrink would say no. I couldn't live with that answer so I refused to answer the question at all if only in my mind.

Betsy and I walked a while to the clearing in the woods. We were quiet holding each other's hand still. I sensed she needed me. I followed her or I led her I guess was the better description since I knew these woods better than her. I opened the brush that led to the pool of water where Adam and I first made love. A time that seemed so long ago it was just a memory in my mind like a dream. I had not been here since that day but suddenly wanted Bets to see it. I sensed that she needed the peace that it would bring her.

Thorns stuck my hand. I released Betsy long enough to pull them from my hand. I took her hand again and we walked further. I could hear the trickle of water as it cascaded over the rocks into the pool below. What would I feel when I saw the water, the rock where Adam had taken my virginity? This might have been a mistake. My stomach began to do flip flops in nervous anticipation.

Betsy released my hand again. Her mouth formed a perfect O as she slid up to the water's edge. She dropped to her knees running her fingers through the water creating a ripple on the surface much like I had when Adam brought me here.

"God this is beautiful," she said.

"I know. Isn't it?" I agreed.

I sat down beside her leaning back on the palms of my hands enjoying the peace of the woods. A rustle of leaves from an animal scurrying through. An owl hooting in the distance. Crickets singing their sweet song.

"What's up Betsy?" I asked.

She gazed at me long and hard. She had something on her mind. Something she didn't want to tell me but she had to. Something that was going to be painful for me to hear. I could see it on her face.

"A condom broke Joy. I'm pregnant."

Wow. Holy fuck...just wow. My heart tripped on a beat or two. I looked out over the water. Calming myself before a panic attack started upsetting my friend who needed me.

"Have you told Adam?" My voice was soft and low.

Tears formed in her eyes. "Joy, he hasn't even told me that he loves me."

I gazed at her. Our eyes locked. I knew what she was thinking. *He hasn't told me loves me because he's still in love with you.*

I stood and grabbed her hand. "Get your clothes off girl."

"What the fuck?" She said. "You've lost your mind."

I began stripping out of my clothes tossing them behind me. Naked in front of Betsy something she was used to with me I dove head first into the pool of water. The cold taking my breath away. The cold stripping me of the pain that this pregnancy would definitely cause me but I somehow had to bury for Betsy's sake. My head broke through the surface with a loud gasp as the air squeezed out of my lungs desperately.

"Fuck this is cold," I gasped.

Betsy looking uncertain was standing in her underwear. "I told you."

"Get your ass in here," I shouted.

She took off her panties and bra and with a heavy sigh she jumped in. Betsy was five feet from me when her head broke through the surface with a loud whoop of *fuck.* I was treading water. Dark had started to fall around the pool. Moonlight would soon dance upon the surface of the water as the nighttime sky was crystal clear.

Her teeth were chattering. "Do you want to tell me why we did this?"

"Don't you feel alive Bets?"

"I feel fucking cold," she replied.

I laughed at her. She had no sense of adventure. "When we go back you need to talk to Adam. Tell him. I will hold your hand if you want. Nothing can be worse than this cold. Right?"

We were close now only a foot separated us.

She shook her head at me. "You're crazy. That isn't really fair of me to ask that of you."

I snorted. "After everything the two of you have done for me I think all is fair."

"Are you okay?" She asked me. Her beautiful blue eyes were seeking the truth.

"I'm fine right now," I replied honestly.

I didn't know exactly how I would be as Betsy's belly started to swell with Adam's baby reminding me of what I had lost.

### Joey

What the fuck had those two been up to? I could see the girls walking back to the farm. As they got closer to me I could see that their hair was wet. Where had they gone?

Joy walked right up to me. Her hair was damp. She cuddled against me soaking my shirt. I kissed her forehead and then looked down at her. Her beautiful green eyes looking soft and sad. She smiled then hiding the hint of sadness. Where the fuck had she been?

I had my sixth beer in hand. Did she know that? Was she keeping count? I knew Joy didn't like me drinking. I wouldn't let it get out of hand tonight. I couldn't not drink with all the boys here. Only Adam didn't give a shit what others thought. The beer helped me relax. It helped me put my demons to rest.

Adam joined Betsy by the pit. He looked just as perplexed by the state of the girls as I was. Betsy wrapped her arm around Adam's waist. I heard him ask if she was all right. I didn't hear her response. She started walking towards the barn taking Joy with her. What the fuck was that about?

### Betsy

I am terrified. I've been in love with Adam for months now, since we started sleeping together after Joy broke it off with him. At first I tried to convince him to work it out with Joy but he wouldn't do it. I tried to convince her to not make hasty decisions but she wouldn't listen then I just gave up and allowed things with Adam and me to progress.

I know Adam cares about me. He is tender and caring but he doesn't love me. I know deep down Adam still loves Joy. I went for a walk with Joy tonight to tell her about the baby because I was concerned about her reaction. I didn't know how Joy would take the news. Surprisingly she took the news well. My girl was supportive and sweet, caring of me and my needs. I was shocked and overwhelmed with love for her.

Besides freaking jumping into the fucking cold water which might have been her way of avoiding it I think she handled it pretty well. She told me she would hold my hand while we told Adam. The party is probably not the best place to tell him but I need to do it quickly. She convinced me of that. So I grabbed her hand and his hand and we were walking towards the barn door leaving Joey looking at us like we were lunatics. Sometimes, that is exactly what we were.

"What exactly is going on?" Adam asked gazing down at us.

She didn't let me down.  No matter how bad it might be hurting her Joy was standing stoic by my side holding tightly to my hand.  The light in the barn was dim which should have made it easier to tell him.  I couldn't see his face so well.  I wouldn't be able to see the emotion on his face when I told him.

"Adam Bets has something she needs to tell you," Joy said softly.  She wasn't looking at him and her grip tighter on my hand encouraging me to spit it out.

The words felt like rocks in my mouth.  I looked at Joy wanting her to tell him for me.  Her gaze locked on mine.

"Bets what is wrong?" He asked.  "I knew you two were up to something before you went on your walk."

His eyes, those big beautiful dark eyes were penetrating and unnerving.  I started to cry.

"She's pregnant Adam." Joy said the words so softly I wasn't sure he heard them.

I looked at Joy.  She squeezed my hand.  I found the courage to look at him.  He ran his hand through his hair.

"When the condom broke," he finally said.

I nodded.

"I think I should leave you two alone," Joy said.

I wouldn't release her hand.  I needed her here.  Her presence comforting me as I had comforted her.  I wasn't sure what he was thinking or feeling.  Adam was good at masking his emotions just like Joy.  They hid behind their high walls well when necessary.

He took our hands apart so that he could hold mine in his.  Joy stood beside me uncomfortably.  I could see her dancing from one foot to another.  I should let her leave but Adam still hadn't said anything.

"What do you want to do Betsy?"

"What do you mean?" Joy and I asked at the same time.

Both Joy and I looked at him pretty quickly questioning what Adam was asking of me.

He seemed even more troubled. "I can't do this with Joy here. Please can we talk alone?"

"I think that is a good idea," she agreed.

I had tears in my eyes as she walked away. Her head down looking at her feet. I hadn't wanted to cause her pain. Adam caressed the palm of my hand with his thumb.

"Betsy I meant do you want to get married?"

The breath I had been holding whooshed out of me. Did I want to marry Adam? I wanted Adam to love me. I wanted Adam to look at me the way he did Joy when he thought no one was looking. I looked at our hands now intertwined. His big thumbs caressing my palms. Adam was sweet and kind. He was loyal to me but did he love me? He cared for me I knew.

"I don't know Adam," I honestly told him.

He seemed taken by surprise. Adam cupped my face with his hand. His eyes were looking into mine, drawing me in. I couldn't hold his gaze. I had to look away from him.

"What is it Betsy?"

## Chapter Two

### Joy

I nearly ran from the barn before the two of them started talking seriously. My heart slamming against my ribcage. I went straight to Joey and wrapped myself around him seeking comfort from him unable to tell him why. He looked down at me with a look that was similar to the one he had as the three of us went into the barn.

"Everything okay?" he asked me. His hand patting my butt intimately. I shook my head affirmative and looked into the fire.

He drained the can of beer in his hand. I settled my body against his back his arm around my waist holding me tightly to him. It was minutes later that I saw out of the corner of my eye Betsy walking from the barn alone. Her head was down. She went straight to the house and inside. My eyes followed her. I turned my head slightly still no sign of Adam.

My hand laid on top of Joey's resting at my waist. He tilted his head towards mine and kissed my cheek. His full lips warm and wet against my face. The faint smell of alcohol on his breath. I closed my eyes. Adam's face flitted before my mind's eye. I cursed myself. He belonged to Betsy. She was pregnant with his child. I belonged to Joey. Would it never stop?

"Can I talk to you Joy?" Adam's voice jolted me out of my reverie.

I opened my eyes. Adam's troubled face appeared before my own. I sighed softly as I pulled away from Joey and started to follow Adam. Joey pulled me back into his arms. His lips covered mine possessively. His tongue dove between mine caressing my mouth. Then he released me just as quickly.

I followed Adam to the lawn chairs scattered on the outer edge of the circle where most everyone was gathered. It was somewhat private. Away from the fire it was getting cool. My teeth were chattering. Adam took off his sweatshirt offering it to me. I put it over my head dropping the shirt into place. I looked over and saw Joey watching us with interest.

"What was that?" He asked.

I looked at Adam with question in my eyes.

What?" I asked him.

"The kiss. Like he's marking his territory? Soon he will be pissing on you." He sounded angry.

"Adam," I said softly not really scolding but sort of. "Are you all right?" I asked tenderly laying my hand on his arm loving the feel of his muscles and strength even if I shouldn't. "Where did Betsy go?"

"She went inside to lay down for a while. She said she's tired. I don't know if I'm all right. I asked her if she wanted to get married."

I wasn't surprised that Adam was being honorable with Betsy.

"What did she say?" I asked my voice low.

He was looking at my hand touching his arm. I should move it but I didn't. "She said I don't know."

*What?*

"Adam why did she said that?" I asked surprised by Betsy's reaction. This should be exactly what she wanted.

He looked from where my hand touched his arm to my eyes. Our gazes locked on each other. "I don't know if you want me to answer that," he said.

"Oh," I replied knowing what my friend was thinking. "She thinks you still love me," I said without thinking of the implications of my words spoken out loud.

His gaze went dark. I finally broke the connection. I looked over to the fire where Joey stood another beer in hand. I had missed him getting that one. How many did that make?

"It's hard for her Joy. She knows us both well," Adam finally said.

My head turned slowly back towards him.

"What do you mean Adam?"

"Dammit I mean that our feelings haven't changed for each other. You know that. I know that. She knows that. Joey for some insane reason refuses to see it."

Adam was now looking at Joey instead of me. My gaze traveled back towards Joey as well. Mr. Goodtime. Life of the party. Everyone loved Joey. Luke was slapping him on the back teasing him about something. Luke stepped between Joey and us blocking our view of him. Mandy moved in beside Luke. He wrapped her arm around Luke's waist. Without thought, he hugged her in return and kissed her temple. My eyes went back to Adam. His head snapped back towards mine.

"Adam how do you feel about Betsy?" I asked him wanting his honesty.

"How do you feel about Joey?" He asked.

I hated it when he did that to me. Trying to turn the tables. Afraid of just being honest.

"Fuck Adam just be honest with me. Tell me what is in your heart for once."

He was angry now. His big dark eyes blazing hurt and furious with me when he turned them on me.

"Fuck Joy I was honest with you when I said our feelings haven't changed and she knows. What more do you want from me?"

I smiled a sad smile at Adam. "What do you feel for her Adam? She's pregnant with your child. What do you feel for her?" I was adamant that he get this out in words that made sense to both of us.

"You know that I care for her. I would say the way you care for Joey?"

He looked to me confirmation. I looked away from him to Joey, my husband. I could barely see him through the throng of people gathered around the fire and him. All laughing and having a good time.

"I feel loyalty towards her. She helped me through my darkest time when you kicked me out of your life."

My eyes traveled back to his.

"I was so fucking careful always using a condom."

"Maybe it's fate Adam kicking you in the ass."

He laughed a disheartening sound.

"Adam, did you think you could date her forever?"

"No."

"Then what?"

"I don't know. We are young. I wasn't expecting this in my early twenties."

I touched his arm again and his eyes dropped to where I touched him. I took my hand away and he took it back. His hand covering mine where it rested on his arm.

"Do you want me to talk to her?"

"I guess."

I rose from my chair and started walking towards the farmhouse not realizing that Adam was following me. At the steps to the porch he touched my shoulder halting my progress. I turned towards him wondering what he wanted now. He looked over his shoulder at our friends, his father, my husband, his best friend, Joey Bonds. He turned back to me and asked something I never thought he would.

"Do you still love me?'

"Adam why would you ask that? Especially now?"

"Just answer the damned question. For once just answer the damned question." He sounded tortured.

I gazed into his face. "It won't make you feel better Adam. We have to stop torturing ourselves."

"Answer me dammit."

"Why?"

"I'm scared Joy. I need your answer."

I touched his face tenderly. I looked over his shoulder. Able to do so because I was standing on the bottom step and he was standing on the ground. Joey was watching us.

"Adam I will always love you," I whispered the words softly never taking my eyes from my husband. His breath caught in his chest. I heard it but I still didn't take my eyes from Joey. "I think of you almost every day. Sometimes when Joey is making love to me it's your face I see. That love is how I get through the day. I made those choices for him. For you and for Betsy. So now we have to help Betsy through this like you both helped me. I'm going inside to talk to her. Go talk to Joey. He's watching us"

Adam looked over his shoulder automatically. Then he looked back at me. His face anguished.

"Adam I told you it wouldn't make you feel better."

"I needed to hear it Joy," he said his voice as anguished as his face.

"And it's tearing your heart out Adam. I know you."

"Like I know you."

"Please Adam. Let me go to Betsy."

He stepped back. I turned towards the house and stepped up onto the porch. At the door ancient and beautiful, the original door that was built with the house my hand touching the etched glass I turned towards Adam who was still standing in the grass beneath the stairs.

"Go Adam."

He ran his hands through his hair frustrated. Still tearing his heart out. Why had I made it harder telling him what he wanted to hear? Why hadn't I kept my thoughts and feelings to myself? I went through the door leaving him standing there. Inside I saw him finally turn and walk to the fire where the others were having a good time.

I ran up the stairs. At the room that Betsy and I had shared I rested my forehead against the door. I took a deep breath. My palms resting against the wood knowing she was inside and she was upset. I knew Betsy. She needed me. She had been there for me when I was at my lowest. Another deep breath and I opened the door.

Betsy was laying on her side facing away from me. Her long hair was down now fanning over the pillow in strands of black hair so dark they glistened with hues of midnight blue. When I opened the door and stepped into the darkened room only the moonlight shining through the room was giving any light. She turned over to see who was entering.

"Hey Bets," I said softly.

"Hi," she responded rolling completely until she faced me.

I climbed onto the bed facing her. Our faces were no more than inches apart. I reached out and touched her cheek.

"Adam told me," I said.

A tear ran down her cheek.

I wiped it away with my thumb.

"What do you want me to say?"

"You love him. You want to marry him perhaps?"

A sob caught in her throat. "I want him to want to marry me Joy. Can you understand that? I don't want to trap him."

"I think he's scared Bets but after seeing me miscarry. All the blood and pain. Who wouldn't be? But I don't think he feels trapped. He's confused by your reaction." I was being honest.

"I want him to tell me he loves me. Is that so much to ask?' She cried.

I put my arm around her and hugged her. No it wasn't so much to ask of her boyfriend of nearly a year.

"Have you told him how you feel?"

She snorted. I took that as no. She wouldn't not when he had his walls built up so high around his heart protecting it after I had shredded it.

"Betsy, you're going to have a baby. You have to think about that first."

"I don't suppose you would have one with me?"

I stared at her like she had lost her mind.

"That is not happening. I feel stronger than I have in months but I'm not ready. I will do what you need for me to do to get you through this but I'm not having a baby with Joey. He isn't ready."

She laughed then.

"Jeez fuck Betsy. Think what you are asking?"

She laughed even harder. Then the subject of what we were laughing about waltzed through the door without knocking. He slipped into bed behind me wrapping his arm around my waist. He snuggled against my back and nuzzled my neck.

"What are you two doing up here?"

I looked over my shoulder and had my lips captured in a searing kiss.

"Do I need to leave the room?" Betsy asked with mock disgust tinging her voice.

Joey's arm reached across my body and pulled her closer to mine crushing her against me. She tried to pull away but he held her tight.

"I've fantasized about a threesome with the two of you," he teased.

I rolled my eyes at Betsy. She looked horrified. "Joey how much have you had to drink tonight?" I asked with disgust.

He just roared with laughter.

"Let Betsy go," I ordered.

He laughed again his voice soft and sexy. Damn him. He released her so she could scoot back into her own space. Her own safe territory. I rolled over and gave Joey a shove. Catching him off guard his ass hit the floor. He grabbed my arm yanking me off the bed on top of him. Then he rolled me over until he had me pinned to the floor crushing me with his weight. I hit at his chest.

"Get the fuck off me."

Joey was in an obstinate mood. He didn't budge. He was staring down at me. His golden eyes taking in my features. Trying to discern what was going on.

"What is up with you guys? Always keeping secrets? I saw you and Adam with your heads up each other's ass whispering. Just tell me what's going on."

I turned my head away from him. "Joseph it's between Betsy and Adam. That is why I was here talking with Betsy. Now get the fuck off me."

I was pushing on him but he was large and not budging. Joey tried to kiss me then but I turned my head. I was pissed at him so he was not kissing me. Betsy reached out and touched Joey's shoulder.

"Joey, get off her before you hurt her."

He turned towards the sound of Betsy's voice then back to me. "Give me a kiss and I'll let you up."

"I'm not kissing you Joey. I'm fucking pissed at you. Now get off me."

"Kiss him Joy so he'll get off you. Don't start anything with him now."

Betsy was getting upset. I could hear it in her voice. I was pissed at Joey. I refused to give in. He wasn't holding my lips hostage.

"No."

I heard Betsy sigh. I could see out of the corner of my eye that she had sat up on the bed leaning against the headboard. Her knees wrapped to her chest comforting herself.

"What the fuck is your problem Joseph?" I was struggling now to get out from under him. "You're hurting me Joey."

"Joey what's going on? Joy said you're hurting her."

It was Adam who had come quietly into the room. His voice was sharp like steel so we all knew he was pissed. Joey climbed to his feet with a swiftness that surprised me. He extended his hand to me. Reluctantly I took it and he pulled me to my feet. We both stared at Adam. Then I looked at

Betsy sitting on the bed. Her head was turned away from us. Her mouth was covered by her hand. Why hadn't I just let the damned fool kiss me?

"Look Joy your savior is here again. Don't you get tired of it Betsy? Adam always saving Joy from me or from herself when she has the panic attacks?" Joey asked meanly.

I gasped turning back to face Joey.

"What's the problem Joey?" Adam asked.

Betsy was now crying.

"You've had too much to drink Joey," I told him. "This is why I hate it when you drink because you get belligerent and paranoid. Did you stop to think that he came to check on his girlfriend you jackass? The one who is upset."

Both men were sizing each other up. Staring each other down. Joey ran his hands across his face in frustration.

"Come on Joey. Let's go back to our party and give Adam and Betsy some privacy."

I took his hand and began tugging him towards the door.

"We'll all go," Betsy said getting up from the bed and coming with us.

She wiped her face with the sleeve of her hoody. I waited for her to catch up to me. I gave Adam a sympathetic smile and took Betsy's hand at the door. We went down the steps together and out the front door. Joey behind us. Adam behind him. She didn't want to deal with him right now so she wouldn't. Betsy could be stubborn that way.

Adam went around us once we were on the lawn. He walked quickly head bent to his father who was standing with Mandy and our friends still surrounding the pig roasting over the open flames. Joey grabbed my arm stopping my forward progress.

"What now?"

Betsy took a few steps forward giving us privacy.

"Take off Adam's sweatshirt. I will give you mine."

I stared at him like he had lost his mind. Joey lifted the hem of his shirt over his head and handed his sweatshirt to me. Then he left me standing there with my mouth open.

"What was that about?" Betsy asked.

"I'm not allowed to wear Adam's shirt. Do you want it?" I asked removing Adam's shirt and putting on my husbands'.

Betsy shook her head no. I folded Adam's shirt over my arm.

"I'm going to move to the farm for a while to give myself some time to think things through clearly. Do you think Luke will mind?"

"Oh no Betsy. Don't do that. Stay with us sweetheart."

I was terrified of her leaving the house that we shared. That would mean Adam and I would be alone several nights a week unless he went somewhere. We worked hard at our relationship but the words exchanged earlier would now hang between us like temptation when Adam's focus needed to be on Betsy.

"Joy I need this for me. Please be supportive."

I stopped walking. Of course I would be supportive of her. She and Adam had been the only thing that had kept me going the last year when things were bleak for me. The days I wouldn't have climbed out of bed they made me. When Joey didn't notice my depression, my anxiety sweeping me into a dark place that was threatening to consume me Adam and Betsy did. They had to be my focus now moving forward.

"I will Bets. I just don't think that moving back to the farm even if for a short period is the answer. I've done enough running away in my life and it doesn't work. Stay and try to work out the right answer for you, Adam and your baby."

She sighed. "I just need some space Joy."

I give. I sighed. "Okay sweetie. I'm here for you."

"That's better."

We walked over to Adam where I promptly handed him his shirt. I shook my head at him. I didn't need to explain. He knew. Adam eyed the sweatshirt that Joey had given me as replacement.

"Is she okay?" He asked with genuine concern and frustration.

Should I tell him? Let her tell him? I looked over my shoulder where Betsy stood talking to Luke. Our lives had become a soap opera. Luke met my gaze across the fire. He was still listening to Betsy. Was she telling him about the baby she carried? He nodded at her then wrapped her in his embrace kissing her temple.

"I think she's asking Luke if she can stay with him for a while."

I turned back to Adam. The look of confusion and frustration on his face only increased. I patted his arm and shook my head explaining that I tried to talk her out of it but she felt like she needed space. Maybe that was the best answer for now. He shook his head angrily. Luke broke up our conversation declaring it time to get the pig ready to slice. We were hungry. Adam and Joey went to help him while I went to Betsy's side.

The girls and I that had attended this party all took chairs around the fire to stay warm. Most of the ladies who attended were wives or girlfriends of either Adam or Joey's friends. We knew them. We had gone to high school with them. Betsy and I balanced plates in our hands and made small talk with them hearing about what they had been doing since graduation from high school.

Sitting next to me was Stephanie Marks a dyed red head married to Benny Marks. They had been married for a year right out of high school. Stephanie was our age while Benny had graduated with Joey and Adam. Benny had even played baseball with Joey. Everyone thought she was pregnant but as the months passed and her belly stayed slim we all realized they married because they wanted to get married.

Stephanie was voluptuous with full hips, a big ass like mine and big breasts which she never failed to expose with her low cut tops. Her dyed red hair was always big and sprayed to hold her style. Her eyeliner heavy and dark. I always thought she could be pretty if she toned it down but Benny liked her so who was I to judge her?

Sitting on the other side of Betsy was Marta Lions. Marta's boyfriend was a friend of Adam who played Basketball with him. Marta had also graduated with us. Her boyfriend graduating with Joey and Adam. His name was Alex James. Marta was dark haired like Betsy with chocolate brown eyes and full sensual lips. She was beautiful like Betsy. More naturally beautiful, Marta rarely wore make-up and wore clothes that were more conservative.

Across the fire because we made her go there because of her smoking was our dyed to the max blonde friend Shay. Shay was dating Bobby Martin, TJ's son. If I didn't know any better there was trouble brewing between them. Shay didn't seem to mind sitting across the fire away from us. She had been brooding all night. She and Bobby had hardly spoken since arriving. Shay was beautiful even with her dyed hair. Her skin still tan from summer, her cornflower blue eyes giving her a surfer girl look. We lived in Ohio. No ocean. No surfing. She looked out of place.

Bobby came over and whispered something in her ear. She stumped out the cigarette glaring at him. She sighed wearily. Something definitely up with them. She glared as he walked away. Back to the table where the boys were sitting. I glanced over my shoulder checking them all out. Hearing their laughter. What did they have to be happy about?

I knew Stephanie and Benny fought a lot. Betsy would be moving to the farmhouse. Apparently Bobby and Shay were fighting about something as well. What the fuck did they have to be unhappy about? Luke approached me. He placed a hand on my shoulder and leaned in close.

"Mandy and I are heading off to bed. Can I speak to you?"

I rose with a sigh of frustration. I followed him back to the porch.

"You're having sleepovers now?" I tried teasing him. He glared at me.

"What is going on with Betsy and Adam?"

"What makes you think I know?"

"If something is going on with you, Betsy or Adam one of you knows it. Now spill it sweetheart. Shorty is upset."

"Luke, please don't put me in this more than I am."

He glared down at me. I hadn't been intimidated like this by Luke Moore in years. "You still haven't started college. I've let it slide because of what you've been through. Start spilling your guts or I'm going to be on your ass like white on rice."

"You know that makes no sense." I could see he wouldn't let it go. "Dammit, all right already. She's pregnant."

"Fuck. Does he not know how to use a condom?" His Pa declared angrily.

I almost laughed and said only with me and realized how funny that would not be. "In his defense the condom broke."

"Fuck," he growled deeply.

"You're going to be a grandpa...again."

Luke took one look at me and crushed me to his big chest asking me how I was handling this bit of news.

"He asked her if she wanted to get married."

"Not do you want to marry me?" Luke said knowingly.

"Right. So she's having all kinds of doubts and doesn't want to trap him. Said she needed space. I tried to talk her out of running away. Told her it was a mistake."

"Like we both tried to talk you out of running away from Adam?" He whispered softly in my hair. He was still holding me.

"Yeah. Yeah. Luke I get it. I fucked up. I got married so I wouldn't change my mind and hurt everyone anyway." I pulled away from Luke. "Don't get me wrong I care a lot about Joey." He nodded. "Adam can't commit. Betsy's still hurt. Joey's acting like a paranoid lunatic because he senses shit between me and Adam. All I did was make everyone uncomfortable." Uncomfortable seemed like the right word.

"That is an understatement sweetheart."

"Thanks Luke."

"How do I make this right for them and their baby?"

Luke caressed my face. "That isn't your place to make things right Joy. Adam and Betsy have to do that if they want to."

"This fucking sucks." I started getting choked up. "I just wanted everyone to be happy."

"I know you did sweetheart. I'm going inside now. Tell Betsy to come in whenever she wants to. I will leave the front door unlocked."

"Luke?"

"What?"

I gazed into eyes that were as familiar to me as his son's eyes. Big, dark beautiful eyes that were more open than they had been a year ago. I thought Betsy and I had helped him become more open. Helped him to put some of his fears to rest.

"I love you Luke Moore."

He smiled a tender smile promising me everything would be right in the world sometime. Only Luke's smile did that for me.

"I love you too Joy Bonds."

Then he turned and walked into the house leaving me standing on the lawn alone and frustrated.

## Chapter Three

### Joey

The party ended at 3:00 AM. Betsy walked into the farmhouse. She was staying here for the night. I turned and looked at Adam. He shook his head indicating don't ask. I looked at the picnic table and saw Joy cleaning up the remaining beer cans and paper plates. The food was all stashed in the fridge.

"I'm done. Let's go home you two. I'm beat," my wife snapped at us.

She started walking towards the driveway expecting Adam and I to follow. I hesitated for a second then she stopped when she realized no one was following her. Adam was looking at the farmhouse.

"Adam give her tonight. Tomorrow we will convince her to come home," she said softly.

He shook his head clearing it of thoughts I assumed. He followed her like the little Pied Piper she was. I saw how Adam looked at Joy. He would do anything for her. I began to follow or rather stagger after them. I knew she hated my drinking and yet I had consumed a case of beer at least. She had lost count I was sure. Hell I had lost count but knew it was close if not more than a case. It was great getting together with our friends though. Some we had not seen because of Joy's illness. I wasn't blaming her. I was grateful she was feeling better.

We had walked here now I wished we had the damned truck. A mile down the lane to the comfort of our bed might as well have been ten miles the way I was feeling. I tripped over something or nothing. Maybe my own feet? They both stopped and looked at me.

"Are you okay?" Joy asked.

"I'm fine."

"Joey how much did you drink tonight?"

"Don't start Joy." I snapped at her.

She sighed tiredly. "It's only because I care."

We walked further. Everyone was quiet. Then Joy asked about Bobby and Shay. She had seen their turmoil too. Neither speaking to each other unless they had to. Shay was pregnant. Bobby had told us and she wasn't happy about it either. She wanted to get an abortion and he had put his foot down. He told her he would leave her if she did. The one thing Shay loved more than herself was Bobby Martin. She was pissed though that he had given her this ultimatum so she was making his life hell. I told Joy what was going on with them. She stopped walking turning towards me.

"You're fucking kidding me."

"No..Nope," I stuttered.

"Wow," she muttered. Then she looked at Adam for a brief second. She turned on her heel and started walking again. We were halfway home now.

"What the fuck is going on?"

I looked between Adam and Joy. They kept walking I stopped walking.

"I'm fucking talking to you," I said belligerently.

"Joey," Joy said softly. She looked at Adam. "Everything is fine. Betsy and Adam just needed some space. Betsy is my best friend of course she would confide in me. Adam asked me if she was okay. Will you fucking relax?"

She took my hand and began tugging me towards the house like an errant child needing guidance. I followed along allowing her to. Occasionally she looked over her shoulder at Adam to be sure he was following. Were we her children? What the fuck? I pulled my hand from hers never so glad to see the house. I cut across the lawn leaving Joy and Adam in the wake of my footsteps. I still felt like there was more to what was going on with Betsy and Adam than they were telling me.

I was upstairs and trying to get my boots off when Joy made it the room. She didn't say anything. She just pushed my hands away and tugged on my boots nearly losing her balance when it came off my foot. She dropped it beside the bed. She lifted my other foot and propped it against her thigh. Then she started pulling it by the heel. It popped off too. She kept her balance with this one though. She tossed the boot aside with the other one.

She took the hem of my shirt, lifted it over her head before tossing it on the chair behind her. She grabbed my tee-shirt at the bottom and started pulling it over my head. I raised my arms to help her get the shirt off my body. When I was bare chested I grasped her ass firmly in my hands and squeezed until she squealed in pain.

"We are not doing this when you are drunk. Hell you couldn't keep your dick hard if you tried with as much alcohol as you've had."

That fucking pissed me off. I stood and unbuttoned my jeans, ran the zipper down the full length yanking the pants down my body. My dick was plenty hard.

"Does this look to you like I'm having any difficulty keeping my dick hard?" I asked drawing her roughly against me.

"Joey, we've been through this once tonight. You.me and alcohol are not a happy time in the making. Go to bed."

She struggled against me a bit. Just enough. I pushed her away from me. I wasn't like this. I didn't force a woman especially not Joy. Not my wife. I walked over to the bed and climbed between the sheets. She stepped out of her jeans. Laid her hoody on the chair. She reached into her drawer and grabbed clean pajamas.

"Where are you going Joy?" I asked softly.

"I will be back soon Joey. I smell like smoke. I want to take a shower."

"Okay babe. I'm sorry."

"You're always sorry Joey after you drink. When will you stop?'

I didn't answer her. I watched her through bleary eyes walk out of the room. She shut the door behind her. I could feel my eyes getting heavier the longer I laid there in the warmth of our bed. My eyelids felt like led weights closing them. I gave way to the alcohol and let sleep take me.

*Joy*

I closed the door behind me and leaned against it. Weary from dealing with Joey's drunk ass. Sober he was sweet and caring. Drunk he was paranoid about Adam or belligerent with me wanting sex. He made my skin crawl when he was drunk. His swaggering attitude when he was drunk reminded me of my...reminded me of Jack Ayers.

The bathroom door opened. Adam wrapped in a towel and only a towel appeared in the hallway. He looked down at his body. His wet hair glistened in the light just above his head. I looked at his body from his toes, his knees, the narrow V at his waist, the six pack abs, the strong pectoral muscles begging me to touch them, to the broad shoulders. I stopped at his eyes boring into my eyes now. His hand went to his waist holding the towel securely in place.

"I smelled like smoke," he said in explanation.

"I had the same plan." I held up the pajamas in my hand showing him.

"I will get out of your way" We were growing more uncomfortable by the minute. "How's Joey?"

"Probably passed out," I told him looking down at the carpet then at him.

He shook his head with exasperation.

I stepped past Adam careful not to touch him. As he walked by me I looked over my shoulder checking out his tight muscular ass. He had a beautiful ass. I had dug my fingernails into it while he thrust his body into mine. I knew what was beneath that towel. My body reacted to the naked image of Adam in my head. My clit throbbed aching for him.

Adam looked over his shoulder catching me checking him out. He quirked his eyebrows at me. I dropped my eyes in embarrassment and slipped into the bathroom. I leaned against the bathroom door catching my breath.

### Adam

I slipped into my room after catching Joy checking my ass out. I leaned against the bedroom door holding my breath. Betsy needed to get her ass back here. We could not be left alone and Joey was going to be at school on Tuesday night. I knew that what we were feeling it was wrong but I also knew what was going on inside my head and it wasn't good.

Dropping the towel I strode naked across the room to the closet and got a pair of sweats from a hanger. I slid them up my body. My plan was going straight to bed but seeing Joy in the hallway had awakened everything in me. I decided to go downstairs for a soda. I walked down the hall to their room first to check on Joey. He was flat on his back arms and legs sprawled across the bed snoring loudly. I shook my head desperately. One of our significant others needed to be aware and be a buffer between Joy and me. Hell Joey just needed some fucking help right now. I was worried about him. I shut the door behind me.

I started down the hallway. By the bathroom door I hesitated. No water was running in the shower. I listened at the door where I could hear Joy on the other side of the door. I knew her sounds. Knew what the hell she was doing. I looked down at my own body reacting to her moans of pleasure. My dick was getting hard. Joy was touching herself on the other side of that door. Fucking hell, and by all that's holy why am I still standing here listening to her?

Softly I banged my head against the hard wood door. Shit she's going to hear me. I took a quick step back from the door. Hands still pressed against the wood. I could still hear her soft little moans of pleasure.

### Joy

I had decided on a bath instead of a shower. The water was steaming hot sloshing about my skin turning it pink. Adam in a towel played with my head in my mind's eye. My hand slipped down to my breasts. I tweaked my nipple causing a zing of pleasure to zap my clit and a moan of pleasure to escape through my lips. *Oh my...that feels so good.*

I didn't do this often, touching myself but Adam had left me one hot mess seeing him in his towel in the hallway. I had to relieve the pressure somehow and unless I jumped an unconscious Joey I had to do it myself because Adam himself was not an option.

My hand dipped lower to the folds between my legs. My fingers found the hard nub and gently I swirled over it until I was splashing water over the side of the tub with my movements. *Ohhhh.* I hadn't realized the sounds were also coming out of my mouth. I thought they were all silent inside my head.

I closed my eyes and remembered Adam...I knew it was wrong...everything in me screamed stop but I couldn't turn it off. I saw him above me. His lust filled eyes boring into mine. His big beautiful dark eyes. His full luscious lips. My god what that mouth could do to me. I missed him. God how I missed him. I felt a tear trickle down the side of my face even as the pressure of sweet release was building in my clit.

I rubbed harder. I slid my fingers inside and imagined they were Adam's fingers. Imagined they were his caressing me as only he could. Then I touched my clit getting fuller and harder by the second. Without conscious thought I moaned his name out loud. Then it all came crashing down on me. The throbbing pulsating release of fulfillment along with the sobbing distress. I covered my face then dunked my head under the water mixing my tears with the water.

When the crying stopped I soaped my body and my hair. I removed the stopper from the floor of the tub and let the water drain. I watched the water swirling out with all my emotions draining out of me too. I sighed then turned on the shower head allowing the water to cascade over me like a waterfall until the water ran clear.

### Adam

Joy was coming downstairs. Her foot hit the bottom stair then she saw me. Her ass literally hit the step her foot had just vacated.

"What are you doing up?" She asked somewhat surprised.

I was sitting on the sofa my thoughts consumed with her. The only light was from the kitchen. My soda can being squeezed tightly in my hand until I had nearly crushed it.

"I couldn't sleep," I told her.

"Me neither. I thought I would get something to drink."

I couldn't resist. "Did you enjoy your bath?"

She gave me an odd look then walked into the kitchen. Her perfect ass with the perfect little shake. Fuck me. Her hair was slightly wet. I knew she had towel dried it until it was just damp. It was wild and loose about her shoulders. She had on pajama shorts and a tank top. I longed to grasp her hair and hold her to me covering her lips with mine. I got up from the sofa. Stay there I told myself. Don't go after her. I rose from the sofa and I followed her to the kitchen not listening to the big head that usually kept me out of trouble.

When I entered the room she looked over her shoulder at me. She was bent over looking into the fridge for something to drink. I told her I checked on Joey. She just snorted. Nothing would wake him tonight. He was dead to the world. I didn't know how much he had at the party but it was a lot. He and Bobby seemed to be having a contest to see who could outdrink the other. Both unhappy with their lives. Both out-drinking their issues.

Joy popped open a soda can – root beer and took a good long drink before sitting it on the counter. Her eyes wouldn't meet mine. I stepped closer to her. What was I doing? I lifted her chin. Her beautiful green eyes hesitantly gazed into mine. My hand still touched her face.

"What are you doing Adam?' She asked her voice soft and sexy.

"Did you enjoy your bath? Nice and relaxed now Joy?" I teased her.

She gasped. She slapped my hand away from her face making me chuckle. She started to grab her root beer and walk away but I blocked her between my arms. Joy looked up at me uncomfortably. Her eyes seeking mine for answers. Hell I didn't know what I was doing. It just felt right. I had missed her. My body ached for hers. My heart wanted her and only her.

Fuck.

I cared for Betsy. I didn't want to hurt her. I knew she was pregnant with our child. Tonight I wanted one last night with Joy. It wasn't fair to her. She was married to my best friend. She should have been mine not his. We had both fucked this up but tonight I wanted to make her mine but I wasn't sure I had any right to do that.

I kept staring into her eyes. She turned in the circle of my arms and sat her soda on the counter. I tilted my head and touched my lips to the slope of her shoulder. I saw her knees give a little. I wrapped my arms around her waist to keep her from going down to the floor. I felt her body tremble in my arms.

"Adam, I asked Luke if there was anything I could do to help you and Betsy work this out so you could be happy if only for your baby's sake because I feel like you haven't committed to her because of me."

My breath was warm against the side of her face. She was breathing hard too. I held her tight against my chest. I rested my face against the side of her face waiting for her to finish. I knew there was more. I knew Joy. Her voice was soft and sad.

"He said I had to let you work it out...." She turned her head just slightly so she could see my profile. "But Adam there is something I can do." She hesitated. "I can not lead you astray. Not make this harder for you."

I tightened my grip on her body. I let her words sink into my brain. I kissed the soft spot below her ear. Her eyes closed and her head tilted back into my shoulder. She nuzzled tighter into my body.

"Now let me talk," I said gruffly. "I'm going to ask Betsy to marry me tomorrow." I felt her stiffen in my arms. I kissed her neck with soft butterfly kisses of my mouth on her skin. I felt her body relax. I heard her soft moans deep in her throat. "I asked her if she wanted to marry me so I will take a different approach with her."

I trusted Joy with everything in me so the next words I was going to say I knew she would keep between us. As painful as they were to say because I felt so much loyalty to Betsy I probably shouldn't speak them out loud but they had to be said between me and Joy.

"My heart will always belong to you Joy." She turned her head away from me. With one finger I made her look back at me. "I care for Betsy. She is going to have my child. I will marry her. Take care of her. Try to make her happy but the heart wants what the heart wants and my heart will always belong to you." The emotion of the moment was starting to overwhelm me. My voice choked in my throat. "Fuck I don't have the right to ask this of you."

A tear rolled down Joy's cheek. I wiped it away with my thumb. My other hand had begun to caress her belly through the softness of her tank top. I turned her face towards mine. My lips covered hers. At first I was gentle with needing the softness to be an expression of everything I was feeling then the passion of it all took over and the kiss became hungry and demanding. She broke away first. I looked at her long and hard not releasing the hold I had on her face.

"What I want to ask you Joy is..." my heart slammed against my ribs. Her breathing was heavy matching my own. She waited for me to ask. Could I? My eyes searched hers. I had to. I wouldn't survive this lifetime without knowing her again. Without touching her like this. Without having her one last time. "I want you Joy. I want to bury myself deep inside you."

She turned in my arms. Her breasts crushed against my chest. Her lips soft against mine. Her breath mingled with my breath. Not really kissing just touching. My hands held her tightly to me. She could feel how hard my dick was. I yanked down her pajama shorts until I felt bare skin. Her ass. I loved her ass. I caressed her firm, bare ass until she moaned against my mouth. I lifted her to me and she wrapped her legs around my waist locking her ankles behind my back.

"Can I take this as a yes?" I asked against her lips.

"I think it is a huge mistake Adam but I can't tell you no."

I crashed into the kitchen wall with her. I grasped her breast with one hand and molded it. I tweaked her nipple through the material. She groaned delighting in the pleasure I was causing.

"Are you sure?" She asked me.

"Are you?"

"No Adam. I'm not but if we don't do this I think I might die tonight."

She began trying to yank down my sweats until I felt my dick free and clear. I lifted her until I could touch the tip of my dick against her center. We both gasped. She touched my face. I closed my eyes. Trying to steady the beat of my heart. The trembling of my body. I slid inside her. My eyes flew open and I saw that she was looking at me. Her eyes full of sadness. I pushed into her hard her back against the cold kitchen wall. She held onto me tightly while I lifted her up and down the length of my shaft.

I knew her. Her finger tips slid softly over my shoulders and down the length of my spine. Her head tilted back on her neck. She wanted to dig in her claws and leave her mark on me but she couldn't. She wouldn't. When her head popped up I could see it in her eyes. I would always be hers just as she was always mine but it could never be. I slammed harder into Joy taking my frustration out on how things had worked out between us. Betsy and Pa both told me to make our relationship right. I had stubbornly refused. They tried talking to her too. She married Joey to be sure she didn't change her mind about us. I thrust harder into her squeezing her ass so hard she gasped out loud.

I felt her muscles tightening around me. I bit softly into her shoulder making her moan. I checked. I didn't leave a mark. Thank God. I slammed into her several more times wanting her to never forget me. The feel of my body fucking her against this kitchen wall...I wanted it forever branded in her memories.

My head went back. I closed my eyes. I thrust into her as she held me tightly to her. Her body reacted as I knew it would. She convulsed around me sending me over the fucking edge too. I climaxed into her. Not protecting her. Not really caring about it either. I dropped my head to her shoulder. I lifted her higher and yanked down her tank top sucking her nipple into my mouth biting hard on it then sucking it just as gently until she pushed at my head. My lips covered hers. Her bared breast brushed against my chest causing a moan deep in my throat.

"This better last you a lifetime because it is not happening again Adam."

She tugged hard on my hair at the nape of my neck. I kissed her roughly. My lips showing no mercy on hers. She bit my lower lip sucking it hard into her mouth. If she kept this up I was going to be hard again and I was still inside her.

I sat her feet gently on the floor. She looked up into my eyes. Hers filled with so much emotion that I had to look away. Tomorrow everything would change but I would always have this memory. I was being selfish for a change because I needed this. She pushed at my bare chest. I stepped back and grabbed my sweats off the floor, pulling them up my body so I was covered.

I didn't know what to say to her to make it better. I didn't know if anything could make it better. She hadn't moved away from me yet. Suddenly she turned to look for her shorts that were across the room. I patted her bared ass as she walked away. My Joy glared at me over her shoulder showing a bit of the feisty girl that I knew and loved. I smiled at her. She just shook her head at me and walked across the room retrieving her shorts from the floor. She yanked them up her body. She turned to find me standing right behind her. I touched her face.

"I'm not going to apologize Joy. I fucked up letting you go last year. Pa and Betsy both told me not to but I was stubborn and now we are both paying the price. You were too distraught. I should have fought for us when you weren't able and now it's too late."

Her hand covered mine. Her eyes lowered to the ground between us.

"Whatever you need to get through to Betsy," she choked on the words, "I'm there to help you."

My lips touched hers. Our kiss was soft and sweet. She pulled away. She stepped out of my arms. Joy turned on her heel and walked to the kitchen door. There she glanced back at me giving me her a bittersweet smile. She started to leave but I called her name.

"What Adam?"

Nothing. I was going to tell her that I loved her but she knew that. "Sleep tight," I said instead.

She looked relieved. Then she was gone without saying a word to me.

*Joy*

I slipped between the sheets lying on my side facing away from Joey. Adam's semen wet between my legs reminding me that I had cheated on Joey something I thought I would never do. Joey flopped over on his side wrapping his big arm around me pulling me tightly into his body. His face was buried in my hair. He grumbled something unintelligible. What had I done? Tears pooled at the corners of my eyes.

## Chapter Four

### Betsy

They all showed up the next morning. I was sitting on the barstool at the island. Luke was making breakfast for us. Mandy in pajamas so damned weird for me she was sitting at the kitchen table talking to Luke.

You could always hear Joey when he made an entrance. The man didn't do quiet. I could only assume Adam was with them. Then I heard his voice. He called my name.

"In here Adam," I said softly.

He came into the kitchen ahead of Joey and Joy. He grabbed me in his arms lifting me off the barstool holding me tight against his chest.

"I have something to ask you shorty." He was gazing hard into my face.

Everyone was staring at us. Joey's hand resting on Joy's shoulder where they stood just inside the kitchen door. Luke standing at the stove spatula in hand was staring at us. Mandy mouth open in anticipation.

His lips descended on mine. A kiss so soft and sweet. Then he looked at me. His beautiful dark eyes gazing into mine for a long time making me uncomfortable.

"Put me down Adam."

"No. I asked you the wrong question yesterday Betsy. Instead of asking if you wanted to get married like it was a chore we needed to do. Today, I'm asking you if you will marry me? Please," he added for good measure.

The room was so quiet you could hear a pin drop. I looked over Adam's shoulder at Joy who had tears in her eyes watching us. I hoped they were happy tears. Did she know about this prior to him doing it? She grabbed Joey's hand resting on her shoulder. I looked back into Adam's eyes.

"Could you put me down?" I asked him quietly.

He sat my feet on the floor.

I took his hand and started for the living room. I grabbed Joy's hand on the way.

"I don't think you need me."

"I do."

I took them both outside to the swing. I forced them to sit side by side. I stood in front of them staring them both down. Adam leaned forward on his knees clasping his hands between his knees staring at the porch. Joy crossed her legs, then her arms across her chest leaning back.

"What you did in there Adam...that was sweet but right here and right now I want you to tell me that you love me and not Joy. Then I will answer your proposal." My voice was broken when I got the sentence out.

Joy looked at Adam out of the corner of her eye.

"Tell her Adam," she begged.

His head snapped around to look at Joy.

"I love you Betsy. I want to marry you," he said but his eyes never left Joy's face.

"Are you fucking kidding me?" I snapped. "Adam how can I believe you when you say the words but you are looking at Joy you fucking dick."

I started to go back into the house. Adam grabbed my arm preventing me from leaving. He looked down at me. "I do Betsy. Please."

I glared into his face. "You do what Adam?"

He cupped my face with his big hands. "I do love you. I do want to marry you."

I almost believed him because he was that convincing.

"Adam you want to do the right thing," I said softly.

"Adam, go inside would you?" Joy said.

He turned to look at her puzzled.

"Go on."

Reluctantly he left us.

"Come here," she told me.

I walked over to the swing and sat beside Joy. She leaned in closer to me and wrapped her arm around my shoulders. Her head rested against my head.

"What more do you want Betsy?"

I almost cried when she asked me that question. I wanted him to look at me the way he looked at her and finally I told her so. She looked at me with pain in her face.

"Bets you are having his baby. He really means to make you as happy as possible. He told me that last night," her voice was soft as she said this. "He wants to make a family with you. Give him that chance. Don't fuck it up the way I did because you will have regrets."

"Is that supposed to make me feel better?" I snapped. "I feel like I'm taking him from you."

"You shouldn't," she said to me. "Are you forgetting I'm married to Joey?" I shook my head no in response to her question. "Betsy, quit being a stubborn ass and go tell him you will marry him."

"I don't know what to do. I never wanted to trap Adam."

"You aren't Betsy."

She grabbed my hand and pulled me from the swing. Then we were walking into the house. Adam and Joey were sitting on the sofa. He apparently had told Joey that I was pregnant because Joey was commiserating with Adam. I scowled at Joey. Joy glared at him too. He left the room uncomfortable with the ladies now staring him down. We both watched him leave.

Adam looked at us. I didn't know what to say or do. I loved him. How could I not? He was sweet and tender. He was a beautiful man in his tight jeans hanging low on his hips. His broad shoulders accentuated by his white tee shirt that fit snug across his pecs. But I had never felt like he belonged to me.

"She's going to marry you," Joy said suddenly.

### She's what?

Adam looked at us like we had lost our minds. I looked at Joy with the same expression myself. She can't answer for me. Joy looked at me daring me to dispute her. She squeezed my hand encouraging me. My gaze returned to Adam.

"Tell me you love me again Adam?" I begged.

He stood from the couch and walked over to me. Joy tried to break the twining of our hands. I gripped her hand harder. I knew it was cruel. I couldn't let her go. I had put my feelings aside to help them both through a rough time now it was her turn. He looked from Joy to me.

"I love you Betsy. I want you to marry me."

Out of the corner of my eye I saw Joy's head drop. I squeezed her hand harder trying to get comfort from her and give her comfort.

"I will marry you Adam," I whispered.

"Thank you Jesus," Joy said softly.

Adam laughed out loud scooping both of us into his arms swinging us around. He kissed both our cheeks.

"Thank you Joy for whatever you said outside to convince her."

"Put me down Adam then you can swing her all you want," she told him.

She was wiggling trying to get out of his embrace but Adam was strong. He kissed her cheek several times laughing at her. Then he set her on her feet. He still held me in his other arm. Joy left the room. Then Adam's eyes stared into mine.

"We're going to have a baby Betsy."

"You don't feel trapped do you Adam?"

"No. Never. Sweetheart, we have a wedding to plan."

"Adam since I'm pregnant could we do something like Joey and Joy did here with just family maybe our friends too?"

"You sure?"

"I'm sure."

"Whatever you want sweetheart."

### Joey

Joy came into the bedroom wearing only her baby doll nightgown in a soft pink color. She was freshly showered. Her hair a mess of wet curls about her face. I was studying lying propped against the headboard. I slapped the book closed and laid it on the nightstand. As she got close to the bed I pulled her into my lap.

"What are you doing Joey?"

I shoved Joy over onto her back pinning her arms above her head. I stared into her eyes. Joy's eyes told her secrets. They told what she was feeling. Right now she was trying to decide if she was interested in what I had to offer. I bit her nipple through the fabric of the baby doll nightgown. She gasped twitching beneath me but not really able to move much because my weight was holding her down. I ground my hips into her letting her know that my dick was hard. I nipped at her nipples again making her squirm and moan. Did she like it?

I rose and flipped Joy over onto her belly. I ripped the nightgown up the back and pulled the pieces from her body.

"Dammit Joey I loved this nightgown."

"Tell me where you got it I will buy you another."

I slid the sheer panties down her legs and tossed them over the side of the bed with the shredded nightgown. I slapped her ass hard then kissed the spot left by my hand. She looked over her shoulder at me anticipating what I would do next. I spread her legs and tested her soft folds to see what she was thinking. She was fucking wet. My Joy was liking the rough play. I slapped her ass again and then pressed soft kisses to the spot.

My eyes met hers over the plane of her back. I bit her ass hard and she nearly cried out loud. I knew when I looked down that it would leave a bruise. I rid myself of my boxers. Dammit I wanted to bury myself in her bare but knew she would freak the fuck out. I started to get a condom.

"No Joey."

"What?"

"No condom tonight. Russian roulette."

Fuck me. I grasped her hips hard in my hands and positioned myself at her entrance. Her firm butt cheeks caressed my dick right before I plunged deep and hard between her silky thighs. She was soaking wet. I put my hands on each side of her waist and held myself above her now.

"Harder Joey. Fuck me harder. As hard as you fucking can," her voice was low and sexy as hell when she said those words. Almost commanding me.

I stroked her hard. I knew it hurt. My dick was large. I wasn't gentle. Joy gasped out loud. She looked over her shoulder at me again. Then I slammed into her again and again. Over and over. We were breathing heavily. She was letting me fuck her without a condom. Her silkiness was caressing my dick. I wasn't going to last long. My head went back on my shoulders. I was trying to focus on something other than her sweet wetness.

"Are you going to come baby?" I asked her.

"Soon Joey," she panted. "I need to reach my clit."

I pulled out of her long enough to get her on her knees. I slapped her hand away.

"I got this," I told her.

I pushed her legs wider. Her perfectly round ass was right there in front of me. The bite mark already starting to bruise. I slapped her right butt cheek then plunged deep into her nearly throwing her forward.

"Fuck Joey."

I held her by her shoulder and began pounding hard into Joy with my dick making her groan. With my free hand I reached around her and stimulated her clit. It wasn't long before she was throbbing against my hand her walls tightening around my dick. Her body convulsing against me. Shuddering with sweet release. I came right behind her shooting my release hard into her. I pulled her back against me both of us on our knees. I kissed her neck. Her shoulder. Then I bit her hard on her back leaving another mark. Claiming her. Marking her as mine. She flinched with the pain. I grabbed her pussy in my hand possessing it. She looked over her shoulder at me. Glaring at me. Then her lips covered mine hungrily.

Just as quickly she released me. She climbed from the bed to grab her panties from the floor. Damn her back and her ass would have a nasty bruise where I had bit her. She didn't seem to mind. I turned giving her a smile.

"Proud of yourself aren't you Joseph?"

She slapped my ass then pulled her sheer panties up her body. She picked up her torn nightie off the floor. Shaking it at me with disgust.

"I told you I would replace it.

She just shook her head at me. She grabbed a tank out of the drawer and yanked it over her head.

"I'm getting something to drink. Want something?" She asked.

"A beer?" I asked teasing her.

"Eat shit Joseph."

I busted out laughing. She flipped me the bird as she closed the door on me.

### Joy

Christ, I need to talk to my therapist about why I liked for Joey to be rough with me during sex. I almost couldn't have an orgasm with him unless he was rough and dirty. Freaked me the fuck out. I turned from the garbage can my feet freezing well all of me freezing to find Adam standing on the edge of the porch in sweatpants. I had just tossed my nightie into the can.

Fuck.

"What are you doing?" He asked like I had lost my mind.

"I had to throw something away."

I ran past him quickly wishing I had more clothes on. My nipples were pressing against the fabric of my shirt because it was damned chilly outside right now. In the living room I looked over my shoulder at Adam following me inside.

"It couldn't go in the trash inside?" He asked incredulously.

I flipped the hair hanging down my back over my shoulder. A nervous habit. Adam gasped.

"Joy did I do that to your back?"

"What?" I had forgotten about Joey biting me. I flipped my hair back to cover it. I went to the kitchen turning on the light with a flip of my hand. I strolled to the fridge and bent over inside to grab a soda off the bottom shelf. I felt his hands on my ass.

I slapped his hands away. "What are you doing?"

I turned to Adam. His eyes were blazing. I felt tears of humiliation burning my eyes. He started to leave the room

"Adam wait."

I caught him at the bottom of the staircase. "Where are you going?"

"What did you throw away?"

"Come back to the kitchen." I took his hand and pulled him with me. "Adam, you can't react this way and keep Betsy happy or your engagement won't last long."

He ran his hands through his hair. "He hurt you again."

I wasn't about to discuss my sex life with Adam.

"You need to trust me that he did not hurt me."

My eyes still glistened with unshed tears. Please don't make me explain anything else my eyes pleaded with him.

"I can see that he left marks on you."

I sighed with exasperation.

"Dammit to hell Adam. You are marrying my best friend. I am married to your best friend. You cannot keep doing this if you want Betsy to believe in you and be happy."

"He hurt you. I can't stand by and watch him do that Joy. Don't ask me to."

"He didn't."

He turned me around and yanked my panties down. He bent over at the waist and examined my ass closely. Then he jerked my panties back up.

"Liar," he ground out between his teeth.

"Holy fucking hell Adam. I feel humiliated enough without having to explain to you that I cannot have a damned orgasm unless my husband is rough in the sack. Are you fucking happy now?"

He looked perplexed. "You didn't seem to have any issues last night," he snapped at me his face so close to mine I could see his pupils dilated with anger.

"Are you going to make me say it?" I asked him.

Adam was looking confused again. He was still holding my arm in a tight grip from where he had turned me around to inspect the bite mark on my ass. I jerked my arm from Adam's grasp.

"I'm fucked up Adam. Can't you understand that?" I said to him. "I can't orgasm for some insane reason unless he gets a little rough with me because he isn't you or unless I'm fantasizing that he's you. If you think I don't know my therapist needs to know how fucked that one is..."I shook my head trying to fight back the tears. "Now leave me the fuck alone."

I stormed from the room not before I heard Adam groan deep in his throat making the tears flow that much harder down my cheeks.

The next morning when I left for work Joey had already left with Betsy. He was dropping her off on his way to the mill. Why was this happening to me? I flew down the steps running late. At the bottom stair I nearly collided with Adam.

He looked like he had not slept well.

"Can we talk?" He said catching me so I wouldn't fall.

"No we cannot talk."

I pulled away from Adam and made my way to the front door. He beat me to it and put his hand on the door preventing me from opening it. Adam was dressed casually. He was working on the farm today. Ratty jeans with holes, a black tee shirt, work boots. He never looked better. I rested my forehead against the front door unable to meet his eyes.

"Joy just give me a second."

"No," I said desperately.

"You realize we didn't use a condom Saturday night."

I started laughing almost hysterically. "Adam, I took care of that last night. I had sex with Joey no condom less than twenty-four hours after you. So if I turn up pregnant too we won't know whose baby it is. So you are off the hook." I jabbed him in the chest. "You already have one woman pregnant. Why don't you worry about her? Marry her and for god's sake leave me alone"

He backed up. A shocked expression on his face.

"You did it on purpose?" He asked an almost hurt tone to his voice. "So we wouldn't know?"

"Actually no I didn't. I had no intention of having sex with Joey last night. He initiated it but it worked out rather well just in case Adam since you already have one woman pregnant it won't complicate our lives with two women being pregnant with your child since you and I cannot seem to remember we need to use a fucking condom or better yet not have sex at all."

"Christ you're crazy."

"Probably," I replied nastily shoving past him.

"Fuck," I Heard Adam say.

"Joy I didn't mean it." Adam was standing on the porch now. He had followed me outside.

I stopped in the yard. Turning to Adam I had tears in my eyes. He stepped off the porch. He was so close to me that he could touch me. He was thinking about doing just that. I took a step back.

"Adam please don't touch me. Please," I begged.

I was barely holding myself together. Too much had happened within the last few days. My emotional state was still fragile. I had been seeing Doc on an as needed basis for the last few months and when he opened I would be making an appointment. It had become as needed. If Adam touched me I would shatter. I recognized that about myself right now.

"I'm making an appointment today when Doc opens up. I need to talk to him," I explained to Adam.

Adam's eyes changed from intense to worry. "Are you okay?"

"I go so I am okay Adam."

"Are you going because of the baby?"

I hesitated in answering that question. Did the baby bring up feelings that I was afraid of? Sure it did but I wanted to talk about other things too. I wanted to talk about the whole rough sex thing with Joey. I wanted to talk about having sex with Adam. Why had I done this? Why did I open myself up to this complication in my life?

"Adam, I have many things I need to discuss with doc."

Would he leave it at that?

"Please tell me you will talk to him about letting Joey hurt you during sex." Adam's eyes couldn't meet mine.

Of course he wouldn't leave it alone.

"Adam," I said only his name pleading with him to let it go. I didn't want to talk to him about me and Joey.

"All right dammit Joy."

""Adam, I will." That was all I would say to him on that matter. "But I need to talk to him about you too."

"That wasn't a mistake."

"Adam, if Betsy and Joey find out ever they will never forgive us. Can you live with that? I can't."

He dropped his head.

I couldn't help myself. I touched his jaw. A tender caress of my hand. God I loved this man. Would I ever stop? Stopping, I thought would be like giving up breathing.

"You're right Adam. It wasn't a mistake," I said softly. "I just don't want them to find out."

My six foot five giant of a beautiful man shed a single tear before he swiped it away with the back of his hand.

"I have to get to work."

I turned my back on Adam and didn't look back. That would have been too hard to look at him again. I climbed into Adam's truck and started it fumbling with the keys because my hands were trembling. I spun gravel over the driveway. Looking in my rearview mirror I saw Adam standing in the driveway with his hands on his head watching me just as troubled as I was.

### Adam

The next morning I was first up so I made breakfast for everyone. I hadn't slept well thoughts of Joy invading my wake and sleep. Betsy and I had dinner with Pa and Mandy at the farm. She wanted to ask him if we could have the wedding at the farm. He agreed naturally. Joy and Joey were invited as always but Joy pretended to have a headache and went straight to bed. I knew her well. I knew she was faking it. She did look exhausted though.

"Hey you. You tossed and turned all night," Betsy wrapped her arm around my waist.

I turned and kissed the top of her head. I did care for her. She was so sweet. She was the only reason I had made it through the heartbreak of losing Joy after she had lost the baby. Damn she was beautiful. She had to be at work at seven this morning. Joey was taking her again. He had to be at the mill at the same time. He had class tonight so Joy and I would be alone. I really didn't know how that was going to work unless we went to the farm and hung out with Pa and Mandy.

"I'm restless right now for some reason."

Joey came to the kitchen at the point cutting off further conversation about my lack of sleep last night which was for the best. It wasn't like I could tell Betsy that Joy was keeping me awake.

"What are you making Adam?"

"Eggs and bacon Joseph," I replied absently.

We were talking about Joey's courses for fall and how they were going when Joy stuck her head in the doorway. She still looked tired. Her hair was pulled tightly back from her face in a ponytail. She wasn't wearing any make-up.

"I will be late tonight guys. I made an appointment with Doc."

She turned to leave.

"Babe aren't you eating breakfast with us?"

She stopped but didn't turn back towards the door. "I'm not hungry Joey. I will see you after class tonight."

Fuck.

"Oh no," Betsy said softly looking away.

We all recognized the signs. When stressed Joy stopped eating. She was so thin after losing the baby her bones were protruding in a painful obvious expression of her internal turmoil. . I put my arm around Betsy.

"Don't worry not yet. She's going to see Doc. That is a good sign. We didn't have to make her go."

"It's the baby," she whispered.

"Why would Joy be upset about you having a baby?" Joey asked clearly confused.

Betsy looked up at me realizing her mistake. My mind searched for an answer to give to Joey.

"No reason Joey. Just more change. You know how she deals with change."

"I guess."

He didn't sound convinced. I handed him a plate with food which diverted his attention. My arm still around Betsy. She was upset that she brought up the baby Joy had lost. A baby

Joey knew nothing about. I kissed her forehead tenderly. She sighed against me.

### Joy

My knees twitched back and forth nervously while I tried to talk to Doc. Doctor Joffrey my friend as well as my doctor stared at me with concern. I knew what he was thinking. He was right. I was slipping. I wasn't sleeping. I wasn't eating. I was stressed. I hadn't had a panic attack yet but I could see them on the horizon.

"Joy, relax. You are safe here. You can tell me anything. Remember that."

I knew that. I wanted to tell him everything but a part of me was still afraid. I had slept with Adam. A big NO. NO. NO.

"Let me start with Adam and Betsy are having a baby."

He sighed. He knew that had to be hard for me. A reminder of what I had lost. I could see the sympathy in his eyes.

"That must be hard for you. You lost Adam's baby. I'm not sure you've dealt with that pain yet. You definitely haven't dealt with losing Adam or your feelings for him."

"No shit."

Doc laughed at me.

"I slept with Adam over the weekend."

He should have been surprised. He didn't show it if was. Doc leaned forward on his knees. He laid his notebook on the table. His eyes dropped to the notebook.

"Why Joy?"

Why? Good question. Because he asked me to? Not good enough. Because he was going to marry Betsy and that would make it permanent that he was no longer mine and never would be? Because I love him desperately?

"Which reason do you want?"

"Why don't you tell me all of them?" He said softly.

I relayed all the reasons that had just gone through my mind.

"Joy, I think at some point you and Adam both need to deal with your feelings for each other or this is going to end in a very bad way for everyone concerned."

"That is all you have to say?"

"Yes."

"Thanks."

I told him my thoughts about the baby coming. I wasn't worried right now. My fear was that as Betsy's belly got bigger reminding me of what I had lost I would melt down. As it became more real to me I would become lost again in the blackness that had consumed me before. He decided we would deal with it then.

Then the hardest part of all. Joey. Sex with Joey. Conflicting emotions about rough sex with Joey. I told him everything. How I could orgasm with Adam with our sweet, tender lovemaking up against the wall in the kitchen but with Joey I had to imagine Adam or Joey had to get rough with me or I couldn't. My cheeks flamed with embarrassment. I felt dirty and disgusting with myself because of my father's abuse.

"Joy," he said. "I think you're making too much of this. Many people enjoy rough sex that has nothing to do with their past abuse. Why do you think you want sex with Joey to be different from Adam?"

**Don't do this to me.**

"You know Joy," he said softly. "If you don't want to admit it to me then at least admit it to yourself."

**I won't.**

"Joy?"

"Fuck," I ground out between my teeth. "Adam holds a special place in my heart. Our lovemaking needs to be different. He was my first. I wanted him to be my only. I have to compartmentalize them Doc. Make sense?" He nodded.

"Joey is Joey. He is the bad boy who holds a different place in my life. Our sex is rough like him making him not like Adam so I can hold onto my feelings for Adam." Tears had begun to flow from my eyes.

"Someday you need to let go of Adam."

"I can't."

Doc sighed. "At least you admitted it. Don't beat yourself up over the sex with Joey. As long as you and Joey are doing things that are consensual then put the rest of it out of your mind. Let go of the past, your father's abuse the things that you are trying to label it with. Accept it for what it is loving two different men in two different ways."

I nodded my head. "Am I going crazy again?" I asked desperately.

He shook his head and gave a little chuckle. "You never were crazy Joy. Just a little mixed up. You did the right thing coming here today. I want to see you next week too until we are sure you aren't slipping backwards."

We talked for another fifteen minutes until my time was over. It might not be professional but when we ended our session I grabbed Doc in a hug and held on tight. I loved this guy like I loved Luke Moore although he wasn't old enough to be my father. He told it to me straight. We made an appointment for the same time next week. Then I left his office.

During the drive home my mind raced at a thousand miles an hour. I pulled into the driveway and parked Adam's truck. Joey was at class tonight. Betsy and Adam should be home. In the kitchen, I found just Adam. Betsy had decided to pick up a second shift while she could. She was feeling good. No nausea yet. I almost ran from the kitchen when I realized that he and I were alone in the house

"How was your appointment?" Adam asked.

I wanted to run from the room.

"Enlightening."

"Care to enlighten me?" He asked.

He was wearing different jeans, a white tee shirt tight across his chest. No shoes. I bit my lower lip to the point that I could almost taste blood.

"No."

He sighed.

"We're worried about you."

"I'm seeing him again next week. We have it under control."

"What is it? Betsy is afraid it's the baby."

I was horrified. "It's not."

"I told her that."

I wanted to take off my clothes and make love to him again. What would he do? He was leaning against the counter.

"What time will Betsy be home?"

"Not until after Joey." He was looking at the floor.

I licked my lips. I started unbuttoning my blouse. Adam's eyes grew wide. I dropped my purse to the floor and slid the blouse off my shoulders never taking my eyes from Adam's face. The silky material fluttered to the ground at my feet. I stepped over it and walked to the living room. Adam had picked up my blouse and purse and was following me. I climbed up the stairs removing my bra and dropping it behind me. Adam picked that up as well. I kicked off my shoes. He was retrieving the trail of clothes as I discarded them not saying a word.

At the top of the stairs with Adam only a few steps behind I unbuttoned my pants and let them fall to the carpet. His eyes traveled to the floor with my pants then back to my face. He displayed no emotion in the dark depths of his eyes. I walked out of my pants and started down the hall. I knew it was wrong. I knew this was dangerous. I knew I couldn't stop myself. Only Adam could stop this from happening and I wasn't sure yet what he was thinking.

He picked up my pants from the floor and followed me to my bedroom. He laid my clothes on the bed. I was naked except for my sheer black panties. He just stood there looking at me. I turned to face him wondering if his heart was beating as hard as my heart.

"What are doing Joy?" He finally asked. His voice so rough with desire I wanted to melt into the floor.

"What does it look like Adam?"

"I thought you said this wouldn't happen again?"

"I changed my mind."

He seemed to be warring within himself. Then he said, "I can't do this in here. This is Joey's bed."

"Let's go to your bed then."

He took my hand in his. I followed him to his room. We left the door open. He started to pull back the covers but I stopped him.

"On top of the covers Adam."

He nodded. I bit down on my lower lip. Adam licked his lips. He pushed me gently down on the bed. He reached behind his head grabbing the collar of his shirt he yanked it over his head tossing it to the floor. His shoes came off next then his jeans and boxers. Adam cut like a Greek statue a beautiful fucking man stood naked before me.

"Take my panties off Adam."

His fingers grazed my hips as he pulled down my panties so gently. His eyes tracing the path down my body. He separated my thighs kissing a path up the inside of one leg. Adam was determined to be as sweet and gentle in his lovemaking to prove a point as Joey was rough.

He nipped softly at the apex of my legs at the tender soft flesh of my inner thighs right before teasing me with his tongue at the core of my sex. My back arched off his mattress. A loud deep moan escaped through my lips. His tongue swirled circles around my clit. Then he sucked hard on it causing my breath to catch in my throat. I literally could not breathe. His hands were gripping my thighs holding me open to his mouth.

Adam inserted two fingers into me sliding gently into my body caressing me lovingly. Gentle like him as his tongue and mouth teased my hard little bud. I rolled my hips against his mouth. Words and little moans of pleasure alternately escaped me.

"Oh Adam, I'm getting close baby."

I tugged on his hair then held him close to me. My body was getting close. I could feel the familiar burn of release building. The hot sweet need climbing to the edge of climax. I was almost there. I was panting for him to make me come. Adam's tongue was warm and wet against me. Long slow strokes up and down my folds teasing my clit and my body trembled on the edge. He held me still. Adam was watching me with his eyes. He was forcing my gaze to connect with him while his tongue and mouth sent me over the edge with such a powerful orgasm that I screamed out his name while everything pulsated around his tongue.

"Adam let me come," I pleaded.

He moved up my body. His dick teasing my sensitive folds causing me to shudder beneath him. Adam covered my lips with his. His tongue dove between my lips. It was sensual and weird at the same time tasting myself on his lips. My arms went around his neck. Holding him tightly to me.

Adam buried himself in me. One big thrust of his body and he was buried balls deep inside me. I gasped against his lips. He began a slow sensual rhythm of his body into mine. Our bodies connected at the right angle so that his dick slid across my sensitive clit creating a plethora of sensations in my already overwhelmed body. I wanted to dig my nails into him. I wanted to bite his shoulder marking him as mine. I tugged his hair instead.

He looked down on me not breaking the sweet rhythm of our bodies making love.

"What is this new thing with you pulling my hair?" He asked gently.

I kissed his jaw. I kissed the sweet spot below his ear.

"I want to dig my nails into you so badly," I whispered.

"And," he replied breathlessly still thrusting his sweet body into mine driving me crazy on the verge of another orgasm.

"I tug on your hair to keep from doing it." I laughed self-consciously. "I don't think Betsy would understand if you had claw marks down your back or your ass Adam."

He dropped his forehead against my shoulder. His thrusts were harder into me. My body responded with my release. My clit throbbed against his dick making him groan deep in his chest. A few more thrusts of his body into mine and Adam climaxed. His body trembled with his release. I held him to me. My hands pressing our bodies together. Then his lips were covering my face in soft gentle kisses. My legs wrapped around him holding him tighter to me.

"You know that I love you," he whispered.

"I know."

He brushed the hair from my face. He kissed my cheek, my neck.

"We can't keep doing this Joy. We'll get caught."

"I know."

"But damn I sure do want to."

I laughed.

"You would be a happy man having your cake and eating it too. Loving both Betsy and me?"

It was a question I think I was asking him. He looked at me seriously. Our bodies still connected. He hadn't left me.

"It isn't like that and you know it."

He was right. I did know that. If he could have me Betsy wouldn't be in the picture at least she wouldn't have been before they created the baby inside her body. Now, things were different. Now we had priorities to think of besides ourselves. There was a baby on the way that had to take precedence over what Adam and I were feeling.

"At my appointment today Adam Doc told me that I needed to admit to myself if not to him that I compartmentalize my feelings for you and Joey."

I pulled him to me so I didn't have to look at him while I spoke. He understood. He let me tell him these things without having to look at him.

"Adam, I need for Joey to continue to be the bad boy both in and out of bed so I can hang onto my feelings for you. I don't want to let go of you," I sobbed. He held me tighter.

"What did Doc say?"

"He told me...Adam he told me that someday...someday I would have to let you go."

I felt his tears wet my shoulder.

"What did you say Joy?" He said roughly.

"I didn't say anything."

We were clinging tightly to each other.

Adam raised his head looking at me. "The right thing to do would be to let you go. Fuck I know that but I can't seem to do the right thing," he said. His hand cupped my face holding it. The desperation in his grasp and in his eyes clear and evident.

"Adam, I can't either," I cried softly my cheek rested against his jaw.

"We'll figure it out together Joy."

"We have to Adam before we hurt everyone we love."

### Joey

I came home from school and Adam was leaning back in the recliner watching television. Joy was asleep on the sofa wearing a cute lavender nightgown covered with the quilt that we kept on the back of the sofa. She didn't even open her eyes when I sat down lifting her feet and placing them in my lap.

"How was her doctor's appointment?" I asked Adam.

"She didn't say much," he replied looking from me to Joy then back to me.

"I don't have to work tomorrow does Luke have work for me at the farm?"

"Yeah he does."

"Great. I need to stay busy right now."

"So you have this year and you're done with school?" Adam asked.

"Yeah pretty cool huh?"

"Yeah. I'm proud of you man."

Adam kept looking at the television. Almost like he didn't want to look at me.

"Everything ok?" I asked.

"Yeah why?"

"You seem out of sorts," I suggested.

He did seem out of sorts. Unable to meet my eyes. Like he was hiding something. Things had changed between Adam and I within the last year and I wasn't sure why. It had to go beyond my drinking. Although that was a great deal of the issue between us I was sure. The drinking was out of hand. I knew this but couldn't seem to find the stopping point. The rock bottom that would allow me to get my shit together.

Then there was Joy. She had my head spinning. Her little performance in the sack had me confused as hell. I didn't know how far to push her. I didn't want to hurt her but I liked the rough play and she seemed to like it too. It made my dick hard to control her. To pin her arms down while I pumped into her. Or to take her face down. I liked that feeling of control but I wasn't sure what she was feeling. Joy was good at masking her emotions. She wasn't good at masking her body's reaction to this rough sex. I could feel how wet she got. I could see her heavy breathing. I could see how her body writhed with the passion building inside her so I knew she loved it. I just hadn't figured out when enough was enough.

I looked at her now. Asleep on the other end of the sofa. Her long dark lashes fanned over her cheeks. Damn but she was beautiful. Absently I rubbed her foot resting in my lap. She moaned softly in her sleep then sat up.

"You were a little rough there big guy," she said sleepily drawing her feet up so that her knees were to her chest. She looked at me then Adam   Joy rubbed her eyes.

"How did your doctor's appointment go today?" I asked.

"Fine," she replied. "I think I will go to bed." She rose from the sofa slipping out from beneath the quilt. Her strap slipped down. She pulled it up. Damn she was beautiful. More beautiful than she realized. Adam did though. He couldn't take his eyes off her.

"Joy," she turned at the sound of her name. I held my hand to her. She came back to me. I pulled her into my lap. She seemed uncomfortable or was just that she was sleepy. She reached behind her pulling down her nightie which had bunched up. I grasped her butt in my hands and pulled her tightly to me. "I just wanted to kiss you goodnight baby." I told her.

Then I laid my lips gently on hers. Her hands rested against my chest. Her palms flat against my pecs. Her mouth responding to mine. She broke the kiss.

"Good night Joey"

I patted her ass and released her. She rose to her feet and walked to Adam's chair. She patted his bare shoulder.

"Good night Adam," she said softly.

"Night Joy," he replied covering her hand with his.

Whatever Adam might be feeling he didn't reveal. He had that damned mask in place. He was good at hiding his feelings behind it.

"Want to watch the news and Carson?" I asked.

He looked at me for a second long and hard like he was considering saying no then he smiled and said, "We haven't done that in a long time. I would love to."

## Chapter Five

### Joy

Betsy was so small in stature that at twenty one weeks pregnant her belly was pretty big swollen with Adam's child.

I was late for my period after my sexcapades with Adam and Joey. Joey was climbing the walls with excitement thinking he had knocked me up. This is the only time in our lives when it sucked living on top of each other. They entire group knew my menstrual cycle. Adam left the house with the excuse that his father needed him when Betsy came home with a pregnancy test for me to use. Joey had asked her to bring one home. They both stood in the hallway while I peed on the stick. I had sat on the floor praying to a god I rarely spoke to unless I needed him but believed in desperately asking him to let me not be pregnant.

Betsy rapped on the door telling me it was time. On shaking legs I had stood to look at that test. One single line. I wasn't pregnant. I nearly hyperventilated I was so relieved. With tears in my eyes I opened the door and handed them the stick. Joey was disappointed. Betsy hugged me to her. No one could figure out why I was so late. My periods were usually regular like clockwork. Most likely god playing a mean game with me. A month later my period came and after that I seemed to be back to normal.

I never knew what Adam was thinking about me being late for my period. We didn't discuss it. We had not been left alone since then either so there had been no repeat performance of our love making. Betsy and Adam were going to get married on New Year's Eve at the farm. Betsy's choice. She wanted to start the New Year with her new life. I was going to be Maid of Honor. Of course Joey would be Best Man just as they had stood up for us. They had decided to invite Stephanie and Benny, Shay and Bobbie and Marta our only other friends were invited. Luke would give Betsy away. This time Mandy would be at the wedding.

Betsy was patient with me letting me feel the baby move inside her. I often wondered who it would look like her or Adam. I was fascinated by the child rolling about inside her belly. I loved her that much more for not getting frustrated with me. They were going to their first ultrasound today. She had asked me to come with them. I thought it was strange to invite me. This should be a private moment between them. She had already told me that Adam was certain he couldn't do the delivery room with her so she had asked me to be there. Maybe not so strange that she had invited me along then. What did I know?

I went. Everything was going beautifully with her pregnancy. She absolutely glowed. I stood by her head when the tech pulled down her pants and tucked in a paper towel. Betsy lifted her shirt so that the tech could squirt gel on her belly. Betsy held Adam's hand. His other hand rested at the small of my back grounding me keeping me from jumping out of my skin. He knew this. I knew this. Hopefully Betsy knew too. My lower lip trembled when the heartbeat, the whooshing, whooshing of their child's beating heart filled the room. A tear trickled down my face. I saw her squeeze Adam's hand. His eyes met hers. He smiled. Then she looked at me.

"You okay?" she asked me.

I nodded. Then I focused on the screen. I could see their baby. It's head. The features that seemed so like Adams' unless I was just trying to see him in the image on the screen. Long arms and legs floated around the image. Little fingers wiggled at us. We laughed.

"Do you want to know the sex of your baby?"

Adam and Betsy looked at each other then they looked at me. I wiped away another tear.

"I don't know why you are looking at me," I said softly.

They both nodded at the tech eager to know what they were having.

She moved around Betsy's stomach.

"There," she said. "Plain as day. You're having a little boy"


## Betsy

The ride home was painfully quiet. I knew Adam was lost in his thoughts. He looked at me from time to time. A gentle smile on his face. The person I was worried about was Joy.

She was far away. I had asked her to go to the ultrasound to see the baby hoping it would make it that much more real to her. Cruel I thought. Probably. I was hoping by the time our baby arrived she would be better. I was so worried about her.

The boys weren't talking about it since that first morning she left without eating. Joy had gone to the therapist again. She continued to see Dr. Joffrey. I had seen it though. She had lost weight. At least fifteen pounds I thought. I wanted to force her ass on the scales to see what we were dealing with but knew it would not be a good confrontation. As much as I had gained she had lost. She didn't seem sad about my baby. She didn't seem happy either. Just fascinated by it. I wasn't sure what to think. Adam didn't want to discuss Joy. If she wasn't dealing with our baby how would she deal with the marriage coming up soon?

I bit my lower lip in concentration. Adam reached across the truck seat and patted my leg. He turned the truck down the lane towards the farm house. Luke and Mandy were waiting for us. I had pictures and video of our baby to show them. Luke's first grandchild. He was supportive of whatever choice we wanted to make. Always supportive always quiet in the background.

Always watching Joy to see if she was okay. We all were if I was honest. I loved her with all my heart but I wanted the focus to be on me for a change. Was that selfish? When the truck was parked next to Luke's truck Joy hopped out. She skirted Adam and headed towards the pastures behind the barns. Adam and I looked at each other. I called her name. She hesitated and then turned towards us.

"Where the hell are you going? It's only forty degrees out. You only have on a light jacket."

"I need to walk," she replied shakily.

Then she turned on her heel and was off again. I knew where she was going. Did he?

"You have to go after her."

Adam looked down at me with exasperation. "She'll be fine. She just needs to burn off steam."

"Adam when she's like this she does dumbass things. She's heading towards that pool in the woods. If she decides to go swimming today she'll die from hyperthermia. Please go after her."

"All right dammit. Are you sure you're okay?"

"Adam, I'm perfect. Our baby is healthy. I'm just worried about Joy."

"Me too."

"Then go after her."

### Adam

I saw Joy slip through the dead thorn bushes and I picked up speed. Damn if I trusted her to not strip down and dive into that water no matter how fucking cold it was. When I arrived at the pool she was sitting by the edge trailing her fingers in the water.

"What are you doing Joy?"

"Imagining what the water would feel like on my skin."

"Don't fucking do it," I snapped.

She looked at me. Her beautiful eyes were round and sad.

"Adam I think I am crazy just like him," her voice sounded broken. "Will you trust me with your child?"

"Yes," he replied without hesitation. "You are not like him Joy. You aren't. You're sad and sometimes you're anxious but you're not like him. Don't think like that. Betsy and I will both trust you with our children."

"I don't think I can do this anymore Adam. The closer it gets to you marrying her the worse the weight feels like its crushing me."

I grabbed her in my arms lifting her feet off the ground. I forced her to look at me.

"I lived through you fucking marrying my best friend and you will live through my marriage."

"You are stronger than me."

She let a tear fall from her eye. I crushed her to my chest. Her tears soaking my shirt beneath my winter jacket.

"What do you want me to do Joy?" I asked her whispering the words into her hair.

"We have no choices Adam. I left us none. I just want this crushing pain to go away. I want to look at you and not feel like I will never stop loving you."

I held her tighter still not knowing what else to do for her.

"Do you still love me?"

"I do," I whispered the words to her for only her ears to hear. "You can't give up on me now Joy."

Joy pulled out of my arms. Her beautiful eyes gazed into mine. She pulled my head down until our lips touched. I wanted to push her down into the cold grass and pull her pants down so I could bury myself inside her but I knew that would only make it harder for her.

I cupped Joy's face in my hands and held her lips to mine. She covered my hands with hers. Our breath like smoke in the air it was so cold. She trembled in my arms.

"You're cold. Let's walk back."

She nodded.

### Joey

Christmas Day we were all going to Luke's for Christmas as usual. Betsy and I were waiting in the living room for Adam and Joy. Joy was in our room getting dressed. Adam was in the shower. I hadn't much time alone with Betsy unless I took her to work which I hadn't done for a while because Joy had been taking her. Bets was absolutely stunning I had to admit gazing at her while I was sitting with her on the sofa.

The baby was active right now. I had my hand on her belly and she was letting me feel him move inside her. It was an amazing thing to share with them. I volunteered to go in the delivery room but had been shot down on that one. Adam apparently didn't want me seeing too much of his wife to be. I didn't know why he refused to be there. You couldn't keep me out when Joy gave birth to our kids.

We heard Adam coming down the steps. Betsy looked at him smiling like only he existed. He stopped seeing me with my hand on her belly.

"Where's Joy?" He asked.

"Still getting dressed," I said.

He turned heading back up the stairs. "I will hurry her along," he volunteered.

Betsy never seemed to mind the connection that the two of them had. She never seemed jealous. I on the other hand always had a nagging thought in the back of my mind what if? What if she and I weren't together? I couldn't seem to shake it. Adam and Joy were tight. I knew it. He knew her before I did. There was an intimacy that existed between them that didn't exist between me and Joy or Adam and Betsy. Did Betsy see it?

I gazed into Betsy's eyes. I saw nothing but bliss. The woman was on top of the world. The child inside her kicked the crap out of my hand at that moment. I leaned over getting close to her stomach my hand still resting there I talked to baby inside. I had heard they could hear you. I wanted the little guy to know my voice.

"Hey little man," I said. "I'm your uncle Joey. I love you already kid. Your dad and I go way back. I've seen you on video you know." I patted Betsy's stomach. "I promise to get you into lots of trouble." I looked into Betsy's eyes. Gave her my best sexy wink. She laid her hand on mine and lovingly patted it.

"He's not kidding Noah."

"Noah huh?" I said.

She nodded.

"I like that name."

"I'm glad you approve Joseph," Betsy said laughing at me.

"Well Noah as I was saying you are going to live with us. I hope for a really long time so I can make you a really bad boy for your mommy and daddy. That is my job."

"Enough Joey."

We looked at the stairs and found Adam and Joy standing at the bottom. Adam had his hand resting on Joy's shoulder. They were watching us and smiling.

"You are going to be a really good Uncle Joey," Joy told me a little teary eyed.

"I can't wait to get my hands on the little guy," I said.

"Let's go," Adam said. "We're going to be late thanks to Joy."

"Thanks Adam. Throw me under the bus."

He swatted her on the butt something I hadn't seen him do in a very long time. I looked at Betsy to see her reaction. She didn't react so I didn't. I gazed at my wife. She seemed to be having a good day. It felt good to see Joy having one. She had started slipping back into depression. Adam, Betsy and I had talked about it once. Then not again. Preferring to bury our heads and hope that she would get better. She was seeing her therapist once a week still so we left her to her own hoping she would continue to get better.

I see her naked though. My girl has lost weight. She was having trouble sleeping again. I didn't know what had set her back other than Adam and Betsy getting married. I didn't understand it. Was she afraid of losing him? They had been friends close friends for a long time. I didn't know what to do for her and it was tearing me apart.

We rode in Adam's truck to the farm. The gifts the girls had bought in the back of the truck. I sure as hell didn't know what had been purchased I wondered if Adam knew. The girls went into the house linking arms while Adam and I carried in the gifts. He loaded my arms first then grabbed the remainder for himself.

"Do you think Joy is better today Adam?"

He hesitated bumping the bed closed with his thigh thinking about her demeanor today. "I guess Joey. I hadn't really thought about it."

I needed reassurance where Joy was concerned.

"Adam, she has lost some serious weight again."

He looked at me with concern. "I know Joey. Betsy has been talking to me about it. She wants to make her get on the scales to see how much."

"What do you think?"

"I don't think that is a good idea." He rolled his eyes.

"Why?"

Adam stopped walking. He looked at me seriously. "Really Joey. She's fragile and you want to force her on the bathroom scales to see what she weighs? What do we do with the number once we have it?"

"I don't know. Adam she was small to begin with but my guess is twenty pounds. She must weigh about one hundred ten or one hundred fifteen at most."

"Damn," he replied. "I can talk to her if you want."

"Nothing Betsy or I have said to her has worked. Maybe you can get through to her or at least convince her to talk to her doc about it."

Adam and I put the gifts under the tree in the living room. We had cut it down in the woods ourselves. A seven foot blue spruce. The girls had decorated it with twinkling lights, old bulbs that had been in Luke's family for years and lots of tensile that he complained he would be cleaning up for weeks once we took the tree down. Garland adorned the mantle red and silver bulbs hung from the garland and stockings with all our names hung form the mantle. The girls had added a stocking for Mandy this year. Next year Noah would have his own stocking.

With dinner Adam served a white wine which I didn't drink so I grabbed a beer out of the cooler on the back porch pissing my wife off immediately. Mandy had made a turkey stuffed with homemade dressing. Sweet potatoes with melted butter, brown sugar and marshmallows melted over top, green bean casserole, homemade biscuits, mashed potatoes and gravy. We had a homemade Christmas dinner. Luke was a fairly good cook ensuring that Adam and I had a great childhood with dinners but nothing homemade. We were drooling at the mouth.

I failed to notice the second glass of wine that Joy had or the third. Adam noticed. They were cleaning up the dinner dishes. She dropped two. He made her sit down.

"I'm fine Adam," she slurred her words.

I walked into the kitchen hearing her. Luke and I had been talking in the living room until the crash occurred.

"I'm sorry Luke."

"Sweetie you don't have to apologize. Dishes can be replaced."

"Joy how much did you drink?" I asked.

"Fuck off Joey. How many beers did you have tonight?"

Wow. What did I do to piss on her campfire?

Betsy joined Joy at the kitchen table. "What's up sweetie?" She asked.

"Joey is always the life of the party. He has cases of beer in one night. I drink three glasses of wine. Drop two plates because they are slippery and suddenly he's asking me how much I've had to drink."

"Sweetie it doesn't matter."

"It does matter."

"Joy could I talk to you outside?" I asked her.

She rose from the chair and followed me outside still furious with me.

I walked out into the yard. She followed me. I turned to her searching her face for answers. She stood looking at me hands on hips.

"What Joey?"

I ran my fingers through my hair. "What the fuck is your problem tonight?"

The nighttime air was cool. Joy was shivering without a coat on.

"You are my problem Joseph."

"Why am I a problem Joy? Because I fucking asked you how much you had to drink tonight?"

"You drink like a fish every party we go to and one damned night I have three glasses of wine and you act all high and mighty with me."

"I'm fucking worried about you Joy."

"Why Joey? Why are you worried?"

I wanted to shake her. Couldn't she see what was happening to herself?

"What is wrong Joy? Why are you doing this to yourself this time? Is it your dad? Is it Adam? Are you afraid of losing him? What is it?"

Her eyes turned cold. She swung at me before I could react and cocked me in the jaw with her deadly right hook. She was small but her right hook was mighty.

"You bastard," she screamed at me.

What the hell did I do? Touch a nerve?

She started to cock her fist back to hit me again and I grabbed her fist bending her arm behind her back. She cried out in pain. I forgot my own strength especially when I was pissed off. I heard Luke's voice. Then I felt his arm on my shoulder.

"Let her go son. You're hurting her."

I released Joy's arm immediately. When she swung around to face me Joy had tears in her eyes. She was holding her shoulder. Still obviously in pain. Luke grabbed her in his arms.

"You all right baby girl?" He asked.

She shook her head no. "I just want to go home," she cried.

"Adam will you take Joy home please," Luke asked.

"I can take her home," I said.

Luke looked at me over Joy's head. "Son, I think you need to let Adam take Joy home. You stay here for a bit and cool off"

I knew better than to argue with him. I watched as Betsy helped Joy into her coat favoring the arm I had bent behind her back. I had hurt her shoulder. She closed the door on Adam's truck. He bent down and kissed the top of Betsy's head. Then strode around the front to get in the driver's side. I watched the tail lights disappear in the darkness.

"Come inside Joey," Betsy told me wrapping her arm through mine.

"I fucked up Bets."

"You both did Joey."


**Adam**

Driving down the lanc I looked at Joy she was staring out the window. I slammed my fist against the steering wheel. She jumped in the seat.

"Lovely performance I put on for the family," she said.

"How's your arm?"

"I'll be fine."

"It still hurts then."

"He didn't mean to hurt me. I slugged him hard the first time. I was getting ready to hit him again."

"Why exactly did you hit him knowing Joey's temper?"

"He opened his stupid mouth."

I didn't push her. God only knows what Joey said. I turned the truck into the driveway. Joy was out of the truck before I had the truck in park. She stomped up the sidewalk to the porch steps. I followed her. I wanted to be sure she was okay before I went back to the farm to get Joey and Betsy. She went straight up the stairs. I hesitated at the bottom watching her go. I wasn't sure that I should follow her. I looked at the floor trying to decide. I had been standing here a minute or two before I took the steps two at a time. I strode down the hallway and opened her bedroom door. She whirled around quickly grasping her shirt in front of her but not before I saw her back and her ribs before she covered them with the shirt.

I stalked across the room and yanked the shirt from her hands. She had picked at her food at dinner tonight. I tossed the shirt on the bed. Grabbing her around the waist I carried her out of the bedroom fighting me every step of the way. Joey was not exaggerating when he said she had lost weight.

"Stop fighting me."

"Where are you taking me?" She asked.

I opened the bathroom door with my free hand. She couldn't weigh much more than one hundred pounds. I sat her down on the bathroom floor.

"Get on the scales," I told her.

"No," she told me with tears forming in her eyes.

"If you don't get on them I will put you on them."

I was staring her down. This had gone too far. Joey should have said something sooner.

"Get on the damned scales now."

She pulled them away from the wall and got on backwards so she didn't have to look. I looked for her. I tried to keep the horror out my eyes when I saw how low the number had become. I covered my mouth with my hand. I lowered my eyes. She stood on the scale trembling. Her breathing becoming raged. She was starting to have a panic attack.

"Come on baby" I took her hand. Her eyes took on the terrified look that meant she wasn't hearing me. I scooped her up in my arms and carried her to her room. I spoke softly to her as I walked down the hallway with her. I placed her in their bed and covered her. I kept talking to her caressing her face.

Her breathing eventually returned to normal. My heart was beating hard in my chest.

"Can I have one of my pills?"

I reached into her nightstand and grabbed two bottles. "Which one?"

She took them both and took the one she wanted. It was the anxiety medication. It made her sleepy I knew. She snuggled under the covers and closed her eyes. I stayed with her caressing her face. Afraid to leave her. I nodded off myself.

"Adam," Betsy's voice woke me.

I stretched and rolled over to a sitting position. My hand had been laying on Joy's stomach. I wondered what she was thinking seeing me like this with Joy. I looked into Betsy's eyes. I couldn't even begin to read what she was thinking.

"How is she?'

I pulled Betsy into my arms and laid my head against her chest. I just needed her to hold me.

"Adam, are you okay?"

"See if you can look at her under the covers without waking her. Where's Joey?"

"I left him downstairs. When you didn't return and you weren't downstairs I didn't know what was going on?"

"What does that mean Betsy?"

"Nothing Adam?" She shook her head tiredly.

She walked to the other side of the bed and lifted them, then she looked at me across the bed with tears in her eyes.

"She weighs one hundred two pounds," I said quietly.

"How do you know?" She whispered.

"Let's go downstairs," I said.

I took her hand at the end of the bed and led her to the hallway shutting the door behind me. I took Betsy in my arms and held her.

"Adam how did it get this bad?"

"I don't know. Joey just mentioned it to me this morning. She's been wearing heavier clothing so we wouldn't notice is my guess."

"How do you know how much she weighs?"

"I went upstairs to check on her. Betsy I saw her in her underwear. I carried her to the bathroom and made her get on the scales. Then she had a panic attack. That is why I stayed."

"Oh Adam I'm so sorry. I really wasn't questioning you."

**You should Betsy.**

I couldn't break her heart though. I couldn't tell her about making love to Joy. We walked down the stairs. Joey was in the kitchen. I led Betsy there to confront him. He was her husband. There was little that she and I could do without him.

"Joey," I said still angry at him for hurting her. I knew she shouldn't have hit him but he was stronger than her. He had hurt her arm badly. The two of them together were volatile and Joy was getting hurt because of it.

"Adam how is she?"

"Her arm is going to be sore in the morning."

"Adam I'm sorry. I lost my temper. My only thought was I wasn't going to let her punch me again."

"Why did she hit you? She said you said something?"

He looked at me then he dropped his eyes to the floor. "I asked her if she was afraid of losing you. I know you two have been close for a long time. You knew her before I did and that is what set her off. She hauled off and punched me in the jaw."

I felt my insides shrivel painfully. I looked at Betsy but her face revealed nothing. I looked back at Joey and shook my head. What had become of us?

"Joey when you told me about Joy this morning I started looking a little closer at her. I will be honest I confronted Joy in your bedroom and saw her undressing. She was in her underwear. Man she is not in good shape. I made her get on the scales. She wouldn't look at the number but I did. She weighs one hundred two pounds. Doesn't she usually weigh around one hundred twenty five or thirty?"

Joey dropped into a chair at the kitchen table. He was devastated. I guess he had seen her slipping away but not realized how bad it was. Betsy and I not seeing her without her clothes on could clearly see how bad it was. He looked up with troubled eyes.

"What do we do?"

"Adam and I are going to just go the justice of the peace. We aren't having a wedding."

Joy appeared at the kitchen door at that moment.

"Why would you do that?" She asked. Her voice was soft with sleep.

Betsy walked over to Joy and took her hands in hers. Joy was wearing a bulky sweatshirt and sweatpants now.

"I think this is too much for you right now."

Joy looked over Betsy's shoulder at me. There were tears in her eyes.

"I know that I'm not doing well but that isn't fair to you or Adam. You deserve a wedding. It's your only one Bets."

"I don't need it Joy."

Joy crumpled to the ground wrapping her arms around her knees. She sobbed into her arms. Betsy dropped to the floor by Joy and put her arms around her. She laid her head on Joy's shoulder. Joey and I looked at each other. Then we crossed the room and sat on the floor by our girls. We wrapped them up between us. Holding them close.

"Don't cancel your wedding," Joy sobbed.

"Sweetie, when is your next doctor's appointment?"

"On Tuesday, why?" Joy looked at Betsy.

"I would like to go with you and talk to Doctor Joffrey if you would let me."

She gazed at Betsy for several long minutes. We all waited to see what Joy would say.

"Joy I think I would like to go too," Joey said quietly.

I looked across at Joey. His eyes told me to go too. I took a deep breath. I knew she told this guy our most intimate secrets.

"I want to go too," I said reluctantly.

"We want you to get better. The only way I won't cancel our wedding is if you let us all go with you," Betsy told Joy.

She swiped her shirt sleeve across her face. We weren't giving her a choice. She looked trapped. She wouldn't ruin Betsy's chance at a wedding and she knew that Betsy would do it too. Joy had that deer in the headlight look right now which made me feel sorry for her.

"All right," she said softly. "The appointment is Tuesday at 5:30 PM."

## Chapter Six

### Joy

Everyone had more important things to do with Adam and Betsy's wedding tomorrow at midnight but they all showed up for my doctor's appointment. I felt ganged up on. Surprisingly even Luke was informed about the intervention. He hugged me to him when he walked in the waiting area.

"We love you just remember that," he told me.

I was standing in the circle of his arms when Doc opened the door to come out to get me. The shocked look on his face when he saw my entourage would have been hysterical under other circumstances. I made the introductions.

"Interesting," was all he said.

He invited everyone into the inter-office to talk. Betsy spoke on behalf of everyone telling Doc what was going on with me. Apparently they thought I was starving myself. Food just didn't appeal to me.

Doc took notes while they talked. He gave them half my appointment. Betsy did most of the talking. He pointedly asked Joey, Adam and Luke certain questions. Then he asked if he could have time to talk to me. Betsy patted my hand before she left. Luke patted my shoulder. The boys just left the room.

Doc looked at me for a second. Then he said, "Want to tell me how you feel?"

"Ganged up on."

"Why?"

"I don't know. They mean well."

He asked a series of questions that led him to make the following statement to me.

"Joy are you afraid of eating?"

I gasped.

"Why do you ask that?"

"Can you answer that?"

"I'm not afraid of eating food doesn't appeal to me."

"I don't believe you," he said.

"What?"

"Joy, you and I are always honest with each other." He nodded. "I think subconsciously you control food because you can't control things like Adam marrying Betsy or your dad hurting you and you losing yours and Adam's baby." He hesitated. "You have to control something so you control your food intake. It's called Anorexia. You're wasting away to nothing Joy," he said. "Betsy wrote down for me what you weigh because you don't want to face how small you actually are. You have body issues. Did you hear Adam and Luke both say they feel you have always had body issues?"

"I have not."

"Where you listening to them?"

"No."

"Adam said you've always thought you had a big butt. His father agreed with him. Said you wouldn't eat lunch or dinner with them at times because of it."

I looked away.

"Joy you know me. I don't pull any punches with you. I'm not going to now. If you don't respond to treatment for this I'm going to hospitalize you. You're too close to a dangerous weight for your body to start shutting down. I intend to tell them that too. What do you see when you look in the mirror Joy?"

"I don't."

"You don't what?"

"The mirror is not my friend. I don't look in the mirror."

He shook his head. "I want you to meet with a nutritionist once a week. I will give you her name. She's really good with girls who have problems like yours. You will continue to meet with me once a week. You have to start gaining weight Joy. Can I call your family back in here?"

And that is exactly what Doc did causing everyone in the room to stare at me with obvious concern. He laid it all on the table telling them exactly how serious this was. He told them about Anorexia Nervosa and the nutritionist's weekly visits plus his weekly appointments. If progressive weight gain didn't happen my ass was going to the hospital and I was sure it was the psychiatric wing he was talking about.

Adam was leaning forward on his knees. He was troubled. I knew his stance. Joey was leaning back. Hands behind his head. He was taking it in thinking. Luke straight back arms crossed over his chest. They all had their signs indicating the state of their emotions. How had things gotten so bad? Betsy was leaning over touching my arm. She needed to touch me when she was troubled.

"I think we should cancel the wedding tomorrow," she said.

"Oh no you don't," I replied. "I agreed that you all could come here if you didn't cancel the wedding."

I could feel the anger, the heat rising up my face.

"Doc help me out here?" Betsy pleaded with him.

He looked at me intensely.

"Betsy if Joy wants this for you the best thing you can do for her is do it. Postponing it will only hurt her."

Tears filled my eyes. He knew what I knew. Eventually Adam would do the right thing. He had to marry her. Their baby was coming in May. His son could not be born without his name. He wouldn't allow him to be born illegitimate. No matter how he felt about me they would be married. I wanted them to get married. It would be better for me when they did. Just getting to that point was difficult for me.

"All right," she agreed.

I squeezed the hand she had resting on my arm.

"The nutritionist will weigh Joy every week and report to someone in your family her progress since this seems to be an obsession she doesn't want to deal with but Joy eventually I'm going to make you face it. I assume that will be Joey?"

"I would prefer it was Luke if Joey doesn't mind." I jumped in quickly with that suggestion.

Joey looked hurt but Luke smacked him on the back. "I will go with her to the nutritionist every week. No hard feelings Joseph. The important thing is that she gets better."

Why did I want Luke? Because I knew Luke wouldn't hound me. He would comfort me. He would hold me but he wouldn't hound me. The others would be on my ass. Luke had his own way of dealing with me. He had his fatherly way that I needed right now.

We ate dinner at Luke's that night. Joey skipped school to be with us. Mandy was there as well becoming more of a fixture in the family. Making it more awkward they watched the food I put on my plate and what went into my mouth.

"Guys we've had one session. This isn't going to change overnight," I finally said unable to bare the scrutiny any longer.

They all looked away. I sighed.

"I feel crazy enough…just like him. I don't need you hovering." I was resting my forehead in the palm of my hand.

"Enough," Adam said. "I've told you before you are nothing like him Joy."

"Adam how do you know?" I nearly cried.

"Because I know you," he said softy.

It was like no one else was in the room. Then I realized the others were looking at us. I became uncomfortable. I took a bite of food to have something to do. It felt like it was stuck in my throat. I washed it down with water. Then realized they were all looking at me again waiting to see if I would take another bite.

I began shoveling food in my mouth until I couldn't hold anymore while tears flowed freely down my face. Then I started choking. I ran to the sink and spit it out. Gagging. Trying not to throw up which would have ruined everyone's dinner. I laid my head on my arms and sobbed. Luke was there lifting my body turning me into his arms. They were all looking at me. I turned my head away looking out the window.

"Come with me Joy. You and I are going to the living room for a bit. The rest of you continue eating without us."

He sat down on the sofa with his arms wrapped around my waist. My head rested just beneath his jaw. I cried until Luke's shirt was soaked. When I was done he lifted my head and looked me in the eyes.

"Better?" He asked.

"I'm humiliated."

"We're your family. You never have to be embarrassed with us," he said tenderly.

He kissed my forehead.

"Why am I broken?" I asked.

"Because life hasn't been kind to you kid. The thing is we need to work on fixing you. I know why you picked me over Joey. They tend to railroad you into things…bullying you then burying their heads in the sand when they think you are all better?"

I nodded.

"I'm going to be with you every second kid until you are better. I've stood by too long again. I won't bully you but I won't let you fool me like you do them."

"I understand."

"I'm going to both appointments," Luke said firmly. "I expect the nutritionist to tell me what you weigh then I'm going to make sure Doc Joffrey knows what the nutritionist says. Got it?"

"She'll send him reports I'm sure."

"That's fine but I want to hear from his mouth that he knows. Okay?"

I nodded.

"We're going to get through this together. Me and you and if they want to help that is fine," he pointed to the kitchen. "I expect you will have slip ups." I nodded. "We'll work through those too."

"I'm sorry Luke."

"What are you sorry for?"

"For being a pain in the ass."

"Listen to me Joy Bonds. I love you like my own kid. That means unconditional love. If you think those two idiots in the kitchen haven't fucked up in their lives your dead wrong."

The two idiots in question cleared their throats causing Luke and I to look their way. They were standing shoulder to shoulder. His hands were still cupped around my face. I turned my head quickly back towards Luke.

"Did anyone tell you could come in here?" Luke asked gruffly.

"No," Adam said but we wanted to know that she was all right."

"They can come in."

They both walked to the sofa. Joey sat beside me his thighs touching me he was so close. The way I was sitting my back was still to him. I leaned into Luke and he pressed my face to his chest. I was still embarrassed. I wanted to hide from them. Adam squatted on the floor in front of his father's legs. He touched my back patting it comfortingly. I kept my face buried in Luke's chest not wanting to look at either of them.

"We can't begin to understand what you are going through Joy," he said.

"No you can't," Luke agreed. "None of us have ever dealt with this type of illness before. We can't make her eat. We can't make her feel self-conscious about eating like we just did," Luke said softly. "We have to be supportive. I'm just as guilty as you two are."

"I know Pa. We should have seen this earlier. We should have seen what was happening."

Adam sounded so sad.

"Boys that isn't what I'm saying. We just need to move forward making the main focus getting Joy the help she needs to get better. And dammit quit watching every bite she puts into her mouth. How would you two feel it you were under a microscope? Hell Adam you eat everything but the refrigerator. Would you like for us to start pointing that out?" He said trying to make a point.

I couldn't help myself I chuckled against Luke. I felt his head move against mine. He was looking down at me.

"We get it Luke," Joey responded for them both.

"I've told Joy I'm going to both appointments every week until we see a significant improvement but that doesn't mean I'm going to police what she's eating."

Adam's dark eyes met mine. I wanted to get lost in them but my husband was sitting next to me. I was being held in his father's arms. His soon to be wife was in the other room. I closed my eyes breaking the connection. Wishing him away. I wished hard enough and my wish was granted. He stood and walked over to the fireplace.

"Joy has to do her part too," he said firmly.

"I'm going to Adam," I said with a little snarkiness of my old self.

"Adam if you think she could have prevented this you're wrong," Luke said.

I turned towards Adam not too far out of Luke's arms but enough I could see his response. His face.

"I didn't say that."

"Sounds like you were implying that son."

"I wasn't," he said tiredly. He ran his hands through his hair. "I will be honest here. I'm scared."

My breath caught in my throat.

"The first time I saw her on Christmas day in her underwear I was terrified we had waited too long. When I put her on the scales and saw how little she weighed, I almost dropped to my knees then I felt guilty that I hadn't seen it."

"I hid behind my heavy sweaters and sweatshirts Adam. I didn't want any of you to see it."

"No excuse Joy."

"I did see it sweetheart and I still didn't say anything to Adam until Christmas day," Joey said.

I turned even more in Luke's arm not letting him release me. I laid my head against the back of the couch and looked into Joey's face. He looked so sad. I touched his jaw.

"Then I damned near ripped your arm off..."

"Joey stop. Don't bring that up now," I said softly. He captured my hand in his and pressed the palm to his lips. There were tears in his eyes. Luke released me to Joey who pulled me into his arms holding me tight against him.

"I'm so sorry baby. I feel like I've failed you."

Out of the corner of my eye I saw Adam lower his eyes. Hiding his emotions.

"Nobody has any reason to feel guilty. Nobody failed me except maybe Jack and Mariah Ayers. Like Luke said let's just focus on me getting better. I'm sorry I keep adding to the mess that is me. I will work on getting better."

I looked over and saw Mandy in the doorway with her arm around Betsy. They both had tears in their eyes. Betsy walked across the floor and plopped down on Joey's lap so she could snuggle with me. It was the only spot that got her close enough unless she sat on Luke which just wasn't happening. He wrapped us both in his arms squeezing us tight. Her nose was against mine.

"We're all one big fucking mess sweetie. Adam is probably the only normal one of the four of us," she laughed. He snorted in the background. "That is thanks to Luke. A shame he couldn't have raised all of us."

"Fuck no," Luke ground out. "You two girls would have been the death of me."

Betsy reached over and pinched Luke on the arm.

"Stop that Shorty before I throw you out."

"You wouldn't do that I'm the mother of your grandchild."

"That you are."

Luke caressed my arm letting me know he remembered the grandbaby that I had carried if only for a short time.

"I love you girls. I want you to know that. Damn you've made me soft in my old age," he added as an afterthought.

Adam laughed under his breath.

"Got a problem son?"

"I work with you nearly every day. There isn't damn thing about you that is soft."

"I'm whipping you into shape boy so you can take over the farm then I can retire."

"Is that right?" Adam told his father.

"That's right."

"You wouldn't know what to do with yourself if you had nothing to do old man," Joey decided to pipe into the conversation.

"I want pie Joy. Do you want pie?" Betsy asked. "Mandy made it homemade. Noah really wants pie."

I knew she wanted us to leave before the boys and Luke started throwing insults at each other. Joey calling Luke *old man* wasn't going down without some mudslinging,

"Let's go to the kitchen," I agreed.

I stood and grabbed her hand pulling her from Joey's lap. It almost felt like old times. Mandy went to the kitchen with us. The men stayed behind. Mandy cut three pieces of her homemade cherry pie. She sat the piece in front of me. It was my favorite pie. I picked for a while lifting the crust playing with it. I rose from my chair. Both ladies pretended not to be interested in what I was doing. With the spoon I retrieved from the drawer I scooped the filling out of the pie and sucked it into my mouth. I nearly licked the pie crust clean. That was the only food I had actually eaten that day. I really did need to work on food consumption. When I finished Betsy pushed her plate over to me.

"I'm not eating yours too."

"Noah is full," she said patting her rounded tummy. "Mandy gave me a bigger piece," she tried again.

"Liar."

She left the piece in front of me and kept talking to Mandy while she ate my crust. Her favorite part of the pie. I rolled my eyes. I scooped her filling out and ate it too then pushed the plate back to her. Betsy was grinning from ear to ear. She scarfed down the crust like a starving dog. Mandy put both our plates in the dishwasher then walked around the table and put both arms around my neck hugging me tight. She would make a great mother if Luke would make an honest woman out of her. I wonder if they talked about it.

"One step at a time," she told me.

A tear fell down my cheek as I patted her arms around my neck.

### Adam

Today was hectic. The girls decorated with Mandy. Pa kept us busy running errands. We picked up the cake and food for afterwards. We hung out at our house. The girls were at the farmhouse since that is where the wedding was taking place at midnight. I wasn't supposed to see my bride today. My insides felt like a twisted knot of nerves. I wanted to make Betsy happy. I cared for her. Our baby was due in a little over four months. She was beautiful, sweet and everything a man could ask for but I still loved Joy. I had gotten good at hiding my feelings for her. I was a great pretender.

We were wearing the same grey suits that we wore to Joey's wedding to Joy. I had no clue what the girls were wearing. Apparently they had gone shopping. Pa giving Betsy the same amount of money he had given Joy when she married Joey. He was loving the girls in his life. He had taken them both in and made them family. I knew he loved them both but Joy had touched him most. Maybe her troubles. Maybe just her. She was something. Tender, sweet, broken and a hellcat all rolled into one.

Everyone practically cheered when we got home and Joy went upstairs to change Betsy told us she ate the filling from two pieces of pie. Of course that was probably all she had eaten all day if I remembered correctly. Pa told us we weren't allowed to hound her about eating. I didn't even know if she ate this morning. Joy had Betsy out the door before Joey and I got out of bed.

She was at the house to pick up the cake and the meal for after the wedding. She flew into the house like a bat out of hell. It was six o'clock. Betsy had cancelled her plans to have our friends come to the wedding tonight fearing it would be too much for Joy. It was just going to be family and Mandy. If she was happy I was happy. Joy was driving my truck. She went upstairs for something. Joey was engrossed in television with Pa so I followed her up the stairs.

"What you doing Joy?" I asked her. She had her back to me sitting on the bed near her nightstand.

She turned looking at me with a surprised expression.

"What are you doing Joy?"

"I'm not doing anything Adam, "she said.

I walked over to the bed and sat down next to her. "What's in your hand?"

"My anxiety pills."

"How many have you had today?" She didn't respond. "Could I see the bottle?" She handed it to me. "Half milligram three times a day. Joy how many have you had today?"

"I'm trying to be there for Betsy Adam. Be the friend she needs today without melting into the ground. Adam cut me some slack."

"We can't let you OD on these damn things. How many have you taken?"

She sighed. "I'm not going to fucking OD." She was irritated.

"Either tell me what you've taken or I go downstairs and talk to Joey and Pa."

"Fuck you Adam," she snapped at me.

I ran my hand through my hair frustrated with her fucking mood swings. Were we going through detox next?

"What's next Joy?"

"What do you mean Adam?"

"Well we've been through it all with you what is next?"

She gasped. You would have thought I had slapped her. I had never been mean to Joy. I loved her too much to ever hurt her but I was at the end of my rope with Joy.

"That was mean Adam."

"I just don't think I can take anything else. I won't survive another issue with you. Watching someone else comfort you…take care of you while I have to pretend to be just your friend. Do you fucking hear me? Now tell me how many of those damned pills you took today?" My voice was shaking as I finished those last few words.

"Five."

I looked at the pill bottle in my hand.

"You're done."

"Just let me get through today please Adam."

"Three a day Joy. You've already exceeded the dose by two."

"I won't take another one until it…until later."

She had tears in her eyes. Her hands trembled.

"Tell me you have never done this before."

"I've never done this before. I swear to you."

"I will make a deal with you. I keep the pills. You get one. You decide when you take it so make it last."

She almost dropped to the ground in relief. I put my arms around her and I held her to me. Could she hear my heart beating hard against my chest? I kissed the top of her head. She clung to the back of my shirt. Her hands clenching the material in her fists. I held her just as tightly.

"Joy are you all right?"

"I'm trying to be Adam. It's yours and Betsy's day. I wanted to be the friend you both deserve."

"Am I just your friend Joy?"

I knew I shouldn't ask. It only hurt us both but I needed to hear her say it.

She buried her face against my chest. My hands still locked around her waist. The words would never leave these lips but no one could stop them from entering my brain. No one could stop them from filtering through my heart. I wanted to be marrying her. I rested my head on hers.

"Are you going to answer me?" I asked huskily.

"Adam don't make me. You know the answer. The answer is what is slowly destroying me."

"Joy, my insides feel like they are twisting into knots," I confessed. "

She pulled out of my arms enough to look up at me. "Maybe you need one of my pills," she said. I wasn't sure if she was serious. I kissed her nose.

"No thank you."

"When the baby gets here you will feel differently. Betsy will be the mother of your child Adam. Things will change." She tried to tell me.

"You are a romantic. You keep telling yourself that Joy."

I gave her the one pill she had to make last. I put the pill bottle in my pocket. I kissed her at the door. I couldn't help myself. It wasn't anything more than a quick touch of the lips but I needed it. She rolled her eyes at me. I followed her into the hallway. Down the stairs. She had me carry the cake out to the truck. I started to head back to the house when she called me back.

"Adam, we'll be okay."

I nodded. I fucking hoped so.

The next time I saw her she was walking towards me standing with Joey in front of the fireplace. She smiled nervously at me. She was wearing a light blue form fitting silky dress with long fitted sleeves that was off the shoulder. The color was amazing on her. Her hair was braided loosely down the side of her head hanging over her shoulder. Joy carried a bouquet of white roses. I winked at her. Damn if she wasn't barefoot. I shook my head at her. She smiled. She took her place opposite me leaving space for Betsy. Joey grasped my shoulder shaking up my thoughts of Joy who even so thin was stunning.

Pa was leading Betsy towards me. She was amazing as well. She was wearing a dress that was tight on the top and flowed loosely down from her breasts allowing lots of room for her growing belly. The color was barely pink. She hadn't wanted a white dress. Her hair was down in soft waves framing her face. A wreath of flowers adorned her head. She looked beautiful.

Pa handed her to me. I kissed her hand. Wanting like crazy to let her know how special she was to me. She had gotten me through the hardest time in my life. I would never forget that. Judge Tony a friend of Pa's and Joy's boss married us. I kept meeting Joy's eyes over Betsy's head. Not on purpose, Betsy was just so tiny it just happened that way. Joy kept looking down so I would have to look down at Betsy.

I kissed her lips when he pronounced us man and wife at three minutes past midnight. Then we all hugged. I whispered to Betsy that she looked beautiful. My wife...the mother of my child was also barefoot. We went to the dining room and had dinner just after midnight. A toast by Pa came first.

"Kids I know I don't say much but I have a lot to say tonight. First I brought this big idiot into my home at ten and raised him alongside Adam hopefully Joey you always realized how much you have meant to me. I know I didn't say it enough."

I looked across the table at Joey sitting next to Joy. He had tears in his eyes. He got up from the table and walked to the head where Pa stood giving his toast. He grabbed him in a hug and held him tight.

"I know Luke. I'm grateful for everything you've done for me. I don't think I've ever told you that."

"I know you are son. I know you are."

They slapped each other on the back in a manly hug before Joey went back to his seat by Joy. I watched her lay her head against his shoulder. I took Betsy's hand in mine and squeezed it tight. Would I ever stop loving Joy like she thought?

"Then these two little girls started hanging out at the farm. They changed the dynamic of my life. Every Friday night they went with me to a football or basketball game. Little Joy here was always cooking up something with me. Shorty was always getting under foot."

"Hey," Betsy snapped at him.

Pa loved to tease her.

"To new beginnings and to my first grandson. May there be many more from both of my sons and their wives."

Joey's head shot up. His eyes had filled with tears at being referred to as Pa's son. He felt like my brother. We had been through a ton together. Why wouldn't Pa feel like he was his son?

"Maybe not by blood Joey but I expect your children to call me Grandpa too. You are like my son. You've been mine since you were ten and moved in here."

He wiped the tears from his face. Joy put her arm around Joey's shoulder and hugged him to her.

Everyone was laughing after that while we ate dinner. I tried not to but I kept careful account of what Joy ate as did the others. She picked at her food. Eating small bites of fish, potatoes and green beans. Leaving three quarters of it. Mandy sat next to me to the right of Pa. She knew what I was doing. She put her hand on my leg getting my attention. I leaned over to hear her.

"Adam," she whispered softly, "Joy ate something at the diner this morning pretty much like she is doing now. She ate lunch with me and Betsy again pretty much like now picking at her food but at least she's eating a little bit again at each meal. That is progress. Stop worrying."

I kissed her cheek. She didn't judge me knowing my history with Joy that on my wedding day I was more worried about the matron of honor than the bride. She patted my thigh comfortingly.

Later than evening Betsy and I cut the cake and fed each other gently the confectionary dream. I was warned by my new wife I would be sleeping alone if I smashed it in her face. She should know me better. That move was more Joey than me. Mandy and Joy cut cake for everyone but Joy. She didn't eat any but I saw her take a big lick of icing from her finger. I chuckled under my breath.

Betsy and I were sleeping at the house tonight just the two of us. Joey and Joy were staying at the farmhouse with Pa and Mandy. Joy disappeared for a while at 3 AM. When she came back she decided it was time for us to go home. I gave her a look. Nothing like being pushed out by the woman you loved. My life was very weird. I put Betsy's coat on her and carried her to the truck barefoot. When we pulled up to the house I carried her to the house across the threshold.

I knew when Betsy flipped on the light what Joy had been up to  White rose petals were scattered on the floor across the living room leading up the stairs. I carried Betsy up the stairs.

"You need to put me down before you hurt yourself," Bets told me.

I rolled my eyes at her. She didn't weigh anything. As far as I knew she had only gained ten pounds since becoming pregnant.

The petals led a trail to our bedroom. Joy had lit candles Tons of them around our room.

"No wonder she shooed us out of the house. She was afraid she would burn the house down."

"Adam," Betsy scolded me.

I put Betsy down on the bed. She took her wreath off her head and laid it on the nightstand. She picked up a bottle.

"Sparkling grape juice," she said excitedly.

She poured some into two glasses and handed one to me. I sat down beside her.

"We have a great family Adam," she said to me.

"We do," I agreed.

I downed the sparkling grape juice and put the glass back on the nightstand. I rose and took off my suit jacket. I went to the closet and hung up my suit and shirt. I came out wearing only my boxers.

"You need help?" I asked her.

She looked a little sad. She smiled half-heartedly and nodded. I pulled Betsy to her feet and turned her around. I unzipped the dress and let it fall from her body. Betsy stepped out of it and I took it to the closet and hung it up for her. She was standing there waiting for me when I returned. Her breasts were fuller and her belly pretty big with my baby. I walked over to her and put my arms around her caressing her where our baby rested in her womb. He kicked softly against my hand.

"You looked beautiful today Betsy."

"Thank you Adam. Joy looked stunning too didn't she? In the light blue dress."

Why did she do this? Every time I complimented her Betsy brought up Joy. I knew what was in my heart. Joy knew what I was feeling. I knew neither of us spoke of what had happened between us. We would not hurt Betsy or Joey with our actions by revealing what we had done recently. Was she testing me?

"She did look beautiful," I agreed using my most noncommittal voice.

Was I supposed to make love to Betsy now? I caressed her breasts not knowing what else to do. She leaned her head against my shoulder and moaned. She covered my hands with hers. Then she asked if we could make love in the morning because she was exhausted. I was never so relieved in my life. I kissed her neck and let her slip into her nightgown. A pretty sheer blue nightgown that left nothing to the imagination. I thought it was pretty. I noticed it as I blew out the candles around the room. We slipped between the cool sheets. So much for consummating the marriage.

*Joy*

I kissed Luke and Mandy at the door to my old bedroom. I kind of missed being here. I opened the door and went inside shutting the door behind me. Joey was already undressed in his boxers.

"You wasted no time."

"I've been miserable in that suit for hours."

I turned my back to him and Joey unzipped my dress for me. I was self-conscious of my body now that the weight loss had left me bony. There was no other words to describe me. Joey kissed the nape of my neck. His fingers trailed down my spine as he unzipped the dress. My body trembled beneath his touch. It had been a month or six weeks since Joey and I had made love. We were young. We should be making love like wild and free. I looked over my shoulder at him. He tugged my braid.

"Want to make love?" He asked softly.

He had never asked me before. He had just taken what he wanted. I smiled at him. I nodded.

He slid the dress down my shoulders. When the dress hit the floor I stepped out of it and Joey picked it up and carried it to the chair across the room where his suit was draped across the back. I turned towards him. He was walking back to me. His golden eyes alight with desire. I smiled at Joey.

"You seem good today Joy. I'm glad."

*I had six anxiety pills today Joey I should be.*

"I am feeling good today Joey."

Joey reached for me drawing me into his arms. His lips covered mine. Softly at first then hungry. His lips devouring mine. He lifted me in his arms and I wrapped my legs around his waist locking them behind him. He squeezed my ass like he always did and I gasped with pleasure. That was as rough as Joey got that night. He carried me to the bed and laid me down. His body covering mine. We continued to kiss. Our tongues tasting, touching each other until he slid down my body kissing his way down.

At my belly button he traced circles around it until his hands grasped my white silky panties ripping them in half.

"Dammit Joey, those were new."

He just laughed before he tossed them aside. He separated my thighs. I knew how skinny they were making me suddenly self-conscious. I was getting tense.

"Joy relax," he said softly.

The lights were on.

"Could you turn off the lights please?"

He did as I asked. Then he was back between my legs pushing them wide pressing soft kisses to the inside of my thighs first one thigh then the other. He separated my folds finding my hard nub. He began licking fast and hard against my slit making me squirm against his mouth.

"Oh hell," I moaned.

I grabbed his head in my hand holding him to me while his mouth worked magic on my body. Joey's tongue slid down the length of my folds leaving a trail of hot wetness behind. He stuck his fingers inside me setting a rhythm to match his tongue.

Joey sucked my clit into his mouth and sucked hard on the little nub. Making my back arch off the bed. Have mercy what he was doing felt so amazing. I was squirming it felt so damned good. My breathing was ragged by this point. I just wanted to explode.

"I'm close Joey. Make me come," I begged him.

He sucked harder on my clit until the familiar burning of my release began building within me. I knew it was close. I tugged on Joey's hair as my body convulsed around his tongue.

He came to me kissing me.

"Baby I don't have a condom. We can't."

"I don't care Joey. I want you inside me now."

I started tugging down his boxers releasing his dick. When they were as low as I could get them he worked them the rest of the way down and kicked them to the floor. Joey rolled between my legs. His body heavy on mine.

"Are you sure baby?"

"I'm sure Joey."

I had to stop thinking of Adam.

Joey thrust into me. I wrapped my legs around his waist drawing him tighter into me. Joey was large hurting me at first. My sensitive clit was getting action again as he rubbed across it with each stroke of his body into mine. My hands went down to his ass. My nails dug into the skin there holding him to me. His breathing increased.

"Christ Joy leave some skin," he said breathing heavily.

His chest rubbed against mine. My nipples growing into hard like pebbles. Joey's strokes into me were long and hard. My body seemed to get wetter with each stroke. My eyes closed. My head tipped back. Adam's face swam before my mind. I tried pushing it out. I tried to focus on my husband making love to me. My eyes flew open. Joey's were closed.

"Joey open your eyes love,' I said.

He did. His golden eyes were full of love and lust. Joey loved me. Guilt filled me that I had been with Adam since my marriage to Joey. I caressed his face. He kissed me.

"I love you baby," he whispered against my lips. His body still stroking mine.

"I love you Joey."

I wrapped my arms around his neck while our bodies connected and he climaxed into me. I didn't need another orgasm. I didn't care. I meant it when I told Joey I loved him. I did. He meant the world to me. They all did so it was easy for me to repeat the words back to him with the meaning that he wanted to hear. He kissed me again crushing me with his weight until I had to push him away or risk death by asphyxiation. He rolled me into his side and was snoring within minutes. I took an hour to find peace that would allow me to go to a place where sleep would be dreamless and not filled with Adam Moore.

### Joey

The next morning Joy was mad when she tossed her panties at me and told me to throw them away. I just wanted to stuff them in my suit pocket and take them home to toss them so no one else would know. I tucked them in my back jeans pocket and headed down the steps.

Luke and Adam were in the kitchen. Betsy was still sleeping as was Mandy. Joy was coming down soon. Luke was frying bacon and eggs. My stomach growled at the smell of the food cooking on the stove top.

"What the hell is hanging out of your pocket?" Adam asked as he pulled Joy's panties out of my back pocket.

He held them up quirking an eyebrow at Joy's torn underwear. "What happened to them Joey?" He asked. Joy walked into the kitchen at that moment. Her torn underwear hanging from Adam's fingers.

"What the holy fucking hell Adam Moore? Joseph all you had to do was make it the trash can with those." She slapped me in the back of the head.

"Damn Joy." I rubbed my head.

She jerked them out of Adam's hand and glared at me and him both. Luke just shook his head.

Adam said, "At least somebody got lucky last night. How about you Pa?"

Luke shook his head at Adam. He wasn't talking. Joy spun around in shock. "After the romantic setting I laid out for you two…Adam you didn't get lucky?" Joy asked in exasperation.

"She was too tired."

Luke sat eggs and bacon on the table in front of us while Joy sat plates and silverware. She leaned over Luke kissing his cheek. He put his arm around her waist giving her a quick hug.

"Your appointments set for this week."

She looked disgusted with him. "Tuesday is the nutritionist at three p.m. and Friday is the Doc at two."

"I'll meet you there since you'll be coming from work. Okay?"

She took her seat across from Adam next to me. Joy nodded. I knew this wasn't going to be easy. The last few days I had been trying to read about her disease. I didn't know what else to do to help her. I just wanted her to get better. Her own plate remained empty while Adam and I scarfed down bacon. I laid a piece of bacon on the plate in front of her. She glared at me. I smiled at her. She looked across the table at Adam. He was watching her too. I knew Luke told us we were going to have to stop this but it wasn't easy to sit back and let her starve herself and do nothing.

"You looked beautiful last night sweetheart," I told her.

She looked over at me and smiled. "Thanks Joey. Betsy picked a great dress for me. I felt beautiful in it."

"You did look pretty," Luke agreed.

"Betsy is sleeping a long time," Luke said to Adam.

"She's tired. She's been working doubles a lot," he replied.

"What's up with that?" Joy asked.

"She's been paying the hospital monthly so when the baby comes our hospital bill and the doctor is paid for."

Joy and I looked at each other. "Stop paying us," I said.

"No," Adam said.

"Adam, when I needed a place to stay your dad didn't think twice about taking me in. He didn't take money from me. My mother's funeral cost him a fortune. God knows what taking care of Jack cost?"

Joy looked at Luke and he just shrugged his shoulders.

"Anyway he took no money from me so why can't you guys stop paying us the monthly contribution? We don't need it. Then Betsy only has to work one shift. That is what family does for each other," she said softly.

Adam was looking down at the table. Joy rose from the table and went around to Adam. She put her arms around his neck and hugged him.

"Adam," she said to him, "what would you do if the tables were turned and I was pregnant and working doubles?"

He looked sideways looking at Joy. He patted her arm around his neck. "I will talk with Betsy," he replied. Then he planted a kiss on her cheek.

"Good."

She came back to the chair beside me and sat down. The two of them together were an oddity. Something I couldn't always figure out. Had she been slipping into depression because of Adam? I glanced over at Joy. She turned her face to me and smiled. Her eyes lazy and soft and filled with what…love? She looked that way at everyone. She turned back to Luke who was saying something to her. She still hadn't touched the bacon on her plate. I nudged her with my elbow. She turned and looked at me.

"One piece." I motioned towards the plate.

She scowled at me but picked it up. I looked across the table at Adam who was watching us. He immediately looked down at his own plate. This was not going to be easy to keep quiet especially not for me.

### Joy

I had changed into my pajama shorts and a sweatshirt and now I was in Betsy's room crawling between the sheets snuggled next to her big belly. We were nearly nose to nose. We used to do this as little girls hiding beneath the covers pretending no one could find us. I usually stayed the night at Betsy's house not wanting her to see what could possibly happen to my father at any given moment.

Noah was kicking softly. I placed my hand on her belly in awe of the soft little kicks of the child inside Betsy. I brushed her hair away from her face with my other hand. She smiled at me.

"What's wrong Betsy?"

Bets had spent a lot of the day in bed. Adam brought her dinner to the house. He spent some time with her upstairs but mostly had been at the farm or downstairs with Joey watching football on the television. I couldn't handle another college football game so I was up here with her now. Rose Bowl or Orange Bowl whatever they were watching now was getting on my last nerve.

"Adam told me about what you and Joey want to do for us."

I laid my hand on her face enjoying the touch of her soft skin. She laid her hand on my face. It was our way of connecting. Our childhood thing for comforting each other. We hadn't done this in years. We rubbed our feet together under the covers.

"You're upset why?"

"I appreciate it so much." Her voice choked.

"You're taking us up on it."

"We are."

"He needed convincing."

"He did."

"You're upset?"

I knew my best friend.

"I'm just emotional. Pregnancy hormones."

"You sure?"

Betsy nodded.

"Are you going to be okay Joy?"

I nodded this time.

"Good cause I can't do this without you. I know I always try to be the strong one but right now I just want to be the weak the one okay?"

I rolled over onto my back and pulled Betsy into my bony arms. She laid her head on my chest and snuggled in. Her arm was across my waist. My arm was around her back holding her to me. When we were girls we had done this to protect each other. To comfort each other. Her parents never being there for her. My parents abusing me.

She meant that much to me which made the fact that I had screwed Adam just months ago that much harder. It wasn't just screwing with Adam. It wasn't just about sex but it still wasn't right. It was still damned complicated though.

We were talking hours later in the same position. Me playing with her hair when Joey opened the door. He stopped dead in his tracks. No one had ever seen Betsy and me this intimate with each other. It wasn't sexual. It was us comforting each other. Us being so close of friends that we didn't need words to know what the other was feeling. Although it did look sexually intimate. We knew it the minute he opened the door even though we didn't move out of each other's arms.

"Did I interrupt something?" He asked.

"Yeah Joey we just finished making out. Dumbass."

"Can I watch next time?"

"Get the fuck out," we both said at the same time.

"Hey Adam and I thought we should check on you both. Do you need anything?"

"No," we said. "Get out."

"Fine I'll go back downstairs. We always thought you two had something funny going on. Now I've seen it."

He backed out of the room and closed the door.

"Dumbass," I said when he was gone.

Betsy just laughed and laughed until the tears rolled down her porcelain like skin. "It does look pretty bad. My parents have questioned our relationship before you know," she said to me. "It wasn't like I could say hey you have nothing to worry about I like dick too much to be a lesbian," Betsy added.

I started laughing then. I remember when Betsy lost her virginity at fifteen. We were finishing up our freshman year in high school. She was kind of going out with a junior who played football with Adam and Joey. She just wanted to get it over with. She told me all about her first sexual experience. I remember listening raptly thinking I couldn't wait. There were others after Tony Sims the junior who took her virginity while she tried to entice Adam into her bed. Betsy definitely liked her dick. Telling me about each sexual conquest that fell at her tiny little feet.

Adam opened the door next.

"Um you two having a party up here? I heard the laughter and from what Joey described I thought maybe I would find naked girls doing god knows what."

"Don't you have a football game to watch?" Betsy asked.

"I had to use the bathroom and heard your giggle fest."

"It feels nice to laugh Adam. I haven't done enough of that recently."

He came into the room and sat on the foot of the bed. We both kind of sat up giving him more room. "It's nice to see you smiling and laughing. Now if we can just get you to eat."

"I ate today."

"A piece of bacon at breakfast that Joey practically force fed you." Betsy took my hand sensing the tension mounting in me. "Dinner was? Oh yeah salad no dressing and half a chicken breast. So you ate all of what three hundred calories today?"

"Adam," Betsy said softly. He looked at her. "Enough." I squeezed her hand gratefully.

"I am trying Adam," I said looking at the comforter.

He sighed deep in his chest. "I'm sorry too. I'm trying hard not to be the food Nazi. So what was the giggling about?"

"Betsy likes dick too much to be a lesbian," I blurted out making us both bust out laughing.

Adam's face turned pink which made us laugh that much harder. It was hysterical to see such a big guy embarrass so easily.

"I'm not even going to ask," he said rising from the bed. "Do I need to make a bed on the sofa or are you planning on sleeping in your own bed Joy?"

"What you don't want to sleep with Joey tonight? We thought we could swap beds tonight?"

"No fucking way. I would sleep in my truck before I would sleep with him."

I was cuddling next to Betsy. We were holding hands again. He was watching us strangely. Adam shook his head. "Are you two okay tonight?" He asked.

"Just feeling like lost little girls," Betsy replied. "We used to do this as kids. Always comforting each other when things were bad. There were times when I just needed Joy to make me feel better. She knew me. I knew her. We would laugh or cry but in the end we felt better."

He nodded. "I get it. I've seen you two together for a lot of years just wondering why you feel so bad today Betsy? Care to share?'

"Pregnancy hormones," was all she would say.

"Okay. I'll be up later."

He started to leave but he came back and kissed Betsy's forehead. Then he left the room shutting the door behind him.

Betsy was still staring at the door where Adam just left.

"What Betsy?"

She turned to me. Her clear blue eyes sad. "Nothing. We've been laughing. I don't want to spoil that."

We fell asleep that way snuggled next to each other. Joey had fallen asleep on the sofa and Adam left him there. When Adam came upstairs to bed he could have gone to Joey's bed but he chose instead to lift me from his side and carry me to my own room. He laid me down on the bed and covered me with the comforter. Sitting by me on the bed he brushed the hair from my face. My eyelids fluttered open.

"Hey," I said.

"Hey beautiful."

"What are you doing?"

"Reclaiming my bed." He smiled down at me.

"Where's Joey?"

"Asleep on the sofa."

"Good night Adam."

"Good night beautiful."

He leaned over and kissed my forehead. My eyes closed as his lips touched my skin. In my head my inner voice whispered I love you Adam. I kept my eyes closed so Adam wouldn't see the emotion evident in my eyes when they opened. I rolled over and pulled the covers up to the chin and fell back to sleep.

### Tuesday Afternoon

Complete terror filled me as I walked to the lobby of the nutritionist office. Luke was standing by the elevators when I arrived. He took my hand and punched the button for the floor that we needed. I followed him into the elevator.

In the office I checked in and filled out paperwork. Then Luke and I sat down and waited to be called. My leg bounced nervously. Luke watched me out of the corner of his eye.

"You okay?"

I nodded.

We waited a while for my name to be called. Emmy Santana was the nutritionist I was meeting today. She was an expert recommended by Doc who worked with many anorexia patients. She helped them develop good relationships with food and monitored weight gain. She was going to work with me to do the same.

"Joy Bonds."

Luke and I both turned in our seats. We stood and he put his hand on the small of my back guiding me towards the door. Once we were in the hallway with the door closed Emmy introduced herself to us.

"Luke Moore," he said extending his hand to her.

"You are?" She asked him.

"I've known Luke since I was fourteen." He smiled down at me. "I guess you could say he's my adopted father."

"That is quite a compliment Mr. Moore."

"It seems like I've raised a bunch of kids that aren't mine by blood but worth every minute."

"Brave man."

"Dumb or brave?  Take your pick."

They both laughed.

"Joy this is always the hardest part.  We need to weigh you. The scale is right here."  She guided us down the hallway a short way.  "Could you take your sweater off please?"  I had worn a heavy cardigan just to weigh more.

"I don't need to take this off do I?" I pleaded.

Luke was already pealing the sweater off my shoulders while I glared at him.

"Shoes too please," Emmy said.

Emmy's bright beautiful smile hid a heart of stone behind it. Her twinkling green eyes not so dissimilar from my own hid an evil that the woman didn't want you to see.  Her long auburn hair was pulled up in a ponytail adding to her innocence. Innocent my ass.  She was tough as nails.

I kicked them off at the scales and stepped on backwards. She looked at me questioningly for a moment.  Then she looked at Luke and something in his eyes made her soften. "For now," she said you don't have to look at what you weigh but soon you need to face facts that you are at a dangerous weight and I will force you to start looking every week.  Got it?"

I nodded.

I looked at Luke.  There was sympathy in his eyes.  He knew it was for my own good but still he was hurting for me. His eyes left mine while he watched Emmy weigh me.

"Dammit Joy," he said softly.

I had lost more weight.  I could see it in his eyes. I felt the tears prick at the corner of my eyes.  I started to step off the scales and Luke took my hand helping me step down.  I slipped on my shoes and grabbed my sweater.

"Joy do you mind if I talk to Luke a minute?"

"Nope," I replied. I went to her office and sat down waiting for them to join me.  The leg bounced nervously again.

Emmy gave me a meal plan to follow which Luke took from me to review. The goal for next week was that I gain five pounds. She didn't want me weighing myself at home. No problem there. I avoided the scale like it was on fire. I avoided the mirror but sometimes when I needed to decide if I should lose weight I used the mirror as my judge and my judge was not good at giving me an accurate account of what my body image really looked like therefore I ate less every day.

Luke and I left Emmy's office. He let me know he would be fixing dinner tonight for me, Mandy and Adam. Betsy was working tonight. She was starting to work late shifts because it was easier for her to sleep late and stay up. Joey was going to be in class.

"We'll get through this," he told me at the truck.

"You keep telling me that. How bad was it?" I asked.

I had to know. I didn't have a number because nobody told me what I weighed when Adam weighed me.

"You've lost two more pounds."

"Fuck."

"You can say that again."


I walked into the farmhouse that night dreading it. Adam, Mandy and Luke were in the kitchen. Adam was sitting at the island on a barstool. I sat my purse on the kitchen table. I knew without a doubt that they were speaking about me. Adam held out his arm and fuck I couldn't help myself I walked into his embrace. Wrong or not I let him hold me. I laid my head on his shoulder. Out of the corner of my eye I saw Luke and Mandy continuing to make dinner not judging us not making assumptions.

"Your father told you," I whispered.

"He did."

He now had both arms wrapped around my waist. I was standing between his legs leaning into him. Hot damn it felt good to be held here.

"What are we eating for dinner?"

Adam looked at me. "Are you eating?" He asked. Luke turned and glared at him.

"It's okay Luke."

"We are having fresh green beans, chicken breasts and a baked potato," Mandy said.

"What am I supposed to eat?"

"All of it?" Adam suggested.

I glared at him. He was so close holding me still about the waist. His beautiful dark eyes penetrating and gorgeous. I could get lost in those eyes. That inner voice still speaking to me whispering I love you Adam. Then my real voice saying shut it. I turned to Luke.

"Well?"

"Eat what you can Joy," he responded. "You know your goal. Gain five pounds."

Adam squeezed my waist.

"What do I weigh Luke?" I asked.

Luke turned from the stove looking at me intensely. It was a big step to have to face the truth of my weight loss. My illness. I sighed. "Go ahead and tell me," I pleaded.

"One hundred pounds today. You've lost two more pounds since Adam weighed you."

I think I would have dropped to the floor had Adam not had his arm around me. "You okay?" He asked. I couldn't talk to him right now. I pulled out of his arms and went to the living room and sat on the sofa. I stared outside into the fields surrounding the farm. I had been coming here for a long time. I had always felt secure here. I wasn't sure even the farm could protect me from myself.

I curled my legs up to my chest tucking my chin into my chest. I wrapped my arms around my legs. What the hell was wrong with me? My weight fluctuated normally between one hundred twenty-five and one hundred thirty-five pounds. I considered myself curvy for a five foot six girl. Joey and Adam had always called me slender. What I had done to myself was brutal. I didn't really see what they did. I knew I was bony now but I couldn't really stop myself. It was like I needed this to punish myself. I rested my forehead in my hand and closed my eyes.

Minutes later I felt him although my eyes were still closed. I wrapped my hand around his when he reached for it but kept my eyes closed. Adam's hand caressed my cheek.

"Where did everything go wrong Adam?"

"Open your eyes Joy."

Everything fit with Adam and me. We were perfect together. I had let him go at my own expense. I could still feel the imprint of his hand on my belly where our child rested in my womb. Yet I had felt the tiny kicks of his child with Betsy in her belly too. It was so fucking complicated and confusing. I wanted her to be happy with him. She was now his wife. Yet I wanted to be happy with him too but I had Joey. I made love with Joey. I was his wife but when I closed my eyes I could only see Adam's face. His love I could only feel in my heart.

"Open your eyes sweetheart," Adam said.

I did and I was looking into his big beautiful dark eyes. I put his hand against my cheek.

"I feel torn apart Adam."

"Talk to me," he said gently.

"I still hurt over losing you and our baby but I let you go. I made the choice Adam. Doc tells me all the time I have to start dealing with all my feelings. So on the other hand I want you to be happy with Betsy. I can't wait to hold little Noah in my arms. I love feeling him kick inside Betsy. It is a beautiful thing Adam."

His thumb rubbed against my face. We didn't move any closer than we were.

"Don't you realize I feel all the same things?"

"When Betsy and I were lying in bed together the other night we were closer than we had been in a while. I thought about her trust in me and the guilt was just as strong in me now as it was then." I hesitated. I needed to tell him about my guilt. I needed to tell someone my feelings the feelings that were consuming me to the point of destroying me. He was the only one I could tell.

"She told me she needed to be the weak one for a while. That is why I was holding her. Adam I felt so guilty for making love with you in September when she found out she was pregnant." He looked down unable to meet my eyes. "I was scared Adam. I was losing you for good. I knew it and you knew it."

That is why it had happened. We would both be married to other people. We would have to let each other go and I was so damned scared of that.

"Adam I love Betsy and Joey dearly you know that but I wouldn't take back those moments with you for anything," I said honestly. His eyes shot up to my face as the tears flowed down my face. Adam brushed away the tears with his thumbs.

"I know we are both married now," I said softly. "I want things to be easy and comfortable like they were but I don't want to stop loving you," I told him. "I know that it is what is best for me and for you but some days I'm convinced that is all that gets me through the day."

Adam pulled me into his arms. Into his chest I whispered "I still have the damned guilt Adam," I laughed sardonically.

He kissed my forehead.

"You aren't saying much."

"It's hard Joy because other than the Doc you have no one to talk to. I thought you needed to just get this off your chest."

"I did."

"I feel like I'm drowning Adam. The whole food thing kind of took me by surprise. When Luke told me what I weighed I was shocked. I've been a little obsessive about my weight. Gained five pounds, ten pounds starved myself until it came off. Always tried to stick around one hundred twenty five. I have a love hate relationship with the scales."

"Joy you have a beautiful body I wish you could see that."

"My boobs have always been too big and my ass…"

He started laughing. I pulled out of his arms and looked at him shocked that he was laughing during such a serious conversation.

"Sorry," he said contritely. "Joy I'm a twenty-two year old male you don't seriously think I'm ever going to say your breasts are too large? Your ass is the best part about you."

I rolled my eyes and shook my head at him before I laid it back on his shoulder. Resting in the curve of his neck where I belonged. Feeling the security of his embrace reveling in it.

"Hey you two dinner is ready," Luke said. He went back to the kitchen. His face revealed nothing about what he was thinking about finding me intimately pressed against his son's chest.

I looked at Adam.

"What do you think he thinks finding me in your arms?"

Adam pulled me to my feet.

"Adam?"

"Pa has been speaking his mind for some time. Before Betsy got pregnant he let me know that you and I had made a mistake ending the relationship. Once Betsy got pregnant he let me know my priorities might have changed but I still had a responsibility to you that included doing whatever was needed to help you get well."

"Did you feel otherwise?" I asked almost hurt that maybe Adam might have felt like I was a burden to him when Betsy was now his first priority. It should be this way I knew but I was a little screwed up after all.

"No," he shook his head at me like I was dumb, "but you know my father. He likes to talk."

I laughed. "I don't think he meant having sex Adam."

He was still holding my hands. "No I don't think he did. I think he would be probably be disappointed that we cheated on Joey and Betsy but maybe he would understand. I just don't know and I don't want to. Can we keep that as our secret?"

I nodded.

"Joy you have to know that Pa loves you like crazy. I've never seen him so upset or feel so helpless when it comes to making you well."

"We've always had something special Adam. I can't explain it."

"I know. You two always snuck off to fix dinner together."

"I clung to him Adam. I wanted a father like him. At times I was like a little puppy dog trailing after him soaking up anything he could teach me about cooking, sports, farming, you name it. I just wanted the love he was giving me. I know it was hard at times when he cut off you and Joey but he wasn't like that with me."

"It was always funny to watch him with you. You always seemed to get under his skin Joy. We were amazed."

"Are you two eating tonight or what?" Luke hollered from the kitchen.

I pulled Adam after me not letting go of his hand. How would they react seeing us holding hands as we entered the kitchen? It was an innocent act. Two friends nothing more. Deep down the love we shared for each other was more. Luke just rolled his eyes when we entered.

"I'm starving you two. Bout time you got your asses in here. You talk roses and shit after we eat. It might be good for you to talk without the others walking in on you,' he said.

That explained what Luke thought of Adam holding me, holding my hand. It didn't give me a clue as to what he would think of Adam and me cheating on our significant others. Adam pulled the chair out for me. I sat down. Luke had already served my plate. Adam sat next to me.

I hadn't eaten much today at all. Honestly I had only had water all day. A small chicken breast lay before me, along with a baked potato and green beans. A protein drink sat on the table too. I opened the can of Vanilla Bean after shaking it. I took a sip. It wasn't too bad. We talked about the appointment with the nutritionist while I drank the shake. Liquids seemed to go down easier than the food. I picked at the green beans, ate three bites of the baked potato and half the chicken breast.

Luke looked pleased. Mandy was ecstatic. Adam wanted me to eat the whole thing. I scowled at him. He and Joey would prove to be the most difficult at handling my illness.

### Friday Afternoon

Luke was waiting in Doc's waiting room when I arrived for my appointment. He stood and hugged me when I walked in.

"How are you doing?"

"I'm good Luke."

"Did you have lunch?"

"I did."

This time I wasn't lying to him. I had eaten lunch at my desk. A chicken sandwich from *Burger King*. I had taken the bread off and thrown it away eating just the patty or at least half the patty anyway.

"Good girl." The thing about Luke was I didn't have to account for what I ate to him. The boys always asked me what I ate. Then I would see on their faces that it wasn't enough making me feel guilty.

Doc opened his door welcoming both Luke and I into the office. Luke held my hand when we stepped through the doorway. We sat in chairs opposite Doc and he asked how things had gone this week. Tuesday and Wednesday night I had dinner with Adam, Luke and Mandy at the farm. Both Joey and Betsy were gone. Betsy at work and Joey at school. Last night I had dinner at the house with the boys. Luke had given them tips on what to fix.

I had my normal protein shake along with the meal they had made for me. It was like old times sitting at the dinner table laughing and talking like we had two years ago before everything fell apart. Once the shake was gone I was faced with the food on my plate. I hadn't eaten anything all day. I felt full from the shake. I knew I would have to fight them both if I didn't eat something I opted for the cauliflower on my plate eating all of it. I was satisfied that I had eaten enough. Joey and Adam were not. A big blow up had ensued with me storming off and locking myself in my room.

I told Doc about the three different dinners. The dynamic of how I felt eating with the different groups. I was comfortable talking in front of Luke because I knew whatever he heard if I didn't want it told to the others he would not tell them. I knew that I could trust Luke.

"Luke," Doc began, "Joy made a great decision when she asked that you accompany her on these visits. I like the effect you have on her."

Luke appeared uncomfortable with his praise. I took Luke's hand in mine and he squeezed it reassuringly. Our glances connecting and then disconnecting briefly.

"I was disappointed that you lost weight in the past week," Doc said choosing his next words carefully, "I'm sure there was more stress helping your best friend get married than you realized so now that the wedding is behind you let's focus on getting better."

"Let's not bullshit anyone," Luke said.

I looked over at Luke in surprise. Doc quirked an eyebrow too.

"I know, she knows, you know so whatever she needs to deal with where Adam is concerned to get well let's put it on the table okay?" Luke said. "I don't want to see her self-destructing anymore because it's eating her alive. I'm a little selfish too it's killing me a little piece at a time."

My heart clinched in pain.

"I'm sorry Luke," I said to him. Tears glistening on my lashes.

"I don't want you to apologize. I want you to get well. I want peace for you Joy."

Doc looked at both of us.

"Luke what do you think would make Joy happy?"

"Adam," he said softly. He looked at me with so much sadness in his eyes that the tears that were just glistening on the edge suddenly spilled over. "I think she would make him happy too. My son lives his life hiding behind a wall that no one but occasionally she breaks through."

Doc was resting his chin in his palm watching intently our reaction.

"I'm sorry Joy. This has to be said."

I didn't respond neither did Doc.

"Unfortunately they didn't listen to me or to Betsy when we told them not to give up on each other after Joy lost the baby. She went and married Joey to be sure she didn't have to hurt Joey by following her heart," Luke got up from the chair and walked to the window. "Unfortunately Joey is a mess at times too but I think he would have fared a damned sight better than you have Joy."

He glanced over his shoulder occasionally looking at me to see how I was reacting to his words. "Adam was nearly destroyed so he wouldn't fight for her. Now I watch Joy killing herself slowly one day at a time and I see him reeling. He feels helpless because he can't do anything about it because a condom broke and he's married to a woman he cares about a great deal but his heart still belongs to her."

"Luke," I started to say.

"Joy, let me finish. I saw how much you two still love each other Tuesday night when you went to the living room to talk. He was holding you, trying to comfort you. I saw it with my own eyes. I don't know how the hell Betsy and Joey don't see it." He shook his head sadly. "I've talked Mandy's ear off about it. I needed to say it to someone else because I don't know what to do about it."

"Luke do you remember when Betsy found out she was pregnant when I asked you what I could do to help them work through their issues." He nodded. "What did you tell me?"

"You have to let them work it out themselves."

"I think this is the same thing."

"I don't dammit."

Doc cleared his throat.

"Luke, I know you feel helpless. I have been telling Joy for months she needed to deal with her feelings for Adam because it was hurting her. She hasn't yet. I know that. Unfortunately neither of us can make her deal with them. We can't make her stop loving him which at this point would probably be best," Doc said.

"Joy why don't you talk about Adam and how you feel. I think when you do you will start to feel better."

"I was telling Adam the other night that I'm torn. I do love him but it is so fucking complicated." Luke turned and looked at me. Then he came back to the chair and sat down with me taking my hand. It was easier to talk to him with him sitting down. "I want to let Adam go so he can be happy with Betsy and Noah but I'm terrified of letting him go at the same time. The closer the time came to the wedding the more I could feel him slipping away from me even though I'm Joey's wife I was feeling this way Luke. How sad is that?"

"I feel like two people. The one who loves Adam with everything in me. The one who has to be Joey's wife and Betsy's best friend. The conflict became too much. I made a mistake pushing him away after I lost the baby. I know that. I can't correct that mistake now," I told him.

"My grandmother always told my mother, Mariah you've made your bed now you have to lie in it so I've made my bed Luke. I've lost Adam for good because he's married to Betsy my best friend. I'm married to Joey not that the ring on my finger has stopped me from loving Adam...like I had hoped it would."

I left it at that to allow Luke to draw his own conclusions about that statement. I hadn't revealed what Adam I had done but I intimated that he and I were more. I was openly sobbing now. Luke drew me into his arms. Doc handed Luke a box of Kleenex. I took one and wiped my eyes. Blew my nose.

"Luke am I a disappointment to you?" I asked tearfully.

I couldn't bear it if he thought I was.

"Kid, you could never disappoint me. I feel like I've let you and Adam down. I wish I had done more to keep you together. I thought it wasn't my place to interfere. Now I see you in marriages that although I don't think you are unhappy they aren't where you should be. I see you both hanging on when it seems futile to do it."

"I know Luke," I agreed. "I think if you asked him he feels the same way that it is hopeless but we can't seem to let each other go."

"Then maybe you should figure out a way to be together?"

My mouth fell open.

"At Joey and Betsy's expense? What about Noah?"

"What about what it's doing to you Joy? Can you love Noah even though he's Adam and Betsy's son? I know the answer to that without you responding. Yes."

"You told me till do us part."

"Hell at this point Joey is going to be a widower if we don't do something to help you. Then I'm going to be dealing with Adam and Joey grieving over your dead ass. I just don't fucking know what to do anymore Joy. Doc?"

Doc was trying to hide a half smile behind his hand. Luke had a way of saying things maybe uncouth but powerful just the same.

"You would miss me too," I declared softly.

"Joy," he said with exasperation. "The point is I don't want you to go anywhere. I'm trying to keep your scrawny ass here with me."

I laid my head on Luke's shoulder. "I just want the pain to stop."

"Me too kiddo," he said. "Me too."

When we finished the session Doc asked about family sessions. I almost sat back down my legs trembling so badly at thought of them all together and my secrets somehow getting out in the heat of the moment.

"Joy nothing like this," he reassured me. "I realize you have things you aren't willing to share with Joey and Betsy. Maybe you would like to bring just Adam sometime. You've talked more with Luke here...honestly talked than I've heard you in a while."

I wasn't sure about bringing Adam alone.  Laying all the rawness on the table.  Examining the feelings and the hurt?  I cringed.  Doc saw the expression on my face

## Chapter Seven

### Adam

Joy was going to be shocked that I was stepping in for Pa but he wasn't feeling well or so he said. So I was going to her nutritionist appointment but maybe it would be helpful for me.

I waited in the waiting area. She walked in and signed in then turned to take a seat and saw me. Her mouth dropped open.

"What are you doing here?"

"Pa wasn't feeling well so I came in his place."

She looked at me skeptically. Unsure of me which I didn't like. I hated it that Joy had locked herself in her room after Joey and I had badgered her to the point that she stormed off.

Her name was called and we walked together to the door. She kept scowling at me over her shoulder. I just smiled determined to be supportive of Joy. She had to get weighed first. The nutritionist Emmy just kept smiling even though Joy's scowl was now directed at her. Joy was wearing a plain wool skirt, tights and low heeled shoes which she kicked off furiously at the bottom of the scales. Her white long sleeved knit tee shirt did little to hide the boniness of her body but the bulky sweater beneath the winter coat hid a lot.

Joy removed her coat shoving it into my arms. "Make yourself useful Adam," she snapped.

I just kept smiling at her refusing to let her rattle me. Then she removed the bulky sweater and shoved that at me as well. She stepped on the scale facing it surprising Emmy I could see. Emmy adjusted the weights until I could see that even she was impressed. Joy cringed at the weight on the scale but a smile spread across her lips none the less. She had gained seven pounds two more than her goal. She was living on the liquid protein shakes I was fairly sure but dammit she had gained seven pounds.

If one of us made one for her without her knowing it we scooped extra powder into the shakes. She hadn't noticed a difference. Thank you Jesus, I whispered inside my head. She weighed one hundred seven pounds.

When Joy stepped off the scales she smiled at me. Then she flung herself into my arms wrapping herself around me. We clung to each to each other. I squeezed her so tightly that she squealed.

"Adam I can't breathe."

"Sorry," I sat her on her feet.

Seven steps forward two steps backward. We were just learning what an uphill battle this fight would be.

*April*

*Joy*

Luke and I attended my sessions regularly. I felt better than I had for a while. My weight fluctuated between one hundred fifteen and one hundred twenty. We had a couple family sessions. They were too stressful for me to have them all in one room together. My family was looking for reasons why this had happened to me. Each one understood different things. The only person who was completely in the dark was Joey. There were some secrets that Betsy didn't know. Some Luke suspected but didn't ask. Adam and I bore the entire truth on our shoulders.

Adam had even attended a session or two with me alone. We talked honestly with Doc about our feelings. The guilt of cheating on our partners. He hadn't been married at the time but I was. The temptation of doing it again. The best thing about Doc Joffrey he didn't pass judgment on us. Adam even talked about his own guilt where I was concerned if he had protected me from Jack we wouldn't be here. Doc tried reassuring him that none of this was his fault. Otherwise, Doc had just listened to us.

Did it changed anything? No. Were we better? Yes because we had talked about how we felt. We talked about the guilt. We talked about the temptation to give in and touch each other. Love each other no matter the consequences of our actions.

I think the thing that mattered most to me was Noah. He was due soon. He was coming in a month. Betsy was no longer waiting tables. Taking maternity leave a month early. Her ankles and legs swollen she was unable to continue working. The delivery was paid for unless there were complications. We had taken the third bedroom upstairs and were decorating it to make a nursery for Noah.

Adam and Joey had painted the walls a soft blue. I entered the room several times a day to take freshly washed clothes and blankets to the room inhaling the fresh paint smell. Picturing the finished product. We were looking for wallpaper boarder for the walls. Betsy wanted to use it in the middle of the wall around the room. The white crib was propped against the wall waiting to be put together.

The changing table already completed was cornered near the three drawer dresser. Diapers were stacked neatly beneath the changing table with wipes, powder and ointment. I opened the powder and a puff of smoke filled the air. I sliced my hand through the air to clear it and put the baby powder back.

I glanced around me. Clothes hung neatly in the closet. Some were put in the dresser like onesies and sleepers. We were almost ready. The boys were going to put the crib together this weekend. Then we just had to find the boarder then curtains and bedding that Betsy wanted and we were done. She still had a month but she tired easily so shopping was a slow process.

"Hey," Joey said coming into the room.

I turned. "What?"

"Dinner is ready. You coming?"

"I am."

I took his outstretched hand and walked into the hallway. "You doing all right?" He asked his voice tender and caring.

"I'm doing great Joey," I told him.

Truthfully I was doing well. I was slim but not scary skinny. My weekly sessions were productive. Doc was preparing me for the birth of Adam and Betsy's child. He was concerned that I might have some setbacks. We were being proactive but I wasn't concerned at all. I was excited by the pending birth of the baby. He gave me something to look forward to in life. Maybe for a time I would stop grieving the child I had lost.

We walked down the steps together. Joey in front of me while I trailed behind. Our hands still loosely linked. I watched my feet on the staircase careful not to fall. My free hand sliding down the bannister caressing the slightly worn wood. We were side by side as we entered the living room and then walked into the kitchen.

Adam and Betsy were already sitting at the kitchen table. We were having pot roast tonight. Adam had cooked dinner. Potatoes and carrots surrounded the roast sending steam into the air. He had just removed the food from the oven and everything smelled wonderful although I still wouldn't allow myself to eat much of it. I sat down opposite Adam.

"I put the clothes away just like you asked," I told Betsy.

We all tried to keep Betsy from going up and down the stairs too much."

"Thanks," she replied.

She looked tired today. I knew she wasn't sleeping well. Her belly was huge because the baby was so large. They were estimating he weighed about nine pounds during the last ultrasound and she still had four weeks to go.

I put a small piece of meat on my plate, two small potatoes and several carrots. I looked up from my plate and saw they were watching me. Still they monitored what I ate. My protein shake sat in front of me. I took a sip of it. I was making it myself these days since I caught Betsy adding more powder to the drink. I had to be able to trust them like they needed to be able to trust me. So to prove my trust to them I was trying to eat a little breakfast with them every day. I didn't always eat lunch but I tried to fifty percent of the time. Baby steps. Everyone was pleased with my progress but still wary of me slipping.

Adam was working hard right now on the farm with Luke preparing the fields for planting. Joey had seven weeks until he graduated with his Bachelor's degree in Accounting. Then he would be studying for CPA Exam. We were all proud of him. I had started my Spring Quarter as a student for Court Reporting. I had really liked the curriculum the first quarter that I just completed.

Judge Tony had turned me onto this field after having me spend a day in court with him during a robbery trial. I found the case fascinating and thought it was something I would enjoy. Luke was thrilled I was finally enrolled in school. Everything seemed to be falling into place finally.

After dinner, most of mine went into the trash can, I cleaned the dishes and put them in the dishwasher. Joey and Adam stayed to help me. Betsy went to the living room to prop her feet. The leftovers in the fridge I sat on the sofa between Betsy and Joey. Adam took the recliner. Betsy propped her feet in my lap while I rested my back against Joey's chest. Adam had turned on the television finding something for us to watch.

It wasn't often that we were all home at once. It was nice like this. It was like we used to be before my father found out that I wasn't staying at Betsy's house and beat me. It was before I realized how much I truly loved Adam. Before I was pregnant with his child. A tear built up in my lashes threatening to flow over onto my cheeks. I wasn't sad. I was happy that we were all together again. Looking forward to Noah coming into our lives. Betsy took my hand squeezed it in hers. I smiled at her.

"I think I'm going to take my walk now," I told them needing to get away before I cried. They wouldn't understand they were happy tears not sad ones.

Joey groaned. "I don't think I could walk a foot," he said.

They didn't like for me to walk alone. Even though my father was dead and buried they still worried about me being alone when dusk was already casting shadows across the farm.

Adam rose from the chair. "I guess it's my turn then," he said with resignation.

"I will rub Betsy's feet for you," he offered his voice rising as if he was pained.

"Like that is a chore," she grumbled.

"You know I can go by myself."

"No you're not," both men said at the same time.

"Let's go then Adam."

I kissed Betsy's cheek. "Be back soon," I told her. Then I kissed Joey's lips softly but without passion. We were too young to let the daily routine of life wipe out the passion this soon. The passion that should still exist between us. Maybe it was me? Maybe he didn't find me desirable. It had been six weeks since we had made love.

Adam and I stepped off the front porch. To combat some of my stresses and fear of gaining weight Doc had suggested a walking program so I walked. Every night for thirty to forty-five minutes depending on my mood and that of my walking partner. Adam was better at walking longer periods than Joey so tonight I hoped we would walk forty-five minutes. We walked to the street and headed north. The road was curvy so we had to walk facing the traffic. There wasn't a lot of traffic on this street but when they did drive on it they tended to drive fast.

Adam walked ahead of me. He was wearing his jeans and tee shirt from today. He had replaced his boots with sneakers. I wore shorts and a tee shirt plus sneakers. His head was down as he watched the road pass by the steps his feet were taking on the road.

"Hey Adam?"

"What?"

"Can I ask you a question?"

"Sure," he replied absently.

"Am I still attractive?"

He looked over his shoulder uncomfortably. "Where's this coming from Joy?"

I didn't want to tell him that Joey hardly touched me anymore.

"Never mind."

He sighed deep in his chest. I watched the rise and fall of his shoulders. "What's wrong Joy?" He asked with exasperation.

"I said never mind."

He stopped walking and I collided into his back. "Sorry," I said taking a step backwards. He took hold of my arm and put me in front of him.

"Start walking and talking," he said.

Damn I should have kept quiet.

"Joey doesn't...he doesn't touch me. Ever...well not ever but not very much," I told him. "It's been six weeks and before that it had probably been six weeks. I don't understand. It used to be a lot more."

I looked over my shoulder and stopped walking. He nearly crashed into me. Well apparently not a good idea for me to walk in front of Adam.

"You were looking at my ass weren't you?"

"The problem isn't you Joy." He ignored my question. "Have you talked to him?"

We changed positions again. Him allowing me to walk behind him. I liked this view better than the road ahead anyway. Adam's butt was beautiful. I could fantasize while I walked about grabbing that butt, digging in my nails and holding on tight while making love. Fuck me I was horny. I made a funny little gasping noise thinking about it and Adam turned to look at me.

"You okay."

"Yep, just fine." My voice sounded shaky to my own ears.

We walked further down the road in silence each lost in his/her own thoughts. I knew where mine were. I wondered where Adam's were.

"How are you and Betsy doing Adam?" I asked him.

He glanced over his shoulder at me.

"Fine Joy," he said quietly.

"That doesn't sound too convincing," I said.

"You live with us Joy. What do you see?" He asked.

"What?"

He had stopped walking again and was looking at me.

"Tell me what you see about my relationship with Betsy."

I stopped for a second thinking about what I actually saw. He was gentle with her. Sweet. Caring. Always kissing her forehead tenderly. Asking her if he could do anything for her. Treating her like she was special.

"I see you being you. Always considerate, kind and thoughtful."

He twirled on his heel and started walking quickly again. I was having trouble keeping up with him.

"Could you slow down? I can't keep up with you."

He slowed but he didn't look back.

"What's wrong Adam?"

"She knows and it is making her crazy. No matter what I do it is never enough," he said sadly.

"She knows what?" I asked surprised by Adam's outburst.

"She knows that no matter how excited I am about our baby coming. No matter how tenderly I treat her or how long I hold her at night or want to make love to her you are always there between us in my thoughts, my head, my heart Joy. Damn you she knows. She has tried accepting it. Now she's just given up."

He looked so defeated.

"Fuck maybe Joey knows it too. Maybe that is why he doesn't want to touch you. It's pretty fucking hard making love to someone when you're constantly picturing that person as someone else."

I gasped. I took a step backwards missed the berm of the road and fell backwards ass over end several times. The culvert was pretty steep.

"Shit Joy. Are you all right?" Adam scrambled down into the culvert.

My back was raw and bleeding where it had scraped against the rocks as I fell. My knees and legs were scraped as was the left side of my face. I laid on my back in the culvert below him and laughed hysterically.

"I'm glad you can find this funny. If you could see yourself you wouldn't."

"Adam nothing is broken. I'm fine. Help me up."

When I stood I realized I might have twisted my knee in the fall. I couldn't put weight on it.

"God you're a mess."

'Thanks. Do you feel better getting that off your chest?" I asked.

He glared at me. "I guess I'm carrying you home since you can't seem to put weight on that leg." He was examining my left knee. It had swelled already.

"Piggy back would be easier for you," I suggested.

I climbed on Adam's back after he grabbed my injured leg first. I guess I wouldn't be walking anytime soon. They would all be happy about that. Adam started walking towards home. I laid my non-bleeding cheek against his shoulder.

"Adam?"

"What?" He said gruffly.

"I'm sorry I made such a mess of things for us."

He looked over his shoulder at me still glaring. Then suddenly he softened. I couldn't help myself. I kissed his cheek. I wrapped my arms around his neck and nuzzled his face. He sighed unable to stay mad at me.

"What am I supposed to say to that Joy?"

"Nothing," I said softly.

He walked on carrying me on his back, me bleeding on him as well as myself. My back bleeding into my shorts. For a while we didn't say anything. He was hardly winded carrying me like this.

"Adam?"

"Now what Joy?"

"I love you."

He looked at me again out of the corner of his eye. A smile twitched at the corner of his mouth. He tried hard not to show it.

"I love you too," he said gruffly. "Even though you're a pain in my ass."

"Thanks," I snapped.

He just laughed then. We saw the house ahead.

"Thank god," he said.

"I'm heavy?"

He rolled his beautiful dark eyes at me. "You weigh nothing. I want to get your back cleaned up. God knows what is in the culvert and get ice on your knee to reduce the swelling. You're probably going to have a lot of bruising on your face," he said checking out my cheek.

Adam hopped up on the porch jolting me. I winched.

"Sorry." He opened the door with one hand and carried me across the threshold kicking the door shut behind me.

Betsy and Joey were exactly where we left them but Joey was rubbing Betsy's feet.

"My god what did you do?" Betsy asked.

Adam sat me on the recliner.

"Graceful here did a swan dive into the culvert about a mile down the road."

Joey tried hard not to laugh.

"Go ahead Joey you can laugh. I did."

"Don't you dare fucking laugh Joseph. Her knee is twice the size it should be. Her face is a mess as you can see and her back which you can't see is worse," Adam warned.

"You carried her all the way back?" Betsy asked getting to her feet with a gentle push from Joey who still hadn't risen from the sofa to see if I was all right.

She walked across the room and leaned behind me to look at my back.

"Ouch," she said lowering my tee shirt.

"You want to get some ice for her knee?" She told Adam. "Joey go get the first aid kit. I will clean her wounds."

When Joey returned with the first aid kit and a wet wash cloth Betsy started cleaning my back.

"You need to take off the tee shirt sweetie. It's soaked in blood."

I looked at Adam then at Joey. I was like what the hell. They've all seen it before. I whipped the shirt over my head and handed it to Joey. Luckily my bra was not sheer or lacy but standard even though the curve of my large breasts were easily spilling over the cups. Betsy started cleaning again.

"Let's take your shorts off too. The blood has soaked into them."

Okay. Let's just get Joy naked in front of the whole house. What panties did I have on? White cotton not granny panties but not sheer, sexy ones either. I stood with Joey's help the bag of ice slipping to the floor. Adam got the job of pulling down my shorts. His eyes showed just uncomfortable he was. I sat back down in the recliner. Joey handed me the ice bag. I could see they were looking at me. What degree of boniness was I since the last time they had seen me in a state of undress?

I looked better. Much healthier I hoped. Betsy distracted me from my uncomfortableness by letting me know she was about to put antiseptic on my raw back. Talk about distraction. Raw burning pain that brought tears to my eyes and almost out of the chair. I bit my lower lip. Joey wasn't good with shit like this. He went outside to the front porch until Betsy was done. She still had to do my face. Adam looked on sympathetically but was careful not to do too much touching in front of Betsy until she finally told him softly.

"Adam since her husband is such a pussy could you at least hold her hand?  This shit burns like crazy.  I want to do it again before I put a bandage on since she was in the culvert.  I don't want any bacteria remaining to infect the wound."

She eyed him just as sympathetically as he was eyeing me. He took my hand gently but kept his eyes averted so neither of us would see what it cost him to hold my hand.

"Oh holy fucking hell," I cried when she poured the liquid on the open wounds on my back.  This time I cried softly against Adam's shoulder.

"I'm sorry Joy," Betsy said softly.

"It's okay," I mumbled into Adam's shirt.

When she had my back bandaged she started on my face. Adam perched on the arm of the recliner steadying me.

"At least we know she can patch up all our kids," I told Adam trying not to cry as Betsy rubbed gently on my bruised and bleeding face with the wash cloth.

They both chuckled.

"I need to rinse this.  I will be right back."

Absently, Adam's thumb traced circles across my back until I shivered.  Our eyes met in the tiny space that separated us sitting on the recliner.

"Are you cold? I could get you some clothes or a blanket?" He asked with a huskiness.

"No not cold," I replied letting him know his touch was causing me to shiver.  Although sitting in my underwear was probably making him just as uncomfortable.  "Maybe you should grab the quilt for me so I can cover up."

"Good idea," he said with relief.

He rose and walked across the room grabbing the quilt the one we had used by the pond to cover ourselves with the one night we had made love outside so Joey and Betsy wouldn't catch us together.  When he covered me I knew he was thinking about that night too.  I pulled the quilt up to my neck snuggling deep within its warmth enveloping myself in the memories it created in my mind. My eyes were closed. I didn't hear Betsy return. She wiped a tear from my cheek. The salt burning my wound on my injured cheek.

"You okay?" She asked looking at me with concern.

"My knee hurts." I said the first thing that came to my mind.

She lifted the quilt then the ice bag examining my knee. "The swelling is going down. Are you sure you shouldn't go to the hospital if it hurts that bad?" She asked.

"I'm fine."

She lowered the ice bag then the quilt. She shrugged her shoulders. Wiping gently again with the washcloth on my face she continued cleaning.

"You've got some gravel in your face. I'll get the tweezers upstairs."

"I'll have Joey get them," Adam told her.

Adam yelled outside for Joey. He scrambled inside wincing at the thought that Betsy had to clean gravel out of my face. He ran up the steps two at a time and brought back the tweezers from the bathroom. He was back outside after that.

"Adam let's go in the kitchen. The lighting is better in there."

I sat in one chair leaning against Adam's shoulder. I wasn't high enough. Betsy had to lean over. She sighed. Her back was beginning to ache.

"Would you hold her in your lap? That will make her higher so I don't have to bend over."

He rolled his eyes. I laughed at his reaction. Stood and hobbled over to him wrapping the quilt tightly around me. He pulled me into his lap with his head behind my back.

"Much better."

"You know you're the only wife who would actually ask that her husband hold a half-naked woman in his lap?" He growled.

She just rolled her eyes at him. "At least she still has a figure Adam. Enjoy it while you can," she tried teasing him.

He glared at both of us. I didn't dare laugh. He looked so grumpy. The sharp point of the tweezers poked at my raw flesh as Betsy pulled gravel out of my face.

"Sweetie you are an absolute mess." She sighed.

Betsy spent the better part of an hour pulling gravel out of my face. With every pinch near my skin of the metal tweezers I flinched and winced. My head ached by the time she was done. One of Adam's arms rested by my thigh and the other was resting across my lap.

"Adam," Betsy said.

"What?" He groused.

"Hold her still. I'm going to put antiseptic on her face. This is going to hurt."

Fuck yes it did hurt. I kicked my legs and tears poured from my eyes after Betsy doused my cheek with the liquid. Adam was rubbing my back with one hand trying to make it better but knowing that nothing would make it so.

"Could you look at her face and see if you think I got all the gravel out?" Betsy asked Adam.

He turned my head. His eyes were sympathetic and compassionate.

"Yeah," he said with a huskiness. Then he lowered his head. "Anything else?"

"Just let me bandage her face. The rest of her looks good. You could carry her back to the sofa. Then she won't have to try walking on that leg again."

Adam continued to hold me. His thumb caressing my back while he looked anywhere but at me or Betsy while she applied a bandage to my face. Living on the farm, working in the fields we had a pretty extensive first aid kit. Luckily Betsy wasn't squeamish about cleaning the wounds. She should have gone to college to be a nurse. She would have made a damned good one.

"All done," Betsy told him.

"I'll carry her to the sofa now."

His eyes never left my face now that his wife and my best friend wasn't scrutinizing us. His emotions were clearly evident when he sat me on the sofa my body wrapped in the quilt. He kissed my forehead running his hand down the side of my face before he straightened. He looked tortured before he turned his back on me.

"Bets, I'm going to shower and change clothes," he called to the other room. My blood was on his white shirt from where he carried me home.

"Okay Adam," she replied.

He took the stairs two at a time not looking back. Within minutes I heard the sound of water running in the shower. If I were a betting woman I would bet the water was ice cold.

I elected to sleep on the sofa. I didn't want anyone carrying me up or down the stairs. I definitely couldn't make it on my own. Sleep wasn't going to come easy for me tonight so tossing and turning would keep Joey awake. Adam's face tortured and angry kept appearing in my mind's eye when I closed my eyelids. All his emotions were playing like a movie in my head over and over.

I was reading a book when the man in question came downstairs at 2:00 AM. He stopped dead at the bottom of the staircase. Adam ran his fingers through his hair. Joey had brought me a tank top so at least I wasn't in my underwear still.

"You're awake," he sounded surprised.

"I'm reading," I told him.

"Can't sleep?"

"No."

"Me neither. I was going to get some water. Want a glass?"

"I'm fine. I don't want to have to pee," I said uncomfortably.

He chuckled then disappeared into the kitchen in tight fighting shorts and no shirt. *Not going to help me sleep any better tonight Adam Moore.*

I sighed and tried focusing on my book, *Thinner* by Stephen King. I loved his novels but tonight I was having difficulty staying focused even on the book.

Adam sauntered back into the living room. He parked his butt on the coffee table and grabbed the book from my hand to read the back cover. He frowned at me and handed it back.

"Really you're reading that?" He asked incredulously.

"I know why I got thin smartass. It seemed ironic to read about a man who doesn't know why he's wasting away."

He shook his head. Not sure that he agreed with me.

"You doing okay?" He asked. "

"I'm fine other than falling into the culvert like a dumbass."

"I'm sorry about that," he said with regret.

"Why are you sorry? I'm the klutz that fell."

"Maybe if I hadn't been so harsh you might not have backed up and stumbled."

I smiled at him. I leaned over and caressed his cheek. "Good thing you have broad shoulders Adam."

"Why's that?"

"Because you feel guilty for all our faults," I told him trying to tease him. "That is a big burden to carry on those big shoulders."

"Not funny," he snapped slamming the water glass down beside him. A little sloshed over the top.

He pushed my hand away.

"I'm sorry Adam. I was only trying to tease you a little so you wouldn't feel so bad," I whispered softly sorry that I had teased him now.

He ran his hands through his hair and said one word "Fuck."

"What is wrong?" I asked him.

"I want to hold you...I want to hold you without anyone watching my every move. Second guessing my every thought or feeling."

I looked at Adam. I knew it would be a mistake most likely but I couldn't tell him no so I gave him what he wanted. I scooted down on the sofa so he would fit behind me. He looked at me strangely.

"Well are you going to just sit there or are you going to hold me?" I asked him.

It wasn't like we were making love although this was dangerous territory for us. Holding could lead to something more if we let it. He sat on the sofa in the space I had made for him. I leaned back into Adam's chest. My head tucked into the curve of his neck. His arm came around my stomach just below my breasts. His breath caught in his chest. I bit my lower lip. His hand was close to my right breast. So close he could cup it. He wanted to. I knew he did. Damn if I didn't want him to.

"I'm just going to hold you," he growled.

I chuckled softly. "I know."

And he did... just held me. All night.

We heard Joey coming down the hallway. I don't know which of us heard him first. I bolted upright as Adam's arms slipped away from my body. He rose from the sofa and guided me back against the pillows.

"I'm going to the kitchen to make coffee," he told me.

He turned to walk away. We heard Joey go to the bathroom. Adam came back cupping my face with his hands. His eyes staring intently into mine. Adam's head bent closer. Our faces so close our breaths mingling. His lips covered mine in a gentle heartbreakingly soft kiss. We heard Joey shut the bathroom door. He was walking towards the stairs. Adam reluctantly released me. His hands dropped to his sides as he straightened and went to the kitchen leaving me alone on the sofa.

"Hey babe. I'm surprised you are awake," Joey said when he got to the bottom step and saw me sitting up, staring out the window behind the sofa.

"Having trouble sleeping," I replied.

"How's your knee?" He asked. "You going to be able to go to work today?"

I uncovered my leg to reveal my swollen knee. With Joey's help I stood. I was able to hobble but only with his help. Adam walked out of the kitchen surprising Joey.

"Didn't know you were awake too."

"Couldn't sleep. She needs to go to the doctor."

"Do you think you or Luke could take her?"

"Yeah we will take care of her."

I looked from one to the other. "I'm here you know."

"You're going to the doctor," Joey said firmly.

He left for work. Adam called Luke to see what the morning was going to be like. He wanted to drop Betsy off at the farm so she wasn't by herself. She came downstairs while he was on the phone with his father. Betsy wobbled over and sat on the sofa with me yawning tiredly.

"How did you sleep?" She asked.

"About as good as you," I replied.

"What is he talking about?" She asked.

"You are going to the farm to stay with Luke. He's taking me to the doctor. Joey had to go to work today."

She rolled her eyes. "I can stay here."

"Good luck with that," I told her. "I didn't think I had to go to the doctor either but wasn't given a choice."

Betsy laid her head on my shoulder. I rested mine on top of hers. "You do need to go," she told me. "Your knee looks bad. What if you tore something inside?"

Betsy brought clothes downstairs to me. I dressed in the living room. I pulled my hair up in a ponytail. Adam was frustrated with me trying to hobble so he scooped me up in his arms and carried me out to the truck making Betsy laugh at the expression on my face.

"Brute force is not usually your style. That is usually Joey's." I was getting grumpy. The pain was wearing on me.

"I don't have all day Joy."

Betsy really laughed at that comment. I scooted over so that I was sitting in the middle. Took her hand, Adam lifted her from behind until Betsy was comfortably sitting next to me. Adam walked around the front of the truck and climbed in next to me and started the truck.

At the farm, Luke came outside. He opened Betsy's door and extended his hand to her not letting her go until her feet had hit the ground.

"Shorty you get any bigger I'm afraid you'll pop." He teased.

"Thanks Luke," she glared at him. "I think I will take my rotund self-inside the house."

"I never said anything about you being rotund."

"You didn't have to."

"Pregnant women," he declared. "So sensitive and you," he turned back towards the truck, "Did Adam shove you down the culvert?"

"Ha ha," I replied. Adam just shook his head at his father's attempt at humor.

"What time is her appointment?"

"Ten," Adam replied.

"You better get going," he replied. Luke stepped back and shut the truck's door.

I waved to him as I attempted to slide back to the door putting space between Adam and me. My muscles were sore this morning. Adam was looking at me out of the corner of his eye.

"Stay here," he said softly.

"What if somebody sees us?"

"It's nobody's business."

"Adam this is a small town. You know they already talk about the four of us living together. Let's not add more to the gossip mill by someone seeing me sitting next to you in the truck driving around town when we are both married to other people and you're expecting a baby any day," I said tiredly. I actually laid my head against the glass so exhausted by everything from the accident yesterday to hiding my feelings for Adam.

He was quiet. Watching the road. What did I expect him to say to that?

"I slept better last night than I have in months." The thoughts in my head slipping out of my mouth. I looked over at him startled that I had actually spoken the words aloud.

"I'm glad," he responded. A half-smile starting at the corner of his beautiful full lips.

"Are you excited about the baby coming soon?" I asked curiously. "You really don't say much."

"Are you surprised? I've always been a man of few words." He chuckled. "Yes I'm excited. I can't wait to hold him. I will be glad when it's over."

"You're scared."

He looked at me quickly and then back to the road. "Out of my mind. I just keep seeing you and all the blood," he said honestly.

I scooted over a little and covered his thigh with my hand. I squeezed comfortingly. He looked down where my hand rested on his leg then he looked quickly to my face before looking back to the road.

"Adam," I finally said. "Your baby's birth will be nothing like what happened to us. You have to know that. Believe that."

He ran his hand through his hair.

"I'm afraid I will just make it worse for Betsy. She needs you there."

"We can both be there," I told him.

"I just can't do it Joy," he said. His voice cracking.

"Okay. I won't push you. I just don't want you to miss what you can never get back again. It's such a special time Adam."

"Joy I know…if anyone knows I do. Every day I want to relive that day over with a different outcome. I think about how old he or she would be. Would it have been a girl who looked like you or a boy who looked like me," he said softly. His eyes never left the road.

Tears, damned tears welled in my eyes. To hell with it. I scooted back over by Adam and laid my head on his shoulder.

"I thought you didn't want anyone to see you sitting close to me in the truck?" He said.

"After that speech I don't give a damn who sees me," I told him. "If anyone asks I had my knee propped up on the seat. You need to stop beating yourself up over it Adam."

"How can I Joy? Me not being where I needed to be cost me everything. I promised you I would protect you both."

I put my arm around his waist and I hugged him. I closed my eyes inhaling his scent fresh and clean just soap smell. Adam was basic in everything he did. He was simple and uncomplicated.

He turned the truck into the parking lot of the doctor's office and parked the truck. He turned to me. One arm went behind me pulling me into his embrace. One hand cupped my face. His lips touched mine tenderly. The kiss went from soft and wet to hungry filled with need and urgency. His ended the kiss and rested his forehead against mine. My hand was at his waist holding him to me.

"I don't think I can stop loving you Joy," he said. He kissed my forehead.

He turned away from me and climbed out of the truck. It probably didn't help matters that we lived together. Seeing each other every day but seeing him every day is how I got through the days. Long as they seemed at times. I scooted across the seat dodging the steering wheel. He didn't let my feet hit the ground. He carried me to the door.

"Please let me walk inside," I pleaded as he reached for the knob. Reluctantly he sat me on my feet. I smiled at him.

Grateful that he had listened. He held me by my waist helping me walk without putting any weight on the bad leg.

I sat down while he checked me in at the desk. When Adam walked over to sit by me he handed me a clipboard with papers to fill out. I hadn't been to the doctor in over a year so I had to fill out all new paperwork. I sighed looking at page after page of documents. When I was done he returned them to the desk. A few minutes later they called my name. He helped me down the hall to the scales.

My favorite part. One hundred ten pounds. Luke knew I had lost a few pounds. He had kept it quiet. I had been walking a lot and eating the same amount. Not much. I had lost five pounds since my last weighing. I turned to get off the scales and Adam was scowling at me.

"Don't give me that look," I told him.

"You're only ten pounds more than when we first went to the doctor," he whispered angry at me.

The nurse looked over her shoulder at us whispering/arguing with each other.

"I'm sure I will gain a few pounds Adam now that I can't walk," I snapped in a hushed tone.

He shook his dark head at me. "We'll talk about this later."

*Oh no we won't.*

He sat me on the table in the room. Adam stood by the table unwilling to sit down. He was angry. The nurse took my vitals.

"Did Pa know?" He asked when she left us alone.

"I'm not throwing him under the bus."

"He knew and didn't tell us."

"He gave me two weeks to get my weight back up or he was going to."

"Why doesn't Joey see the weight loss?"

"Why didn't you see it last night? I was in your arms in my underwear."

"I was concentrating on not getting a hard on while holding you nearly naked with my wife standing over us not really focusing on your body Joy," he said being brutally honest.

"Oh."

"Yeah. Oh."

His hands were planted on either side of my body. He was gazing intently into my eyes.

"Adam, you knew there was going to be setbacks. I'm working on it."

He kissed my cheek. Then he straightened. He couldn't be caught in a comprising position with me. The doctor knew all four of us. Several minutes later the doctor knocked. She was short and slender like Betsy. Brilliant red hair and freckles. Round, metal glasses were perched on the end of her nose. She was looking at my chart. Betsy and I saw her for most everything. Betsy had switched to an obstetrician only to deliver Noah.

"Joy you took a tumble I hear," she said.

"I did."

"I want to remove those bandages and take a look at the contusions. Also, you do realize you haven't had a pap smear yet? I think it would be a good idea to do one today if you're up to it. We talked about it after you lost the baby but you didn't come back for your checkup."

Adam's head swiveled towards mine and he was not happy.

"Sure why not," I said sarcastically.

"Let's look at the knee first."

She examined it bringing tears to my eyes. The damned knee hurt like crazy.

"Joy I think it's dislocated. I want an X-Ray to be sure."

Adam carried me down the hall where her technician did an X-Ray. Then he carried me back to the room where he sat me on the table. We waited in silence for Doctor Ray to return.

"Are you going to say something?" I finally asked.

"You didn't come back for a check-up after you lost the baby?"

I shook my head no. I hadn't wanted to talk about losing the baby or to even think about it. No one realized what was supposed to happen. No one pushed me so I hadn't gone. Not that it was their responsibility.

"Joy, what if something had gone wrong after the miscarriage? Anything that could have been serious?" He was leaning close too close. His eyes full of emotion and fear.

I had to look away. "Adam," I said softly. "At that point I really didn't care."

He took a deep choking breath. That hurt him. I could tell. "I would have cared," he said straightening.

Doctor Ray came into the room. "Well Joy, the knee is dislocated. Since it's naturally bent at the moment I want to get the girly stuff out of the way first since I probably won't get you back here for a while," she said knowingly. "Then I will straighten the leg and put you in a splint for three weeks. You'll be on crutches."

"Can I go back to work?" I asked.

"I'd like for you to be off for a week to rest the knee giving it time to heal. Then you can go back."

She reached into a cabinet. She handed me a soft cloth gown. "Undress completely. I will be right back. I will check out the contusions while we do the exam."

She left the room. I looked at Adam. He looked at me.

"I don't suppose you can do this yourself can you?"

"Not really."

"Fuck. Where do you want to start?"

I lifted my top over my head and handed it him. He tossed it to a chair behind him. I reached behind me and unclasped my bra. I took my arms out of the straps but held the cups in place so at least I didn't flash him. He helped me get the gown in place opening in the front. I pulled it tight around my body.

Adam lifted me from the table steadying me while I reached under the gown and dragged my shorts and panties down my legs. He helped me step out of them. Then he grabbed them off the floor laying them with my shirt and bra. Adam grasped me around the waist lifting me back onto the table.

"That wasn't so bad," I said.

"Who says?" He grumbled. "I know you're naked under that flimsy gown."

I laughed softly at him. His hands were pressed to the table surrounding me. Doctor Ray came back to the room making him move away.

"Adam I assume you don't want to stay for this part?"

"Hell no," he replied.

I tried to scoot to the bottom of the table. "Hey Adam," I said stopping him from leaving.

"What?" He asked grumpily.

"Could you at least help me get into position before you step out?" I asked helplessly.

"Sure why not."

He got me settled butt at the bottom of the table. Legs in the stirrups. He shook his head frustrated with the entire situation and stepped into the hallway shutting the door a little too hard.

"Is he all right?" Doctor Ray asked.

"Adam?" I asked – who else? "Yes, he will be fine."

Doctor Ray did a pap smear, a pelvic. Everything looked fine. She did a breast exam showing me how to do self-exams in bed or in the shower. Explaining the importance of doing regular self-exams especially since I was notorious for not going to the doctor. She said this with a hint of sarcasm letting me know she wasn't pleased that I had not returned after the miscarriage.

"Can you sit up on your own?" She asked.

"Not likely."

"Ok let me get Adam. Then I want to look at your face and back."

Adam stepped back in and helped me sit up. "Everything okay?" He asked worriedly.

Doctor Ray spoke before I could. "Adam everything looks fine so far. I want to take a look at Joy's contusions now. Then I will straighten her leg and put on the splint. I think she will need you then," she said kindly. He nodded knowing it was going to be painful when she did that to my leg.

Doctor Ray knew my history with Adam. As my primary care she knew my history of mental illness, Anorexia Nervosa and my miscarriage. She also knew he was now married to Betsy and they were expecting a baby any day. She was kind and gentle about our situation no matter how crazy or complicated it had to seem to her.

Doctor Ray removed the bandage from my face first. She looked at it thoroughly

"Looks good. You guys did a great job of cleaning the wound although the ER would have been preferable."

I rolled my eyes. Adam turned his back to us when she pulled my gown down and removed the bandage from my back.

"Kiddo when you do something you sure do it right," she told me. "I'm going to cover this one again. I don't want your clothes sticking to it. Your face you can leave uncovered."

She pressed the bandage back in place retrieved tape from a drawer and secured the gauze tightly to my back. Adam looked over his shoulder. I caught his eyes out of the corner of mine.

"Why don't you get dressed while I get the splint?"

She helped me get the gown back in place then she left the room. Adam lifted me to the floor. I balanced on one foot. He guided my bad leg into my panties first then he helped me get my other foot in. I pulled them up my body. The gown came open revealing my breasts right in Adam's face. I pulled the gown closed again.

"Sorry," I said.

He just grumbled. He grabbed my shorts repeating the same process this time I held my gown closed. He lifted me back onto the table. He handed me my bra and shirt. I let the gown slide down when he turned his back but when I looked up he was peeking over his shoulder.

"Hey," I said hooking my bra behind my back.

"I should get some reward for today.

"Adam." I kicked out with my good foot and nudged him in the ass. He just chuckled at me. I pulled the tee shirt over my head ending his show.

He walked over by the table and stood by me.

"You know this is going to hurt."

"Thanks for the warning but I suspected as much."

He kissed my temple casually. I took his hand because I was starting to feel nervous and he held it tight comforting me.

Doctor Ray returned with the splint, a black heavy device with metal rods that she opened and stretched out on the table. Adam helped me lay down with my legs stretched out before me. My bad leg still bent at a forty-five degree angle.

"You ready," the doctor asked me.

Adam leaned over the table and turned my head towards him still holding onto my hand. He whispered softly to me our foreheads almost touching while the doctor took hold of my leg placing it over the splint. She looked over her shoulder then straightened my leg causing my knee to pop. I cried out nearly passing out with the pain. She buckled the splint around my leg.

"I'm sorry Joy. I know how badly that hurt," she said while she buckled me into the splint. She showed Adam how tight the splint had to be. "She can take it off to shower no other reason."

I was sobbing. My knee throbbed painfully. She gave me ibuprofen and a drink of water plus a prescription for painkillers if needed. I didn't want them if I didn't need them. With my personality drugs were the last thing I needed; recognizing my own weaknesses was not a problem. Always dealing with them sometimes was.

Adam helped me to an upright position. I rested my head on his shoulder still in pain and still crying softly not sobbing like before. Doctor Ray handed him crutches I was to use for three weeks plus a note to give to Judge Tony excusing me from work.

"Whenever Joy is ready you guys can check out at the receptionist desk. Take your time."

"Thanks Doctor Ray," Adam told her.

He put his arms around me holding me to him while his head rested against mine.

"I've been able to hold you a lot in the last twenty-four hours. You should fall down more," he said teasing me.

I laughed which came out somewhere between a sob and a very unattractive snort. His hand big and strong comforted me rubbing across my back. I leaned back to look into his eyes. His hands were still wrapped around my body. I placed my hands on his face and pulled him to me. I pressed my lips to his. This kiss in itself was wrong but I needed to let him know how much I appreciated him helping me today. Our breathing quickened. His hands became more urgent on my body. Finally I pulled back. Our lips still close. Our hands still touching each other.

"I don't think Doctor Ray intended for us to make out in her office," I told him.

"No, probably not. Ready to go?" He asked.

"Yes, I'm ready."

He checked me out at the receptionist desk. Maneuvering the truck was an interesting experience since my leg would not bend. Adam sat me on the seat and asked which way I wanted to sit facing him or not? I decided not would be okay. I scooted myself back until I was sitting up against his shoulder with my legs straight in front of me stretched across the bench of the truck. I looked over my shoulder and smiled at him. There wasn't anything I could do but lean against him. We were quiet on the ride home. Lost in our thoughts. He turned into the driveway which surprised me.

"I thought I would take you home first. Get you settled then go get Betsy. She can keep you company while I work with Pa this afternoon."

I nodded. He parked the truck close to the porch but in the yard. Then he carried me into the house. "Upstairs or down?" He asked.

"You know I think I would really like to be in my bed."

"Your bed it is," he said. He carried me up the staircase carefully so he didn't bump my leg in the process. Down the hall to my room, I opened the door for him. He kicked it shut with his foot. He placed me gently on the bed.

"Want to sit with me for a minute?"

"I don't think that is a good idea."

"Oh," I replied casting my eyes anywhere but at him.

"Joy, I can only do so much. I can only take so much," he said with obvious strain. "Right now I just want to take our clothes off and bury myself in you and that is wrong on so many levels."

"I get it Adam." My voice sounded breathy.

"I really don't think that you do."

I stared at Adam. Didn't he think that I saw in him and felt the same consuming need? Didn't he think that I still loved him as desperately as he seemed to love me? Wanting to just hold me last night in his arms was such a simple request. Something easy to give him but had we been caught it would not have been so easy to explain. The intimacy of the situation would have been evident to our spouses. The people we never wanted to hurt. How do you stop loving someone as much as Adam and I loved each other?

"Adam," I said softly looking at the comforter. "I think I do. It isn't just about the sex or wanting you so much at times that I ache for you knowing Joey can't make you disappear from my heart or my mind. Knowing he can't possess me the way that you do," I added. "It is so much more. It's about the feeling I had of you holding in me in your arms last night. Getting so comfortable I fell asleep. You being there today to comfort me when most likely no one else could have nor would I have wanted them to."

He ran his hands through his hair. "Stop or I'm going to do something we will both regret."

"I don't think I could regret anything more than I do giving you up," I whispered sadly.

Adam ripped his shirt over his head. I knew then I had gone too far. Regrets would be for later. We needed each other. He unzipped his jeans and dropped them to the floor at the same time that he toed off his sneakers. I was already removing my shirt and bra tossing them over the side of the bed when he met me on the bed.

His hands caresses my face, my breasts. His tongue licked my jaw, my neck. He took a nipple into his mouth and sucked until I was squirming beneath him holding his head to my breast. His hands jerked down my panties tossing them aside. I started on his boxers. We had to be quick. He had to get to the farm to get Betsy. Later I would have to face her and pretend nothing had happened. Later I would have to face Joey too.

Now I just had Adam. His boxers were around his ankles his dick teasing my folds. I separated my legs difficult with the heavy splint on the one leg. Adam thrust into me hard and fast. His head thrown back in pure ecstasy. I grabbed his ass careful not to dig my nails into him like I wanted to. I couldn't leave any marks on his beautifully sculpted body.

I was soaking wet around Adam's dick.

"You feel so damned good Joy," he said thrusting into me.

I moaned in response. I was focusing on him, the feel of him so long since he had been inside me. So wrong that he was now. His dick slid over my clitoris with sweeping powerful strokes better than his tongue making my climax quick. I convulsed around Adam hard surprising him.

"I'm going to come." He wasn't wearing a condom. I was too close to my fertile cycle. Not really sure how close but not willing to take the chance.

"You have to pull out Adam," I said huskily. "I could get pregnant."

"Fuck no," he ground out shaking his head.

"Adam," I pleaded. "You have to." He kept thrusting into me feeling so fucking good. Holding him in but pushing him away too. "Adam," I said his name again. "We can't take the chance."

"Fuck," he growled thrusting a couple more times into my body. He finally rose to knees with a force that rocked the headboard into the wall. With his head thrown back, his hand on his dick he came all over my belly. He covered me again with the weight of his body and kissed me urgently.

He pulled back staring into my eyes. "I fucking love you with everything in me. How the hell are we going to survive this?"

"We just are," I told him. I didn't know what else to say to him. I had no answers. I loved him just as passionately. He was kissing me again not wanting to leave me. "You have to get Betsy before somebody questions us."

"Fuck all right."

He climbed out of bed and started picking up his clothes. I loved his ass and had a nice view of it right now as he retrieved clothing from the floor. He went to the hallway and got a washcloth; bringing it back warm and soapy. He washed me, my belly, and my folds caressing me with soft loving strokes of his hand. Then he dried me just as tenderly.

"Want all your clothes?"

"My panties and my shirt."

He helped me back into them and threw the others in the laundry basket in the closet. He kissed my forehead and then he left me alone with my thoughts. My guilt but no regrets. I could never regret loving Adam

## Chapter Eight

### Joey

Two weeks since Joy's accident falling into the culvert. I knew the crutches and the splint were a fucking pain in the ass. Hers and mine. She was having trouble sleeping.

Two weeks until Betsy's due date. She had trouble breathing when she climbed the stairs. The baby was pressed on her bladder so she felt like had to pee all the time. She was also having trouble sleeping.

Adam and I were about to lose our minds with the two bitchy women in our lives. Joy scared to death she might gain an ounce was barely eating since she couldn't walk. She was drinking her protein shakes like a champ asking how many scoops of protein powder we had put in the drink. Just one we said every time although our fingers were crossed mentally if not behind our backs.

Betsy had put three scoops in one time she made it. Joy had almost fallen into the tub trying to weigh herself something she rarely did at home. She weighed one hundred twenty pounds having gained ten pounds since her doctor's visit.

My girl was still slender. I wish that she could see what I see. I hadn't touched her in weeks. Afraid of hurting her. Feeling unsure of whether she wanted my touch. So many confusing thoughts going through my head.

I stepped out of the shower after a long day at the mill. Soon no more mill for me. I wouldn't fucking miss it either. Five more weeks till graduation. I had a job lined up. I had all summer to study for the CPA. I wanted to take the exam as soon as possible.

Dammit, I had forgotten a towel. Adam and Betsy weren't home so I stepped out of the bathroom dripping wet and headed towards my bedroom where Joy was resting after working all day. Her knee aching.

The door opened just I reached for it and Betsy stepped into the hallway screaming as soon as she saw me in all my naked glory. Not screaming because I was naked but screaming because I had startled her. She scared me with her screaming and I jumped back.

"Good god Joey you aren't normal," she said unable to take her eyes off my junk.

"Stop staring Betsy," I growled not sure what to do to cover myself.

Adam was standing at the top of the stairs now trying not to laugh.

"Hey Bets," Adam called down the hall.

Without looking away from my dick she said, "Uh yeah Adam?"

"You know it is kind of insulting that you are staring at another man's dick with so much enthusiasm," he teased.

I glared at him. "Jackass." I heard Joy laughing her ass off in the bedroom. "Shut it Joy," I snapped at her.

"Sorry Adam but I've never seen anything like it," she sounded as amazed as she looked. "Who knew he was hiding this inside those jeans?" She pointed at my junk.

Adam almost dropped to the floor he was laughing so hard now.

"On your way little momma," I told her as I gently shoved her down the hall and went to the bedroom slamming the door shut behind me. Joy still cackling like a chicken at my expense.

"Behave," I told her. She knew I was sensitive about it.

"We could make money off your junk Joey," she said trying to stop the laughter.

"Funny," I told her grabbing boxers from the top drawer of our dresser.

"Five dollars you can look and ten dollars you can touch. If we get you hard first they would really be amazed and pay big bucks for that," she teased.

"Go fuck yourself," I told her not appreciating her humor.

"Come here," she told me realizing that the size of my penis which most men would be proud of was the one thing that made me damned uncomfortable.

She wrapped her arms around my neck and kissed my cheek. "I'm damned proud of that dick Porn Star," she said mischievously.

That was it. I rolled her over and smacked her ass hard. She looked over her shoulder at me with a twinkle in her eye. "Do it again," she said with a deep husky sexiness that made my dick hard. She wiggled her ass at me.

I yanked her shorts down her body. Then ripped her panties in half. She glared at me. I knew she hated it when I ripped her underwear but pure need was fueling me with urgency to get inside her. I spread her legs and pulled her to the edge of the mattress practically lifting her off it. I smacked her ass again hard living an imprint on her butt cheek. She moaned deep in her throat. My dick was now so fucking hard it was ready to explode. I jammed it into her loving the feel of her slick, moist wetness. I groaned.

"Do I need to get a condom?"

"I'm good," she told me.

I didn't know what that meant but I was one happy man. I buried myself in her deeper making her squeal. I slapped her ass again loving the sound and the feel of my hand on her bare skin. It made my dick that much harder and made her pussy that much wetter. I leaned over Joy and started a slow steady rhythm pumping my body into hers. My hand on her shoulder caressing her. I grabbed a handful of hair and tugged on her head until she was looking back at me. Her hand went underneath herself to touch her clit and I was nearly lost.

I wanted to see her face. I pulled completely out and flipped her over gently, pulling her ass closer to the edge of the bed as I slid back into her softly. Joy ran a finger across her clit while I thrust my dick into her soft, wet center. Her legs were up on my shoulders making her tight surrounding me. I thought I would lose my mind she felt so good. Joy moaned. Her hair was spread around her head like a fan. Her arms flung over her head.

"Touch yourself again," I demanded.

She smiled at me. Then her finger found the hard little nub and she caressed herself. I knew her tells. Her signs. She was getting close.

"You about to come baby?" I asked sliding in and out in a slow steady pace my dick so hard I thought I was going to come inside her at any moment.

"Fuck yes," she ground out between her clinched lips. Her eyes closed.

"Open your eyes Joy," I told her. "I want you to see me."

"Just make me come Joey."

I grabbed her jaw. I knew it was hard when she flinched. I loosened my grip. "I want you to look at me while you come," I told her roughly.

She opened her eyes. Those beautiful green eyes never once left my face as her finger brought her clit to throbbing satisfaction. Her body convulsing around me sending me over the edge with her.

I heard Adam yell, "Pizza's here." I fell on Joy with my entire weight crushing her into the mattress. I kissed her roughly. She was mine. All mine. Nothing and no one would ever take her from me.

Downstairs, at the kitchen table Betsy kept looking at me differently. I would take a bite and catch her staring at me. So what she had seen me naked. Joy was still giggling over Betsy's reaction to my junk. Betsy laid her pizza down.

"I'm sorry I just can't get your dick out of my head," she said still amazed. "I've never seen one so big."

I glared at her.

"I told you he was big did you think I was lying?"

"Do we have to talk about the size of Joey's dick at the dinner table? Really ladies," Adam almost groaned.

"I agree with Adam," I said uncomfortable myself with this conversation.

"He's sensitive about it," my wife told Betsy.

"Why?" Betsy asked. "I thought you guys were proud of your penis."

"Joey was teased so badly when we were kids about the size that it traumatized him," Adam offered.

"I'm not traumatized," I disagreed. "Think about Betsy's first reaction. You're not normal. I've heard that my whole life. I hate it."

"Well Joseph," Betsy said. "After I have this baby I wouldn't mind trying that out just once. Can I please have some of that?" She looked at Adam begging him for permission. She was teasing of course but he didn't take it that way.

He dumped his piece of pizza on the plate. Then he got up from the table. "I think I will go to the farm. I forgot something I was supposed to help Pa with."

We watched him stalk out the front door.

"Think I went too far?" She asked Joy and me feeling more than a little uncomfortable I thought.

"Yep," Joy replied rolling her eyes.

"Joy deals with him best maybe she should go to the farm and talk to him," Betsy said sighing.

"Maybe we should just let him cool down," Joy said.

"Would you talk to him Joy?" She begged.

My girl sighed. "Whatever you want."

After dinner I took Joy to the farm to talk to Adam. We went inside where we found Luke who let us know that Adam full of piss and vinegar was in the barn burning off steam. Joy went to the barn alone to talk to Adam while I talked to Luke.

After a while I went to the barn to see if we could all go home. I didn't walk all the way in. I turned at the door and met Luke coming out of the house.

"Will you bring those two home?" I asked him.

"Sure. Everything okay?" He asked me.

"Yeah I have studying to do. They aren't done talking."

"Okay Joey. I will bring them home," he said uncertainly. I don't think he believed me. I just wanted to get the intimate scene I had witnessed out of my head.

### Joy

I walked into the barn finding Adam shirt off shoveling hay into the stalls for the horses. His head low. I could tell the wheels were spinning a thousand miles an hour. I hobbled with the splint still on my leg the length of the barn until he looked at me catching sight of me or hearing me.

"What are you doing here?" He asked.

"I'm checking on you. Your wife sent me."

"Oh you mean the one that wants to take a spin on your husband's dick. That one?" He asked.

I couldn't help but smile. "You are more than adequate in that department Adam," I said definitely checking out his package.

"I wasn't fishing for compliments."

"Then what is wrong?"

"I know you have sex with him. I know that. I have to live with that. I have sex with Betsy. I feel like I have to. We're both married. That is what married people do. This is so fucked up."

"Where are you going with this Adam?" I asked tilting my head to the side trying to understand. Trying to give him my full attention but his half naked body was definitely distracting me, giving me thoughts that weren't good considering my husband was in the house and could decide to join us at any moment.

"When she was sitting there begging me to let her have sex with Joey…"

"She wasn't serious Adam," I cut him off.

"I don't care. When she was saying that shit I was like hell why would she want to be with me."

"Adam, she's having your baby. Betsy loves you."

"I'm not talking about Betsy Joy."

**Oh.**

"Would it make you feel better to know that just looking at you right now, no shirt, jeans low on your hips, a little sweat covering your chest makes me want to throw you down in the straw and fuck your brains out?" I asked.

He looked shocked.

"Why?"

"Why what?"

"Why would you want me over Joey? He's going to have the great career. He's smart. He's got a huge dick to satisfy you with."

I busted out laughing.

"It's not funny."

I tried to stop laughing. "It is funny Adam. If I don't laugh I will probably sit down and cry and not stop. We're both married to other people when we should be married to each other," I said. He dropped his eyes to the floor of the barn covered in bits of straw that had fallen from his pitch fork. "We do what we need to do to make our marriages work because it is the right thing to do when all we want to do is be with each other. I should be having your baby not Betsy and probably Adam if Noah wasn't involved I would say screw it and screw them but I can't do that to him just as I couldn't do it to them after I lost the baby. So as far as Joey's career or his intelligence or the size of his dick this conversation is ridiculous. You two have never been in competition in my mind."

He dropped the pitchfork to the floor. He took a couple steps towards me. I took two towards him. He met me the rest of the way. Adam wrapped his arms around my waist and pulled me into his embrace. His chin rested on my shoulder. His hands were on my body one on my waist and one just at the curve of my ass. Was it intimate? I didn't think so at the time but I guess to my husband who I hadn't heard come into the barn it did appear so. He came, he saw, he went in a big hurry.

I knew this because as we were standing there just like this Luke came in as well. He didn't leave. He cleared his throat. Adam stepped away from me. He grabbed the pitchfork from the floor and turned his back to get his shirt from one of the stall doors where he had tossed it earlier.

"I get it you two. I really do. Life's a fucking bitch but I told you not to give up on each other. I told you both," he said passionately. "Now you're both married to someone else. Adam you are expecting a baby with your wife in a matter of weeks." Adam still hadn't looked his father in the eye.

"You can't be hanging out in the barn hugging her with your hand almost on her ass with no shirt on when your best friend and your husband could and did walk in and see you. From my perspective it was a pretty intimate embrace I just saw. From his perspective he's wondering what the fuck is going on between you two."

"I'm sorry Luke," I said.

"I'm not the one you should be apologizing to."

Frustrated, Luke ran his hand over his face. Both hands were now planted on his lean hips. "Kids look it breaks my heart to see you going through this but I can't stand by and watch everyone get destroyed all over again. I think everybody is on pretty stable ground right now. Can we keep it that way?" He asked.

"Pa exactly how am I supposed to stop thinking about her? After all this time, she is all I want?"

I was shocked by Adam's admission. I whirled around to look at him. He hadn't told anyone but me how he felt. Luke ran his hands through his hair making it more unruly than it usually was.

"Adam I don't know. Maybe you and Betsy need to move out so you aren't under each other's noses."

"No," I cried. Then clasped my hand over my mouth at my outburst. Tears welled in my eyes.

"I see. You both torture yourself keeping each other close. You don't really want to get over each other do you?"

Adam walked up behind me. He placed a hand on my shoulder to comfort me. Neither of us said anything to Luke. We didn't answer his question because we had no answers for him.

"There is nothing else for me to say to you two. Just be aware that you give off vibes that let all of us know how you feel about each other. The air crackles with the emotions that you two put off as hokey as that sounds coming from me."

He turned to walk out of the barn. His face a mask of sadness when he turned back. "I have to take you home when you are ready. Joey left you here."

Adam and I looked at each other. Joey really was upset.

"Luke will you take me home now?"

"I will walk home later," Adam said.

He was giving me time to soothe Joey.

"Let's go," Luke replied still irritated with Adam and me.

Betsy was sitting on the sofa watching television. I plopped on the coffee table to talk to her for a second. Then she decided to come upstairs with me when she realized that Adam wasn't coming right home.

I left her at her bedroom door and went to my own room. Joey was sprawled on our bed in his boxers hair wet he had showered apparently studying now. He didn't look up when I entered our bedroom. I crawled into bed beside him. I tried snuggling next to him and received a cold shoulder. I kissed his neck, sucked his earlobe into my mouth. He slammed the book shut and laid it on the table beside him. Joey was looking at me out of the corner of his eye. His intensity was somewhat frightening.

Joey was angry. I didn't want to encourage him when he was angry. That didn't work out too well on our wedding night. He was sorry afterwards but I had learned my lesson. I started to get off the bed and he caught my arm pulling me backwards. The heavy splint on my leg slowing me down.

"Where are you going Joy?" He asked quietly.

"You're pissed. I'll come back when you're not angry with me."

"Why should I be angry with you?" He asked.

"You shouldn't be," I said calmly.

"So if you walked in on me with my arms around a woman, my hand nearly on her ass you wouldn't be pissed? Oh and I had no fucking shirt on either," he added.

I bit my lip. How was I supposed to answer him? I started to get up again and he stopped me.

Joey pinned me face down on the bed. He was holding my arms over my head with one hand as he yanked my shorts down then my underwear were ripped to shreds.

"Joey," I begged. "Not angry. You promised not to do this when you were angry."

"You're mine god dammit," he replied. "You're my wife."

He rammed himself into me hard and hurtful. I cried out but he didn't stop. I could feel my flesh tear at his forceful intrusion into my body. There was blood on me and on him. That is what stopped him. He backed up and released me. I flipped over onto my back. Joey pulled his boxers up.

"What the hell have I done?" He asked himself. He ran his hands through his messy hair. "I'm no better than him." Horror was clearly evident on his face.

"Who Joey?" I asked my voice trembling.

Joey went to the closet and got dressed. I laid on the bed crying. One arm over my face. When I realized he was leaving I got up from the bed and grabbed my shorts. My panties were trashed. I pulled my shorts up, snapping them and zipping them before I limped from the room after him calling to him. Betsy came out of their bedroom after me. Asking me what was happening.

We followed him to the front door. I was slower coming down the steps because I came down with Betsy holding her hand making sure she was safe on the staircase. At the bottom, he put his hand on the doorknob and hesitated.

"I just need to get out for a while Joy," Joey said softly. He was hurting.

"Don't leave," I begged him.

"I hurt you again," he said. "I promised I wouldn't." His voice was desperate.

"Joey you leaving is not a good idea when you are this upset. You will start drinking. I know you."

He turned and looked at me. My hair a wild mess. My face puffy from crying. Adam tried to come through the door. Joey took a step back to let him come in.

"What's going on?" He asked. He looked at all of us for an answer.

"Nothing," I responded. "I was trying to keep Joey from going out."

"Why was Joey going out?" He asked.

We all looked uncomfortably at each other.

"We had a fight," I explained. "I don't want him to leave."

"Joey man stay here," Adam said. "Let's talk it out."

Joey's face was impassive. I thought maybe he had changed his mind then he drew back and punched Adam in the jaw hard cursing at the pain in his hand. Betsy and I both cried out at the same time as Adam's head snapped back with the blow of Joey's fist.

Adam glared at Joey. "Feel better?" He asked his friend rubbing his jaw.

"Not one fucking bit." He shoved Adam out of the way and walked out of the front door. I went after him but couldn't stop him.

Back inside Adam turned to me, "What was that about?"

"It doesn't matter," I said.

"Did he hurt you?" He asked.

I shook my head no unwilling to make the situation worse by telling them what he had done. I walked slowly up the stairs neither of them tried to stop me. I drew a warm bath and climbed into the steaming water. I drew my knees to my chest and sobbed into my arms. My life was a mess and I didn't know how to make it better. I was only nineteen soon to be twenty. Life shouldn't be this damned hard.

Betsy knocked on the door half hour later.

"Come in," I told her.

She sat on the floor like an elephant whose legs had collapsed. I tried not to laugh at her. She was so big with Noah poor thing had no other way to get down there on the floor.

"You aren't getting up by yourself you know," I told her.

"I will call Adam."

I looked down at my naked self and then at her.

"Close the curtain."

I just shook my head.

"I saw the bed. There's some blood on it. What did he do to you?"

"Tell me Adam didn't see it."

"He saw it."

"Fuck."

"Do you want to be with Adam?" She asked her voice breaking.

"Betsy," I cried, "You and Adam are having a baby soon. I would never do anything to come between you."

"I don't think you do it intentionally."

This was probably the first conversation we had in a while.

"What do you want me to do?" I asked.

"Maybe we should move out?" She suggested.

"I don't want you to. Not now."

***Not ever.***

"I don't want to either. I think I will need your help with Noah."

I raised my head and looked at her.

"I want to help with Noah."

She smiled at me.

"Bets Adam thinks he can't do anything to make you happy."

"He told you that?" She asked.

I was holding my head in my hand.

"Yes," I replied.

"I told you after you two got together that I still had feelings for him would you be honest with me. Do you still have feelings for him?"

I tilted my head back on my shoulders and looked at the ceiling. "I still have feelings for Adam." My green eyes met her blue eyes. "Feel better Betsy?" I asked her.

"Hand me the washcloth."

"What?"

"Just hand it to me," she said.

She took it from my hand. She soaped it up really bubbly and began to wash my back. Then my arms and neck. It was as if I was her child.

"Wash your front," she said handing the cloth to me. I took it and washed my breasts. "Where did the blood come from?" She asked.

"My vagina most likely," I said. "He tore something in me I think. He was pissed."

I washed my legs. I was sore when I reached between my legs to wash myself. Adam knocked on the door and then opened it. Betsy was blocking his view of me but our eyes met over her head and his spoke volumes. He was getting weary of the battle. So was I.

"Are you ladies all right?" He asked.

"Fine," I said. She nodded in agreement.

"Can I do anything?"

"I think one of you helping me bathe is enough," I replied and Betsy laughed.

"Want me to leave?" Betsy asked. Her blue eyes twinkling.

"No," I said grumpily.

"Everything will be okay," she told me and Adam agreed.

I finished my bath got out and dried off while Betsy continued sitting on the floor talking to me. I dried the floor and wrapped the towel around me. Then I tried to get Betsy off the floor by myself. Between the two of us giggling and me nearly losing my towel we decided we needed Adam's help. I opened the door and yelled for him.

It was easy for him to lift her off the floor. He wrapped her in his arms and kissed her temple. I left the bathroom unable to watch the tender moment between them. I put on pajama shorts and a sweatshirt and went downstairs.

"It's a nice night," I told them. They were sitting together on the sofa. "I think I will step outside for a bit. Sit on the porch swing."

"Do you want company?" Adam asked.

"Up to you," I replied.

They came out with me. Betsy deliberately sat on one end while I had sat on one end thinking she would sit next to me. Adam sat in the middle. He put his arms around both of us and hugged us but he whispered the words, *I love you* to Betsy. She turned surprised at his admission. I smiled and turned my head. I knew what he was doing. I knew he had to take this path no matter what he felt for me. If things were ever going to be right in our world we had to move on if only we were pretending. I had gotten good at pretending. I could do it so could he.

At 1:00 AM Adam and Betsy went to bed both kissing my head before heading up the stairs. I kept watch for Joey. At

2:00 AM I saw his truck lights as he turned into the drive parking beside Adam's truck. The television was on but the lights were off in the living room. At first he didn't notice me. He started to walk into the kitchen I called his name. Joey turned. His hair was messy. His gate not quite steady. I had seen him drunker than tonight.

"Come here," I told him.

He came over and scooped me into his arms and sat down with me on his lap.

"Where's your leg splint?" He asked.

"I'm sick of the damned thing."

He shook his head like I was a naughty child.

I placed my hands on either side of his face and cupped his jaws lovingly. "This will never stop you know."

"What?" He asked confused.

"You and I arguing. Things getting out of hand because we both have tempers. One of us is always going to explode."

"I hurt you," he said disgusted with himself. "I saw the blood."

"Joey in the course of normal sex you could cause a tear like that."

He laid his head against mine.

"I would say I'm sorry but I don't think it's enough."

"Can you try to understand something?"

"What?"

"Adam and I are always going to feel about each other the way we do because we've been close for a really long time," I explained without lying but without saying the whole truth.

"I'm married to you though and he's married to Betsy. Nothing was going on in the barn but me comforting him. I realize how it would seem to you but can you try talking to me for a change instead of trying to fuck away your anger? Cause right now I won't be able to fuck you for a really long time until I heal," I kissed his cheek. Nibbled on his earlobe causing him to tremble in my arms. "That's a real shame Joseph cause you and I need a really nice slow fuck right now." I could feel his dick getting hard next to my leg. I licked along his jaw.

"You are bad Joy."

"Yes Joey Bonds. I am and you won't have any of me until I heal because you hurt me. So enjoy your hard on jackass."

I got up and walked to the steps. At the bottom step I turned and glanced over my shoulder, "I love you Joey," I said before I went up to our room.

"I love you Joy Bonds."

### Chapter Nine

### *Joy*

Noah made his entrance into the world a couple weeks later at midnight with me beside Betsy as I promised. The doctor laid him on Betsy's stomach. He was long and big not scrawny at all like most newborns. He wailed at the cold new world he had entered. I touched his tiny hand. Betsy's eyes met mine and we both had tears in them.

Noah had a head full of dark nearly black hair that stood on end just like his father. I thought for sure he looked just like Adam. She did too. I was so overwhelmed I had to sit down for a minute. While the doctor finished with Betsy the nurses took Noah and cleaned him. When they brought him back Betsy told me to take him. The nurse handed him to me.

Noah was no longer crying. His cheeks were pink. His eyes were puffy from birth but they would be big and beautiful like his daddy's eyes. His full little lips were also Adam's lips. I looked over the baby in my arms and Betsy looking beautiful but exhausted said, "He's beautiful. Isn't he?" I agreed.

Once Betsy had been sewn because of the deep incisions to get Noah out they covered her. I knew she was hurting. I handed the baby to her and walked over to the door where Adam, Luke and Joey were waiting for word of Noah and Betsy. All three men rose quickly to their feet when I opened the door.

"They're both fine. Come in," I told them motioning with my hand.

Adam was first through the door. He slid into the bed beside Betsy wrapping his arm around her shoulder. Luke put his arm around me holding me close. He kissed the top of my head. His first grandchild was born. Adam kissed Betsy tenderly on the lips his hand resting on his son. I felt tears stinging my eyes but I sniffed them back.

"Adam," Betsy said. "Do you want to hold him?"

"Son, I think he looks like you," Luke noticed.

"God help him," Joey smarted off. We all turned and glared at him. He just laughed.

Betsy handed their son to Adam who looked more than a little uncomfortable holding the baby who didn't look so big in his arms. His face showed his complete awe at his son. He touched the tiny hand now sticking out of the blanket and Noah wrapped his fingers around Adam's larger ones. His eyes were large and full of wonder when he looked up at us.

"He's amazing," he said holding his son's hand.

We all laughed.

"I think we should leave them alone Joey," I told him.

"Can I at least hold him before we go?" He asked.

"You can hold him when they come home," I argued wanting to get out of the room and go home.

"Joy let him hold that baby," Betsy said.

I stood by while Adam lifted his son into Joey's arms. I stood there holding it together while Joey held the baby that was so beautiful my heart was breaking into a thousand pieces. I was going to be fine. I was happy for them. I just needed to leave for a bit and pull myself together. I just needed to have a few minutes or even better a few hours by myself. Luke took a step closer to me so he could put his arm around me. He whispered in my ear, "You doing all right?"

I nodded. I had to be. I wouldn't hurt them, not today. Today was too important. I bit down on the inside of my cheek to help myself focus on something other than the pain inside my heart. I tasted blood inside my mouth I was biting so hard.

"I think that Joy and I will go get coffee in the cafeteria," Luke told them. "That will give Joey some time to hold Noah. I can hold him when we get back."

He guided me out of the room. I started breathing again once we were in the hallway. We walked side by side silently. We didn't need words.

"Have you eaten today?" He asked me. I looked at Luke. He took my hand and squeezed it. "You haven't have you?"

I wouldn't lie to him. I shook my head no.

"We'll get something besides coffee in the cafeteria then," he told me gently.

I nodded yes. I was afraid to speak. Afraid that the tears I was holding in would turn into sobs.

We bought food in the cafeteria and sat down at one of the tables. Luke held a plastic chair for me to sit.

"I'm taking you away from Noah," I complained.

Gently he said, "He will still be there when I get back upstairs. I could see you were about to come apart at the seams."

"I was trying not to. They've been there for me."

"You have been there for them as well even if you don't realize it right now. The four of you are pretty damned tight." He looked at me over the rim of his cup.

I guess.

I looked at the plate in front of me. Hospital food not the greatest but I knew Luke. He wouldn't let me out of here without eating something. I didn't have my protein shakes to be my crutch. The mainstay of my diet these days. He didn't watch me eat like the others measuring the bites that went into my mouth. He didn't make me crazy with it.

I took a bite of the chicken, kind of tough and tasteless I decided after popping it into my mouth. Followed it up with some mashed potatoes no gravy, dry no taste. I ate all of them because the chicken tasted really bad.

"How are you guys doing?" Luke asked.

Which guys? All four of us or just me and Adam?

"We're doing fine."

"Doing fine or pretending to do fine?" He asked.

I shoveled more food into my mouth. Luke quirked an eyebrow at me. "Is this how I get you to eat? Ask you uncomfortable questions?" He asked with a hint of humor in his voice.

I stopped chewing for a second and contemplated what he said. I chuckled trying not to lose the food in my mouth.

"Probably a bit of both but you know us," I said after swallowing.

He rolled his eyes.

When he was satisfied I had eaten enough and wasn't going to eat more he cleared the tray for me while I refilled our Styrofoam coffee cups. When he reached my side I handed him his cup. We walked back to the elevator and rode back upstairs in silence. He placed his hand on my lower back guiding me through the elevator doors when they opened.

"Feel better?" He asked.

I did. I didn't feel like I had the crushing weight on me like was there previously. We opened the door to the room and found Joey was still holding Noah. Adam was sitting on the edge of the bed his arm around Betsy. I smiled at them.

"I want one Joy," Joey said so sweetly.

It wasn't a toy but he made it sound like one. Betsy and Adam both chuckled but in their eyes I could see the concern. I still didn't feel ready to have a baby. I just smiled at him and rolled my eyes.

"It's Luke's turn," I told him.

He rose from the hard fake leather chair where he was sitting. He handed Noah to me. I looked down at the little guy swaddled in the not so soft hospital blanket and turned to Luke. So sweet. Sleeping peacefully in my arms.

"Here gramps." He raised his eyebrow at me.

"I think we can come up with a better name," he said taking Noah into his arms.

When Betsy or I was holding him Noah looked big but when one of the men held him he looked so small. I walked around the bed and snuggled in next to Betsy kicking off my shoes first. She put her arm around me and I laid my head on her shoulder.

"You did really good Betsy," I told her.

"I couldn't have done it without you."

"Um ladies what about me?" Adam asked. "I did have something to do with him."

"You had the easy part," I told him teasing him.

"Noah does look like Adam," Betsy said to me.

Adam looked over his shoulder at us like we needed to see his face for confirmation. The baby did look like him.

"He does," I confirmed not meeting Adam's eyes. Still wondering what our child would have looked like. Was he?

"You staying with Betsy and Noah tonight?" I asked him.

"She wants me to go home. She's sending Noah to the nursery so she can get sleep before she comes home."

"Then we will see you at home," I said. If he were mine I wouldn't let him go but that was her decision. Betsy was warm and loving but no nonsense.

"Yep," he replied nonchalantly.

I had to drag Joey home promising him he could hold Noah first when he came home tomorrow. He was going to be impossible now that Noah was here.

We walked through the door at our home and I was right. He wrapped his arms around me. Snuggling my neck. Kissing my shoulders. He wanted to get started right now making a baby. I pushed out of his arms and went to the kitchen. I grabbed the protein powder from the cabinet. He followed just watching for now. Arms crossed over his muscular chest. I glanced over my shoulder at him. Then I filled a glass with ice and water and dumped the powder into the glass. Eating was the only control I had over Joey not getting me to have sex with him. It was manipulation but all I had right now.

He watched me drinking it down slowly. Joey crossed the filed floor.

"That isn't going to work," he said.

He took the glass from my hands. It was right in the middle of my cycle and we had begun to sometimes have sex without condoms so tonight when he had baby making on his mind I wouldn't get him to wear a condom. I pushed him away and tried to side step him. He grabbed my arm in his grasp. I smacked at him which only fueled his intensity and need. Joey shoved me roughly against the kitchen table until my back was laying on it.

'We eat here," I said struggling to get up.

"I'll scrub it down with Clorox later," he growled pushing me back until I was flat on my back.

His fingers fumbled with the button on my pants until he had them undone then he was tugging down the zipper. I was trying to push his hands away. "Not tonight Joey." He yanked my jeans down my body and tossed them over his shoulder. His fingers were warm against my skin as his hands slid my panties down my body leaving me bare to him from the waist down.

"I was gentle with your panties."

I glared at him. Then he ripped open my shirt sending buttons flying everywhere. I watched them fly through the air landing in various locations throughout the kitchen. Joey released the clasp of my bra and my breasts spilled out into his hands. He grabbed them roughly kneading them between his long strong fingers until I was moaning.

"You like that," he said huskily.

"I don't want to do this tonight not without a condom," I said.

He ignored me.

"Dammit Joey I mean it. I'm not ready for a baby yet. I need to keep focusing on my health. We are young. We have plenty of time to have our own baby," I declared.

When he didn't like what I said he was rough not mean but rough. Joey bit hard on my nipple making me gasp. I looked down to see if he had drawn blood. He hadn't but it sure as hell felt like it. I slapped him hard across the face for biting me. The thing with Joey and me we were like fire and oxygen. We were combustible materials waiting for that ignitable material to set us off. He rubbed his cheek where my hand had left an imprint.

His full weight was on me pinning me to the table then. His mouth was on mine kissing and biting with a hunger that was of anger not passion. I turned my head when I could taste blood. He had bit my lower lip hard. I felt tears sting my eyes. I wasn't going to cry dammit. I pushed at him but he wouldn't move. He was rock hard and he was beyond reason.

Then we heard the front door and I panicked.

"Get the fuck off Joey. Adam is home."

He stood and yanked me to my feet. He looked around him for the panties he had tossed. I pulled my shirt closed. He walked over to the fridge and grabbed my underwear off the floor. He tossed them to me. As I was about to slide them on Adam walked in the door. I stepped behind Joey.

If I had kept my head down he might have turned and walked out but he saw my lip. He stepped further into the kitchen. He was so close he could reach around Joey and touch me. He did. He cupped my jaw and turned my face to his. Joey's back was stiff. I could see Adam's face hard as stone. His eyes blaring with fire and anger. While I stood there holding my shirt closed holding my panties in one hand bare assed.

"What did you do to her Joey?"

"Leave it alone Adam," Joey told him.

"It's all right Adam," I reassured him.

Joey couldn't see him do it but he ran his thumb across my full swollen lip where he had bit me.

"It's not all right Joy." He dropped his hand from my face. "Are you going to turn out like him?" He asked Joey.

*Him who?*

Joey shoved Adam hard and he went tumbling through the kitchen door into the living room nearly falling on his ass. I took that moment to get my panties on. I didn't have time for anything else. I followed the boys into the living room who were now having a shoving/shouting match. I tried to get between them but even at nearly five feet six I was no match for their size or strength. I ended up on the floor on my ass. Adam saw my breast.

"Goddammit Joey what are you thinking?" He asked as I pulled my shirt closed.

"I don't need your shit Adam. You aren't so god damned perfect."

"I never said I was perfect but damn Joey I don't hurt my woman."

Joey drew back his fist and hit Adam in the jaw. I was still sitting on the floor. I watched Adam's head snap back.

"Stop it," I screamed from my position on the floor.

Both of them turned and looked at me Adam rubbing his jaw. Joey glaring down at me then at Adam. We had been playing house, living grown-up lives while growing up ourselves. Things felt like they were imploding around us and I didn't know how to stop it.

"I'm out of here," Joey yelled as headed for the door.

"You have to stop running away Joey," I told him.

"You prefer his company anyway Joy," he snapped at me before he went through the door slamming it behind him.

I laid back on the floor and let the tears fall from my eyes. I should have just had sex with him. None of this would have happened. Adam walked over to me. He sat down on the floor next to me. I felt his hand on my bare stomach and I flinched. He didn't move it one way or another. He just pressed it into me holding me together. We were silent except my occasional sobs. When I stopped I sat up and wiped my face on my sleeve.

"All better?" He asked me.

"Yes, I need to find all my buttons and clean the table."

"Huh?"

"My ass was on that table. I don't know about you but I don't want to eat at it until I've cleaned it."

He nodded understanding.

"Joy?"

"What?"

I rose to my feet. Adam remained sitting on the floor. "I think we should go to the farm."

"What do you mean?"

'I think it would be nice to hang out with Pa and Mandy if they don't mind."

"Don't trust yourself with me or don't trust me?" I asked.

"Right now I just want to hold you but that would not be a good idea."

"No it wouldn't. I'll change clothes."

"I'll get your buttons off the floor and clean the table."

### Middle of the Night

Adam and I were sitting in the loft, side by side. The doors opened our feet hanging over the edge of the opening. We had been talking for hours like we had just two years ago when my life still felt like that of a normal teenager not a married wife. We hadn't come to any conclusions. We hadn't really expected to. It just felt good to talk. Some of the weight lifted. He talked of Noah and holding him in his arms. The feeling it had given him of overwhelming unconditional love.

Joey pulled up to the farm in his truck while we talked. I started to get up then I hesitated. The door to Joey's truck opened and he staggered out of the vehicle. He slammed the door shut. He tripped going up the steps. At the front door I heard him call my name. Adam looked up at me. I sat down beside him.

"I can't handle a drunk Joey."

He nodded.

So we watched Luke handle a drunk Joey. He guided him out to the truck. We weren't close enough to them to know what he had to say to Joey. Luke had his hand on Joey's shoulder. I could see Joey's head shaking back and forth no. Then he was in Luke's arms. I could see Luke holding him to his chest. I looked at Adam. I couldn't do it. Not again tonight.

"Please don't make me," I begged Adam.

"I'll go," he said. "You coming home?"

"Not tonight," I said. "I'm going to stay here."

I followed Adam to the ladder.

"Adam." He hesitated. "I wanted to thank you."

He reached out a hand to me. Our hands touched. He pulled me close. Our lips touched softly. Nothing passionate or hungry. A tender kiss full of emotion. A brief kiss that said I would do anything for you. Then his dark head disappeared over the edge of the loft. I walked back to the open doors. I stood in the shadows. I saw Adam run across the yard to Luke and Joey. They talked then Adam took Joey into his embrace holding him. Then he guided him into the truck and climbed in after him. Luke watched the truck drive down the lane as I did from my perch in the lot.

Luke walked across the yard. I returned to my seat with my feet dangling over the edge. Luke joined me within minutes. I glanced up as he sat down beside me. Our shoulders touching. Our thighs only inches apart. How many conversations had we had like this?

"He's sorry," he said in a deep husky voice.

"He always is," I replied.

Luke took my hand and held it in his. I stared down at our joined hands. Suddenly Luke leaned in and kissed my temple.

"I don't have any wise words to say to you about this situation. Adam told me what he walked in on. I'm disappointed in Joey."

"Luke," I said softly, "it's like he loses his mind every now and then. I can't reach him when he's like that."

"Joy, he was beaten pretty badly by his stepfather on a regular basis for six years until I took him in." Adam stopped talking. He stared into the distance. Looking for words to describe the anguish Joey felt. "He watched his mother drink herself to death. It was something he couldn't control. He's pretty messed up. Honestly, he's better with you in his life."

I knew there was a connection I had with Joey. This was the most I had heard about it. No one wanted to talk about

Joey's past least of all him. He used alcohol the way I used food to control the inner demons of his childhood. I didn't know what to say. Was he better with me in his life? That was part of the reason I had pushed Adam out because I knew that Joey had feelings for me. I hadn't wanted to ruin their friendship. I hadn't wanted to hurt Joey.

"I need for him to talk to someone," I told Luke.

"I think that is a good idea."

I shook my head up and down. "I'll talk with Doc the next appointment to see what I can do about getting Joey to talk to somebody."

"You need to go home," Luke said. "He needs you."

"I just want to stay here tonight."

"I know you do and I want you to but I think it would be better if you went home," he said softly.

I sat by Luke for a while contemplating what I would do. Finally, I decided I would do as he asked. I climbed to my feet. Took his hand and pulled him to his feet. Not that he needed me to help him. I just did it. We climbed down the ladder with Luke behind me. In the yard he said he would take me home but I insisted I wanted to walk.

"Call me when you get home."

I smiled up at him. "No one is going to get me between here and there," I told him.

"Humor me will you?"

"Sure, sure," I replied. Luke took me in his arms and kissed my forehead.

"Joy," Luke said. I turned at my name. "You know I love you like my own kid."

"I know Luke. I appreciate that." I started to walk then I turned and said his name. He was still standing where I left him watching me walk. "You know I love you too right?" I asked.

Luke chuckled. "Yeah kid I know."

"Good," I replied.

I started walking down the lane. I stuck to the side of the dirt road. The sound of gravel crunching beneath my feet. The sky an inky black with a quarter moon providing little light to guide me. Sounds along the way messed with my mind spooking me. I wished I had let Luke take me home. I was halfway home no reason to turn back now.

I walked into the yard. My heart racing slightly. I kept looking over my shoulder. I stepped onto the porch, the light left on for me. Out of the shadows a man stepped. Broad shoulders, so wide I had never seen another's with shoulders this wide. His red hair buzzed short to his head but his beard hung to the middle of his chest.

"Excuse me young lady?" His voice deep and gravelly.

I nearly jumped out of my skin. "You startled me. What are you doing lurking in the shadows?"

"I'm sorry. I didn't mean to frighten you. Do you know Joey Bonds? He used to live here."

"I do and he still does."

"He does?" The man's brow wrinkled. He was thinking.

"How can I help you?" I asked him.

"Who are you?" He asked me softly.

"Who are you?" I asked.

"My name is Markus. I haven't seen Joey since he was a kid. I'm probably the last person he would ever want to see."

He was soft spoken. A broken man I thought. His largeness didn't frighten me. I stared at him trying to access his danger. I knew it when I saw it from dealing with my father.

"I'm Joy Bonds. Joey's wife."

He took a step towards me hand outstretched. I put my hand in his and we shook. Immediately he released me.

"Looks like Joey got himself a pretty little wife. Nice too," he suggested.

"Thank you," I told him. "Would you like to come in?" I asked.

"Sweetie I don't think that would be a good idea." He chuckled sarcastically.

The front door flew open startling me more than Markus had. I was standing on the second stair still leading to the front porch. Adam came out his magnum pointed at Markus. His hand trembled. He grabbed me around the waist and yanked me behind him.

"Adam Moore," Markus said. "I would know you anywhere. You look a great deal like your Pa, Luke Moore." His head dropped to his chest. "You still thick as thieves with Joey?"

"What the fuck are you doing here?" Adam's voice was deadly calm even though his hand shook.

"Adam," I said but got no further.

"Go inside," he cut me off.

"What is wrong?"

"Get the fuck inside," he snapped.

"Go inside little girl," Markus said softly. "Thank you for your kindness."

I backed up to the house not sure I should leave Markus with Adam. I didn't know who he was. Why he was so tense. I backed into a hard body. Joey's hands came around my shoulders gripping them hard.

"Joey, are you all right?" I asked looking into my husband's terrified face.

He didn't take his eyes off Markus. He nodded. He was sober. Sobered instantly I assumed by the sight of Markus. Who was he? Joey turned me into the house. He shut the door on me firmly.

*Joey*

Fuck, I screamed over and over in my head although no words would come out of my mouth. I had left my pistol in the house. When Adam had yelled at me that Markus was standing on the front lawn talking to Joy I thought he was joking. It couldn't be. I had grabbed my pants and running down the hall I slipped my feet into them. No shirt, no shoes I stood on the porch next to Adam who had his gun aimed at Markus.

"What are you doing here Markus?" Adam asked again.

"I just got out a few days ago."

"And you're here why?" Adam asked his voice hard as steel.

I was still unable to say anything. The monster of my nightmares was standing on my lawn. The man who had ruined my life. Taken my brother's life was standing before me. Staring at me then Adam. He wanted to say something.

"I'm sorry Joey," he said with profound sadness.

I ran my hands through my hair. I found my voice.

"What the fuck?" I said.

He held his hand up in front of him. Appealing to me to listen to him. "Joey, I had a lot of counseling by a cleric in prison. We became friends. When I made parole this month he suggested I seek your forgiveness."

He had gotten parole? Why hadn't I been notified?

"Why?" I asked incredulously. What difference could forgiveness make in my life?

My forgiveness of him would not bring my brother back. It would not erase the torment he brought to my life, my mother's life and Jamie's short life.

"Listen Joey. I can see the pain I've caused in your eyes. If I'm right you need to let it go son before it destroys you."

"You don't call me son," I ground out between my teeth clenched so tight my jaw hurt.

"I'm sorry Joey." His eyes could not meet mine. "I have to live with what I did to you, your brother and your mother. How is she?"

"Dead." One hard word that caused him so much pain. I could see it in his eyes. Good. He deserved nothing less.

"I'm sorry."

"You keep saying that," I spat. "But your words cannot make things right Markus."

"I know that Joey." He hesitated. He was contemplating what to say. "Joey, I'm dying. I have pancreatic cancer. I'm not seeking treatment. I think the more I suffer for my sins the better." I agreed. The anger and the hate for this man eating away at my gut.

Adam began lowering the gun in his hands. I glanced to my right. "Don't fucking lower that gun," I told him. He raised his arm back to eye level holding his wrist with his other hand. "If your arm is tired. I will hold the fucker."

"I'm not giving you a loaded gun Joey," Adam declared. Markus actually chuckled.

My eyes went back to Markus. Appealing to me with his eyes to hear him out. My legs wouldn't hold me. My ass hit the porch with a thud. Adam lowered the gun to his side and sat beside me. Markus stood in front of us staring at us like he was remembering two ten year old boys.

"Joey when you are sitting in a cell twenty three hours a day and you have time to think about your life you start to see where you went wrong. Father Pat helped come to terms with the wrongs that were committed against me that made me the man I was. He helped me come to terms with the man that committed the crimes against you and Jamie." He actually had tears glistening in his eyes. My jaw dropped. I felt no sympathy for him. I couldn't forgive him.

"I see in your face you are hardened against me. I don't blame you. I never expected anything different Joey. Before I die I just needed to say these things to you. To say my peace. Joey if nothing comes of this visit but one thing it is that I want you to let go of the pain I caused you. I will deal with my own guilt. I don't need your forgiveness if your life turns out differently than mine. That is all I want. Don't let what I did destroy your life."

"So this is all a coming to Jesus meeting you wanted to have you cold hearted bastard," I screamed. I jumped to my feet.

He wasn't so intimidating now. He was only three inches taller than me not towering over me like he had when I was a ten year old boy. I was standing in front of him. I shoved him with both hands in the chest. He didn't shove me back. Why the fuck not? I was a man now. I wanted him to provoke me so I could hit him. I wanted to smash my fist into his face as he had so many times when I was just a kid and couldn't defend myself.

"Joey would it make you feel better to take a shot at me?" He asked.

Fuck yes! My head screamed so loudly my ears rang with the exclamation.

"Go ahead son," he said not taunting me. "Hit me. Get it out."

He called me son again. He did it again to taunt me so I would hit him. I was never his son. The only father I had known was Luke Moore. I stood and drew back and punched him in the jaw my knuckles cracking against the bone and flesh. I thought my hand was broken. I grabbed my hand and held it against my chest bent over at the waist. I cried out in pain and frustration.

"Joey, stop," Joy cried running past Adam to me. "What is wrong with you?"

She looked at my hand.

"It's okay little girl," Markus said. "I deserved that and more."

His jaw was red and would bruise but he hadn't even flinched.

"You've said your peace. Now leave," Adam said coming to stand beside me and Joy.

"I will and you have nothing to worry about. I won't return," he said softly not looking at any of us.

When he was out of sight I dropped to the ground my forehead resting in the dewy grass. I rocked on my knees sobbing into my hands fairly sure the one was broken. I heard Joy say Adam's name in question. Her soft hand touched my bare back.

"I will get a shirt and shoes for him. We need to take him to the ER," he said.

### Early Morning

Coming home from the hospital hand in a splint until the swelling was down I was on pain meds but my mind kept racing to the events of earlier tonight.

Inside we said goodnight to Adam and climbed the stairs to our room. Joy shut the door behind us. I toed off my sneakers kicking them against the door of our closet. I yanked one arm out of the shirt and whipped the shirt over my head. My injured hand was inside the shirt not through the sleeve. I tossed it on the floor. Joy walked behind me and picked it up. She opened the closet door and tossed the shirt inside in the laundry basket.

"Want me to help you with your jeans?" She asked softly. Her voice caressing me, soothing my jangled nerves.

I nodded.

Joy walked over to me. She ran her hand across my bare chest causing my breath to catch in my throat. She softly touched my jaw with her fingertips. Her beautiful green eyes met mine. So much emotion was evident in the depths of her gorgeous eyes I had to look away. Her hand moved lower to my waist. My eyes dropped to my waist. Her slender fingers were fussing at the button on my jeans. It came undone. She unzipped my pants allowing them to fall to the floor with a soft touch of her hands at my hips.

My eyes flew back to her face. Her eyes were searching my face for answers. Was I all right? I leaned down our earlier argument gone completely from our brains. She hadn't asked me any questions about Markus. I was glad because I wasn't sure I could tell her who he was or what he had done to me and my brother. A brother she didn't even know that I had. His existence causing me too much pain.

Then my lips touched hers tenderly. Soft wet moist lips met mine in a gentle kiss of understanding. She knew I needed her. She broke the kiss and yanked her shirt over her head. Joy wasn't wearing a bra. With my good hand I grasped her breast in my hand tweaking the nipple between my fingers.

She groaned deep in her throat. A sound that excited me because I could make her feel that way.

She reached out and grasped my waist with her hands digging her fingers into my flesh. She had tiny hands but damn they were strong. With one hand I reached down and undid her shorts. The zipper slid down easily enough between the fingers of my good hand. Her shorts fell to the floor. Joy stepped out of them kicking the garment aside as she did so.

My hand slid lower over her belly into her silky panties. She gasped at my touch. I stepped closer to her. My hand met the soft curls beneath her panties where she was warm and wet. I slipped a finger inside her and her hands slid to my shoulders. Her head tilted back on her shoulders revealing her soft tender neck. I leaned over and pressed soft kisses to her throat while my fingers slipped in and out of her body.

"On the bed," she groaned. "My legs won't hold me."

I laughed. Allowing her to lay on the bed. Her silver hair spread out around her like a fan. She looked like an angel. My angel. I sprawled across the bed between her legs gently spreading them apart as wide as I could to give me space. I nipped at her inner thighs gently with my teeth making her squirm beneath me. I used my good hand to separate her soft folds. I pressed my tongue firmly against her soft little nub making her back arch off the bed. Only having one hand was the only frustration for me. I couldn't stick my fingers inside her like I wanted. I couldn't feel her moist, hot insides while I sucked her clit into my mouth making her call out my name.

Joy grabbed my head in her hand and held it tight to her hot center while I sucked hard on her clit making her breath come in short little gasps of air. I knew she liked this.

"Fuck Joey. What are doing to me?" She cried out. Loud so loud that I was sure Adam heard her down the hall.

### Adam

Fuck me. She was loud. You would think with a broken hand he couldn't fuck her but somehow he had found a way. Joey was fucking what was mine although she wasn't mine. The thought twisted my gut and my heart. She was his.

The woman that was mine was in the hospital. Betsy had just given birth to my son. I had a beautiful woman and a beautiful son and they would be coming home tomorrow or today rather. In a few short hours. I kept telling myself over and over that I had to get Joy out of my head. Out of my heart. It was the best for both of us but I couldn't. It was torture living here wanting her and not being able to have her. It would be torture not living here not knowing if she was all right and Betsy wanted to be here.

I should have fought harder for Joy when she pushed me away after we lost the baby. I should have given her some time then forced her to let me back in but my heart had been shattered. My gut twisted in knots. I had lost her and our baby in one night. I could still see her body and my clothes covered in blood as she miscarried our child. I opened my eyes unable to bare the image playing behind my eyelids.

Fuck I could still hear them. Our walls were not that thick. Their room not so far down the hall. I ran my hands over my face digging my palms into my eyelids rubbing furiously until my eyes felt raw. I climbed out of bed unable to sleep. In my boxers I slipped out of my room and shut the door. I went downstairs at least I couldn't hear them downstairs. I lay on the sofa my hand behind my head. I lay in the dark just staring into the blackness. A single tear trickled down my cheek. Angrily, I brushed it away.

### Joy

Joey climaxed and fell asleep nearly on top of me. I rolled him onto his back and covered him with our greyish blue thick comforter. I couldn't sleep so many unanswered questions in my head. I climbed out of bed grabbed my panties off the floor and slid them up my body. I pulled my tee shirt over my head. My hair was down now an array of wild curls around my head.

I left our room closing the door behind me. I padded barefoot down the hall stopping at Adam's door wanting to go in and talk to him like I had so many times before but I couldn't. We had to start moving forward. We had to put our feelings behind us. Nothing would change. We could never be together. It was destructive to allow these feelings to continue. Reluctantly I walked on. At the top of the stairs I turned on the light and went down the steps my hand caressing the worn bannister like it was a soft glove. At the bottom I stopped dead in my tracks when dark beautiful eyes met mine.

"Adam," I said his name a little breathlessly.

"Joy, what are you doing up?" Adam sat up on the sofa spinning around so his long legs were in front of him.

"I needed something to drink," I replied.

"You worked up a thirst with Joseph?" He asked not able to keep the hurt out of his tone.

"Oh Adam," I said. "I'm so sorry."

I wouldn't have wanted to hear him and Betsy making love. His head dropped. He wasn't able to meet my eyes. I crossed the room and wrapped my arms around his shoulders. His head rested against my breast. He didn't touch me at first. He just let me comfort him. Suddenly his strong arms went around my waist and I gasped. I laid my head on Adam's dark head. My hand caressed his naked back. It wasn't sexual. It was two people who loved each other deeply comforting each other.

"I'm sorry Adam," I repeated.

His voice was rough when he replied, "For what Joy?"

"For hurting you. For everything going back to when I lost the baby," I said softly.

His arms tightened around me.

"It shouldn't have ended that way," I whispered. "I wasn't strong enough to fight for us."

Adam pulled me down onto his lap so I was straddling him.

"I just want to hold you," he said to me when I looked at him questioningly. "We can't go back. I know that. I have a son now."

He leaned back against the sofa. There was more space between us now.

"He's beautiful Adam," I told him.

"He is. Isn't he."

Adam's hands were on the curve of my butt holding me in place. His eyes were so full of pain and emotion. Pain because of me. Emotion for his newborn son. A mixture of them tearing him apart. I knew him.

"We have to find a way to stop feeling this way Adam," I told him so softly my voice was barely above a whisper.

He chuckled sadly. "Don't you think I would have done that already if I could Joy?" He replied.

His jaw covered in whiskers was set hard like he was gritting his teeth. I touched him and he sucked in air like he was in pain. I had just wanted him to relax. I was making it worse.

"Do you want to leave here Adam?" I asked.

"Fuck yes," he replied with so much feeling that my head shot up meeting his gaze. "And no I'm not sure that I could do that to you or Betsy. I feel like I'm going crazy sometimes."

"Why?" I asked trying not to cry.

"Why what?"

"Why do you want to leave?"

"Do you really need to ask?"

"I guess not," I replied.

I rose and he reluctantly let me go. I sat on the sofa next to him. I leaned against Adam. This was more comfortable. Less intimate that me straddling him.

"Did you think of me when you were fucking him?" He asked.

I wasn't shocked that he asked that. I often imagined Adam when Joey was making love to me. "You don't really want to know that?" .

I didn't respond. This conversation wasn't getting us anywhere. I shivered getting cold in just my tee shirt and panties. I pulled the quilt off the back of the sofa and covered myself. "Do you want some of the blanket?" I asked him.

"I'm warm enough," he replied.

I snuggled inside the blanket. Did he imagine me when he was making love to Betsy? What good would it do me to know the answer to that question? We were just hanging onto something that we couldn't have. We were both married now to other people. He had a child with Betsy. She was my best friend.

"Would you say it for me?" He asked. We had been quiet for a while.

"Say what Adam?"

"Say that you love me."

I whipped my head around. Tears glistened in the corners of my eyes. It wouldn't help either of us for me to say those words to him. His big dark eyes were pleading with me to say the words. I looked away. My heart felt like it was breaking into a million pieces. I did still love him. I wasn't sure that I could ever stop. I glanced back at Adam. Our eyes locked on each other.

"I love you Adam." The words were easier to say than I thought. He leaned over and kissed my forehead. He didn't respond in kind and I didn't press him for a response.

I leaned back against Adam and snuggled under the blanket. Adam's arm was around my body. His hand rested just below my breast caressing me. The gentle movement of his thumb on me lulled me into a deep relaxing sleep.

### Several Hours Later

"Adam, Joy, wake up." Luke shook each of us gently.

It was morning. We had fallen asleep on the sofa in each other's arms. Luke had found us. Luckily not Joey. I sat up and Adam's hand slipped to my side beneath the blanket. His fingers lingered on my bare thigh. I looked over my shoulder at him. He was trying to wake himself. He rubbed his eyes with his free hand.

I looked up into Luke's eyes. He wasn't judging us. We hadn't really done anything but still I was ashamed. I knew what we wanted. I knew I was comfortable where I was. I knew that he had me where he wanted me too. In his arms. Did Luke know that too? Probably. Luke knew us well.

Luke sat on the coffee table.

"Where's Joey?" He asked.

"Sleeping," I replied. "We had to take him to the ER last night."

"ER?" Why?'

"Markus showed up here last night Pop," Adam explained. "Joey punched him in the jaw. Broke his hand."

"Markus?" Luke repeated the name with surprise. "Everything all right?"

"Yes, he's on parole. Dying of cancer. Wanted Joey's forgiveness."

"Really?"

"Yeah," Adam responded.

I had the feeling I was missing a great deal about this Markus fella that no one wanted to talk about.

"How did that go?" Luke asked.

"His hand is broken," Adam said meeting his father's gaze. "How do you think it went?"

Luke ran his hand across his face. "Do you think Markus will go away now?"

"Yes I do," Adam replied.

I still didn't ask. "I'm going to check on Joey."

I stepped past Adam's feet between him and Luke. I could feel his eyes on me as I walked up the stairs to my bedroom.

### Adam

Pa was watching me watch Joy leave the room. I could feel his eyes on me. I couldn't tear my eyes away from her. Finally when she was no longer visible I met my father's gaze.

"Son, what are you thinking?" he asked.

"I'm not apparently," I replied.

I folded the blanket that Joy used to cover herself while she was wrapped in my arms and put in the back of the sofa.

"Your wife just gave birth to your son and you're here holding Joy in your arms all night I can only assume."

"Nothing happened Pa," I told him meeting his gaze now.

He shook his head at me. His sadness at the situation was clearly evident in his eyes so much like my own.

"Adam you have to get over her," he said.

"Why?" I asked.

He shook his head at me again.

"Because it is destroying both of you," he said forcefully.

"Tell me how I do that. Tell me Pa. How do I stop loving her?"

Pa's eyes were sad when finally he looked away. He looked at the floor then back to me. He was uncomfortable. He didn't have the answer.

"How do you feel about your wife?" He asked.

"You know I care a great deal about Betsy," I snapped. "I wouldn't be here today without her. She helped me through the most difficult time of my life when Joy broke it off after she lost the baby."

"But you don't love her," Pa said sadly.

"I didn't say that," I said. "I feel like I love her but I love her differently. She's very special to me."

"Like your best friend Joey is special to you," Pa said.

"They both are that," I replied.

"Son, your life is a mess."

"Thanks Pa."

"Be grateful it was me that woke you too up and not Joey."

"I am."

*Early Afternoon*

Joey, Joy and I drove to the hospital to pick up Betsy and Noah. Joey insisted we all go even though Joy and I wanted space from each other. Her words still echoed in my head. She loved me. I hadn't told her I loved her too even though I do. I didn't know if she wanted me to tell her. I thought it might make it harder for her. It might make it harder for me to continue on with our daily lives if I said the words out loud even though I made her say them to me.

We walked down the hallway towards Betsy's room. Joey leading the way. A spring to his step. The fucker. His good hand intertwined with Joy's hand. I walked behind them. He pushed the door open with his splinted arm and guided Joy through the open door. He followed her holding the door for me. I followed him into the room. Betsy was sitting on the edge of the bed holding Noah. She was staring at our son. Our son who looked a great deal like me.

I walked over to her and pressed a kiss to her forehead. She smiled up at me. I touched Noah's cheek. He was content being held in his mother's arms.

"How are you feeling today?" I asked her.

"Pretty good actually Adam," she replied smiling up at me. Guilt tore at my gut. Her eyes locked with mine. She had given birth to my son yesterday. Earlier, I had held her best friend in my arms. The woman I loved with all my heart. "Do you want to hold him?" She asked.

"He seems to content with you," I replied.

"Hold him Adam." She stood and transferred our child to my arms. I juggled him a bit until I was sure he was comfortable in my arms.

I looked at Noah. He was long and scrawny I thought even though the girls said he wasn't but he was beautiful. A thatch of dark fly-away hair covered his small head. His cheeks were rosy. He had my full lips. Very little about Betsy stuck out in his face. Maybe time would change that. I kissed his forehead holding him to me. He was my son and I loved him.

Betsy walked over to Joy. They were talking quietly. Joey came over to me to check out Noah. Joey touched his cheek.

One of Noah's hands had escaped the swaddled blanket. He stuck his finger in Noah's hand and he wrapped his fingers tight around Joey's finger.

"He's precious man. You know that?" Joey said his voice husky.

I met Joey's eyes over the bundle of my son I held in my arms. "I know Joseph."

"I can't wait to be a father," he said.

I was shocked. I tried to mask the feelings his statement sent through me.

"I've been trying to convince Joy but she's not ready. Maybe last night did the trick?"

***Don't push her man. You don't know what she's been through***. I knew my feelings were selfish. I didn't want to watch her get big with Joey's baby.

A nurse came into Betsy's room with a wheelchair. "Ready to go Mrs. Moore?" She asked.

"More than ready," Betsy replied.

Joey grabbed Betsy's small bag in his good hand. Betsy climbed into the wheelchair. Once she was settled I placed our son in her outstretched arms.

"Want me to take that?" I asked Joey.

"I got it."

"Joey, what did you do?" Betsy asked just noticing his splinted arm for the first time.

"My fist came into contact with something hard. My hand is broken."

"Do I dare ask?"

"No," he said.

She laughed. "I miss all the excitement," she said.

She had missed nothing. I was glad she hadn't been there. It was tense enough worrying about Joy and protecting her from Markus if necessary without having to worry about Betsy too.

My eyes met Joys across the top of Betsy's head. She smiled at me. Her beautiful green eyes were filled with a hint of sadness that her smile didn't reflect. I could see what she was thinking. She was remembering being in my arms, falling asleep. The feeling of peace and security. The feeling of belonging where she should be not where she was.

Suddenly Joey's arm snaked around her. Her gaze went to his face and her smile was directed at him. I looked down and found Betsy looking up at me. I bent over and touched her shoulder. I pressed my lips to hers. I wanted to reassure her or myself. I didn't know which. When I stood to my full height my wife smiled at me. She was happy. That is what I needed. Her happiness.

Joy and Joey sat in back of my truck with my son. Joey was acting like an idiot with the baby. Joy was quiet. I kept checking her out in the rearview mirror to see if she was all right. My eyes met hers a couple of times and she would look away. Betsy reached across the seat and touched my leg. I looked at my wife. My Betsy. I smiled at her. I patted her hand resting on my leg. Pa was right my life was a mess.

Joy carried the baby into the house. She cooed softly to Noah as she walked up the steps. I held Betsy's hand walking into the house. Joey brought up the rear carrying Betsy's bag.

Inside, Betsy just wanted to rest for a bit. I carried her bag upstairs and helped her get settled leaving Noah with Joy and Joey downstairs. In our room I shut the door. I laid the bag on the cedar chest at the foot of the bed.

"Do you want me to unpack that for you?" I asked.

"Not now," she said tiredly. "I just want to lay down."

Betsy kicked off her shoes. She climbed onto our bed and rested her head against the pillows. She looked beautiful with her dark hair fanning out against the white pillowcase. Her light colored eyes clear and sparkling even though she was tired. Her cheeks having a natural rosy glow. She was beautiful. I sat on the edge of the bed next to her. I ran my hand across her cheek lovingly. She leaned into my caress.

"Should you go check on our son?" She asked.

"I think Joey and Joy can handle him," I said. "Unless you want rid of me."

"I would like to rest," she said. "That won't happen with you in the room."

I was surprised. She was kicking me out.

"Okay," I replied. "I will leave you alone."

"Don't be hurt Adam."

"I'm not Betsy," I replied. "I understand."

I wasn't sure that I did. But I knew that I was hiding out from Joy so I would leave her alone so she could rest. I walked down the stairs where I found Joy still holding Noah close to her breast like he was the most fragile thing in the world. Her soft voice cooing to him. He was awake. She was turned sideways in the sofa's corner. Her knees propped up. She was alone.

"Where's Joey?" I asked.

"In the kitchen. Fixing himself lunch."

"What about you?" I asked.

"I'm not hungry," she replied.

I raised my eyebrows at her. She hadn't eaten anything this morning. "You need to eat too."

She scowled at me. "I'm enjoying Noah."

"I see that," I said softly.

I walked over to the coffee table and sat down on the edge. "Joey said he's been talking with you about having a baby," I said.

Her eyes met mine. I could see the haunted look in them. I patted her leg comfortingly.

Her finger was encased in my son's tiny hand. She wiggled it gently back and forth. "I'm terrified Adam."

"I know sweetheart."

"You would understand," she said softly meeting my gaze.

"You have to do what makes you comfortable in your own time but you won't be able to put him off forever."

"I know," she said her voice breaking. "It's just too painful."

I knew she was remembering the feel of our baby starting to grow inside her. She was afraid of falling in love with another child only to have it ripped from her again.

"You know it will be different this time."

Her eyes were on Noah. She was watching his expressions change wondering if he was going to cry. She shifted him just a bit which seemed to make him content. Her eyes suddenly met mine.

"My rational mind says it will. My irrational mind hasn't quite gotten there yet," she replied.

"Hey, what are you two talking so seriously about?" Joey asked barreling into the room in his usual loud manner.

"How cute Adam's son is," Joy replied.

"He is cute," Joey agreed. "Even if he does look just like Adam."

"Thanks man," I replied sarcastically.

"Can I hold him?" Joey asked. "Joy can put him in my good arm."

'Sure Joey. You can hold him," I told him.

Joy looked at me skeptically. "He can hold him," I told her. "Then you can get some food." I pointed at her letting her know I meant business. She needed to eat something.

Joey was on the top of the world and over the moon at holding Noah. Joy placed him carefully in Joey's good arm that was propped against a pillow. His face transformed from cocky and arrogant to complete mush and adoration at my son in an instant. I shook my head. Who would have guessed a small baby could transform Joseph Bonds so completely.

I took Joy to the kitchen with me. I dug through the refrigerator pulling out different items to prepare sandwiches for us while she sat at the kitchen table. I turned she was playing with a curl hanging from her pony tail. She was stunning. I don't think she realized what she did to me.

"You okay?" I asked.

She nodded.

I fixed us both a sandwich and put them on the table. Hers in front of her. She scowled at the food on the plate.

"You're eating that."

Her scowl deepened.

I plopped into my chair across from her. I took a bite of my sandwich. Joy got up and crossed to the fridge. She took out two cans of soda. One diet for her one regular for me. She brought them back to the table and sat down. She popped them both open handing mine to me. She took a long drink from her can.

"Thanks," I said.

"You're welcome," she replied.

"Joy," I began. Her eyes came up to meet mine. "You know…" I wasn't sure I should finish.

"I know Adam," she said softly looking at her sandwich.

"How do you know what I was going to say?" I asked.

Her voice was soft when she replied, "You were going to say that you loved me too weren't you?"

I laid my sandwich down. That was exactly what I was going to say. How did she know?

She smiled sadly. She took a bite of her sandwich. She swallowed hard like it was painful. "It doesn't change anything Adam. Does it? We're still married to other people. I guess it does me some good to know your feelings. I'm not guessing what they are. Driving myself crazy even if I can't act on them."

Our gazes were locked on each other. Is that what she had been doing? Guessing how I felt about her? We were driving ourselves crazy. If only we could find a way to let these feelings go. I knew how she felt about Joey, the way I did about Betsy. I could see it in her eyes when she looked at him. There was a tenderness there when she looked at Joey. She cared for him. She had let me go to protect him and to protect me. She hadn't wanted to come between our lifelong friendship.

Joy took another bite of her sandwich. I watched her swallow again. Another painful hard swallow. She took a swig from her diet soda. Her eyes met mine across the can. She sat the drink down on the table.

"I can't eat anymore Adam," she said.

"You only had two bites Joy." I was exasperated with her

"Please," she begged.

"Fine," I said reluctantly. She rose from the table. Turned and grabbed her soda and left me in the kitchen to eat alone.

## Chapter Ten

### Joy

I hadn't told anyone. I was nine and half weeks pregnant. Joey had gotten his wish. That night when he broke his hand and we had sex after trying to force me to have unprotected sex with him had gotten me pregnant. Why hadn't I told anyone? Because I had been spotting the entire time. At first my doctor had told me it could be the egg implanting. Then my numbers were kind of low so we were waiting to see if it was a viable pregnancy. I hadn't even told Betsy. In two weeks I could possibly hear a heartbeat. If no heartbeat then the doctor told me tenderly that we could discuss my options. I knew what that meant

Options, a cold word. I needed to tell someone. Luke was the best option. I drove to the farm instead of stopping at the house to talk to him after work. I parked the car in the drive next to Adam's truck. I got out of the car and walked towards the barn. Adam came out as I got close.

"What are you doing here?" He asked.

"I wanted to see Luke," I said softly.

"You okay?" He asked.

It would be so easy to tell him what was troubling me. To seek his comfort. Besides being the man I loved he was my best friend. He understood me almost better than Betsy at times. Things were going well for us. We were all getting along now. All acting like the happily married couples we were supposed to be. I couldn't risk it.

"I just wanted to talk to him about something. Is he here?" I asked.

"He took Mandy out to dinner and a movie."

"This early?" I glanced at my watch verifying the time to be sure it was actually 4:00 PM. I felt tears prick my eyes. I had finally worked up the nerve to tell somebody and he wasn't here.

"You know Pa. Matinee pricing for the movie. Early dinner afterwards."

I chuckled.

"Yeah. I hadn't thought about that. I guess I can talk to him tomorrow." I turned on my heel to walk away.

Adam grabbed my arm stopping me from leaving him. "Joy, what's wrong?" He asked.

"Adam, I can't tell you." I sniffed trying to hold back the tears. I started to walk away again but he wouldn't release my arm.

"Why not? You've always been able to tell me everything."

"We're all getting along well now. I don't want to screw it up."

I tried to pull out of his grasp. He held on tighter. "What is wrong? Are you sick?"

I shook my head no. Unable to look at him.

"Okay you're freaking me out now. What the hell is wrong? You came here to talk to Pa about something that is obviously serious."

I rolled my eyes. "I'm scared Adam. I needed his advice."

"Scared about what."

"Walk with me," I told him.

We sat on the picnic table. I stared into the distance. I had lived here at seventeen when my father beat the crap out of me. Here I had found my peace. I rested my chin in my hand.

"Are you going to tell me what's wrong?"

"I'm pregnant," I said softly.

So many emotions crossed his face. Adam looked shocked. Then he looked hurt. Then he looked like he wanted to be sick.

"That is why you are scared?" He said huskily.

"No Adam," I said taking his hand in mine. "My numbers are low."

"I don't know what that means."

I sighed. "As your pregnancy progresses your numbers get higher as your hormones increase. Mine are not. Mine were low to begin with. I've been spotting since day one. The doctor said at first it could be the egg implanting." I glanced over at Adam. He was looking at our hands. He looked up at me. His eyes big and dark so beautiful were sad. "I go to my doctor on Tuesday if they don't hear...don't hear a heartbeat the baby...the pregnancy," I amended, "isn't viable. She and I will discuss my options."

"You haven't told Joey have you?"

"No."

Adam rubbed his free hand across his face.

"Why? Can I ask?"

"Because they told me the pregnancy might not be viable."

"Shouldn't you want to share that with him?"

"He's not good with the painful stuff Adam. Only the good times."

"You can't go through this alone Joy."

"That is why I was going to tell Luke."

"Not me or Betsy?" He asked.

"I couldn't tell you without telling him," I cried softly.

"Okay, Joey's a big boy. We're going home we're telling Betsy and then we're telling Joey tonight. She and I will be there with you. You can't go through this alone. "

He took my hand and walked me to my car. He pushed me gently inside.

"I'll see you at the house. I'm right behind you."

He climbed into his truck. I started the car with trembling hands and backed out. I drove to the house and parked my car there. I sat behind the wheel until Adam opened my door. He took my hand and helped me out of the car. Betsy was holding Noah when we walked through the door. She looked up as we entered the living room.

The room felt too big suddenly.  She was sitting in the recliner.  I sighed heavily.

"What's wrong?"  She asked looking concerned.  "I can put Noah down."

"You don't have to," I told her.

"I will take Noah.  She needs to tell you something."

I looked at Adam.  Then at Betsy.  He bent over and took the baby from her.  She stood and walked over to me.  "What is it?  What is wrong?"  She touched my cheek softly.

"I went to the farm to talk to Luke.  Adam knew something was wrong.  He made me tell him," I explained.

She started to chuckle.  "I'm sure he did."

He raised his eyebrows at us.  He was holding Noah's finger in his big hand.

"Now tell me what is going on?"  She said softly.

Suddenly the tears started.  Just a gentle trickle of tears escaping my eyes then full blown sobbing.  She looked at Adam because I couldn't speak for the tears that were choking me.

"She's pregnant."

"That's not good news?"  Betsy asked him.

I shook my head no.  She looked at Adam.

"Why not?"  She asked.

He dropped his head looking at his son.  A healthy baby boy.  A child I loved with all my heart.

"She said the pregnancy," Adam's voice broke.  "The pregnancy might not be viable."

Betsy gasped.  "Oh sweetie no."

She pulled me to her.  She held me tight in her arms.  We slid to the floor together.  Betsy rocking me in her arms.  "Not again," I whispered to her.

"I know," she said.

Betsy held me while I cried. When the tears dried up. She pushed me back so she could see my face. She wiped my face with her sleeve and pushed my hair back from my face.

"Now tell me what is going on?" Betsy said gently.

"My hormone levels aren't increasing like they should," I told her. I laid my head in her lap. I couldn't look at her. She rubbed her hand across my hair.

"It's okay Joy. I'm here for you."

"I've been spotting since the beginning. On Tuesday I go for my next appointment. They should be able to here the heartbeat if it's viable." I choked on the words. "If it isn't they will discuss my options."

"Oh baby we will all go with you."

I nodded.

"She hasn't told Joey," Adam said.

"I get that," Betsy said softly. "Come on sweet girl. Let's get you upstairs." She lifted me to a sitting position. She stood and extended her hand to me. I took it gratefully. She guided me upstairs. Betsy opened my bedroom door and led me to my bed. She helped me undress. She put my clothes on the chair and got a tee shirt for me. Betsy put it over my head and left me alone to drift off to sleep.

### Adam

Noah's finger was still wrapped around mine. I was just looking at him. Thanking God for him. Praying that Joy would be okay through this. Why her? Of all the things that had to happen to her. Why this? I didn't hear Betsy's feet on the stairs as she came back down to me. She sat on the coffee table. I still didn't see her. I was lost in thought.

"Adam," she said my name three times before I finally glanced at her.

"What?"

"We need to tell him when he gets home." She glanced at the clock on the wall. "Which will be in half hour."

'Really. We should tell him?" I said incredulously.

"Adam, you know she can't do this."

Betsy was looking at me knowingly. She and I knew what Joy had gone through losing the baby previously. My baby. He did not. We were both concerned what this was going to do to her. I was surprised she had made it this long without telling anyone.

"All right," I said reluctantly. "We tell him."

"Give me Noah," Betsy said. "I will put him down."

### Half Hour Later

Joey was home right on time. He was happy now. Wearing his dress slacks and button downs. Working behind a desk. He had everything he wanted except for a baby. We were about to give him that and take it away in the matter of minutes. I asked him to sit down. Betsy sat next to him. He looked between us uncomfortably. Joey didn't do uncomfortable. He didn't do the serious stuff well.

"Joey," Betsy began. "Joy told me something today that I need to tell you. She's too upset to talk about it. We need to be there for her because the next week could be pretty traumatic for you both."

"What the hell Betsy?" He said. "Where is Joy?" He asked.

"She's lying down upstairs in your room."

He got up. I stepped in front of him. "Let Betsy tell you first Joey. Then you can go see her."

"Fuck what is it? Just spit it out Bets."

"Joey, she's pregnant."

"What?" He turned towards Betsy. "That's great news."

Betsy reached to Joey. He took her hand and she pulled him back to the sofa with her. "Joey, she's upset. She's been hiding the pregnancy from you from all of us because it might not be viable. Joey, I would say it most likely isn't."

He shook his head. A frown furrowing his brow. "What the hell does that mean?"

"She said she's been spotting from day one and her hormone levels aren't where they should be. She goes on Tuesday for her doctor's appointment they should be able to hear a heartbeat. If not they will discuss options with her."

"What options?" He asked his eyes filling with unshed tears.

"Joey I don't know. She doesn't know."

"Fuck," he cried. "She said she wasn't ready. Why didn't I listen to her?"

"Joseph, this isn't your fault. It isn't anyone's fault. Sometimes it just happens."

Betsy pulled Joey into her arms. She held him while he cried softly into her chest. I stood there watching my best friend sob in my wife's arms. I couldn't remember another time when I had seen Joey cry. Betsy looked at me over his head. She could do nothing but hold him while he let out the emotions overwhelming him at the moment.

Suddenly he sat up. He wiped his face on the sleeve of his shirt. He rose from the sofa. Joey stopped in front of me. I pulled him into my arms and hugged him. He clung to me like we did when we were kids and afraid of Markus. It had been that long since we held each other like this.

"I love you man," I told him. "Bets and I are here for you guys."

"I know. We're going to need you both too."

"I know," I said.

He stepped around me and headed up the steps two at a time.

### Joey

Joy was lying on her side. Her long blonde hair flowing behind her on the pillow in a mass of curls. I toed off my shoes and climbed in bed beside her on my side so I was facing her. Her eyelids fluttered then opened. I put my hand on her cheek.

"Joey, they told you," she said closing her eyes.

"I wish you had told me," I said huskily. "I'm so sorry baby. So sorry you have to go through this."

She leaned into my hand. Her eyes still closed. A tear slipped beneath her lashes and rolled down her cheek.

"I don't think I can do this Joey," she said softly so softly I didn't think I had heard her.

"Do what sweetheart?" I asked.

"What they will want me to do if there's no baby."

I swallowed hard.

"What?"

She clung tighter to my hand. "I guess a D&C," she said. "I asked the nurse before I left what options the doctor was talking about. That is what she told me."

I didn't know what a D&C was. "Any chance you will miscarry on your own?" I asked her.

"I don't know," she sobbed. The tears were coming harder and faster.

"Hey baby," I said to her. "Let's take this one day at a time. Okay?"

She nodded. I was getting antsy. I needed to get away.

"Do you want to come down to eat dinner?"

She shook her head no.

"Okay baby. Why don't you go back to sleep? I will come up and check on you in a little while."

She nodded.

### Adam

He left her upstairs alone to deal with the pain because that is what Joey did. He came down. Betsy and I were preparing dinner in the kitchen. He fell into a chair at the kitchen table. He looked at us like his world had come to an end.

"How is she?" Betsy asked.

"Upset. Betsy what is a D&C?" He asked.

"Is that one of her options?" She asked.

He nodded. "She said she asked the nurse. She told her that would be one of her options."

Betsy turned back to what she was doing. "Joey a D&C is where they scrape the uterus to rid it of the cells and anything left of the pregnancy." She turned around and looked at him. He had his head in his hands.

"Could she just miscarry on her own?" He asked.

"She could but she might still need a D&C."

"Why?" He asked. "She seems terrified of having one."

"I don't know. I've just heard that some women do."

"We need to tell Luke. He'll know what to do. What to say to her. I don't know what to say to her Bets. I always say the wrong thing."

Betsy nodded. "I left him a message. He's out right now. I asked him to come here when he got home."

We sat at the dinner table and ate the meal that Betsy and I prepared. The food going down to my stomach like a lead weight. Joey seemed to have no issue with consuming the meal but that was Joey. Betsy picked at her food too. Mandy and Pa showed up at our house while we were sitting at the table not eating. He walked in and straight to the kitchen.

It was still odd to me seeing my father in dress clothes. He had worn khakis and a dress shirt to take Mandy to a movie and dinner. His hair was combed not messy like usual. He was shaved not scruffy. He and Mandy had been dating for a long time. I wasn't sure why they hadn't taken it to the next step and gotten married. She was single with no children. Joey and I were grown men, me with a child of my own. He had no reason to not marry her. I didn't ask him though. Pa was private that way.

"Now what is wrong?" He asked his voice relayed his sense of urgency. He knew something was wrong and he knew who it involved immediately scanning the room and finding her not there. "Where is Joy?"

"She's lying down Luke," Betsy told him.

"What's wrong with her?" He asked his concern now evident on his face as well as in his tone.

Betsy relayed today's events to him regarding Joy's pregnancy. He knew what Betsy and I knew. She had already lost one baby. This was going to devastate her. He patted Mandy's arm as he slipped by her. He left us with Mandy and went upstairs to see Joy.

### Joy

I heard a knock on my bedroom door. I turned over on my back and flipped on the lamp on my night stand just as Luke walked through the door. I sat up my hair fell over my shoulder hiding most of my face. I wanted nothing more than to hide from the world right now. Luke walked over to the bed. I held my hand over my face. He sat on the edge of the bed and pulled me into his arms.

Luke my rock through the last couple years. The one that knew me, protected me from my own father, became a father to me. Telling me what I needed to hear even when I didn't want to hear it.

"Want to tell me about it sweetheart?" He asked.

"I'm not going to be able to keep this baby either Luke," I told him my heart breaking.

With this baby I had tried to not let myself get attached. I knew from the beginning something wasn't right. Still my heart hurt at what was happening in my body. It brought up painful memories of my baby with Adam. My previous loss. Would I never hold my own child?

Luke rubbed my back. My cheek rested against his shoulder. My tears wetting his shirt.

"We'll get you through this Joy," he said.

I leaned back so I could look at him. "The doctor told me I had options if it isn't viable. It sounds so cold Luke." I rested my forehead in my hand.

"I know it doesn't seem fair especially since Betsy and Adam have this healthy baby they just brought home but you will have a baby someday. I know you will," he said.

"I just don't understand. I had no control the first time. Jack took care of that. Everything was going well then. This time I have no control either but it's my body betraying me Luke."

His dark eyes met mine. They were full of emotion and compassion. His hands wrapped around my arms. He was fierce when he said, "Joy you listen to me. You did nothing wrong. Sometimes these things happen. If you are ready for a baby you and Joey can try again in a month or two."

"No," I cried. "I can't go through this again. Not after this."

"Sweetheart, you need to give yourself time."

Another knock. Another visitor. Adam Moore came through the door. He was looking concerned.

"They sent me upstairs to check on you," he said. "Betsy is feeding Noah. She was worried."

"Where is her husband?" Luke asked.

Adam looked uncomfortable as he contemplated his answer.

"Pa you know him. He doesn't do this stuff well."

I sobbed/laughed at the same time. I laid my head against Luke's shoulder.

"It isn't funny," Adam declared.

I fell back against the pillows then. My hair fanning around my head. I placed one hand on my forehead. He was right about Joey. Joey was good for a laugh. Betsy was good at organizing us. Adam was our strength. What was my role?

"I'm going to talk to Joey," Luke declared.

"Don't bother Luke. He's great at cheering people up but dealing with the emotional side of life? The thought of losing a baby he's going to be lost. He comforted me for five minutes and left me alone. That's his nature."

Luke had stood and stopped by the side of the bed. "He's about to get a kick in the ass then sweetheart."

He walked out of the room. Adam wasn't sure what to do. Should he stay? Should he go? He chose to stay. He walked over to the other side of the bed and stretched out. He opened his arms to me. I slid over and laid my head on his chest.

"How are you doing?" He asked.

"Not great," I replied.

"I'm sorry this is happening to you," he said softly.

"I wish I understood why," I said.

"Me too.

We stayed like that for a long time. Adam just holding me. Comforting me. I prayed that if this baby wasn't going to make it that I would just miscarry it naturally. Betsy came into my bedroom carrying Noah. She didn't flinch or even acknowledge that I was in her husband's arms. She walked over to the side of the bed where there was some space.

"Scoot," she said. "I want to get in here too."

I laughed softly. I sat up. Adam sat up. I leaned against the headboard. She sat down with Noah in her arms. I peeked over her shoulder at Noah.

"Can I hold him?" I asked.

She handed him to me. I juggled his little body in my arms until he and I were both comfortable. His wide eyes were bright and alert. He had his daddy's eyes. Such beautiful eyes. I ran a finger down his face. A tear fell on Noah's face and he scrunched up his face like he might cry. I giggled softly at his face.

"You know we are here for you," Betsy said.

I laid my head against hers. I was grateful for her friendship. I was grateful for Adam. I didn't know where I would be without them sometimes. The thing with Joey was that no matter how much he loved me he was not good at the serious things. He tended to bury his head and come out when the fury was over letting everyone else deal with the pain. He had done this with my illness. He would do this with my miscarriage. I pressed a soft kiss to Betsy's cheek. I leaned the other way and nodded my head so Adam leaned my way. I pressed a kiss to his cheek. His eyes closed as my lips pressed against his skin.

"Thanks guys. No matter what Luke says to him you know I'm going to need you."

Saturday morning I woke with intense cramps. I didn't know whether to be happy or sad. I was in the bathroom by myself. Joey was still in bed. Adam and Betsy were downstairs with Noah. I pressed a hand to my belly and breathed deeply.

"You weren't viable," I said softly and sadly.

I walked out into the hallway and had to stop by the railing. I grasped it hard in my hand. I took a few steps down the staircase when the pain eased enough to allow me to. The staircase turned and I came down a few more steps before I had to sit down. Betsy was sitting on the sofa. She could see me. She was holding Noah giving him a bottle.

"Adam," she called his name urgently. "Get Joy. She's on the steps."

He stepped around the corner seeing me. He ran up the few steps and lifted me in his arms. I cried against his neck. The familiarity of it too much. He took me to the sofa and laid me down.

"Go get Joey," she told him.

He acted confused. His stared at me for a second. Then he turned on his heel and disappeared up the steps.

"You okay?" Betsy asked.

"It hurts," I told her.

She rested Noah's bottle against her chest so her hand was freed. She laid that hand on my leg. It wasn't long before Adam returned without Joey.

"Where is he?" She asked.

"He'll be down in a second," Adam replied. He sat on the coffee table between me and Betsy. "What do we do?"

"Joy do we need to call your doctor?" She asked.

I nodded. The pain was becoming more severe. I turned on my side and pulled my knees to my chest. Betsy put Noah in Adam's arms and went to the kitchen where she called my doctor. Five minutes later my husband still hadn't come downstairs.

Betsy came from the kitchen into the living room. She glanced at the staircase as she walked to the sofa and sat down. She told me what the doctor said. I could go through this for days. I should make an appointment on Monday. If the bleeding became too severe I should go to the ER. She couldn't know for certain without an exam but I was probably miscarrying my baby. No probably about it. The non-viable pregnancy was ending.

Betsy kept looking at me then the staircase. She patted my hand. Finally she rose to her feet. "I'm going upstairs. I'll be right back."

### Joey

I pulled on a pair of shorts and now I sat on the edge of my bed staring at the floor. Joy was miscarrying our baby. Was it ever even a baby? My head was spinning with so many terrifying thoughts. I wanted to go downstairs to be with her to give her the comfort I knew she needed but I wasn't good at this stuff. My emotional walls came up when she needed me. I was terrified. I sat on the edge of the bed wringing my hands worrying about her but unable to move. Wanting to go to but unable to make my feet take the steps necessary to go downstairs.

Our bedroom door flung open crashing into the wall behind it. Little Momma walked across the threshold of our bedroom and stood in front of me hands on hips. She was pissed. I had known her since she was fourteen. Six very long years I had known this girl and I loved her. I knew when she was pissed and right now she was pissed at me. That was an easy one.

"I know what you're going to say," I told her.

"No Joseph Bonds," she said. "You don't. Your wife is lying on our sofa downstairs in pain. She is hurting. Dammit we have been there before with her going through shit after her father killed her mother then she shot him. Where were you then?"

I looked at Betsy. Hurt clenched at my gut. I loved Joy with everything in me. I just wasn't good at this deep emotional stuff. It turned my insides out. It reminded me of my mother agonizing over losing Jamie and I could do nothing to help her. It was a helpless out of control feeling that she couldn't possibly understand. That's why Adam let me get away with it. He got it. He knew my mind's inner workings. He knew what made me tick.

"Do you get what she is going through right now while you hide away up here being a pussy?"

Fury started to build inside me. I stood and walked over to Betsy standing just inside the doorway. She wasn't fazed one bit by the difference in our heights or my current fierce expression. The problem with knowing someone as long as I had known Betsy. She knew me too. She knew I would never hurt her.

"Did you stop to think how this affects me too?" I asked.

"Oh really Joey. Cry me a river. Joy is the one who has to suffer right now. She's cramping pretty bad right now." I started to turn my back on her. She grabbed my arm turning me back towards her. "You're going to listen to this. I called the doctor. She'll start bleeding heavily. The doctor said it could last a day maybe two or three. If the bleeding gets severe we should take her to the ER. How exactly do we know what is severe?" She asked. "Do you know?"

I yanked my arm away from Betsy. I walked across the room and grabbed a tee shirt from the dresser. I put it over my head and followed Betsy out of my bedroom while putting my arms through the sleeves. She had shamed me. What if something happened to Joy?

In the living room Luke and Mandy had joined Adam. Mandy was holding Noah. She was sitting in the recliner holding him. She acknowledged us first. Luke turned and looked over his shoulder at me. I could see the look of disappointment on his face. I wasn't where I belonged. I should be at Joy's side. Adam was the only one trying to understand my side, my feelings and my fears.

Betsy leaned on the arm rest of the recliner. I walked over to the sofa and knelt on the floor by Joy's head. She was lying on her side. Curled into herself, her face pale. I brushed back her hair which was down. She was still wearing her pajamas. Luke was leaning over on his knees. He was worried about her. I could see it on his face.

"Are you all right baby? Can I do anything?" My voice was soft not loud like usual.

She closed her eyes when my hand brushed her cheek. I could see the pain etched around her eyes. I ran my hands through my hair and across my neck. What else did I say to her? She was losing our baby. What did I say to make it better?

### Joy

Poor Joey. Betsy had drug him downstairs. He didn't know what to say to me. He didn't know how to deal with his feelings or mine. Joey was Mr. Goodtime not Mr. Let Me Fix Your Troubles Baby. I smiled at him. Through the sharp cramping in my back and lower belly I smiled at him. Reassuring my idiot husband that everything was all right. I gave him the out he needed.

"Joey just do what you need to do," I said.

I heard Betsy's sigh across the room.

Joey kissed my forehead and nearly ran from the room. "You'll let me know if I can do anything," He asked before he disappeared up the stairs.

Adam and Luke both watched him leave. Adam brushed his hand across the back of his neck. He leaned over me giving me a long hard look.

"Why did you let him off the hook?"

"Adam, I'm in pain." I almost started crying. "The last thing I need right now is Joey hovering because he was forced to trying to say the right thing while he says everything wrong. I'd rather lay here by myself and suffer alone."

"You're not alone," Betsy said angrily. "But someday he needs to step up to the plate."

"I know Bets," I said holding back the tears. "Just not today. Okay?"

They all went to the kitchen to get coffee leaving me in peace. Everyone but Adam. His wife didn't seem to mind that he was staying with me. His hand found mine under the blanket that I had pulled to my chin.

"You know she's right about him?"

My gaze met his. My eyes were pleading with him to let it go for now.

"All right," he said. "You will let us know whatever it is we need to know as things progress?" Even Adam was uncomfortable.

"I will let you know if I start to bleed too heavily. So far I'm still just spotting and cramping. This isn't like before when Jack beat me Adam. We didn't really know if I had internal injuries to go along with the miscarriage."

"I know," he said. His thumb caressed my hand. "I feel just as helpless."

I sighed. "I get it. I feel helpless too. Why don't you go to the kitchen with the others maybe I can get some rest?" I suggested.

"If that is what you want?"

My husband ran out that evening for a while. He didn't really say where he was going. My family stayed with me. Luke and Mandy went home near 9:00 PM long before Joey came home.

Betsy put Noah down for the night after giving him a bottle. She helped me to the bathroom downstairs. I had begun to bleed heavier since the last trip to the bathroom. Betsy waited for me at the door. The choking sound that escaped me I couldn't hide from Betsy. She walked to me and helped me pull my pants up. We walked back to the living room together, me leaning on her.

"Adam, help me," she said unable to hold me up. The pain was intensifying.

He was on his feet quick then scooped me into his arms. He strode over to the sofa and laid me down before covering me. Adam looked at Betsy. He was looking for answers.

"It's not bad. I don't need to go to the hospital," I said reading his expression. His concern.

She threw up her hands. "It isn't like I looked Adam," she said when he looked from me to her.

I laughed softly. "Would you relax?" I told him. "It hurts worse but the bleeding isn't that heavy. I won't bleed to death on you guys. All right?"

"Noah needs you," Betsy declared. "You better not."

"I won't."

Betsy went to her bed that night at eleven. She got tired of waiting on Joey to see if he would return. She told Adam to stay up with me in case I needed anything. They didn't want to put me in our room alone and it didn't seem appropriate to have Adam stay there with me. Since Joey hadn't returned home yet I stayed on the sofa with Adam at the other end under his watchful gaze. She had kissed my forehead before slipping up the stairs telling me to wake her if I needed her.

"How are you feeling?" Adam asked when Betsy disappeared up the stairs after kissing him softly on the lips.

"Damned crampy," I replied uncomfortably.

"Brings back memories doesn't it?" He asked.

Adam was holding my feet in his lap. He rested his head against the back of the sofa. He needed a haircut. His long thick strands of black hair were touching below the color of his tee shirt. He was starting to look like a hippie. His jaw was scruffy with unshaven whiskers. I hadn't seen him this scruffy since I had lost our baby and he fell apart for a while.

His question brought more than a bit of emotion welling in my eyes and in my heart.

"I didn't get attached to this baby Adam. I'm not saying it doesn't hurt." I looked down the length of my body. I gazed into his eyes. "It hurts."

"I know it does Joy," he said. "That is why I'm pissed that Joey's not here. I'm here. It's fucking killing me to see you go through this again. I feel like he should be here dammit."

"He doesn't know what I went through before. We hid that from him. That isn't really fair."

"He does know what you are going through right this very minute Joy."

"I know," I said softly.

I pulled my knees harder into my belly. I just wanted this to be over. I had to pee. It had been hours since I had used the bathroom afraid of seeing the blood again. I sighed.

"You're going to have to help me to the bathroom," I told Adam.

He rose from the sofa. "Want me to carry you?"

Oh hell yes I did. I felt safe in his arms. I wanted desperately to be there surrounded by his strength because right now I didn't feel strong at all.

"Can I just lean on you?" I asked.

He pulled me to my feet. "Whatever you need Joy." Adam's voice was husky. His arm wrapped around my waist. He half carried me to the bathroom anyway. He stood in the bathroom door with his back to me.

"Adam," I said his name letting him know that I was ready to go back to the living room.

He wrapped his arm around my waist. Adam kissed the top of my head. "Joy I wish you didn't have to go through this."

"Me too," I said.

He walked me back to the sofa and guided me down. He covered me with the blanket.

"Will you hold me Adam?"

He hesitated just for a second. Then he lifted my head and sat down beneath me. He guided me into his arms so that my head rested across his lap but his arms were around me. We fell asleep that way.

Joey came in at 2:00 AM. Not really drunk but drinking. He was sarcastic and angry. He slammed the front door making Adam and I both jump. We were wide awake now. I was still cramping bad.

"Why am I not surprised that it's you comforting her?" He asked angrily.

He plopped down in the recliner staring at us with golden eyes intense but Adam wasn't intimidated.

"Listen Joseph if your ass was where it needed to be then I wouldn't be here taking care of your wife. My wife wouldn't have been here with us until eleven waiting on your ass so we could decide where Joy should sleep so lose the attitude."

"Adam," I said his name with a bit of fear. I could feel the blood overflowing. I didn't think it was too heavy just too heavy for what I was wearing. "Could somebody get Betsy please?"

Joey jumped out of the chair and started up the steps. I didn't know if it was the look on my face or what that moved his ass as fast it did but fast he moved. Adam turned me. "What is it sweetheart?" He asked.

"I'm bleeding heavier. I'm getting blood on the couch," I said. Afraid to move.

He looked terrified. I could see it in his face too. Betsy came running down the stairs with Joey behind her. She hesitated at the sofa. She looked down at me. She was scared too. "What do you want me to do?" She asked.

"I don't know," I said.

We were two kids pretending to be grown-ups. I was scared. I lifted the blanket that covered me and showed her the blood that was covering me. She gasped.

"I don't know Joy."

She ran to the kitchen. She dialed the farm. I slapped my hand over my face. Adam was still holding me in his arms. Both he and Joey were looking at the blood. I pulled the quilt back over me. I closed my eyes tiredly and sighed.

"Mandy and Luke are coming."

Minutes later they ran into the house. Fear on Luke's face. We had all been through so much with me being the cause of so much of the turmoil. Mandy was gentle with me. She checked out the blood that I was losing. She asked Adam to carry me upstairs to the bathroom. She and Betsy helped me get cleaned up. Then they put me to bed. Betsy went downstairs to tell the men that I was doing okay. Mandy stayed with me she caressed my cheek and then kissed it gently.

"You're okay sweetheart. If it gets heavier than that you need to go to the ER."

"How do you know?"

Her gaze dropped to the comforter she had just pulled over me. "I had a miscarriage once. A while ago. Before Luke. I know it's scary. It should be over soon. You were in the hospital the first time and you were in shock. So you don't remember."

I smiled at her. I leaned over and hugged her to me.

"Mandy, thank you."

"Anytime sweetheart."

She left the room. Mandy left me alone. Luke came to tell me goodbye. He sat on the edge of the bed. He took his hands in mine.

"You okay now sweetheart?" He asked.

"I'm sorry we got you out of bed in the middle of the night. We were scared."

"I forget sometimes that you four are just kids really." He laughed a soft sad laugh. "I don't care that you woke me. Joy you might not be my daughter by blood but I love you like my own daughter. If you need me I want you to know that you can call me at two am or ten am." His eyes misted over.

Luke rose from the bed and leaned over me. He kissed my forehead cupping the back of my head. I felt loved. I felt like his daughter. More than I ever felt like I had belonged to Jack Ayers.

I slipped down under the covers and laid my head against the pillows. Adam and Betsy came into the room next. They both kissed me goodnight. A peck on the cheek letting me know I was loved by them as well. They went to their room exhausted. Before they left I asked if Joey was coming upstairs. They said he was but they left my bedroom door open just in case I needed them.

He did come to our room. He climbed into our bed fully clothed even his shoes were still on his feet. He didn't say anything. He put his arm out for me to slide into his body. I nearly cried. I rolled over into the nook of Joey's warm body. He held me tight against him. We didn't talk. I could hear the steady beat of his heart against my ear. His breathing soothed me and for once I slept soundly in his arms.

## Chapter Eleven

### Betsy

I had been Joy's friend since we were little girls. I had cleaned wounds that no child should ever clean on another child's body because she insisted my parents couldn't find out about her dad's abuse. I loved her like she was a sister. I knew I couldn't live my life without her in it. The best thing would have been for me to step aside and force her and Adam to get back together but I hadn't. I had fallen in love with him. Then I had gotten pregnant with his child.

Now I was married to Adam Moore. Should we move into our own home? Most likely but I couldn't bring myself to leave Joy. I didn't know what would happen to her without us. I often wondered what would happen to my marriage if we left. I wasn't sure that Adam could live without seeing her. So I kept them close.

Was it difficult? At times my heart would feel like it was being gripped in a vice so hard I thought my life was being squeezed out of me. Seeing her lying on his chest was one of those times. He was comforting her. That is what I told myself. She was losing her baby. Joey wasn't stepping up to the plate like he should. I climbed into bed with them and she took Noah from me. He comforted her. Her heart was breaking. I couldn't help her any other way so I gave my son to her.

Adam was tender hearted. He was sweet and kind. He loved big. When he loved he loved with all his heart. Did I have a place in that big heart of his? I did. He was good at making me feel special. I could almost believe he loved me but then I would catch site of him looking at Joy. I knew then that although Adam Moore might love me he didn't love me like he loved Joy.

What should I do? I knew what I should do if I had an ounce of respect for myself. What did I do? Absolutely nothing because I knew Adam Moore was an honorable man and his priority would be my son and me. Then Joy no matter what feelings he might have for her.

Joy's presence in the kitchen took me out of my revelry. She looked pale and worn. She looked sad. I hoped this miscarriage didn't set her back emotionally.

"Sweetheart, how are you?" I asked taking her hand in mine.

Joy took a seat next to me. "Bleeding is still pretty heavy but the cramping is letting up," she replied softly.

I did love her. We understood each other. We were still holding hands. I pulled her into my arms. I held her close. Her head rested against my shoulder. I caressed her long blonde hair. She always wanted to look more like me and I wanted to be more like her. The thought gave me a little chuckle now as I held her. She leaned back looking at me with a puzzled expression.

"Thinking about us as kids," I said. "Thinking about us now."

She smiled although her smile didn't appear to be a happy one.

"Thank you," Joy told me.

"For what?" I asked gazing into her eyes. Her beautiful green eyes. I knew why the men had fallen for her. She was mysterious in beauty and fiery in temperament. Her eyes drew you in. She was damned beautiful.

"For always being there for me?"

"That is easy," I told her and meant it. I couldn't imagine being anywhere else.

"So where is Joey?" she asked. She knew he had gotten up early and left the house.

I sighed. "He left as I was coming down the stairs. He said he was going to the library to study for the CPA exam."

She shook her head sadly. "Glad I'm doing better today."

"Me too or I would have gone to the library and drug his stupid ass home," I said.

She laughed at me. A soft delicate sound not like my own brash laughter. I smiled at her. We were so different. She might be fiery but she was quieter than me. She was thoughtful. I was loud and obstinate. I got my way by being a bully which was funny since I was all of five feet two.

Adam walked into the room carrying Noah. "He's all clean and changed. Ready for a bottle."

"Can I give it to him?" Joy asked eagerly.

"If you will eat," I demanded. I wasn't sure she had eaten anything yesterday.

"How about a shake?" She asked hopefully.

"I will make it while I make Noah's bottle."

She stood to take Noah from Adam then she looked over her shoulder. "One scoop Betsy Moore."

"I promise." I crossed my toes lying through my teeth. God knows what else I would get her to eat today. She was getting two or three scoops if I could get away with it.

Adam handed off Noah to Joy. He kissed her forehead tenderly and watched her walk to the living room before walking into the kitchen with me.

I was preparing the bottle for Noah and the shake for Joy when Adam's strong arms snaked around me. He pulled me against his chest. Involuntarily, I leaned into his body. Adam's body was rock hard. It felt inviting and warm to be held in his arms. He nipped at the curve of my neck. His hand went up to cup my breast.

"Let me finish this," I told him brushing him away.

He dropped his arms to his side. I wasn't sure why I was constantly pushing Adam away. I loved him. I wanted him. I definitely didn't want him to end up with Joy but at times I thought I might be pushing him away so that he could be where he wanted to be. I looked at him over my shoulder. What the hell was I doing?

### Joy

I felt human today. I was in much less pain. I was blocking out the emotional pain of losing my child. My child that wasn't viable. It just felt wrong. I held Noah in my arms tracing the soft curve of his cheek. His mouth opened turning towards my gentle caress. He was hungry. I smiled at him a look of tenderness crossing my face. He was my comfort in this difficult time. He was my happiness when I might have fallen into darkness again. He was my hope. It was a lot to put on such a little guy.

Betsy walked into the living room. She handed me Noah's bottle in one hand. I popped it into his mouth resting it against my chest. In her other hand she held out my shake. I took it and sipped it gently. I shook my head at her.

"What?" She asked innocently.

The shake was thicker and richer. I had developed a taste to know when they put more than one scoop in the shakes. I shook my head again and rolled my eyes but I continued to drink it anyway. Adam chuckled softly at Betsy. He plopped in the recliner after sitting a coffee mug on the table beside him. She climbed into his lap surprising him I could see. I focused my attention on Noah not on them. His innocence was a beautiful thing. I wanted to protect him. Let him have it his entire life. I didn't want him to know the pain that we had known. My heart swelled in my chest and tears formed in my eyes looking at the little guy.

"Hey," Betsy said softly. "Are you okay?"

I nodded. "I am. Just thinking about how sweet and innocent he is. I never want him to know the pain that we have known."

Betsy gazed at me across the room. She smiled at me. "He won't," she promised. "He's going to have a golden life not like us. His parents won't ignore him. They won't hurt him."

I looked across the room at her. She had been hurt in her own way by the Carters. Their lack of interest in her had hurt her deeply. We had relied on each other for love and support. What child had to do that? They provided a roof over her head, clothes on her back and food. That was it. Her father was a cold man. Her mother doing what her father told her to do. Her father demanding her mother's time and attention. She was an only child like me.

"I just had a really odd thought you guys. We're all only children. Do you think that is why we're so close?" I asked Betsy and Adam.

Adam seemed to be far away. Thinking of something. She looked over her shoulder at him. She brushed his hair away from his eyes.

"What?" He asked.

"Are you all right?" Betsy asked him.

"I'm fine," he replied. "Where is Joey speaking of our other partner in crime."

"He went to the library to study," Betsy told him.

Adam's face was tinged pink as his anger grew. "You're kidding right?" He asked.

Betsy shook her head no.

"Adam," I said softly. "It's okay. I have you and Betsy. I'm better today than yesterday. Much better. He knew that before he left."

"It's not right dammit."

"It's the way he is," I said. "It's the only way he can deal with it."

"Too fucking bad," he snapped.

We were quiet after that each of us lost in our thoughts. Noah finished his bottle. I sat him up on my knee and held him, his chest against my hand. I patted his back until he burped loud and proud causing a chuckle from his parents. I just shook my head. Who would have thought that a tiny baby could make so much noise? I smiled at Betsy and Adam.

"He's a Moore all right," I said.

Adam chuckled harder.

I put Noah on my shoulder and continued to pat his back. His head rested on my shoulder. I could see his eyes were open looking at me. His head wobbled a bit as he tried to hold it up. He was a strong boy. He was beautiful and he was precious.

Luke walked through the front door coming to the house to check on me. Startling us when he opened the door. We were all lost in our separate thoughts. Thinking about our own issues and emotions.

He was casual, dressed in usual jeans and tee shirt, his scuffed boots familiar and worn.

"How are you Joy?" He asked.

"I'm feeling better today," I replied.

"Where is Joey?" He asked looking around the room.

I chuckled. Betsy responded, "For the third time this morning he went to the library to study."

Luke looked annoyed as had Adam. He sat down on the sofa near me. He appeared tired probably because we had woken him in the night. "Where's Mandy?" I asked.

"She went home," he said. "She has some work to do."

"When are you going to make an honest woman out of her?" I asked teasing him.

He scowled at me. "Did you ever hear if it isn't broken why try to fix it?" He asked.

I slapped at his shoulder. "Would you like to hold your grandson?" I asked.

"I think I would," he replied. I passed Noah to him. The little guy grunted as I did so. He had comfortably started napping on my shoulder. "You know you two produce a mighty beautiful kid," he said to Betsy and Adam. He looked uncomfortably at me.

I smiled at him. "I tend to agree. He is as sweet as he is beautiful. It is hard to put him down."

Luke's dark eyes filled with emotion gazed back at me. Then he looked at his grandson in his arms. Noah always looked small when Luke, Adam or Joey held him. He was over nine pounds so he wasn't small. I caressed his mop of dark hair lovingly.

Luke looked across the room at Adam and Betsy. "When are you getting a haircut?" He asked Adam. "You're starting to look like a damned hippie."

Adam just laughed at his father. I liked the longer hair and the whiskers on his jaw. It made him sexier than he already was. Not that I should be looking at him that way. He was Betsy's husband. I needed to focus on my own husband.

Betsy agreed with me and told Luke so. "I love the longer hair," she said. Adam's hand went around her waist drawing her to him. He kissed her shoulder. I looked at Luke and smiled. What else could I do? Pretend it didn't hurt. Pretend I didn't want to be the one sitting on Adam's lap. Pretend I didn't want his arm around me. I didn't want his lips to be pressed to my body. I sighed not really a sad sigh but not a contented sigh either.


### Adam

There is one thing about me that pisses Joy off. I have a great memory. Not only did I remember from the doctor's appointment for her knee but I remembered from Betsy's phone call to her doctor she was supposed to have a follow up appointment after this miscarriage. She was pissed at me right now because I had reminded everyone that she needed to make an appointment. She was glaring at me across the kitchen table. I had given her a week. She hadn't made the appointment. If looks could kill I would be a dead man. I just smiled at her kindly and continued eating my dinner.

"I'll make the appointment in the morning if you don't," my wife told her.

For some reason we didn't understand Joy had an aversion to the doctor. She just plain didn't like going. Now Joy's death glare was concentrated on Betsy. My little wife wasn't fazed one bit. Hell, if Joseph Bonds couldn't intimidate her when he was pissed off then a littler Joy Bonds with less piss and vinegar wouldn't scare Betsy. I watched the interaction between the two women for a second before Joy finally finished the conversation.

"I will make the damned appointment," she snapped.

Joy got up from the table and scraped her food into the garbage can. She grabbed her shake and her diet soda from the table and took off. Betsy and Joey looked at me then at each other. It was always like walking a tightrope with Joy.

You never knew how far you could push her before sending her plummeting to the ground.

### *Joy*

I took my drinks outside to the front porch. I plopped my ass in the porch swing. One foot I propped up on the swing. One foot I rested on the floor boards of the porch to slide the swing back and forth in a gentle motion. Adam came outside minutes later. He sat beside me on the swing. I stopped rocking long enough to let him sit. I didn't look at him. I couldn't.

"I'm sorry," he said.

"For what? For caring enough to make me do what is right even when I don't want to?" I asked.

He laughed at me. "And it pisses you off."

"Yes it does." I finally looked at him. His big beautiful dark eyes that a woman could get lost in. I had lost myself in them so many times. Too many when I shouldn't have. "You care more than Joey," I said.

"I don't think that's true. He just doesn't know how to deal with things."

"You're the same age. What is his excuse?" I snapped.

"Joy I've had a much easier life than him. I don't need to hide behind walls to protect myself."

I gazed at Adam. His childhood might have been better but Adam knew pain. He had held me in his arms while I miscarried our baby. My blood had covered his clothes. His heart had broken into a thousand pieces when I told him we couldn't be together. He stood by stoically while I married his best friend. Adam knew pain yet he continued to be the responsible one. He continued to take care of all of us.

"If you say so Adam," I finally said.

His eyes met mine. Our gazes locked on each other. Our eyes saying what our voices could not.

"How are you feeling?" he finally asked.

I looked away. "I'm fine."

"Emotionally?" He asked. He took my hand. His thumb caressed my palm. I felt my breath quicken. Why did he have such an effect on me?

"I'm fine. Really Adam I am."

"I don't believe you," he answered back. "We aren't waiting until it's too late this time Joy. Until you are so bad you're almost ready for the hospital because you weigh barely over one hundred pounds."

I turned back to Adam but I couldn't look at him for long. I laid my head on my bent knee and closed my eyes. I had lost another baby. I felt his large hand touch my back tentatively at first. Then firmly to let me know he was there for me. He was comforting me. Adam and I were best friends before we became lovers. I hung on to that thought as I kept my head down and my eyes closed letting him comfort me. A few tears slipped from my eyes.

"Adam," I whispered. "I am doing okay."

I was. I hadn't had a panic attack in weeks maybe months. I was taking my medication like I should. I was feeling stronger. This was a major setback for me, I knew and I acknowledged that I was sad but I wasn't depressed. I wasn't falling to pieces like I had before. I was bending but not breaking.

"Joy," he said my name in a husky whisper.

I looked at him turning my head in his direction.

"I can't..." he struggled with what he wanted to say. "I love you so damned much you know that." I nodded with so much hesitation. Why was he telling me this? "I can't watch you do this to yourself anymore. Please tell me you mean it. You're breaking my heart."

I was surprised by Adam's words. I had hurt him so much with my actions. Not intentionally but I had. He had tears in his eyes. I raised my head and dropped my foot to the floor. I hooked my arm around Adam's neck and pulled him to my chest. I kissed the top of his head as he cried on my shirt wetting it. Adam hadn't cried since I had lost the baby. Not like this at least.

I held him to me. I comforted him. I looked up and found Betsy and Joey standing on the porch watching us with concern. Adam raised his head when he saw them. He leaned over on his knees and covered his face. My big strong Adam was hurting. I had caused it. They looked at him with concern. My hand rested on Adam's back caressing him, comforting him still even though he was no longer in my arms.

"Adam," I said his name. He looked at me sideways. "I promise. I am okay."

He nodded. Betsy walked over to the porch swing. She sat beside me. She smiled at me. Then she hugged me. She had tears in her eyes too.

"You'll tell us if you're not," she begged.

"I will try. But right now guys I'm better than I've ever been. I'm at a good weight. I feel positive. I'm dealing with this better than I've dealt with other things in the past. I really am doing well."

She nodded. Grateful that I was well.

"That doesn't mean you two can leave on your own if that is what you were thinking?" I snapped.

She laughed at me. "We're growing old together. We're never leaving," Betsy said.

"Dammit," Adam said shaking his head while Joey laughed. "I had hoped someday to live in separate homes."

"Why?" Betsy asked. "I love seeing Joy and Joey every day."

"I love seeing Betsy everyday but I could live without him every day," Joey said sarcastically.

"Thanks Joseph," Adam replied. He rolled his eyes. He gazed at me and Betsy. I knew what he was thinking if she didn't. He needed the separation from me at some point in his life. I knew some time in the future we would have to make the break.

"You can't go far," I whispered taking Betsy's hand in mine.

Adam looked at us. He looked at our intertwined hands. He shook his head with exasperation. "We won't," he promised. He might want some point of separation from me but not a complete one. Even he couldn't do that.

*Chapter Twelve*

*Adam*

Noah was turning one year old today. Betsy had given me a long list of items she needed for the party that was taking place at the farm. I left Pa with all the farm work today but he was okay with that since it was for Noah.

Currently I was at the grocery store picking up his cake. It had a train on it with brightly dressed clowns hanging from the windows waving. Betsy wasn't one to get the latest fad or popular TV character for our son's first birthday. It was actually pretty cute. She had seen it in some magazine she received on a monthly basis.

Joy and I? Well we had gotten good at burying our feelings. An occasional touch that made me crave more of her. I thought she felt the same way because she always lowered her eyes. Not willing to let me see the depth of emotion that she tried to hide in those beautiful green eyes of hers. An occasional look of longing that was broken by somebody saying something breaking the spell between us.

The feelings for Joy hadn't gone away. They were being ignored. Then there was Betsy. I made love to my wife with my eyes open because closing them brought forth images of a silver haired woman that invaded my dreams. Sometimes, I woke at night trembling from some damned realistic dreams of a naked Joy in my arms loving me like nothing had bad happened between us. Like we weren't married to other people. Like we weren't married to the wrong people.

I saw how she was with Joey. Tender and caring even when he didn't deserve her. When she told him she loved him it was with the same inflection that she used for Betsy or my Pa. She rarely told me that she loved me anymore but in private when she did it was with the emotion of a woman who loved a man. I think that had happened twice in the last year. In a moment of weakness she had said the words. Once I had grasped her arms pulling her to me and kissed her forehead releasing her just as quickly.

Desperate moments in time getting us through another year of our lives. I ran my hands through my hair. It was definitely too long again. Maybe I would stop at the barber shop today if I had time.

### Joy

Noah is turning one today. Betsy has given me a long list of tasks to do today. What else could I do but make today the most special day for a special little boy? Noah had started walking. I loved helping him. His little fingers wrapped around mine while we took tiny steps across the grass at the farm. If he fell down he wouldn't cry. Always making me smile.

Then Noah smiling at me taking my face between his tiny hands. Kissing me all over my face. We giggled together. Him calling me *my Joy Joy*. I was captivated by him. Apparently I was meant to love the Moore men because they all had me wrapped around their fingers.

Adam and I spent most of our time trying hard to hide our feelings. No looking or touching. Being happy with our lives that I had created for us because we had to because of the fateful day Jack intervened in my life changing my path forever. When the occasional touch happened I would have to look away, lower my eyes to keep anyone from seeing the effect that man had on me still. I knew I couldn't keep the passion, the longing out of my voice so I rarely told him I loved him anymore. It was just too much. Too painful.

Once we got caught, me coming out of the bathroom him going in and he pushed me back into the interior of the small space. Just for a second. To touch me just for a heartbeat. I breathed through it trying not to melt into his arms. I had told him I loved him in that moment. The words escaping from my mouth even though I thought they were still only playing inside my head. He had kissed my forehead tenderly. Then he released me letting me go on my way before things got out of hand. No one hurt. No one the wiser. It had only happened one other time when we were alone.

### Joey

Today Noah turned one. I had my CPA certification. I was working long hours. I was currently at the office just for half a day. I had to be at the party or two women would have my head.

I had two tasks to do on the way home for Noah's party. Pick up a birthday card for Noah from me and Joy and pick up a meat tray from the butcher's shop fresh deli cuts of meat for sandwiches. My only two tasks to ensure Noah had a great birthday. I couldn't be late.

I loved the little guy. When I held him, gave him a bottle, changed him it made my heart clench in desperate need. I wanted a child with Joy. It had been months since her miscarriage. She was adamant that we use birth control. She wasn't able to take birth control pills she had tried them. They gave her migraine headaches so it was up to me to use condoms. Condoms every time. She was back in panic mode. Terrified of getting pregnant and I didn't know how to change her feelings. I wasn't sure if we would ever have a child.

Otherwise, my relationship with Joy was solid. Happy. She was sweet with me. Tender with me. In bed our sexual relationship was different. She wanted it rough. I was never sure where to draw the line. She excited me and scared me at the same time. She was like two women. A sweet gentle firebrand with a quick temper out of bed. A naughty whore who liked her ass spanked in bed. She couldn't get off unless I was rough with her. Damned freaky I had to admit. Made my dick hard as steel. I loved this woman who made me crazy as hell to the point of distraction.

Then there was Ria Jackson. A woman at the office. A bright single woman who loved to flirt with me. She was part of my department. My employee. Against company policy. A major distraction at times during meetings. A dark haired beauty with chocolate brown eyes. Just a flirtation I told myself. I am married to a beautiful woman named Joy. Ria knew that.

### Betsy

Today was Noah's first birthday. I was going to open a can of whoop-ass on the first person who screwed up was late or didn't get what I needed done. This was my baby's first birthday. I was already at the farm organizing things. Luke and Mandy chasing after Noah who was shuffling / running from his grandpa.

Joy was running around taking care of her tasks. Her eyes were bright and happy. She was better. Healthier. Her hair was down flying about her in springy curls of silver blonde. Her body was slender but not scary skinny. We still watched her food intake though. We still walked on egg shells careful that we didn't miss anything. She was better than she had been since she had miscarried the child she and Adam were going to have.

Her and Adam? They were careful. I saw the careful glances directed at each other. The hidden feelings they tried so hard to keep anyone from seeing. Joey thought it was a lifelong friendship they shared. Seven years of sharing everything. I knew the truth. I knew the secrets we kept from him. I knew they still loved each other and for our sakes mine and Joey's they avoided each other. They buried those feelings.

Me and Adam? He was honorable my Adam. I had a tender feeling for this man who did the honorable thing. He had married me when I got pregnant. We had created a family for our child. He was devoted to me and Noah. Adam was always taking care of all of us. He always put everyone's needs first before his own whether it was me, Noah, Joey or Joy. He took care of us. He was our rock. He was our strength. I adored him. Was he mine? I wasn't sure that he ever was or ever would be but he did everything in his power to make me think he was mine.

"Cake," he said walking up behind me. "Where do you want it?"

"Wow it turned out better than I expected."

"It is cute," he said smiling down at me.

"Just put it on the picnic table over there," I directed pointing with my free hand.

"Sure," he replied.


### Joy

It was a child's birthday party. Who decided beer was a good idea? Oh that is right my husband that is who. I was fuming that Joey arrived with the meat tray and the birthday card plus three cases of beer. Damn him. Would he never get away completely from the drinking? He had hot and cold moments with alcohol. Highs and lows. Obviously right now he was having a low if he needed alcohol to get through Noah's birthday. Both Adam and Betsy told me to let it go.

Noah toddled up to me smiling brightly. His arms reaching for me before he actually was to me. I scooped him up in my arms and kissed his neck. He laughed his beautiful childlike giggle filling the air. He leaned back away from me and gazed into my eyes. His love for me evident in his big dark eyes. His little hands grasped my face. Sweetly he smiled at me.

Softly he whispered like it was secret, "Loves you my Joy Joy."

My heart felt like it was swelling to the three times its size in my chest.

"I love you my Noah."

He threw his arms around my neck hugging me then he was off again. His vocabulary for a one year old was amazing. He spoke clearly no baby talk. He had to know at least one hundred words. The boys like to say it was because Betsy and I never shut up of course he was going to talk early. He was just so smart.

"Joey," Betsy yelled across the yard. "I think you have competition. You better start treating Joy right."

He looked puzzled. Beer in hand. He was standing with some of our friends and Luke. The Marks', the James' and the Martins' all came with their kids. Of course Mandy was here too. She and Luke seemed to be somewhat cool tonight. Something was wrong in Luke's world that he didn't want to talk about. I wished I knew what was ailing him because he was downright grouchy these days.

"My son just declared his love for your wife," she told him. "He's getting pretty possessive of her."

Adam chuckled. Luke was looking at Mandy with a far-away distant look that had me puzzled and Joey? Joey just shook his head at her and waved her away like she was bothering him. I just shook my head at him. Sometimes he could really irritate the piss out of me.

The wives all moved to the table where Betsy and I were standing.

"Shay what is up with you girl?" Betsy asked. "You're grumpier than Luke these days."

We all sat down at the picnic table. I heard the beer can tab pop and looked across the yard where the men were standing. It was Bobby Martin opening a beer can, not Joey. I met Adam's eyes briefly and looked away. Luke caught Noah up in his arms. Mandy walked over to the table with the ladies. She sat down next to me.

"You okay?" I asked.

"Just tired sweetheart," she replied patting my hand.

"Everything good with you and Luke?" I asked.

She nodded but not happily. I could see it in her eyes. "Are you sure?" I asked.

"I am sweetheart." She was dismissing me. Telling me to let it go. She wasn't going to talk.

Then I heard the news that explained Shay's grumpiness and Bobby guzzling beer as fast Joey. Shay was pregnant again. Shay didn't like being pregnant. She loved her son but she didn't like being pregnant. Her boy blonde and blue eyes like her was running after Noah right now. Timmy named after TJ his grandfather was a wild one but cute as a button. When Shay was pregnant she made Bobby's life hell.

Alex and Marta James had a dark haired boy Shane, a few months younger than Timmy and Noah barely able to walk. He spent more time falling down. His dark eyes and long lashes were Marta's features. Everything else was all Alex. Marta was expecting again as well. She had just found out she was pregnant.

Stephanie and Benny Marks were expecting their first baby in seven months. Stephanie had already gained ten pounds. Everyone had baby brain including Betsy. She was trying to convince Adam they should have another and me that Joey and I should have one too.

Something in me was definitely missing. An emptiness consumed me but I wasn't sure a baby could fill that void.


*Adam*

Noah was winding down. He had blown out the candles, opened the presents. Chased around the farmyard with Shane and Timmy. Now he was being held by Joy. Everyone had gone home. He was cuddled against her breast. Every now and then he raised his head and nodded at her eagerly. He had a length of her hair in his hand not pulling on it but letting the curls run through his fingers until it sprung back in place making him giggle. Her eyes were just as bright as his. He laid his head back down on Joy's chest.

I lowered my eyes soaking up every minute my son spent with her. Not wanting to reveal too much I was feeling to those surrounding me. When he grabbed her face and called her, *my Joy Joy* I understood his feelings. She had that effect on me. She had that effect on my Pa as well.

Betsy slipped in and took Noah from Joy. She stood and kissed Noah's forehead. She was putting our son down in grandpa's house. I gathered he was staying the night here. I knew what that meant. She was in a baby making mood. Sometimes I thought Betsy only wanted sex when she thought she might get pregnant. I didn't know why we couldn't just enjoy the one we had. What was the hurry? He was just one year old today.

Betsy brought Noah to me so I could kiss him good night. I took him in my arms and held him tight to my chest. "Pop, Pop," he said softly. I kissed his forehead. "I go night night."

"Momma making you little man?" I said to him.

He nodded solemnly. "Party over," he said.

"It is Noah. You sleep tight buddy."

"No bed bugs bite."

"That's right," I replied.

I handed Noah back to Betsy. I kissed her temple before she walked away with our son. I watched her leave. She was a sweet woman. I knew I was a lucky man. She was beautiful as well. Her body slightly curvier after giving birth to Noah. Her hips swayed as she cuddled Noah against her. She kissed his temple tenderly. She was a good mother to our son.

Then a silver haired beauty walked into my line of vision. She slipped beneath my father's arm. She could do this with him. Be free. He wrapped his arm around her holding her against him. Pa loved Joy. She was like his own daughter. He brushed her hair away from her face. She had started wearing her hair down instead of in ponytails like usual. It hung to the middle of her back. The curls bouncing wildly about her beautiful face.

Her green eyes danced as she talked to him. He threw back his head and laughed at her. She just smiled at him. Her hand rested at his waist. She squeezed him tight and he returned the hug. When was the last time I had held her? When I pushed her into the bathroom needing to hold her. To touch her. To feel her without prying eyes. It had been months.

Joey walked over to them. He was drunk. Pa handled him well when he was drinking or drunk. Suddenly Joy's smile faded. She hated the drinking. Joey's behavior when he was drunk reminded her of Jack. He tended to be more obstinate more out of control when he was drinking. More violent. Betsy came outside and walked directly to me. She saw where I was looking.

"Everything okay?" She asked glancing at the three of them.

"So far," I answered.

"Joy looks like she's about to crawl out of her skin. Maybe you should rescue her."

I glanced down at my wife. Had she lost her mind? Joey drinking. Me rescuing Joy from him, would lead to nowhere good. "You're kidding right?"

Betsy sighed. She put her hand on her hip and glared up at me. "So you're willing to let her suffer? Or worse?" Betsy said with her snappy tone of voice. "Cause we all know that when he's drinking she always seems to get hurt."

Why did she do this to me? No I didn't want Joy to suffer. At any time in my life did I ever want Joy to be hurt or to suffer but right now my father seemed to have the situation under control. My father didn't provoke feelings of irritation in Joseph that I seemed to whenever I intervened.

"Pa has things under control."

Then suddenly he didn't. Joey was trying to manhandle Joy. She was pushing him away. Pa was trying to get him to back off. He shoved Pa and that was when I had to intervene because the only thing right now keeping Pa from knocking Joey on his ass was Joy.

"Joseph, why don't you come with me?" I asked trying to take his arm. Where I was taking him I didn't know but getting him away from Pa before fists starting flying was first and foremost in my mind.

"I don't need to go anywhere Adam. I just wanted to a little loving from my wife. I don't see the problem with that," he slurred.

"The problem is you're drunk Joey," Betsy shouted.

*Great. Way to go Betsy. Antagonize the drunk. That was the answer.*

"Shut up shorty," Joey snapped glaring at her.

"Make me jackass," she barked.

"Will you stop?" I said to Betsy throwing up both hands.

"Whatever happened to getting him help Joy?" Pa asked irritably.

*And that made things so much better.*

"I don't fucking need help," he yelled at Pa.

"That is what happened," she replied to my father.

He walked over to Joy standing near Pa. "You do not discuss me with anyone." He was in her face. She wasn't afraid. I could tell but Pa couldn't see her face.

"Back the hell up Joseph," Pa said pushing Joey back and that is when the fists started flying with Joy right in the middle of things. Betsy crying she was going to get hurt. Did she? Of course she did because instead of getting out of the way she tried to break it up.

Joy was lying flat on her back in the grass not moving. "Jesus Christ Joey," Betsy screamed at him. "What did you do?"

He stood still as a stone statue. He knew the minute his fist connected with her fragile jaw. Betsy ran around them and straight to Joy but I was already there. I lifted her in my arms. She was out cold. Joey had cold-cocked her accidently of course.

Pa wiped his face where Joey had split his lip with the first punch. Mandy came out of the house running across the lawn to where we were. Luckily everyone had gone home and missed my family's fabulous fiasco of a fight. I patted her cheek. Betsy laid her hand on my arm.

"God Adam is she all right?" she asked me trying not to cry when Joy didn't open her eyes.

Pa knelt next to us now. Joey was still standing over us looking in horror at what he had done. Mandy ran to the picnic table and came back with a cloth she had dunked in the cooler. It was wet and cold. Mandy handed it to Betsy. She wiped it across Joy's face. Her eyelashes started to flutter.

"What the hell happened?" She asked in a husky voice.

"Your husband missed my father and hit you. Knocked you out cold."

"Damn my jaw hurts."

I was still holding her in my arms. I was allowed right now to do it so I was and I was going to take full advantage for as long as I could.

"Do you think maybe next time fists start flying you could get out of the way?" Betsy asked tearfully.

"I didn't want Luke to get hurt," she said.

Betsy and I looked at each other across her body. We both tried not to laugh. Pa threw back his head and roared. "Little girl I hate to tell you but I can handle Joey much better than you."

Joey was still standing. Watching us. Hands on top of his head. I knew him. He was trying to keep them from trembling. He had knocked out his wife. She had been unconscious. So far he hadn't said a word.

"You ready to try sitting up?" I asked softly.

She looked up into my eyes. She smiled sweetly then almost cried because it hurt her face. I cringed. She nodded. "Help me sit up dammit," she said. Betsy and I each took her arms and helped her sit. "Whoa," she said. I kept one arm around her back just in case.

"Head still spinning?" Betsy asked.

She nodded holding her head.

"Do you need to go to the hospital?" Luke asked.

"Oh hell no," she told Pa.

"Adam why don't you carry her into the house? At least she won't be sitting in the grass getting her ass bit by mosquitos. We can determine what to do in there."

Her husband still hadn't moved. I gathered Joy in my arms and stood with her. She was easy. Light as a feather. Betsy walked along behind us. Mandy right beside her. I could tell Joy was looking over my shoulder.

"Luke isn't coming."

"Will you quit worrying about Pa? He can more than handle Joey. Right now the fight is gone from Joey. It isn't every day that you knock your wife out cold."

She laid her head on my shoulder. "It was an accident."

"He was acting like an ass."

She looked up at me. Her beautiful green eyes met mine. "I know," she said softly.

Pa walked into the house a few minutes after I laid Joy on the sofa. He walked straight to her. "Are you still dizzy?" He asked.

"I'm better. You need to let Betsy look at your lip."

He touched it. "I'm fine."

She drew her legs up and he sat down by her. "I know he needs to blow off steam. I understand he has a lot of pressure on him. His job. His past. Whatever drives his demons? But he cannot drink."

"He hasn't in a while," she defended him.

"Every damned time he does he hurts you. You know that. Do not defend him," Pa said forcefully.

She reached out to Pa. She took his hand. She laid it on her cheek. "I'm not." But really she was.

Betsy climbed into my lap. I leaned back in the recliner and held her just watching what was going to happen next.

"It is one thing if he wants to hit me or take a swing at Adam."

*Hey. Don't put me into this. I've take enough hits recently.* I rubbed a hand across my face remembering.

"Joy the minute he hits one of you girls accidental or not I have to put my foot down before you seriously get hurt."

She was looking at Pa. I couldn't tell what she was thinking. She looked across the room at Betsy and me. She was biting her lip. Her jaw was turning purple already where he had hit her. I tightened my arm around Betsy. She laid her head against mine.

"I don't know what to do to help him," she said forlornly.

Pa patted her leg. "First thing I told him outside is that he needs to put the alcohol down permanently. Some people are not mean to drink and Joey Bonds is one of them sweetheart."

"What if he can't?"

"Joy he has to and if he can't...then sweetheart he needs to leave or you do," Pa said forcefully. "You have a home to come to always."

Betsy gasped softly. If she hadn't been sitting on my lap I wouldn't have heard her. What was she thinking? If Joy left Joey would I leave her? I tightened my grasp on her. She talked about it a lot. Yes, I had done the honorable thing but it went beyond that. She was my wife. It was a lifetime commitment. That is how I was raised. No matter what I felt for Joy.

"Where is he?" Joy asked softly.

"He's in the yard thinking."

"You told me this was forever. To be sure," she said her voice breaking. She was still holding my Pa's hand.

"And I just told him I would tell you to leave his ass if he picked up another beer."

She kissed my Pa's hand. "I love you Luke Moore. You know that?"

"I love you too Joy."

"I need to go outside and talk to him."

*Really?*

"Adam and I will sit on the porch."

*Again really?* I was the last person that needed to be in Joey's vicinity.

So Pa and I sat on the swing together while Joy walked unsteadily to the picnic table. Pa looked over at me.

"I think she needs to go the ER."

"Good luck with that."

"She's a stubborn little thing," he said to me.

"That doesn't begin to describe her."

We sat in silence for a while. From the porch we weren't able to hear Joey and Joy but I knew they were talking. I glanced at Pa.

"You still love her don't you?" He asked quietly.

"Do I have to answer that?"

I wanted to keep my feelings to myself. Private. Buried in my heart where they belonged. I rubbed my hand through my hair.

"You don't have to," he said.

"Do you think they realize it?" I asked.

"They being Betsy and Joey? Or is Joy included in that question as well?" He asked.

I sat back in the swing. My shoulder touched my Pa's shoulder. We were almost the same width now that I was a man. I could remember as a child sitting with him on this very swing and wondering if I would ever be as big as him. I was actually taller but cut like him broad with a thin waist. Joey was just big all over. Broad shoulders, barrel chested, big biceps, big thighs.

"Joy knows how I feel," I replied. "The same way she feels."

"Oh," my Pa replied. That was all he said for a minute. "If they know they hide it well."

We both worked hard to keep our feelings buried deep so our spouses wouldn't be hurt. She felt like I did. Our marriages were a commitment. A commitment we made. A commitment we took seriously. Had we screwed up? If they knew about the times that we had been together making love they would be crushed. Sometimes the temptation was too much so we just avoided each other.

### Joy

I walked across the yard. Joey was sitting on the bench at the picnic table staring at the sky. His arms crossed over his powerful chest. He didn't look at me.

"Have you figured out that I'm a fuck up?" He asked.

"Yeah I got that a long time ago," I responded.

He laughed. "Are you all right?"

I walked over to him and climbed into his lap.

"No, I'm not."

"I see your protection came out with you," he said glancing at the porch swing where Adam and Luke sat watching us but not watching us.

"Yep."

Joey's arms went around my waist. He drew me against him. "I can't tell you how sorry I am that I hit you."

"Joey, do you know how sorry I am that you actually took a swing at Luke? After everything he has done for us. You actually took a swing at him. He loves you like a son. I'm more upset that you hit him than me."

He buried his face in the crook of my neck. My hair fell over his face. Joey actually sobbed on me. His large hands gripped my back almost hurting me with the intensity.

I cupped his head and I held him. "Promise me that you won't drink again."

He nodded. His breath warm against my skin. "I promise. Luke told me you would leave me if I drank again."

I laughed softly. "Am I worth it Joey?" I asked him.

"Fuck yes," he said. "I've loved you since you were fourteen. You bout drove me crazy until you turned eighteen."

I laughed uncomfortably and I had loved Adam. I had given him up for Joey. To protect him. Concerned for him and Adam's relationship. I kissed Joey's head. He would never know what I had given up for him.

## Chapter Thirteen

### Joy

I knew something was going on between Mandy and Luke. She hadn't been at the farm since Noah's birthday. I was worried about him. He had been seeing Mandy for around ten years. Was she tired of waiting for him to commit? As much as I loved Luke Moore Mandy was a saint for waiting on his ass that long.

I left work at five o'clock as usual. I was stopping by the farm to see how Luke was doing even if he wouldn't talk to me. Adam had tried talking to him too but he wasn't having any of it. He wouldn't talk to either of us. I drove through town. I saw Adam's truck at the mill picking up feed. I pulled in beside him.

"Hey," I said as he threw a bag into the back of the truck.

He walked over to the car and leaned in. "Hey yourself. Where are you headed?" He asked.

"To the farm," I replied. "I was going to see how your father was doing."

"I've been gone for a couple hours running some errands," he replied. "He was a bear when I left."

"Have they broken up?" I asked him.

"Your guess is as good as mine. You don't think he talks to me."

Damn. "Are you almost done?" I asked.

"Yeah. That was the last bag. I just need to pay. I'm right behind you."

"Okay. I'll see you at the farm."

He told me goodbye. Then he walked to the back of the truck and closed the gate. I watched him walk inside to pay. He had a grace that was unusual for such a large man. When he disappeared inside the mill I put the car in reverse and backed out.

We still fought the attraction we had for each other. The love. The night Joey had knocked me out he had held onto me longer than he needed to. I had laid my head on his shoulder stealing a moment when I could just like him. It made life a little easier when I couldn't seem to stop loving him.

How things could have been different had I made a different choice after losing the baby? What would have happened to Joey? Would he have survived? Become a raging alcoholic? Killed himself on the motorcycle I had gotten him to sell?

The window was down, my hair blew about my face. I loved the fresh air blowing inside the car. The feeling of freedom that it gave me. I pulled the car into the lane next to my house. Betsy was home with Noah. I couldn't wait to see him. Joey was working late tonight. He had been working late a lot now that he had been promoted to manager of his department.

I drove past the house and saw the pond. My mind remembering Adam carrying me to the far side of the pond where we laid on sleeping bags under the stars. Remembering us making love. My heart beat a little faster in my chest. Involuntarily my body throbbed remembering the feel of him inside me. I squeezed my thighs together wanting the feeling to continue.

I turned into the drive and parked next to Luke's truck. I climbed out of my vehicle. There was no sign of Luke in the fields when I passed by. I put my hand over my eyes looking for him. I didn't see him. I called his name. No response. I ran up the porch steps and opened the front door.

"Luke," I called his name. No response. I turned and looked around again. I saw the barn door open.

I walked down the porch steps. I laid my purse on the hood of my car as I walked towards the barn. My dress shoes not the easiest to walk on gravel and dirt.

I leaned inside the door and called for Luke. No response. I stepped further inside the barn. The familiar smells of hay and horses filling my nostrils. I walked down the length of the barn checking the stalls looking for Luke calling his name. I turned the corner and saw his boots sticking out of the stall at the end.

Panic filled me as I ran to him. He was unconscious. I dropped down beside him. Luke was pale. His skin cold and clammy. I touched his chest. He wasn't breathing. My own breath caught in my throat. I gasped wanting to scream but nothing came out. I felt for a pulse at the base of his throat. Nothing. I laid my head on his chest and was met with silence.

Then the sound that had wanted to escape through my lips before did. I screamed one word. No. I kept screaming it over and over. He was too young to be dead. I lifted him even though he was heavy into my arms and rocked back and forth with him in my arms. I sobbed. My tears splashing onto his face and shirt.

I heard Adam call my name. Call Pa. Then I realized that he had heard my sobbing. His booted steps were heavy on the wooden floor of the barn. He skidded to a halt. He ran his hands through his hair.

"What the fuck happened Joy?" He cried.

"I don't know Adam," I answered. "But he's gone." I was sobbing again. "He's gone."

"No." Adam climbed over Luke's body. He was directly across from me now. He did all the things I had done. He felt for his father's pulse. He listened to his chest. He looked at me with such profound sadness that my heart broke into pieces. I was still holding Luke's body in my arms. "I'm going inside to call 911. I'll be right back."

I nodded.

Adam returned sitting outside the stall. His back against the wall. His head hanging low. Fifteen minutes later Sheriff John Sims arrived I knew him from when my mother had died. He came to the farm to tell me. He came with TJ Martin and paramedics. The paramedics wanted to take him from me. I wouldn't let them. I held him tighter in my arms. I wouldn't let him go. I sobbed on his chest. Holding him to me. They couldn't take him from me.

"Adam, can you do something with Joy?" I heard the Sheriff ask calmly and softly. "Son the paramedics need to check him out."

"He's gone Sheriff," I heard Adam say. "But I'll get her out of here."

"That's probably a good idea son."

I felt Adam's hands wrap around my waist. "Come on Joy." He pulled harder on me. Unwrapping my fingers from his father's shirt. He lifted me to my feet. His arm was around me holding me to his body while I sobbed. My heart broken.

I heard the sheriff say to TJ, "Call the coroner."

I cried harder. Adam scooped me into his arms and carried me out of the barn. His own tears wetting my hair and face. I clung to Adam. My grief overwhelming me. He sat on the bench by the picnic table with me in his lap. We clung to each other.

Betsy's car was flying up the lane towards us. Still Adam and I clung to each other. She jumped out of her car frantic. Noah was in the backseat in his car seat. She ran across the yard leaving her car door open.

"What happened?" She screamed.

I tried to move but Adam's grip on me was too tight. He raised his head looking over me at his wife. My best friend. Luke had taken us both into his home. "Pa's dead."

"What? No," she cried.

Her hands began to tremble. She walked over and sat beside us. Her body shaking. Adam kept his hold on me but put an arm around her and held her tightly too. He needed us both at that moment.

Luke's body was removed. We had called Mandy at home. The only number we had. Left her a voicemail to call the farm. Called Joey at work. Got his voicemail. Left him a message to call the farm. Betsy decided to take Noah back to the house.

"Take care of him," she told me before she left. "He's too quiet." She was talking about Adam.

I hugged her tightly to me.

I was on the phone with the funeral home when I realized that Adam had disappeared. I confirmed some arrangements and told them we would be there tomorrow to finalize everything.

I walked to the front door opened it and saw Adam walking across the field. His head was low. His shoulders slumped.

The phone rang. I took a last look at Adam and ran to the kitchen to grab the receiver. Mandy was frantic when I answered.

"What's wrong?" She asked as soon as she heard my voice.

Dear God. I took a deep calming breath. "Mandy Luke..." A sob caught in my throat that choked me.

"Joy what about Luke. Is he all right?" She asked her voice shaking.

There was no easy way to say this to her. I still couldn't believe it. My heart was shattered. Something had happened between them. She hadn't been coming around the past few weeks but I thought they would work it out given time but now there was no more time. This wasn't the way it was supposed to be. "He's gone Mandy. I found him in the barn tonight. He's gone."

Her cry filled my ears making tears of intense sadness that I didn't think I had left in me flow down my cheeks. They dripped onto my chest. Then the line went dead. "Mandy?" I said her name three times then I hung up the receiver. I laid my head on the wall next to the phone and I cried.

I kicked off my shoes and left them on the floor by the wall beneath the phone. I ran through the house. I closed the front door behind me. I knew where I was going. I was going after Adam. I knew where he was. I ran down the steps of the porch. I didn't hesitate. I took off across the fields towards the woods. I didn't stop until I reached the thorny bushes. My hands were cut and bleeding by the time I got through them. I pulled out the thorns after I got through.

I could hear the water now. I ran down the path towards the sound. Towards Adam. I stopped in the clearing. He was sitting on our rock. The rock where he had made love to me the first time. My breathing was loud and raspy. His head came up.

"What are you doing?" He asked.

"Looking for you."

"You shouldn't be here," he groaned.

"Why?" I almost cried.

"Because we are vulnerable right now. We just lost Pa. Joy, right now I want nothing more than to lay you down on this rock and bury myself in you so I can feel something other than the pain."

I walked closer to him. I stopped when I was standing right in front of him. I ran my fingers through his long black hair. The strands falling back into place perfectly no matter how long it was. I loved the feel of his thick dark hair on my fingers. I caressed his cheek keeping my hand cupped on his jaw. Adam turned his face into my hand closing his eyes. His lips caressed my palm. I loved his lips. I slid into his lap and his arms came around me. Clutching me to him.

"This is wrong."

I knew it was wrong as much as he did but everything in me screamed for him. Wanted his touch. Craving his body buried in mine. Wanting to forget the pain in my heart.

"Tell me to leave and I will," I whispered.

Adam's hands were on my ass clutching me to him. "Fuck you aren't being fair. I'm not that strong Joy."

He lifted me and laid me gently on the rock. He unbuttoned the blouse I was wearing. Laying the sides open baring my breasts covered by only my sheer purple bra. Adam's hands covered the flimsy material. Pinching my nipples through the fabric. He released the clasp and my bared breasts were suddenly in his hands. Then his mouth was on my nipples. First one then the other. I held his head to my breast while he kissed and nipped at them.

"We can't do this," he said sounding tortured. He rested his head on my bare chest and I held him to me. All thoughts of Joey and Betsy gone from my head. Adam was all I could think of right now.

I could feel his dick hard as steel against my stomach. Aching for my body as much as I ached him. He moved down my body pressing kisses on my stomach as he went.

"What are you doing?" I asked. I thought we weren't going to make love. I thought he had made up his mind.

"I have to see you. I have to touch you. To taste you. I fucking want to bury myself in you."

He lifted my skirt to my stomach. Adam slid my panties down my body. His fingertips grazing my skin as he did so. He laid them beside us on the ground. His hands strong and large separated my thighs. He dipped his head and touched his lips to the inside of my thigh.

"Joy, I'm lost."

"I'm sorry," I said. I didn't want him to be hurting.

"For what?" He asked huskily.

"For coming here. I didn't want to torture you. To hurt you. I needed you. He's gone Adam. He's just gone. I needed you so damned much."

He choked on his tears. He turned his head and kissed the softness of my thigh again. His hand brushed across my sex. My back arched off the hard rock I was lying on. Adam's mouth hot and wet touched me. Kissed me. Sucked on me until I was squirming. My hand went to his head holding him to me while the powerful sensations of his mouth took over my body. I throbbed against him my release hard and strong and he groaned.

Adam got to his knees. He unbuckled his jeans and dropped them with his boxers as far as he could while still on his knees. His dick was free. He grabbed my hips and slammed into me as I wrapped my legs around his waist. Adam wasn't gentle with the strokes into my body. He was rough and hard taking me with all the pain that he was feeling in his heart.

His head went back on his shoulders as he slammed into me. Our breathing was loud and hard. I was practically screaming his name. Luckily no one could hear me in the silent woods. Adam's hips moved faster. His body thrusting harder into me. His grip on my hips fierce. The groan that came from his chest was deep as he reached his own climax.

Adam cried my name as he thrust into me several more times until he couldn't thrust anymore. Then, he fell on top of me. His lips settling over mine not gently. They were hungry and consuming. Taking everything they could before he released me. He sat hard on his ass beside the rock. I laid there for a second before I sat up and pulled my skirt down.

"Are you angry with me?" I asked.

"No. Myself. I wish I had more self-control where you are concerned."

I touched his shoulder. "I think our self-control has been amazing."

He looked over his shoulder. He grabbed my panties off the ground and handed them to me. I stepped into them and slipped them up my body.

"Adam, we should get back to the farm. They will be looking for us eventually."

"You head back first. I need a minute."

I stood and helped him to stand. Not that he needed my help. He yanked his pants up his body and fastened them while I watched.

"What are you doing?" He asked.

"I don't know," I said. "I don't want to leave you."

"Go on. I will be along soon."

"Are you okay?" I asked.

He nodded. Gently he pulled me to him. His lips pressed against my forehead. "I love you Joy. With all my heart. I wish sometimes that I didn't. It would be much easier but I do."

My hands rested at Adam's waist. I felt the tears prick my eyes. I squeezed him gently. He let me go. Then I started to walk away. I turned on my heel before I had walked five feet. "Adam," I said. His eyes were locked on mine. "I love you too and I never wish that I didn't. Sometimes it's the only thing that gets me through the day."

Then, I left Adam alone in the woods.

Adam returned to the farm an hour later. I was asleep on the sofa. He woke me gently shaking my shoulder. "Hey Joy let's go home."

"That wasn't really soon you know?" I said stretching tiredly.

"I needed some time alone."

"Are you okay?" I asked taking his outstretched hand and letting him pull me to my feet.

I grabbed my shoes from the kitchen and my purse from the side table. I followed him to the front door. We shut and locked it. He looked down at me. The farm house seemed empty without Luke. I knew he felt it too.

"No regrets Joy," he said.

At first I wasn't sure what he was talking about. Then I realized he was talking about what had happened in the woods.

"Me or you?" I asked.

"Both."

"Okay."

He pressed his hand to my lower back and guided me down the steps. I left my car at the farm and rode to our house with Adam. He pulled in beside Joey's truck. He was home and hadn't come to the farm? I looked across the seat at Adam as he put the truck in park. I opened my door and jumped down to the ground grabbing my shoes and purse off the seat.

I followed Adam up the steps of the porch. He opened the door for me and I stepped in front of him and walked through the door. Betsy's eyes were the first that I met. She rose from the leather recliner. Her favorite place to sit. She walked across the room and grabbed me in her arms. We hugged tightly for several minutes. Guilt filled me, causing tears to flow down my cheeks. Betsy thought they were for Luke.

Joey was sitting on the sofa holding Noah. I could tell he had shed a few tears tonight as well. When Betsy released me I crossed the hardwood floor to the sofa and sat down next to him laying my head on his shoulder.

"Babe, you okay?" He asked.

"Exhausted. I fell asleep on the sofa at the farm waiting on Adam."

"Where was Adam?" Betsy asked looking between us.

"I went for a walk. I just needed to be alone. I woke her when I got back to the farm."

"The farm seems so empty without him," I cried softly.

Joey comforted me while I cried on his shoulder.

**Five Days Later**

We buried Luke at the local cemetery. The wake the night before had been open to the public. The four of us standing by an open casket. Mandy joined us from time to time. Otherwise she sat in the front row of chairs looking shell shocked pretty much feeling like the rest of us.

The lines to pay respects to Luke Moore at the funeral home were long. A two hour wait at one point in the night. So many people grieving along with us. We never felt more alone in our lives. The boys wore their grey suits that they wore when we had married them. Betsy and I chose blue dresses that we purchased just for today. Blue being Luke's favorite color.

Noah was staying with Bobby and Shay Martin. They had arrived early to see us and give their condolences. Then they left the funeral home with Noah in tow. He was happy enough to leave with them because he had a playmate in their son Timmy. He didn't understand what was going on. He didn't understand where Grandpa was.

Luke was forty-two years old and he was gone from our lives leaving an empty void that we were struggling to understand. Preliminary results of an autopsy showed major heart disease that had been left untreated. In the barn, he had suffered a massive heart attack. If one of us had been with him might he have survived? We would never know. Adam was doing a lot of soul searching about not being there. He was more quiet than normal not even talking to me which had everyone concerned.

I knew they were watching me closer as well. They were waiting to see if I would fall back into my old ways. Would I start starving myself? Would I have panic attacks? I made an appointment with Doc to be sure I didn't fall into my black void of emotional turmoil. I was taking the steps to ensure my health both mental and physical stayed intact.

At the end of the night we had walked to Adam's truck. Betsy and I holding hands with our husbands on either side of us holding our hands. Noah was staying the night at the Martin's home.

That night I was sitting in the dark on the sofa covered by the quilt trying to come to grips with the fact that Luke was gone. He had left a huge hole in my heart. I had left my bed so I didn't wake Joey or keep him awake tossing and turning. I heard Adam coming down the steps. His footsteps on the stairs light for a big man. I knew it was him. I knew his gait versus Joey's. My knees drawn to my chest. My head rested on my palm. My arms cradling myself.

He stopped in the living room. Seeing me in the moonlight shining through the window casting shadows across the room.

"What are you doing?" He asked softly.

He was in boxers bare chested. His hand rested on his chest. I might have startled him I think.

"I can't sleep."

"Me either."

He walked over to the sofa and plopped down at my feet. His arms were crossed over his chest. I reached out and touched a strand of his hair letting it slip between my fingers.

"You really need a haircut," I told him.

He laughed softly. "Pa had been telling me that for weeks," he said. "I may never cut it again or cut it all off now. Still trying to decide."

I quirked my eyebrow at him. He couldn't really see it in the dark though.

"I keep going over and over in my mind if I stayed too long somewhere. Maybe if I had gotten home earlier could I have saved him?" He said his voice filled with intense sadness.

I rested my hand on his shoulder. I didn't squeeze it or pat him I just rested my hand there. Eventually he covered my hand with his.

"You realize that is like saying if I stayed with my parents instead of moving to the farm with Luke my mother might still be alive."

His head turned towards me. I could see his surprise. "Do you really feel that way?" He asked.

"Sometimes," I replied quietly.

"You might also be dead," he said matter-of-factly.

"Adam we have no way of knowing if you were with Luke when he had the heart attack if he would have survived. You have to know that and believe it," I said forcefully. "He made choices. He was great at telling me I needed to go to the doctor, to the hospital even. You both are but he wasn't good at taking his own advice."

Adam chuckled. "No he wasn't. He ignored the signs that he had high blood pressure. The headaches. He didn't take care of himself."

"He was too busy taking care of the farm and us." Our hands were still resting on his shoulder. "Are you okay Adam? You've been so quiet since he passed." My voice showed my concern.

He looked at me. Then he was pulling me towards him. My back to his chest. I snuggled into his arms. We were both hurting so much over Luke's loss. He held me tightly. At first he didn't say anything. His lips caressed my hair in a gentle sweet kiss.

"I don't know how I am," he said sadly. His words a whisper against my hair. "I'm just lost without him. I now have the farm to run. He kept making jokes that he was preparing me to run it so he could retire. What if I'm not ready?"

His arms wrapped tighter around my middle. I rested my arms over his holding him to me.

"You've been doing this since you were a kid. You know what to do," I replied.

He nodded. We were silent after that. There were no other words to say. Our spouses found us like this the next morning. Holding each other. Consoling each other. Did it hurt them? Probably. Did they say anything to us? No. Betsy woke us letting us know we needed to get ready to go to the funeral home for graveside services. This part of the funeral was private just for family.

### At the cemetery

The sun was shining. The morning air cool but not cold. It was actually a beautiful day that we had to bury Luke. We stood by the open grave his casket being lowered when my knees buckled. I would have fallen to the ground had both Joey and Adam each not taken one of my arms holding me on my feet. I saw them over my head exchanging worried glances.

Then, they dropped dirt on his casket. I followed behind unable to bend down and pick up the dirt in my hand. It would have made it too final in my mind and I wasn't ready to let Luke go. I hadn't accepted the fact that I would never hug him again. See his smile or see his scowl for that matter. Then I heard the pastor telling us what a great man Luke was. His words sounding like the roar of the ocean on a stormy day in my ears so loud I couldn't hear anything else. Overwhelming. Frightening. Devastating.

### After the Graveside Services

Adam walked out of the Martin house carrying Noah. He handed him to Betsy in the back seat who buckled him into his seat between us. He was happy not understanding that Grandpa was no longer with us. I felt a tear trickle down my cheek. I wanted his sweet innocence for myself. I wanted to not have to bear this pain in my heart. His little hand reached over and covered my arm. I felt his little fingers tickling me. I turned my face to him.

"No cry, my Joy Joy," he said.

I wiped away a tear. I saw Adam look in the rear view mirror at me and I had to look away.

"I stopped Noah," I said choking on the words.

"Loves my Joy Joy," he said so sweetly. Joey looked over the back of the seat at me. I knew what he was thinking. We needed one of those. I smiled through my tears at Joey. Maybe he was right.

"I love my Noah," I whispered huskily.

Betsy reached across the car seat and grasped my shoulder. I patted her hand. I turned my head towards the window so Noah wouldn't see more tears. In the background of my mind I heard him talking about playing with Timmy Martin and how much fun he had.

At the house Adam extended his hand to me helping me from the truck. Joey did the same for Betsy. Noah was still busy chatting about his stay at the Martin house. I stepped out of the way to allow Adam to shut the truck door. We walked into the house the four adults quiet. Lost in thought. Missing Luke with every passing minute.

Mandy hadn't come to the graveside services. Betsy called her as soon as we walked in the front door. That was the first step Mandy took in separating herself from us. As painful as losing Luke was we were immediately forced to deal with the loss of Mandy too. She cut us out of her life week after week. First not coming for Sunday dinner. Then not taking calls and rarely returning them until she quit calling back all together. We finally stopped making an effort. A picture of Mandy and Luke in a perfect silver picture frame stayed on the side table long after it should have been removed but nobody could seem to put the damned thing in a drawer.

## Chapter Fourteen

### Betsy

Six months since Luke's death Adam has been withdrawn from everyone but Noah and Joy. Joey and I often find them asleep on the sofa together. Joy and Adam that is. Although since the first time the night before Luke's services at the cemetery they haven't been in each other's arms. They are usually asleep on opposite ends of the sofa.

I know there is a bond there. It has been there since Joy and I were fourteen when she met Adam Moore. I can still see her blonde ponytail bouncing back and forth as she traipsed behind him. Him giving her a look over his shoulder. I had known it even then. He had loved her. She had both of them wrapped around her little finger. I can see now what I should have seen then.

I know they both lost Luke. We all did but it was harder on the two of them than any of us. They shared the tightest link to him. I can only assume they have been talking most of the night. His big body takes up most of the space on the sofa. Sometimes Joy's feet are draped across him because she has no other room. It is damned hard I tell you seeing them console each other when I want him to come to me. I know Joey feels the same way. He and I have talked about it.

So being fearful that I was losing my husband I did what I had to do. Knowing this was a vulnerable time for him I seduced him. We used no birth control. I knew he wasn't ready for another child at the moment but I needed it. I needed the reassurance that another child would bring to our relationship. I had missed three periods.

So I sat in the bathroom by myself waiting for the pregnancy test to confirm that Adam and I were going to have another baby. Hating myself for my insecurities that led me to this point. Knowing deep in my heart that with or without another child Adam would never leave me. Regretting that I had taken advantage of him. I glanced at his watch I held in my hand. Time was up.

I knew the results would be positive. I don't know why I had waited so long to do the test. I had missed three cycles. I was never late. I stood and walked over to the bathroom sink. I picked up the pregnancy test. It was positive. I didn't know whether to laugh or cry. I tossed the stick in the trash can and went downstairs finding Joy fixing a protein shake getting ready to start her day at the courthouse. She was a court reporter now passing her classes and exams.

She was dressed for work wearing a black straight skirt and short sleeved red top. The red looked great on her. She wore open toed black pumps on her feet. Her hair was loose and down. Curls flying madly about her face. The only make-up she wore was a bright red lipstick. She looked stunning while I looked like somebody's mommy. Black leggings. Loose fitting tee shirt. Hair a tangled mess. No make-up and barefoot. We hugged briefly then she went back to her shake making.

How would she respond to my news? Would she be happy for me? She adored Noah. I loved how they responded to each other. She had no jealousy of the baby that I already had with Adam. Honestly, I didn't really think that she wanted to take Adam from me. Maybe just share a little piece of him? I was fairly sure they had not stopped loving each other but as his wife I really didn't want to know what that love entailed.

"Hey can I talk for a minute?" I asked deciding to test the waters with her first.

"Sure, I have time. I don't need to be at work for an hour."

"I'm pregnant," I told her.

Her face showed no change in expression at first. Was she shocked? Upset? Then she smiled a genuinely happy smile and I knew she meant it when she walked over to me and wrapped her arms around me and said, "Betsy I'm really happy for you and Adam. I think it will good for him. For all of us to have something good to look forward to."

"Why don't you and Joey have a baby?" I suggested taking her hands in mine. "We could have this one together."

"I think you have a head start on me," she answered softly.

"He wants a child so badly Joy," I said.

"I know."

Her eyes dropped to the floor. She and Adam did the same damned thing when they didn't want you to see what they were really feeling. They lowered their eyes. They hid their emotions, their feelings. Their true feelings. They both hid behind a mask, a wall they built to protect themselves or us. I wasn't sure which. I knew that only they allowed each other behind that wall to see the truth.

Joey walked into the kitchen. Dressed smartly in a navy suit today. He had taken over his department becoming the success he had always wanted. He hadn't touched a drop of alcohol since the day he had knocked Joy out in the yard at the farm after Noah's birthday party. He was working so many hours though he rarely home before seven or eight o'clock.

"Can I tell him?" I whispered. I probably should have told Adam first but he was already at the farm. Noah and I would go there later and tell Daddy the news.

She leaned against the counter watching me. Joy nodded her head nonchalantly sipping on her shake.

"Joey, guess what?" He turned from the coffee maker a look of perplexed interest on his handsome face. "I'm pregnant again."

He sat his cup down and stepped over to me. He hugged me briefly then he kissed my forehead. "That's great news Bets. I'm really happy for you and Adam."

"I'm trying to convince your wife we should have babies together this time."

His smile faded. "Good luck with that one," he said sarcastically. Joey stepped back to the counter and picked up his coffee mug.

Joy turned her back on us hiding whatever she was feeling. I sighed in exasperation at what was becoming of my family. The only one I had left in this life.

### Later that afternoon

I took Noah and lunch to the farm to see Adam and to tell him about the baby. I put our food on the picnic table. He waved from the field behind the barn. Then he stopped the combine he was driving and climbed down. Adam grabbed his shirt and drew it over his head. I don't think he realized how handsome and sexy he was.

He was close to being able to wear a short ponytail but I kind of liked it on him adding to his ruggedness and virility. My hand on my hip I ogled Adam as he walked across the field around the barn greeted by our son who was running at him excited to see his father. Adam scooped him into his arms and kissed him.

What would this next baby be? Who would it look like? Noah so obviously resembled Adam. Still holding Noah Adam leaned in and kissed my cheek when he reached me.

"This is a nice surprise." He smiled down on me. "How's my girl today?"

He was sweet and gentle. Always kind to me. Always making me feel special. Why had I been so insecure? Because deep down I knew the truth that I was second in his heart.

"Funny you should ask," I said.

He raised a thick dark eyebrow at me. His hands still wrapped around our son's bottom holding him to his broad chest. Noah's little arm around his father's neck.

"I'm pregnant," I said softly.

His eyes bulged a little like he was surprised. He swallowed. Then the mask came down. "I guess I'm not surprised," he said a little gruffly thinking about the lack of birth control.

I expected a little bit more than that as a response. Did I expect him to jump for joy? No. But not this gruff response.

"I'm trying to convince Joy to have a baby too so we can have one together," I said. Go big or go home, I thought to myself.

"I think you should let Joy make up her own mind when she wants to have a baby."

"Doesn't Joey get a say in it? He's desperate for a child."

"It's her body," he reminded me. "She has to live with the consequences of whatever happens. It's her decision first."

"Or maybe it's because you can't stand the thought of seeing her pregnant with another man's child," I snapped. Then I gasped and slapped my hand over my mouth. Distressed that I had said that to him.

"I'm going to pretend that you didn't just say that to me," he said angry and glaring down at me. Tears welled in my eyes as Adam walked away with Noah. "Let's see what your Momma has prepared for our lunch little man."

Deep down I knew Adam's main concern for Joy was another miscarriage. We had been through enough with her second miscarriage and now Luke's death. No one needed anymore tragedies right now.

He sat down with Noah and they ate lunch together. I kept my distance upset that I had been so mean. Adam buckled Noah into his car seat after lunch. When he straightened he said to me, "Did you make your doctor's appointment yet?"

"No, I haven't," I replied softly keeping my eyes averted.

He turned my chin up forcing me to look at him. "Let me know when so I can go with you," he said gently. Adam never stayed angry long. He kissed my nose before guiding me into the front seat of the car. He shut the door. Adam watched me drive down the lane before he headed into the house.

### Adam

I stood with my hand on the phone debating with myself. Finally I picked up the receiver and dialed her work number. She answered on the third ring.

"Joy, it's me," I said. "Would you meet me in the woods after work? Go the back way. Think you can find it?"

I didn't know what I was doing other than I just needed to talk to her. Maybe to hold her. To spend one hour with her without hiding how I felt about her.

### Waiting on Joy

I sat on our rock waiting for her. I had been here for an hour just absorbing the woods. The sounds. The sights. The peace. The trickle of water behind me reminding me of anther time so long ago when I brought her here.

I heard the rustle of bushes and turned to find her making her way through the thicket and brush barefoot in her black slim skirt and bright red top. She had pulled her blonde curls up on her head in a loose bun. Tendrils cascading about her face. She had on red lipstick and no other make-up. The sight of her taking my breath away.

"What is wrong Adam?" She asked as soon as she reached me.

"Where's your shoes?" I asked taking her in from head to foot.

"Black pumps aren't meant for walking in the woods," she laughed softly. She sat beside me on the rock. Her hand went to my shoulder. Then she leaned on it. "Are you going to tell me what is wrong?"

"Betsy is pregnant," I replied.

She leaned away from me for a second. "I know. She told Joey and me this morning. Is that why you are so upset?" She sounded surprised and concerned.

"She said she's trying to convince you to have a baby too." I hesitated. Did I tell her what else she said? Her words that had cut me to the bone.

"She is and Joey is starting to apply pressure too," she said sadly. "I'm afraid of another miscarriage."

I knew my girl well. She would tell me what she was thinking. We had secrets from everyone else but not each other.

"When I told her that it was your decision for that very reason she snapped at me."

"What did she say?" Joy asked.

I swallowed hard. "Maybe I didn't want to see you pregnant with another man's child."

"Ouch." She looked sad for a moment. Then she laid her head back on my shoulder. "I don't think that is it Adam."

I wanted her. I dreamt of her. With her sitting by me now her head resting on my shoulder I was at peace. I was living my life day by day filled with regret when I had no choice but to continue on. I turned my head and kissed her forehead.

"So you want to tell me why you drug me out into the woods?" she asked me.

"I just needed to see you. To do this without anyone watching or questioning me," I said honestly.

Pa's death had hurt. The wound deep and painful. I knew that both Betsy and Joey were hurting too but not like me and Joy. I knew she understood what I was feeling.

"Is this about what she said or about Luke's death?" Joy asked.

I glanced at her sideways. Then back into the woods. The sunlight was still bright and dappling the water's surface.

"Want to go skinny dipping?" I asked.

"Now me coming home soaking wet would be very difficult to explain Adam," she said teasingly. "Although a very tempting offer."

"I want to go back to that time when the seventeen year old and the nineteen year old kid made love on this rock." My voice sounded wistful and full of longing.

I heard her soft sigh.

"I was so mad at you Adam Moore when we got back to the farm and you asked Joey to take me home."

"I was mad at you," I clarified. "I thought you didn't know what you wanted and I had just taken your virginity. Talk about feeling lower than dirt."

She looked up at me. Those big green eyes. "I knew Adam. I just didn't know how to handle it so no one was hurt."

I turned back to the woods staring into the depths of the shadows revealing small animals like squirrels and birds flitting from branch to branch.

"Do you know what else I love?' I asked. I felt her head shake against me. "I love how you and Noah are together."

She chuckled against me. "He is easy to love Adam." Her voice was soft and relaxed when she responded. "My heart melts when he calls me my Joy Joy."

"You're mine Joy." Not that I minded sharing Joy with my son.

"Always," she replied.

We sat on the rock just talking. Joy resting her head on my shoulder. Talking about something Noah had done. Talking about Pa. She had loved him as much as me. Her eyes lit up when she talked about him. Tilting her head back laughing at something. Her laugh a soft sweet sound. Cooking with him when we had dinners on the weekends. Sitting with him during one of our games in high school.

"Do you know how relieved I was when he told me to sit tight he would be right there to pick me up when I ran away from Jack? I never looked back and he never let me."

"He adored you Joy. Don't you know that?" I said my voice quivering with emotion talking about Pa. His loss so fresh in me even though it had been six months.

"I loved him Adam. He stood by me through all the crap."

"You mean the Anorexia and the depression?" I asked.

"I do."

"Do you feel like we didn't?" I wondered aloud.

She looked at me contemplating her answer. "No, I know the two of you were always there for me. Sometimes you and Betsy keeping me on my feet but Luke was different. He handled me differently."

"He handled all of us differently. Especially Joseph."

"He did have a way with Joey. Now what do we do with him if he doesn't behave?" She asked.

I ran my hand over my jaw. "Starts drinking?"

She nodded at me.

"I can't make that decision for you. I won't stand by and let him hurt you again though."

"When Luke told me I could leave him and come home to the farm if Joey didn't straighten his act up your wife almost choked."

"I know. I was sitting there very close to her."

"You know what she was thinking?"

"I can guess."

"That will never happen," she said softly.

"I know." But I had these moments when I could pretend. "Will you come again to the woods if I ask you?"

"As long as it's not thirty degrees outside…yes. Maybe even then if you really need me."

I took her hand in mine. I pressed my lips to her palm then held it then to my chest. Near my heart.

"This was nice Adam," she said.

"Yes, it was Joy."

And we didn't have sex.

### Joy

I drove around the farm on the main road until I reached the house. I pulled into the driveway and parked. Climbing out of my car I grabbed my shoes and my purse and walked across the lawn to the porch. Betsy was sitting on the swing with Noah asleep in her arms.

"I almost didn't see you there," I told her. I was startled.

"How was work?"

"Great. How was your day?"

"I told Adam," she said. "At first he wasn't so excited. I think."

"I'm sure he was happy Bets. You probably caught him off guard."

"Did you think any more about having a baby too? Wouldn't it be great if our kids grew up together?"

"I'm afraid Bets." She went through both miscarriages with me. "What if I miscarry again?"

This conversation was exhausting. Between her and Joey I was feeling some pressure to have a baby.

"How far along are you?"

"I've missed three periods."

"You're just now finding out?" Why had she waited?

"I am."

"Why?"

"I screwed up Joy. Adam wasn't ready for another baby. I forced his hand so to speak because I was insecure."

Good God Almighty. We were a screwed up bunch. I put my arm around Betsy and we swung back and forth. It was the most relaxing part of my life spent on this swing or on the swing at the farm except for the visit to the woods with Adam.

"You have nothing to be insecure about. You know that. Believe that."

"I'm trying. About a baby for you."

"God woman will you drop it for now please. I just need some time."

"It's been a year," she told me.

I laid my head against hers. I watched Noah sleeping peacefully in her arms. His beauty. His smell were appealing. She handed him to me. She was playing dirty.

"He adores you."

"I adore him," I said absently looking at the toddler in my arms. I leaned closer to the arm of the swing so I could prop my arm. He was heavy.

"I'm going inside to start dinner. You okay?" Betsy asked me.

"More than okay. Thank you," I told her.

She left me then. Betsy went inside to start dinner. I rocked on the swing holding that sweet boy in my arms. I knew this is what Adam looked like as a child. His sweetness captivated me. His softness I kept caressing with my finger careful not to wake him. I didn't even notice Adam pull into the yard and park the truck. I didn't notice him walking up the porch steps.

"You'll make an amazing mother Joy."

I looked up at Adam and smiled. Pretending like I hadn't just seen him in the woods. Hiding out with him. Enjoying him like he was mine if only for an hour. I was relaxed and at peace from having that time with him. He appeared so as well.

"So what is this?" He asked softly. His voice deep and husky. Smooth causing warmth to spread through my body. My blood warming in my veins. I was so damned attracted to this man. I ached for him.

"This is your wife trying to convince me to have a baby with her," I said smiling at him. "She's like a little bug buzzing around my face. She won't give up easily once she's made up her mind."

"I'll talk to her," he said obviously irritated with Betsy.

"Don't Adam. Promise," I begged.

"If you say so."

Joey's car was turning in the driveway when Adam decided maybe he should go inside. I put my hand on his arm letting him know he should stay. I didn't want him to run away. No matter what did or didn't happen in the woods.

He was a handsome guy my Joey. He had swagger. In his suits he was something to behold. They fit him well. It was easy to love him. Deep down Joey was kind. He wouldn't hurt anyone intentionally. The times he had physically hurt me usually he had been drinking. They were accidents or him defending himself when he bent my arm behind my back to keep me from hitting him again. He didn't know his own strength. He was my big lug.

Did I love him? I did. I took care of him the way we all took care of each other. A sadness filled me. I lowered my eyes to the child in my arms. I did love Joey not the way he loved me though. It wasn't the consuming love I felt for Adam. It didn't have the burning desire attached to it. When he walked into a room he made me smile. I owed him much more than I had given him. He wanted a child of our own. Maybe it was time to give that to him. God couldn't be so cruel to take another baby from me.

"How was your day?" I asked him as he walked up to the porch. My voice soft and inviting.

Joey raised an eyebrow at me. He picked up on the tone. I smiled letting him know in that smile, in the twinkle of my eye that he was getting lucky later. He smirked at me acknowledging that promise. Joey loosened his tie. He leaned over Noah touched the softness of his head gently so not to wake him then pressed his lips to mine.

"I'm going in to take a shower," he said tiredly.

"Dinner will be ready probably in about forty minutes." I was basing this on when Betsy went inside and started cooking.

"Even better. I'm starving. Do you want me to take him and put him in his crib?" He asked.

I looked at Noah sleeping in my arms. He was hot sitting on the porch. The August air warm but not as hot as usual. I didn't want to give him up.

"I think I will just move inside to the air conditioning. I want to hold him."

He nodded. "I will see you at dinner."


*Joey*

I went to the kitchen first and said hello to Betsy before I headed up the stairs. I walked down the hall to our bedroom so I could hang up my suit first. In my boxers I stood in front of the mirror gazing at my body. I turned around and scrutinized my back. My head low I headed for the shower.

Standing beneath the spray my mind kept replaying this afternoon's events. Ria, one of the best of my accountants sitting in my office, door closed came around my desk. Her long dark hair straight and silky hung to the middle of her back. She turned my chair around so I was facing her.

"What are you doing?" I had asked her.

She proceeded to show me what she was doing. Ria had been flirting for months. I was actually younger than her. I had made manager after six months on the job because of some cost cutting recommendations that had saved the company millions of dollars. I had more in mind. They loved me. I was doing what I had dreamed of doing. Becoming a success. Working on my master's degree at a much slower pace than I had my bachelor's degree. I was going to be somebody.

So why did I let Ria unbuckle my pants? Her long thin fingers wrapped around my cock. She gasped at my size. I still couldn't believe it. I had cheated on Joy. I let this girl with her big dark eyes suck me in. She was beautiful. I had no excuses.

Once Ria had my dick out of my pants my mind was on nothing but getting her out of her panties. Her ass was small and firm. I palmed it thinking what it would feel like to leave an imprint on it. I didn't really know what she was into so for now I just touched her. I definitely was an ass man.

She dropped to her knees in front of me. We were supposed to be reviewing numbers for a board meeting. Everyone knew not to disturb us. The meeting was too important. No one would walk in on us. No one would know that she was sucking my dick like a pro. Except me. I knew.

Then she guided her skirt up her long, lean but muscular thighs. She was a runner I think. I seem to remember her talking about running some marathons. I'm young. Successful. I have a beautiful wife at home. Why was I letting this woman risk it all? Something was missing. Ria with her full pouty lips and her smooth skin tempted me once too often and I finally succumbed.

I yanked her to her feet. My dick throbbing to ram inside her hot center. I pushed her panties to the floor. She stepped out of them. I sat her back on my desk spreading her legs wide. I don't think I would sit here day after day and not see this beautiful girl spread out on my desk like this.

My mouth sought her warm center. I licked her until she was moaning so loud I was sure they could hear her outside my office. I had to shut her up. I rose and kissed her lips. She licked mine like she craved the taste of herself on my mouth. Fuck she was hot. My pants fell to my feet. I didn't have a condom in the office. What the hell now?

"Don't worry," she told me. "I'm on the pill."

I wrapped my arm around her waist and I buried myself inside her. She gasped.

"Good God Joe," she said. At work everyone called me Joe not Joey which was immature. "You're amazing. I love that big fucking cock of yours," she whispered huskily.

I smirked. I rammed myself into her hard and fast. She had no control over our bodies' movements sitting on my desk with my hand anchoring her to my body. Her legs wrapped around my waist taking all of me into her with every forceful thrust. I was cheating on my wife. The thought kept playing over and over while I slammed into Ria but I kept pushing it down into my subconscious.

Besides cheating on Joy. I was risking my job fucking Ria on my desk where anyone could walk in on us. I gazed into this crazy beautiful woman's face. I reached under her blouse and tweaked her nipple through her thin bra. Her head tilted back and her eyes closed. Her body trembled as she came around me. Her muscles tightening on me.

"Fuck," I growled. "You feel so good."

I knew that I would fuck Ria again. Preferably not on my desk. I was a dog. I knew it. Even when I knew all I wanted was Joy just waiting for her to turn eighteen I was fucking around with other girls.

Ria put both hands on my ass while I pumped into her the last few times that achieved what I needed a mind blowing orgasm. The kind where your vision goes black. Your head feels like it will explode if your dick doesn't first. I filled her with every ounce of me I had and it was fucking amazing.

We were breathing heaving when I dropped her legs to the floor. I reached down and grabbed her panties handing them to her. I yanked my boxers and pants up securing my belt after zipping my pants. What had I done? She kissed my jaw that was already showing signs of whiskers even though I had shaved this morning.

"That was something," she said. "I knew it would be. Who knew what you had this hiding in those suits?"

"That cannot happen again..." I looked into her beautiful eyes. "At least not here. We can't risk our jobs."

She quirked an eyebrow at me. "That's half the fun Joe."

She was damned enticing and damned dangerous I decided. Fuck I was in trouble.

I stepped out of the shower and wrapped a towel around my waist. She knew I was married. I had a picture of me and Joy on my desk. I think that was part of the fun for her. Having something she wasn't supposed to have.

I walked down the hall to my bedroom. I dropped the towel on the floor and grabbed boxers out of my dresser drawer. Unless I mistook Joy's expression she wanted sex tonight too. I was a dirty, dirty dog. Fucking two different women in one day. The only one should have been my wife.

### Joy

I slipped on a sheer light blue teddy. I had every intention of seducing my husband tonight. The matching panties left little to the imagination. I curled up on the bed waiting for Joey to come to me. He was watching the news with Adam. He promised no Carson tonight.

The silky material tickled my skin where it touched it. I found myself exploring my own body while waiting on him. My need causing an ache between my legs. I rubbed my hands across my breasts. I squeezed them twirling my nipples between my fingers. One naughty hand traveled south and slipped into my panties where thoughts of Adam filled my mind's eye much to my shame.

What if Joey came up? What if he caught me? Would he be excited seeing me touch myself? I was so wet when I inserted a finger between my folds testing my body's reaction to this new form of play. I touched my clit and my back arched off the bed. I ran my finger over and over the hard little bundle of nerves that created so much pleasure in my body. I moaned out loud.

Joey walked through our bedroom door. I was squirming on the bed. Touching my clit. Touching my nipples. Flicking them with my fingernails. He stopped dead inside the bedroom watching me for a second. I licked my lips. My mouth dry.

"What the fuck are you doing Joy?" He asked in a hushed whisper.

"What's it look like Joseph?" I answered sweetly. "I couldn't wait for you."

"Jesus Christ woman. I'm hard as steel already."

"Come closer Joey."

He did. He walked over to the bed and sat down. His fingers grazed my hips as he pulled my sheer panties to my ankles then tossed them to the floor. His eyes were intense and focused on what my fingers were doing to my sex. Rubbing softly. Dipping inside then rubbing again. I moaned deep in my throat.

"What the hell happened to you tonight?" He asked.

"Don't you like it?" I asked. My hair had come out of the loose bun I had put it in.

"Fuck yes I love it. You've never done anything like this before."

"I'm so close Joey," I moaned.

Touching, rubbing dipping my finger inside myself. I squirmed beneath my own touch. Joey stood and took off his shorts and boxers. He ripped his shirt over his head. He was naked. His cock getting harder by the second. I watched him take himself in his big hand rubbing the length of his shaft getting himself harder and I came undone. I came with such force that I thought I was going to explode. My head pounded. Colors danced before my eyes. My pussy throbbed as blood pounded in my clit.

"Joey, get inside me while I'm still throbbing."

He climbed up my body. Started to reach for the nightstand to get a condom. I stopped him. He looked at me with a puzzled expression.

"No condoms now. I want a baby of our own," I said the words so softly I wasn't sure that he heard me.

Joey's look at me so intense, so filled with love almost made me come again. His hand cupped my face. I could feel him hard against me.

"It will be fine this time Joy," he whispered in my ear.

I tried to believe him. I wanted to. I grasped his ass holding him to me. Joey entered me softly not rough like we usually did. I spread my legs wider to accommodate his size. My sensitive clit being rubbed with every stroke of his body into mine. It didn't take long before I was throbbing against him a second orgasm blowing my mind.

Joey continued to rock my body with his in slow even strokes. He sat up taking me with him until I straddled him. When his dick hit my center it felt like he was going straight through my center he was so deep. I groaned against his shoulder.

Joey grasped my hips rocking my body hard on his dick. I tilted my head back getting lost in the sensations taking over my body.

"Holy hell Joey. I'm going to come again," I groaned as my body trembled around him. My muscles tightened on his cock. My clit throbbed another furious rhythm on him.

He chuckled. "I love watching you come undone," he said. He was leaning back on his hands letting me use him. Letting me ride him to an overwhelming release for a third time.

"I'm not going to be able to walk tomorrow," I gasped. "Would you come already?"

Joey leaned forward grasping my hips in his hands. He guided the rhythm that he needed to come. My body began to tremble against his as my hips ground against him. My center was soaking wet and ready for a fourth orgasm. He stiffened. The muscles of his rock hard stomach were coiled tight. A sure sign his own release was close.

He flipped me onto my back. My legs in the air Joey held them tight while his hips ground against my ass. His eyes closed. He tilted his head back. He slammed into my body until he growled low in his chest.

"Fuck," he said as his body released into mine.

A few more thrusts of his hips and he was done. He released my legs and slowly crashed down on my body. His lips took mine eagerly. Hungrily. I wrapped my legs around his body holding him close. I hoped we had made a baby tonight. Betsy would be thrilled but I wasn't telling her shit until it actually happened or she would drive me crazy.

## Chapter Fifteen

### Joy

I got my period two weeks later. I have to admit that I was sad. Since I was staying at a pretty healthy weight my periods were pretty regular so we could try again in a couple weeks. I still hadn't told Betsy a thing. She was still bringing up that I needed a baby too. I just gave her a smirking grin that would have done Joey proud.

I walked downstairs feeling crampy and crabby. The three of them were already eating breakfast with Noah in his highchair. I planted a kiss on the little man's head. He smiled at me. I could see the love he had for me in his big dark eyes. I grabbed coffee and no breakfast this morning. Not even a shake. I felt too crappy to eat. They all looked at me when I sat down with my mug. I rolled my eyes.

"Cut me some slack. I started my period this morning," I told them. "You know how I am on my first day. My back hurts. My stomach hurts."

"You're a bitch," Betsy offered.

"Thanks," I gave her a smile dripping with sarcasm. "Little ears."

"I know. I know," she replied. The guys just smiled at us.

Joey rose from his seat and put his dishes in the dishwasher. He walked to my chair where he cupped my head and kissed my forehead so tenderly.

I could see in his eyes, in his face what he was thinking. *Maybe next month.* His lips touched mine briefly before he straightened to his full height.

"I gotta go," he said. "I have an early meeting."

"See you early tonight?" I asked.

"Maybe. I will let you know later."

### Joey

I called Joy telling her I was working late. Ria was pressuring me to spend time with her. I agreed to meet her at her apartment for an early dinner after work. I had to break this off. It had only been a few weeks. Sex on my desk. Sex in my truck. I was cheating on my wife. It had to stop especially now that Joy wanted to have a baby. I couldn't risk losing her. I couldn't risk my marriage period. End of discussion.

I walked up to Ria's front door and knocked. I had removed my suit jacket and tie leaving them on the seat of my truck. She opened the door wearing only tiny shorts and a tank top. Her long dark hair piled loosely on her head in a sloppy bun. She was beautiful. I had to end this tonight. No question. I kept telling myself that as I entered her apartment.

She lived in a small space. Neatly decorated with some paintings she had probably picked up at a bargain store but they were modern and cool. Her sofa and end tables were worn but expensive looking. We walked through her living room into her dining room. She motioned for me to take a seat at her table. Ria was finishing dinner.

I watched her in the small galley kitchen finishing the preparations for our meal. She walked over to me and slid into my lap. My arms went around her. My head was saying speak to her. Tell her this has to end but my body was craving her. My dick starting to throb wanting to go deep inside her. I wanted to hear her soft moans get louder as I made her come on me. *Shit this was no good.*

Ria wrapped her arms around my neck. "My bedroom is through there," she said pointing over my shoulder. My gaze followed to where she was pointing.

"You know we shouldn't be doing this? I'm married." There I had said it.

"I know but you want to Joe. Don't you?" She whispered huskily into my ear. Kissing the spot below my ear.

Fuck yes. I did want to. My dick was hard as steel. She was amazing. Ria was wild in bed. Full of passion and heat. In the office she was cool under pressure. So fucking smart. She was my employee grounds for both of us being terminated according to company policy.

Ria began to unbutton my dress shirt. Her hands slid the material down my shoulders until my upper body was bare. I reached for the hem of her tank and lifted it over her head.

She wasn't wearing a bra. I flicked my tongue across her hardened nipples and she ground herself against me. I stood with her in my arms. Ria wrapped herself around me. She nipped at my neck, my earlobes which she knew made me fucking crazy.

I carried her to her room. My hair a mess from her fingers running through it. Her chocolate brown eyes were twinkling when I dropped her on the bed. I toed off my dress shoes leaving them beside the bed and stepped out of my pants dropping them on the floor. I yanked her shorts down her body. No panties. She was naked before me. Spreading her legs for me to take her.

I crawled up her body and entered her swift and hard. Her nails raked my back in desperation. "No marks," I reminded her. "My wife can't find out about this." I thought I saw a hint of sadness before she masked it with desire as I filled her body with mine until we both dropped off the edge at the same time on a wave of intense pleasure. Our bodies trembling. Hers tightening around me then pounding out her release. She moaned as I released everything I had into her body.

I rolled off her onto my back. She was wild. Exciting. She was beautiful. She was forbidden. I thought that made her that much more exciting to my warped mind. Ria rolled over next to me. She snuggled into my side. My arm came around her holding her to me.

"I came here tonight to tell you it was over," I told her.

She raised up on her elbow to look me in the face. "And?"

"And I had no intention of fucking you first. I can't seem to get enough of you Ria." I brushed back a strand of her thick dark hair.

"Joe, we are good together. Don't break it off."

"I have to," I told her kissing her nose. Her cheek. The spot in the curve of her neck.

"I can see how much you want to."

I laughed softly. She was right about that. A part of me didn't want to give her up just yet. I knew that I had to eventually. Joy would be pregnant sometime in the near future. I couldn't run around with Ria screwing her brains out behind Joy's back if my wife was pregnant with my child.

I'm shallow and I know it. I shouldn't cheat on my wife but I've never been great at commitment. I have loved Joy since Adam introduced her to me. She was mine. Other women had turned my head since we married but I hadn't cheated on her until Ria. Something about this woman just got under my skin.

Ria Jackson was trouble. I was risking everything to bury myself between her legs and I knew that I could lose it all. Ria was like riding the motorcycle at one hundred miles an hour on the curvy roads around Pointe Royal. Wild and dangerous. I felt freer than I had in a long time when I was with Ria. I rolled her onto her back ready to go again.


### Joy

It was 11:00 PM. I sat on the front porch steps in only my pajama shorts and a tank top wondering where the hell Joey was. The evening was cooler for August. The temperature about seventy degrees. A tiny bit of perspiration clung to me.

Betsy had gone to bed at 10:00 tired from the pregnancy. She was about sixteen weeks now. She was stunning with a glow about her now that she was pregnant again. It definitely agreed with her. Only mild nausea which lasted about six weeks. The tiredness her only complaint so Adam and I picked up some of her chores forcing her to rest. Taking care of Noah more which wasn't a chore for me.

Adam walked through the front door joining me on the porch. He plopped his big frame down beside me.

"You're worried about Joey?" He asked.

I nodded. I was afraid he was drinking again. It wasn't like him to be so late.

"I'm sure he's fine."

"Did you check on Noah before you came out?" I asked.

"Yep. And Betsy. Both are sound asleep."

"She is more beautiful when she's pregnant," I said.

"She does glow," he agreed.

His hands were clasped between his legs. His thick muscular thighs brushing against mine from time to time while we sat there not really talking. He glanced at me sideways. His big dark eyes revealing so much. He was comfortable. He liked this time we could spend together. When no one was watching us. No one could see our feelings. Our emotions that we usually buried.

"So you and Joseph...trying to have a baby?" He asked.

I turned towards him. How had he known? "Did Joey say something to you?"

"No. It was the look that passed between you this morning when you said you had started your period."

I chuckled softly. "You know only you would have picked up on that."

"Obviously Betsy didn't or she would have been harassing you like crazy. What changed your mind?"

"Noah," I replied honestly.

He looked at me long and hard. Then he nodded like he understood me.

"I want what you have in him. I want to hold my own baby Adam. I love Noah like he were my own. You know if anything happened to you and Betsy we would care for him like he was ours but I need this too."

"I know," he said looking off into the distance. "I wish I could give it to you."

I sighed softly. *Me too*. I didn't say the words out loud. I covered his hands with mine and leaned my head against his shoulder. The love that we had was what fate or Jack dealt us along with a little of my own stupidity. We just had to keep dealing with it. We had no choice. No other options. We were both married to other people. He was expecting a second child with his wife. My best friend.

At times I told myself he was mine first to ease the guilt I felt when I thought about the cheating. It was a poor excuse for it though. No matter how Adam and I felt about each other we should be true to our wedding vows. Our spouses. We kept those feelings in check once again until Luke's death. I hadn't been able to stop myself from following him to the woods. I wanted to feel him inside me. I had wanted him to make me forget the pain of losing Luke.

"You're mine Joy," he said softly. Reminding me? Reminding himself. Even though we couldn't really belong to each other.

"I know," I answered honestly.

I was his. My heart belonged to him. My body too. Even giving myself to my husband, to Joey at times felt like a slap in the face to Adam. It was what I had to do. It wasn't hard. He was a beautiful man. It was hard because he wasn't Adam. Did Joey ever feel the little piece of me that I held back? I hoped not. I had sacrificed my happiness so he could be happy. I tried to make him happy.

Joey's truck turned into the drive. I lifted my head from Adam's shoulder. He put my hands in my own lap. Then he smiled at me tenderly.

"Want me to go inside?" He asked.

"No."

Joey lazily walked to the porch suit jacket hung over one shoulder. Tie dangling from his other hand. His shirt rumpled and untucked from his pants.

"What are you two doing out here?" He asked. "Kind of muggy tonight to be sitting outside."

"It's actually really nice tonight Joey. I was worried about you and Adam was keeping me company."

"Where's Bets?" He asked.

"Asleep," Adam answered. "She's tired."

He nodded.

"No need to worry about me Joy. I wasn't drinking." His eyes couldn't quite meet mine or if they did he looked away quickly. I glanced at Adam out of the corner of my eye. Did he notice Joey's case of nerves?

"What were you doing?" I asked softly.

"I told you I had to work."

I nodded. Not sure if I believed him.

"I'm going in to shower. Are you two staying out here?" He asked uncomfortably or tired? I wasn't sure which.

"For a bit," I replied. "At least I am."

We both watched Joey walk into the house and softly shut the door behind him. Adam and I said at the same time, "Did he seem nervous to you?"

Then I said, "I wonder what he's up to?"

### Adam

I'm always first up because I have to be at the farm early. There are animals to feed. Fields to take care of. Other things that start early in the day and end late at night sometimes. I was making coffee when Joey joined me.

"You're early," I said.

He grunted.

"What's wrong with you?" I asked him.

He ran his hands through his hair. "Tired I didn't sleep well last night."

I gazed long and hard at my best friend. I knew him well. Something was on his mind if he wasn't sleeping.

"You upset about something?" I asked.

"Just work," he replied.

"So you and Joy trying to have a baby?" I stated.

"Did she tell you?" He asked looking at me while he re-tied his dress shoes.

"She didn't have to. I saw your disappointment yesterday when she told us she had started her period."

"Yeah I was disappointed. I really want a baby with Joy."

"Why?" I asked.

Joey looked at me like I was crazy. "What do you mean why?" His tone was harsh. He wasn't comfortable with my questions.

"I think it's pretty simple Joseph. Why do you want to have a baby with Joy?" I repeated.

"Why are you asking?" He was becoming irritated with me.

"Just wanted to be sure you are doing it for the right reasons. Especially when she's taking a huge risk. She's really scared she will have another miscarriage."

"What do you think my reasons are Adam?" He asked standing so we were almost eye to eye. He was only an inch and a quarter or so shorter than me. We were both big men.

"I'd like to know Joseph."

"Fuck this shit," he growled. "I've got to be at work. I'll be home early tonight. Please tell Joy." He grabbed his suit jacket off the back of the chair and disappeared into the living room.

Fucker. I knew what his reasons were. I wondered if he would repeat them out loud to me. He wanted a child I knew. He wanted one now. His *desperation* as Betsy called it was because he had an itch. I don't know if he had scratched it or not but he definitely had an itch. I knew Joey Bonds. I knew how he operated. I knew from years of experience with him and other women. He was thinking a child would cement their relationship and force his hand. It would stop his itch.

I walked out onto the porch carrying my mug of coffee. Joey just a few steps in front of me. I called his name. He was irritated with me when he responded turning on his heel. He shoved his arms into his suit jacket. Shaking the lapels straitening them until the jacket hung like a second skin on him.

"I've known you a lot of years Joey. I've seen you with a lot of women. Do not hurt Joy."

"Where the fuck did that come from?" He barked at me glaring because I knew the truth.

"My hunch. With you my hunches are pretty damned accurate."

"Fuck you Adam," he growled between clenched teeth before he took off for the truck.

Yeah Joey had an itch. He could do whatever he wanted with that itch as long as Joy didn't get hurt. Who was I to say anything to him about where he stuck his dick? I had put mine where it didn't belong in his wife. I raised my eyebrow in concern. I watched Joey's truck pull out of the drive and start down the main road towards town.

I bet he will be coming home early a lot from now on. For a while at least. I shook my head as I went back inside.

### Joey

I saw Adam standing on the front porch watching me as I pulled out of the drive. I slammed the heel of my hand into the steering wheel. I needed to cool it with Ria. Damn Adam. He thought he was so perfect. Psychic shit he had where I was concerned. How did he fucking know?

A lifelong friendship is how he knew. He knew me better than anyone. They both could see my nerves last night when I came home so late. I hadn't meant to stay at Ria's until 10:30. Too late. She was like a drug. Addicting. Her body craving mine. Mine craving hers. We had sex at least six times last night before I cried uncle. She was on fire.

Her chocolate brown eyes were amazing when she was in throes of passion. I was a dog. I knew it. She knew it. Adam knew it. The only one who didn't know it was Joy. Maybe Betsy too. I might have pulled the wool over her eyes too.

I steered the truck mindlessly towards the highway. My hand rested on my forehead. Today, I was telling Ria we had to cool it. At least for a while. I wouldn't tell her that part. I had to make her believe it was over.

### Joy

I literally bumped into Adam on the way out of the kitchen this morning. He was heading to the farm. I had just taken Noah to Betsy in their room. Kissing him goodbye was the highlight of my mornings.

"Joey said he will be home early tonight," he told me.

I quirked an eyebrow at him. Threw a hand on my hip. "Hmm," I said. "Suddenly he can come home early? Interesting."

Adam lowered his eyes and walked around me to the kitchen. My black pumps clicking on the tile in the kitchen as I walked up behind him. I tapped him on the shoulder. He turned and glanced down at me.

"What?" He asked.

"What do you know?" I asked.

"I know nothing," he declared vehemently.

"Really?" I watched Adam's face carefully. "I think you are lying to me Adam Moore."

He put both hands on my shoulders. I blinked a couple of times trying to clear the swarm of emotion that he caused by his hands on my body. "I really know nothing."

He had looked me in the eye. "All right. I believe you."

I smoothed my royal blue silk tee shirt down. I had paired it with an A-line black skirt. My legs were bare, no stockings. I crossed my arms over my ample breasts pushing them up unintentionally of course. When I saw Adam's eyes pop I lowered my arms to my sides.

"I have to get to work," I said leaving him in the kitchen alone thinking god knows what because I knew what was going through my mind.

### Adam

I hated lying to Joy but no good would come of me telling her my hunches or suspicions. My guess was that Joey would be home early more often now so no harm, no foul. Right? I told myself.

I walked to the front door. Joy was gliding down the steps like she walked on air. Her hair was pulled to the side in a ponytail the hung over one shoulder revealing the gentle slope of her neck. I looked down at my jeans near my zipper. Fuck, I was getting hard.

I had better go tell my wife goodbye before I got into trouble. I thought of our school librarian Mrs. Hauke as I took the steps two at a time cooling my libido. She and Ruby who worked at the corner drug store had a lot in common. Both very nice women but not the most attractive.

I opened the door to my bedroom. Betsy was propped up in bed. Noah stood up and yelled, "Pop Pop."

"Hey little man. How are you this morning?" I grabbed him up and twirled him around. I leaned over and kissed Betsy. "Babe you all right?"

"I feel a little crampy this morning. Adam, I had some spotting."

"I won't go to the farm," I immediately told her feeling more than a little frantic.

"No, you go. I'm going to call the doctor later when she opens."

"Then I'm staying until we talk to her," I said.

She nodded uncertainly.

### Early Afternoon

We dropped Noah at Shay Martin's house while I drove Betsy to the doctor. I held her hand and kept reassuring her everything was fine even though inside I was scared. I was always the strong one. I was always making things right so I hid my fear.

Betsy's doctor examined her. She did an ultrasound showing us on the screen not that I could see what she was talking about Betsy had a condition called placenta previa. The placenta was covering part of her cervix. It could correct itself as the pregnancy progressed. She might need a C-Section if it didn't correct itself before this baby came. She looked terrified at that thought of surgery. I was plain terrified.

She asked if we wanted to know the sex of the baby. It was willingly showing off for us her doctor told us. I left these things up to Betsy. I didn't care what we had as long as it was healthy and Betsy was all right. Betsy finally nodded in agreement. She wanted to know.

"A boy," she told us.

Another son.

"You okay with that?" I asked her. She nodded with tears in her eyes.

"Another boy. Not that we could do anything about it if I wasn't happy," she said holding on to those tears.

"He'll keep Noah company," I suggested.

"Yes he will. Maybe the next one will be a girl?" She said.

"Can we have one at a time?" I asked her unable to keep the exasperation out of my voice.

She laughed softly.

*Joy*

I arrived home to find Adam up to his eyeballs with cooking dinner and Noah crying. I picked Noah up and carried him to the kitchen. I looked around unsure of what was happening. He looked at me and sighed.

"Thank God you're home."

"What is going on?" Where's Bets?" I asked.

"She's lying down. We ran into a little glitch today."

"And what might that be?" I asked bouncing Noah on my hip. His sticky hands clinging to my shirt while he started to wind down from crying so hard.

"I had to take Betsy to the doctor today." He stirred multiple pots on the stove while he talked. "She has placenta previa."

"What the hell is that?" I asked panicking. "Is she all right?"

He proceeded to explain the complication. Everything was fine but she had to take care of herself for the next forty-eight hours. Bed rest. Then after that as long as she was feeling well she could be up and about. She's spotting. They would like to see that stop."

"Oh Adam. But everything is all right?" I questioned him.

"Yes for now."

"I'm going to run upstairs and change and see her. I'll take Noah with me."

Adam walked across the kitchen. He sighed, relieved that he finally had help. Then he kissed my forehead.

"Thank you. Thank you so much."

"You should have called me. I could have come home a little early."

I carried Noah up the stairs to my room. I sat him in the middle of my bed. Poor baby. He had a rough day. Seems like his Daddy did too. I hung up my skirt, dry clean only. I put the sticky shirt in the laundry basket. I grabbed a pair of pajama shorts and a tank and threw them on in the closet so I could strip out of my panties and bra. I played peek-a-boo with Noah while I was in the closet until he fell over laughing at my antics. I left my hair in the pony-tail I had styled it in this morning.

"Come on little man. Let's go see your Momma."

I carried him to Betsy's room. She was reading a book. "This is going to suck if I have to do this too much," she said.

I laughed at her.

"How's Momma's little man?" She asked Noah.

He cuddled in the bed next to her while I sat on the outside edge. I patted her stomach softly.

"Everything okay in there?" I asked.

She rubbed her belly. "Declan is just fine for now."

"Declan?" I said raising an eyebrow.

"Adam didn't tell you? Another boy."

"Ah Betsy, good for Noah but I know you wanted the girl this time," I said.

I leaned over and she hugged me.

"I'm sorry the placenta previa sounds like it's going to put more pressure on Adam which means he's going to rely on you."

"I owe you guys. I will be fine. We will be fine. The most important thing is to cook that little fella as long as possible and for both of you to be all right," I added.

She took my hand. "We will be Joy. No worries."

I nodded. Then I grabbed Noah up in my arms swinging him around. "One of us will bring you dinner in a while," I told her.

She shook her head absently. Her nose already back in the book she had been reading. I called Joey's office number from the kitchen to see if he was really going to be home on time. He answered on the first ring.

"Are you leaving soon?" I asked.

"I am," he answered.

I told him about Betsy. Then we ended the call. He promised to leave work within a half hour putting him home in an hour.

### Joey

I hung up the phone with Joy and rested my head in my hands. Everyone had left for the day but myself and Ria. I asked her to come to my office. If I met her anywhere else I knew what would happen. She and I would fuck. She was too much temptation.

She opened my office door and shut it behind her. She was damned beautiful with her smooth skin, her chocolate eyes and her thick dark hair. My wife was beautiful too and I was going to lose her if I didn't break this off. I hadn't slept last night thinking of what I was doing. She walked her hips sash-saying as she made her way around my desk. I stood and put a hand up.

"We need to talk," I said.

She looked disappointed. Her hand on the desk she slid it seductively around the top as she walked to a chair on the other side. She took a seat crossing her legs. Beautiful long legs. Tempting long legs.

"Ria, I'm married. I'm not leaving my wife ever for anyone. You are fun. Exciting and drop dead gorgeous. I should never have allowed my head to get turned around. Joy and I are trying to have a baby. I can't do this anymore."

She rocked her leg back and forth irritated with me. "So we just work together with this chemistry between us? We work pretty closely together. Do you think you can handle it?" She asked.

"I can. I hope you can too. I didn't sleep last night worrying about my wife getting hurt by this. I can't do it."

"But you did do it."

"I did Ria. I'm sorry if I hurt you."

"You did Joe. You are hurting me but I'm a big girl. I can handle it."

"I'm glad. I enjoy working with you. There are so many more things I want to do. You're smart. We can do lots of great things together."

She looked annoyed. "I'm sure you think so."

I should have kept my dick in my pants. She left my office. I gathered my things together. I met her at the elevator leaving for the night. Ria looked at me sideways a few times while we waited for the elevator.

"You're sure about this Joe?" She asked.

"I am."

The elevator doors closed when we stepped through. I allowed her to go first trying to be a gentleman. We had six floors to ride down together. After two she stepped in front of me. Close, too fucking close. I could smell her perfume. A light fruity scent. She pressed closer until her breasts were against my chest.

"You're sure about this Joe?" She asked.

I nodded yes but I was still looking down at her with longing. I was sure she could see it. Then she cupped my balls through my pants and ran her hand the length of my shaft.

"You're sure about this Joe?" Ria asked me again.

One more floor. Fuck no I'm not sure but I have to stop it now. "I'm sure," I said through clenched teeth. Clenched so tight my jaw hurt. Then the elevator doors opened so I could sidestep her and leave the confining space. This wasn't going to be easy. She wasn't going to make it easy on me.

I walked to my truck a little stiffly because my dick was fucking hard as rock thanks to Ria. I deserved every minute of my torture.

I pulled into the driveway thirty minutes later on time or earlier than what I had said I would be. Everything would be all right now. I just couldn't fuck Ria again.

## Chapter Sixteen

### Joey

Joy was fertile again. Once she decided she wanted a baby she was relentless. She climbed in the shower with me one morning ready to fuck my brains out. Water has a negative effect on a woman's lubrication. She turned off the water and drug me out before I finished my shower.

I backed her against the bathroom door and entered her there. She wrapped her legs around my body and held on tight. Until Adam knocked on the door. He didn't know that Joy was in there with me. She giggled softly while he grumbled outside the bathroom door about me taking so long.

"I'll be right out dammit."

I climaxed Joy did not. She took my towel and wrapped it around herself. Pulled me down for a kiss and left me naked in the bathroom. Dammit. I peeked out and followed her down the hall as Adam walked out of his bedroom.

"Joy?" He said her name. We both stopped dead in our tracks. I didn't care if Adam saw me naked but I didn't want little Momma coming out anytime soon and catching me standing in the hallway. "You were both in there? Jesus Christ." He rolled his eyes. "The rest of us have to use that bathroom too."

"Sorry Adam. Just don't touch the back of the bathroom door." She tiptoed to our room with a little mischief to her step.

I followed my Joy to our bedroom chuckling at Adam's face.

When we got home that night from work she was ready again. She was changing clothes when I joined her in the bedroom. This time was a little more exciting. A lot more relaxed. I tossed Joy on the bed in her bra and panties. The matching set red and lacy. Fucking beautiful. I ripped the panties from her body tearing them into two pieces.

"Joey," she scolded me. "They were a set. You ruined them."

"Sorry baby."

I can't help myself sometimes. I love to rile the woman up before sex. She slapped at me. I held her hands down. She struggled against me. I lay on top of her so she couldn't move.

"Now what?" I asked.

She struggled for a second then she gave up. "You win. Is that what you wanted to hear?"

It was. I leaned in and kissed Joy softly and gently. My kiss full of love and tenderness. She fucking bit my lip. I tasted blood.

"Really Joy?" I sat up letting her get up as well. Then, she slid into my lap and ran her thumb across my lip. "I'm sorry," she said softly.

"You're a brat."

"I'm a horny brat," she teased.

Joy began unbuckling my pants. She slipped off my lap and pulled my pants down. Her hands were soft against my skin as she pulled my boxers down too. She pushed me and I was flat on my back. She took me in her hand and slid up and down the length of my shaft. Then her soft wet mouth covered me. She sucked taking all of me into her mouth.

"Oh hell Joy," I said grabbing a fistful of hair holding her head to my dick.

Her mouth continued to move up and down on me while her tongue caressed me. I was moaning deep in my chest. She was perfect.

"Joy, I'm getting close. Stop."

"What do you want me to do?" She asked.

"Get your scrawny ass on my dick," I said.

"My ass is hardly scrawny," she said climbing on top me. I smacked her ass as she settled over my dick taking it all inside her.

Joy rocked on my dick hard, circling her hips, grinding against me until I thought my head was going to explode.

"Christ woman, you're killing me."

I took her hips in my hands and guided them in slow hard circles while I thrust into her. Her hands rested on my chest pushing into me to support her weight. I was close. My balls felt like they were tight in my body ready to let go. The muscles in my belly tightened. She was panting. Her breathing coming in hard gasps of air. I had wanted to control this and she had quickly turned things around on me. She controlled me.

When I thought I couldn't hold out any longer. Joy's muscles tightened around me. Her clit exploded on me and I lost it. I gave her everything I had and then some. Was she happy? Hell no. She wanted it again after dinner. I just fell back on the bed. She really was going to kill me.

Joy dressed and told me she would meet me downstairs.

### Joy

I think Joey's had enough of me. I walked downstairs and helped Betsy and Adam with dinner. The small one turned and looked at me when I walked into the kitchen.

"So Joy, what is up with you and Joseph F-U-C-K-I-N-G," she spelled the bad word in front of little man, "like bunnies?"

"Not a damned thing," I played innocent.

Adam looked over his shoulder at me. This was hard for him. I could see it in his eyes. I lowered mine and bent to kiss Noah on the head. Joey walked into the kitchen. I had nearly bitten through is lip. I owed him more than a blow job and a quick fuck. His lip was swollen and bruised looking.

"Getting a little rough Joy?" Betsy asked.

I turned and looked at her with a puzzled expression.

"Joey's lip."

Adam looked over his shoulder again. Mumbling something about him deserving it probably.

"Thanks Adam. Let her bite you and see how you like it."

I was sure Adam said *Fucker* beneath his breath. Betsy raised her eyebrows at both Joey and Adam. Then she giggled as she saw the look on Adam's face then mine too flushed with embarrassment. I couldn't tell them that he was holding me down. That is why I bit him. Adam would get mad so I grinned and I let her tease me and Joey. If I got a baby out of this it would be worth it.

### Adam

Jesus Christ in heaven they are doing it again. Betsy looked at me sideways. One eyebrow raised. She was twenty weeks pregnant. Halfway there. Scared to death to have sex because of the placenta previa afraid we would somehow hurt the baby.

So I was listening to the soft moans of Joy getting fucked by Joey. Pure torture. Getting fucked for the third time today. If she didn't get pregnant this time I was going to be one crazy motherfucker before she did become pregnant.

I listened for a few more minutes before telling Betsy I was going downstairs to watch television. In the living room, I slid into the recliner to watch the news.

Joey came downstairs first wearing basketball shorts. Hair a bloody mess. Nail marks down his back I noticed as he went to the kitchen to grab a soda. He hollered from the kitchen asking if I wanted one too. He brought them both to the living room.

"She's going to kill me man," he said plopping his big frame on the sofa. He crossed his legs and rested his soda can on his bare chest.

"There are worse ways to die," I suggested grumpily.

He looked at me funny from across the room.

"She's ready now for a baby and it's like she's a mad woman. Once a day just isn't enough?"

I really didn't want to discuss this with him.

"I haven't had sex in four weeks. I don't want to hear your complaining," I grumbled. "Especially since I've been more than aware of you and Joy entertaining yourselves multiple times today reminding me of what I'm missing."

Joey started laughing. Then he noticed his wife standing at the bottom of the stairs. "It isn't nice to discuss people behind their backs," she said with a snarky attitude.

"How much did you hear?" I asked.

"Oh I heard big mouth over there complaining about me killing.him. Life's tough Joey."

Joey laughed even harder.

"You want a black eye to go with that lip mister?" She asked.

I had to smile. She was starting to act like her old self. Fiery and feisty when we riled her which didn't take much. Never had. Little Joy had a volatile temper. I had been missing this side of her. She could be this way one minute and soft and gentle the next. Right now she just looked damned beautiful. Hands on her hips glaring at us both. Her curls a wild mess about her head. Looking like she just been fucked. I wish it had been me though.

"Get over here," Joey commanded. "You can cuddle with me while we watch TV."

I was hoping she wouldn't do it. I didn't want to have to watch them cuddle after being forced to listen to them have sex. She declined. *Thank you Jesus.* She went to the kitchen for a glass of water.

She returned to the living room with her water in hand and climbed over his feet settling herself in the corner of the sofa. Joy covered herself with the quilt off the back of the couch. The quilt we had taken to the pond with us to make love under the stars so long ago. Damn I was semi hard thinking about it. I pulled my legs up on the recliner so neither of them would see my dick. Not like I could get up and leave the room now.

We were quiet watching the news. Joy sipping her water. She cocked her head to the side her gaze locking with mine. She smiled. I wondered what she was thinking. Joey started drifting off. Snoring softly. Eventually he got up. Kissed Joy's lips and headed upstairs to bed leaving us alone. This was not a good idea.

Joy continued to sip on her water holding the quilt to her chest. It didn't matter how much she covered I knew what was beneath that quilt. I swallowed hard. We had made love in the woods after Pa died. Desperate for each other. Wanting to make the pain go away. It wasn't right. She closed her eyes. What was she seeing now? Was she imagining what I was? Her beneath me. Her softness enveloping me. Fuck I was going to need a cold shower.

"I think I should go to bed," she said huskily.

Joy threw aside the quilt and rose from the sofa. The vibes in the room intense. She started walking towards the kitchen. To return her glass I thought. I couldn't take my eyes from her face, her body as she disappeared into the kitchen. I rose from the recliner and followed her. I just wanted to touch her just once before she went to bed. That was it. Nothing more. I was starving for her.

She was putting her glass in the dishwasher. She straightened and turned towards me. I was standing in the doorway to the kitchen. Her eyes were big and round and full of wanting. I licked my lips. I couldn't make love to her. We couldn't risk it. We couldn't keep doing this but I just wanted to touch her. Joy walked to me.

"Let me by Adam," she said tentatively. I was blocking the door with my body.

I reached out cupping the back of her head with my hand beneath the massive curls on her head. Her soft silky hair cascading over the top of my hand. I closed my eyes for a second getting control of myself. I thought neither of us were breathing in that moment. I bent my head to her and gently kissed her lips. Her hands went tentatively to my waist. Holding me loosely. Not encouraging me but not letting me go either. She responded to me softly. Her mouth opened to mine allowing my tongue to dance with hers. Then I had to pull back or I would lose control. I continued to look into those beautiful green eyes of hers.

"You're mine," I whispered.

"I know," she answered.

I stepped aside releasing the hold I had on her. Her hands fell to her sides. She walked past me and then turned gazing at me with interest.

"Why did you do that?" She asked me so softly.

"Because I had to," I answered.

### Joy

I had Betsy in the bathroom with me standing guard over the pregnancy test while I sat on the toilet seat lid down of course. I was late by a week. I didn't know which of us was more nervous. Me or her? The men in our house didn't keep track of things like women's cycles so neither of them had guessed. Betsy was aware I was late after three days. After a week she produced a pregnancy test. It was a Saturday morning Joey was still sleeping and Adam was in the kitchen with Noah preparing breakfast.

"God how much longer Bets?" I asked.

"One minute sweetheart," she said. "You know you're pregnant."

"We'll see," I responded.

She was holding Adam's watch in her hand timing the test. A watch he never wore. Not knowing the time would drive me batty. He seemed to know close enough without the watch what time it was so he never wore one. It was one of his strange abilities.

"Ready?" She asked.

"As I ever will be," I responded nervously.

She picked up the test and let out a scream of exaltation that brought Joey out of bed and Adam up the stairs knocking on the bathroom door wanting to know if she was all right. They didn't know I was in the bathroom with her. She opened the door. I was still sitting on the toilet. My knees shaking. She kept looking at me wanting me to say something. I couldn't. I was too upset. Good upset not bad upset.

The test was positive. I was upset happy not upset sad. I was pregnant. Sitting on the toilet seat in the bathroom with two men peeking in at me wondering what was going on I said a little prayer to God that he protect the child growing inside me. Then I took a deep breath and let it out in a deep whoosh.

I was going to be all right.

"Are you going to say something?" Betsy asked.

"As soon as I can speak more than a few sentences," I replied still in shock.

"Can I tell them?" She asked softly. She was so happy for me and they were looking at us with concern.

I nodded.

She held up the pregnancy test in front of their faces. "She's pregnant."

"Fuck yes," Joey hollered grabbing Adam in a hug that prevented me from seeing Adam's face. I didn't know what he was feeling. I was always conscious of him. Always worried about him.

Joey released Adam and came to me. He scooped me up in his arms and hugged me against him. Twirling me around the small space. "Everything will be fine this time," he whispered in my ear.

I actually believed Joey when he said it. I thought this baby would be all right and I started to cry. I didn't know why. I just started to bawl my eyes out. Joey put me down. "Are you all right?" He asked.

He looked to Betsy for help. She walked over to us and took me in her arms. "It's all right sweetheart," she said soothingly. "This time it will be all right."

She was holding me so that my face was facing the bathroom door. I finally got a good look at Adam who was sprawled across the doorway. Strong muscular arms resting above the doorframe. He winked at me which made me want to cry harder. He was all right too. That was important to me.

Suddenly we heard whimpering from the kitchen below. A tiny voice calling Momma, Pop, Joey or Joy Joy. Anyone who could hear him. We all looked at each other in confusion. Adam's look of horror that crossed his face was comical. He had left Noah in the kitchen alone when Betsy screamed at the positive result of my pregnancy test.

"Jesus, I'm an idiot," he growled before he turned and ran down the stairs. We all followed him.

In the kitchen he had picked Noah out of his high chair and held him close to his chest. "Pop is sorry little man. I didn't mean to leave you alone for so long."

We all stood in the kitchen doorway and watched Adam console Noah with smiles on our faces. Adam didn't make mistakes like this one. Noah had his head laying on his father's shoulder while Adam caressed is back lovingly. Joey stood behind Betsy and me. Somehow we would make it through this parenthood thing together.

### Two Weeks Later

### Joy

We rarely used locks on things like bedrooms or bathroom doors. Thank you Jesus because I woke up two weeks later to the worse case of morning sickness I had ever had. I threw Joey's arm away from me and bolted from the bed. Somebody was in the shower but at that point I could have cared less. I dropped to my knees in front of the toilet bowl and lost the contents of my stomach.

It was Adam in the shower. He stuck his head through the curtain. "Are you all right?" He asked with obvious concern. Water dripping onto me and the floor.

"Do I look all right?" I asked flushing the toilet without thinking.

"God dammit Joy you just scalded me," he yelled.

"I'm sorry," I cried. Then I really cried big crocodile tears streaming down my face while I held my head in my head trying not to vomit again. My stomach feeling like I had just gotten off a roller coaster ride.

"I'm sorry for yelling at you." He actually squatted down in the shower and patted my shoulder. "Baby are you all right?"

I shook my head no. There wasn't much he could do but pat my back since he was naked in the shower. Betsy appeared in the bathroom doorway.

"What's wrong? I heard you shout." She rubbed her eyes sleepily. Then she tried not to laugh.

"It really isn't funny," Adam said.

"It is," I agreed. "The boys are going to be crazy by the time they get through two pregnancies in the same house. Bright idea you had here Betsy."

"Morning sickness?" She asked.

"Bad," Adam said still rubbing my back. "She flushed the toilet without thinking. Got a little toasty in here."

"I'll bet. I will go get her some saltines," Betsy said.

"Wake up Joey," I said. "Let him get the crackers."

Betsy left the bathroom. Joey stopped by the bathroom with Betsy behind him. I was afraid to leave the toilet afraid my stomach would betray me again. He kissed the top of my head lovingly. *Just get me the damned crackers.* I smiled weakly at him from my spot on the floor.

Betsy plopped on the floor next to me when Joey left to go to the kitchen. Adam looked at us strangely. "Finish your shower Adam. We aren't going anywhere. I don't think she can."

"Wonderful," he replied.

"Adam you're just showering unless you had other things in mind," Betsy snapped.

I just shook my head.

"Not me," he declared. "I'm not given any privacy to possibly whack off and take care of my own needs."

Betsy started laughing. I couldn't help myself I giggled too. He jerked back the shower curtain a little.

"Glad you ladies think I'm so funny."

We just chuckled. Joey returned with the saltines. He handed me a pack. I nibbled on the cracker. He ran his hands through his hair. Looking at us really strangely.

"What Joey?" I finally asked.

"Are you really going to just sit there and eat crackers? Adam is showering."

"All Adam wants to do is whack off in the shower," Betsy declared. "It's our job to torture him."

Joey almost choked when Betsy said that. I shook my head trying to focus on the crackers and not vomiting again. Adam snorted in the shower. He turned off the water.

"Would someone mind handing me a towel or would you like for me to step out naked and grab my own towel?" He asked grumpily.

Joey looked around for the towel. Joey didn't know it but I had already seen Adam's stuff. Everything he had I knew intimately so towel or no towel made no difference to me. He picked up Adam's towel from the counter and handed it to him through the curtain.

"Thanks Joey," he grumbled.

"I come in?" Noah asked rubbing his eyes sleepily.

"How did you get out of the crib Noah?" Betsy asked.

"Crime out," he replied honestly. He sat on his mother's lap and laid his head against her chest. His thick black hair standing on end in the back. His blue pajama shorts askew like he had a rough night sleep.

"My Joy Joy sick?" He asked checking me out.

"No little man," Betsy replied. "She is having a baby like Momma. Sometimes the baby makes her feel bad for a little while."

"My Joy Joy not having a baby," he replied very matter-of-factly.

*Uh Oh.*

Adam opened the shower curtain, towel wrapped around his lean hips. He had run his fingers through his hair making it nearly perfect. I hated him right now for his perfect hair.

"Well ladies," Adam said. "Now what?"

"He'll get used to the idea," Betsy replied easily.

Joey looked confused. "He wasn't upset about your baby was he?" He asked Adam and Betsy.

Betsy chuckled. "Nope," she replied. "He's just not willing to share Joy."

Noah rose and walked over to me. He plopped down on my lap. My stomach revolted but I kept from throwing up by breathing deep. I put my arm around his little waist and hugged him then kissed the top of his head.

"My Joy Joy not having a baby," he repeated adamantly.

I looked over his head at Betsy then up at Adam and Joey. Joey reached for Noah. "I'll take him down for breakfast," he suggested.

"I think that's a brilliant idea. Your wife looks green," Adam replied before he wove his way through the throng of people in the bathroom and disappeared into the hallway.

Noah allowed Joey to take him. Betsy stayed with me. My stomach felt awful but I didn't throw up again. We stayed in the bathroom though talking while I leaned against the tub and sucked on saltine crackers.

"Do you think Noah will be okay with this?" I questioned Betsy really concerned by his reaction.

"Yes," she answered looking over at me. "He will be fine. He'll have months to prepare being a big brother to Declan before your baby comes. I'm positive he will be fine."

"Are you ready to go downstairs?" Betsy was getting uncomfortable sitting on the tiled floor.

"I was just going to ask how long you two were planning on hanging out in here." Adam had returned.

"Help me up big guy," she told him. She held her hand up to him. Adam took it and pulled her easily to her feet.

"Do you need assistance?" He inquired of me as I still had my ass parked on the floor.

"I think I can make it," I said.

I climbed to my feet and immediately my world began to spin Adam caught me before I dropped to the floor or into the tub.

"I think you should put her in bed," Betsy said to him.

"Good idea," he responded.

She backed out of the bathroom giving him space. Adam lifted me into his arms and carried me to my bedroom. Betsy opened the door for him and he went in alone with me. I wasn't sure where she disappeared to.

"I know I'm so drop dead handsome and all but swooning in my presence was a bit much don't you think?" He teased before he deposited me on the bed.

"Yeah that was it," I agreed with Adam. I still clutched my little pack of saltines to my chest.

"You afraid somebody is going to steel those from you?" He asked.

"Maybe," I replied. "This is worse than the first time. Last time I didn't have any morning sickness. I guess another indication that things weren't quite right?"

Adam sat on the edge of the bed. "Maybe," he agreed.

"Maybe things will be okay this time," I said hopefully a little too softly.

"I know it will Joy." He sounded confident his hand resting on my leg.

"Hey Betsy said you almost passed out," Joey said busting into the room.

Adam lifted his hand from my leg and rose from the bed. Joey was going to get all protective now that I was pregnant.

"I'm fine Joey."

I noticed that Adam left us alone in our bedroom.

## Chapter Seventeen

### Joey

Office gossip I heard at the water cooler suggested that Ria was pregnant. I nearly choked on my coffee as I passed by. I went straight to my office passing by her cubicle not saying a word to her just wanting to check her out.

Joy had made it through her morning sickness like a trooper. It was rough on her. Betsy had never been like this with either boy so there were many mornings when she was sitting on the bathroom floor while somebody was in the shower with Betsy sitting on the floor by her holding her hand. Joy was eighteen weeks pregnant. We were going for an ultrasound next week. They expected to be able to tell the sex of the baby if we wanted to know. It would supposedly look more like a baby than the clump of cells at her first ultrasound. She wanted to find out what the sex was. I didn't care. As long as she made it through this pregnancy without miscarrying I was happy with whatever sex we got. Every week I breathed a little easier.

Until I walked by the water cooler, my happiness with mine and Joy's baby blown to pieces by a little piece of news. Maybe it wasn't true? Wouldn't Ria have told me? She had tried at first to break me down and get me back into her bed. When she realized it wouldn't work Ria was all business barely meeting my eyes during meetings. We had accomplished three of our goals for the new year. She had been setup for a promotion to Senior Accountant. I thought things were going well. Then this.

At the end of the day I saw her at the elevator getting ready to leave. I asked if she could stay for a minute. She looked uncomfortable. I tried to see around the suit jacket she wore to see if she had a belly. Joy was shorter than Ria. Ria was also more athletic maybe she hadn't gained any weight? I was dreading this conversation as she followed me to my office. Ria set her items she had been carrying in one chair and sat in the other. I shut my office door behind us.

"Are you pregnant?" I asked. No sense in beating around the bush.

Her head snapped around like she had been slapped.

"Good news travels fast," she sniped.

"Did you tell somebody in the office and expect me to not hear it?" I asked incredulously.

"No Joe, I told no one. Someone caught me throwing up here at the office several times. They put two and two together along with the little belly I got going on that you haven't seemed to notice."

"What are you going to do about the baby?" I asked sitting behind my desk asking her the question like I was asking about the effective interest rate method of amortization.

Her face flushed with fury. "What exactly do you mean Joe? I'm almost twenty-one weeks pregnant. I'm keeping my baby." She was snippy when she finished speaking.

Damn, this was not going well. I was putting her o the defensive. "I didn't mean anything by it."

"I'm sure you did."

"Why didn't you tell me?"

"You were so ecstatic Joe over the news that you and your wife are expecting a child it hardly seemed appropriate that I tell you about my news," she declared with anger and hurt.

"I thought you said you were on birth control pills," I said wearily.

"I lied. Are you happy? I fucking lied. I wanted you so much. I wanted this baby. I thought I could trap you if I got pregnant. Happy?" Ria crossed her arms over her chest in a defiant air. "I thought we could make such a great team."

I leaned back in my chair. Shocked by her outburst.

"You knew I was married Ria," I said sadly.

"My head knew that Joe. My heart didn't listen so well."

"I don't know what to say," I said. She was having my baby too. What the fuck was I supposed to do now?

"Nothing," Ria said trying to hold back the tears. "You say nothing."

"I can't really do that Ria. That's my baby too."

"As you said Joe. Your wife is expecting a child. Your wife. I'm nothing to you."

"Don't say that," I cut her off.

Her hands were trembling now. Her voice soft and husky. "Consider this my resignation. I'm leaving town. I've been thinking about it for a while now. You just helped me make up my mind. I think it's best for everyone if I just go home to my family."

"Where is that?" I asked.

"I don't think...I don't think you need to concern yourself with that Joe."

"Ria," I began. Could I live with not knowing my child? Could I live with knowing there was a part of me existing in the world a boy or a girl that I didn't know? It would destroy Joy if she knew. "Ria, don't rush into anything. Give me a few days to think this through."

"Please don't do this. Just let me quit. Go home to my family. Don't make me give two weeks' notice. That would be too hard for me. I screwed up. I got myself into this." She stood. I stood. "Let me get myself out gracefully."

"What if I want to know my child?" I asked feeling a sense of panic and dread fill my gut.

"I will let you know when the baby is born but I think that is all that is appropriate."

I stepped around the desk while she gathered her things. "Please don't do this," I begged. "Just give me a couple of days to think about the right way to handle this."

"Joe," she laughed bitterly. "The right way to handle this would have been for us to not do what we did in the first place." She sounded so sad when she said those last words. She turned on her heel and walked out of my office. I walked around my desk and plopped down in my chair running my hands through my hair.

"Fuck," I shouted to the empty space. What had I done?

*Later that evening*

I walked through the front door and found Joy in a panic. Adam was still at the farm. She ran down the steps.

"Careful babe. You might fall," I said softly. Still upset about the days' events.

"You have to go to the farm and get Adam."

"What's wrong?" I dropped my briefcase by the chair.

"I've called 911 Betsy is bleeding heavily. You have to go get him," she said. I could see the terror on her face.

"I will baby. I will. Everything will be okay. I promise." I kissed her forehead quickly. She bolted back up the stairs. I was worried she would hurt herself on the steps.

I raced to the farm in the truck. I saw Adam in the field. I started laying my fist on the horn. He saw me and stopped the tractor he was on and looked at me. I stopped the truck and climbed out. I waved my hand for him to come to me. He was scared. From here I could see it on his face. He ran across the field leaving the tractor where it was.

"You did turn it off didn't you?" I asked him.

He nodded trying to catch his breath. "Joy or Betsy?" He asked finally able to breathe.

"Betsy," I replied. He climbed into the truck. "She's bleeding. Joy called 911."

"Fuck," he ground out between his teeth.

I backed into the field and whipped the truck around and pulled back onto the lane. When we pulled into the driveway the ambulance had arrived. Joy was holding Noah in the hallway while the paramedics were in the bedroom with Betsy. Adam touched her arm and Noah's back before he went into the bedroom with them. I walked to Joy and took Noah.

"Go in there with them," I told her.

"I don't know," she said reluctantly.

"I do," I declared.

She looked at me gratefully and gave Noah a kiss before she disappeared into the bedroom. I kissed Noah myself. Man I loved this little guy. I had felt his brother move inside Betsy. She was always accommodating with me letting me feel him move inside her. I was nut about it. I knew I had driven her crazy. There was something about her pregnancies that enthralled me. I had been that way with Noah too. Couldn't wait to feel my child move inside Joy. I would never know what Ria's child felt like beneath my hand. What a fucking mess I had created.

I carried Noah downstairs to the kitchen. I dropped my suit jacket in the recliner and pulled off my tie leaving it in the chair as well.

"Joey, Momma ok isn't she?" Noah asked me.

"Yeah little man. She will be," I replied hugging him just a bit tighter to me. I put Noah in his high chair. "What sounds good for dinner Noah?"

"Mac and cheese," he said happily.

I just laughed at him. "I think we need something more than that buddy."

"Mac and cheese Joey," he repeated slapping his hands on the highchair tray.

"I hear you buddy. I hear you." I saw the gurney taking Betsy out of the house. "I will be right back little man. Just going to the living room for one second."

Adam followed behind. "You've got Noah," he said frantically.

"Yeah man. Little man and I are fine."

Joy came flying down the steps nearly falling down the last two but she caught herself using the bannister. Adam and I at the same time said, "Dammit Joy be careful."

"We're going to the hospital. I will call you later. Love you," she said, words running together, not acknowledging she nearly wiped out on the steps.

I watched her and Adam climb into his truck and pull away. I went back to the kitchen to Noah.

"Mac and cheese Joey." The little man demanded.

"Mac and cheese it is little man."

*Joy*

I grabbed two sodas from the vending machine near the waiting area where Adam and I waited. Betsy was in surgery. I walked back to the waiting area and stood over Adam who was leaning on his knees head bent low. He looked up at me. His face troubled. His eyes glistening with unshed tears. He laid his head just above the curve of my belly on my chest. His arms went around me.

"I'm so scared," he whispered.

"Me too," I said. "They'll both be all right."

"Promise?"

"I do Adam. It can't be any other way."

I held him for a while. Me just standing between his legs holding Adam. Both of us afraid for Betsy and Declan. Finally he pushed me gently away. "Sit."

I took the seat next to him and held onto his hand. He kissed the top of my hand. "Thank God for you and Joey," he said.

"We're lucky to have each other Adam. Since Luke died I've realized it even more. How lucky I am to have all three of you."

He nodded.

It was an hour later when the doctor came out to see us. He looked grim. Adam rose before I did. My hand slipped from his. I rested my hand at the small of his back holding onto him. Grounding him. His body was trembling.

"Adam, your son is doing great. He's a big healthy boy." I heard Adam's breath release from his chest.

"Betsy?"

"She's weak. She lost a lot of blood. I'm sorry Adam We had to do the hysterectomy. We couldn't stop the bleeding. Adam, we had no other choice."

Adam looked at me with concern.

"She's alive Adam."

He nodded.

She was young. Too young for this to happen. I wasn't sure how she was going to respond to this news. No more babies. I looked at the floor half listening to the doctor talk to Adam. He told him we could see her in half hour when she was taken to recovery. Half hour. Seemed like an eternity to Adam and me.

A nurse came to us next. She took us to the nursery so we could see Declan. She handed him to Adam first. I had to stand on my tip toe to see his face. I pulled off his little cap to see he had the same wild ass hair that Noah had. Thick and black like Adam's head of hair. Same dark eyes, same full lips but there the resemblance to his father and brother ended. I thought the rest of him might be his mother other than he was big. Much bigger than Noah had been. He was a whopper.

"He's beautiful Adam," I said putting Declan's cap back in place. Caressing his cheek.

"Want to hold him?" He asked.

"When you're done."

He slid him into my outstretched arms. I guess he was done. We didn't have long before they would take us back to see Betsy. I gazed down on him resting on my belly. He squirmed a little in my arms.

"Can you believe it Adam? Two beautiful boys. I wonder what Joey and I are having."

"A gorgeous little girl like her mother," he responded quietly. "Someone to lead my two boys around by the nose."

I laughed at him. "Gosh I need to sit. He's heavy."

Adam guided me into a rocking chair that was close. I sat down with the heavy boy in my arms trying not to disturb him.

"What does he weigh Adam?"

He walked over and looked at his card in his crib. "Twenty-four inches long and ten pounds four ounces."

"Damn boy, you are a big one. I thought your brother was big boy," I said smiling at the little guy in my arms.

Adam walked over to the rocking chair. He ran a long finger down his son's face. All kinds of emotions ran across his face before his gaze met mine.

"She's going to be devastated Joy. She's too young for this to be happening to her."

One of the nurses let Adam know that we could see Betsy. She was in recovery. I kissed Declan's brow and passed him to Adam who also pressed a kiss to his son's forehead before laying him in the crib. He took my hand and we left the nursery to see Betsy. She was out of sorts from pain medication. Yet we still convinced her that Declan was fine. She wasn't sure what else was going on and we didn't tell her. There would be plenty of time. Adam and I decided to stay with Betsy for the night. From a payphone in the hallway, I called Joey to check on him letting him know what had happened.

"Hey babe."

"Joey," my voice broke.

"Is she all right?" His voice sounded fearful. "Tell me she's all right."

"She's okay but Joey, they had to do a hysterectomy."

The line was silent. He said nothing.

"Did you hear me Joey?" I asked.

"Yeah babe. I heard you. She'll be all right though? The baby is all right?"

I was nodding my head. Tears falling down my face. "The baby is...Declan is beautiful Joey. He's a big boy. Over ten pounds. Wait till you see him. Betsy will be fine."

"Her life is what is important babe."

"She's so young Joey."

"I know sweetheart."

I wiped the tears from my face with my sleeve. "How's Noah?" I asked.

"Sleeping like a baby," he said proudly. "Fed him mac and cheese. Bathed him. Read him three stories and put him to bed."

"Mac and cheese Joey?"

"That is what the kid wanted," he said in his defense.

"Joey, what are we going to do with you?"

"Love me," he replied easily.

"That is easy," I said to him. "I'm going back to Betsy's room now. We'll see you tomorrow morning some time. Betsy won't come home for two or three days."

"I'll see you tomorrow. Love you babe."

"Love you Joey."

I hung up the telephone receiver and stood there for a moment to collect myself. Betsy was still in and out of it but I didn't want her to get any idea that something was wrong. I went back to the room and found that Declan had been brought to the room. Adam was holding him. There were two comfy chairs side by side on the far side of Betsy's bed. I took one next to Adam and just watched him holding his son. He was much more comfortable with Declan than he had been with Noah.

"Noah and Joey doing okay?" He asked me.

I laughed softly. "They are fine. He's fed, bathed and in bed."

"Good." Adam looked at me quickly then back to Declan.

"I would tell you what he fed him but I'm sure you've done the same."

Adam raised his eyebrows at me. "Mac and cheese," he guessed.

"Noah's favorite," I replied.

Adam laughed softly. "He has Joey's number."

"That he does," I agreed.

I had never been happier sitting with Adam. Sharing Declan. Caring for Betsy. Helping her sip water from a cup. Hold Declan when she was alert enough. Sleeping in chairs side by side waiting for either Declan or Betsy to need something. Dreading the moment when we had to tell her about the hysterectomy.

### Joey

It was odd being in the big house all alone. Just Noah asleep in his room. I had checked on him once or twice. Adam had talked to me about them moving to the farm before our baby came. He felt like it might be time. Nobody was living in the farmhouse. It was huge with six bedrooms and three bathrooms. Betsy wanted to fill those bedrooms with children. I was sitting in the recliner thinking about her two beautiful boys wondering what to do about Ria's child. I hadn't been able to completely accept in my mind that it was mine as well.

Even though it was 10:00 PM I rose from the recliner and went to the kitchen. I dialed Ria's home number which she had written in my planner. She answered on the third ring. Her soft voice husky with sleep. I told her it was me. I could hear the sigh that escaped her before she started to speak.

"Joe, what do you want?

"Ria, we need to talk."

"We said everything that needed said today." She sounded tired and sad.

"I'd like to see you and talk to you please." I was practically begging her to hear me out.

"No. There is nothing that can be done to make this right Joe. I screwed up."

Maybe she had but there was a child involved. I at least needed to help her with that child.

"I could help you financially."

"You know I don't need it," she whispered into the phone.

"What am I supposed to do Ria?" I felt helpless. Frustrated at the situation.

"Joe, you're supposed to let me leave town like I want. Have a baby with your wife and enjoy your life."

A thought suddenly occurred to me.

"Have you had an ultrasound? Do you know what the baby is?"

She was quiet for a minute. Was she debating telling me?

"I have Joe and I know."

I felt the tears well in my eyes. The emotion of the moment choking me. "What are you having?" I asked.

She was silent again. Would she tell me?

"A boy," she replied softly.

I laid my head against the kitchen wall. The tears silently gave way. I was having a son with Ria.

"Ria…"

"Joe no. I'm leaving town. It is the best for everyone. I told my parents tonight about the baby. They are thrilled. I'm going home to them. They will help me get on my feet. Watch the baby while I work. We'll be just fine."

"I won't be," I replied.

"I'm sorry."

She was crying softly now.

We talked for an hour. I wasn't able to convince her that she should stay. I didn't know what to do. I couldn't offer her anything but financial support. She didn't want that. She was hurt. She wanted love. I couldn't give her that. I wanted to know my son. I couldn't do that without possibly destroying what I had with Joy. She promised to send a picture when he was born. She promised nothing more.

I laid down on the sofa and covered myself with the quilt. I didn't think sleep would come easily that night. My thoughts were filled with my son that I wouldn't see. I wouldn't know. I didn't know how to make things different. I thought about going to Ria's apartment tomorrow to try to convince her in person to stay but I wasn't sure it was a good idea. I didn't know where that would lead to. She still had a hold on me. Pulling me back into her bed would not get us anywhere. I just wasn't sure I could let her leave.

### The next morning

"Joey," a soft voice calling my name waking me from a deep sleep. A gentle touch on my shoulder.

I jerked. Startled out of sleep. I bolted upright. I ran my hand through my hair.

"Joy, you're home."

"Adam made me come home. I'm exhausted. I'm going to rest for a while and go back later. He thought maybe we could take Noah to Shay if she's willing and you could come with me."

"I would like that," I answered.

I rose from the sofa. She started to walk away. I called her name. Joy hesitated turning towards me. I walked to her and wrapped her in my arms just wanting to hold her. She didn't know why. She didn't know the heartache I was feeling. If I told her would I lose her? Could she forgive me? I kept silent and held her tightly.

"Are you all right?" she asked me.

I nodded.

We checked on Noah. He was sleeping soundly. Joy told me Adam hadn't told Betsy about the surgery yet. He was dreading it. I could understand that but she was alive because of it. We had to help her understand that. We went to our bed and Joy stripped down to her underwear. She was exhausted and didn't bother putting on anything else. She climbed into bed in her silky panties and matching bra. I slipped into bed beside her pulling her to me. My hand cupping her rounded belly. I hadn't been able to feel the baby move yet although she had felt little flutters of movement.

Absently my hand caressed her where our child rested inside her. Her skin smooth and soft to my touch. I kissed the curve of her neck. I wasn't trying to entice her into sex. I just wanted her to be close to me.

Joy rolled over facing me. She laid her hand on my face. Her head tilted towards mine seconds before her lips captured my lips in a warm gentle kiss. My hand rested at her waist loosely just holding her. Her hand went up to my hair. Joy ran her fingers through my hair letting it fall back into place while her lips caressed my lips in a sensual slow tease.

Joy pushed me onto my back. She crawled on top of me straddling my hips. My dick grew hard as she ground herself against me. My hands went up to cup her face. Her beautiful green eyes filled with desire locked only on me. How could I have cheated on her my mind asked?

I removed my hands from her face and unclasped her bra. Her breasts a little fuller from the pregnancy spilled into my hands. They were more sensitive as well. She moaned as I played with them. Joy let the straps slip from her shoulders. She tossed the bra onto the floor. I rubbed her nipples and kissed them until she was squirming on me like a crazy woman gasping for breath.

"Oh Joey," she kept moaning my name. It was such fucking beautiful sound.

I pushed her onto her back. I slid her panties down her legs my fingertips touching as much skin as I could along the way. I tossed the panties on the floor with her bra. With my tongue I flicked her nipple with my thumb I rubbed her sensitive clit until she was groaning in a husky breathy way. I inserted my fingers inside her and continued to play with her while watching her come undone on my hand. I loved this part. Her face a myriad of pleasured moments crossing her beautiful features. Her green eyes simmering with desire. Her breath coming in short gasps. Her body arching off the bed.

Then she closed her eyes. Her head tilted back on the pillow. Her mouth opening as she gasped. Her body throbbing on my hand. I flicked her nipple with my tongue to increase the climax of her body and she moaned deep in her throat. I didn't stop rubbing on her clit until she squealed for me to stop. I removed my shorts. Stroked my dick a couple of times making sure it was nice and hard. Joy was soaking wet for me ready for me. Waiting for me to take her while she was still sensitive. She loved for me to get inside her when she was still sensitive from an orgasm.

I rolled on top of her. Holding myself above her so I didn't squash the baby. I was a big guy. I buried my dick inside her warm wet folds. Closing my eyes I reveled in the feel of her surrounding me. I groaned as I penetrated her, the feel of her. Joy groaned with me.

"Damn you feel good," I told her.

She chuckled softly as I began to stroke her body with my own. I kept the rhythm slow and steady driving her body crazy with my own. We both needed this. She had been frightened she would lose her best friend last night. So much blood. I was losing my son. So much pain. We both needed to block out something with this…a good fuck.

I held Joy's hands above her head pushing her breasts out. I licked them making her moan as I continued to thrust into her body.

"Let my hands go," she said.

I did and she dug her fingers into my ass as she wrapped her legs around my waist.

"Leave some skin Joy."

She laughed at me. "I am Joey. I am." Her hands moved up to my back. Her breathing was getting raspy again. Her muscles tight. She was getting close to orgasm again. I knew her signs. I pushed my body up on my hands pushing my pelvis harder into her pelvis. She gasped.

"Oh fuck yes Joey. Harder baby."

"It won't hurt the baby?" I asked.

"No," she said holding me tighter, urging me deeper into her body.

I thrust harder and faster into her. Her legs tightened around me. I closed my eyes. Her beautiful green eyes were replaced by big chocolate brown ones. My heart raced. My eyes shot open. I slammed into Joy harder. She gasped as her body clenched around me and her body found sweet release taking me with her. I called her name several times before I stopped thrusting into her. Sweat glistening on both of our bodies. I rolled to my back taking her with me. I held Joy close. We slept until I heard Noah calling for help. His way of saying he wanted up. I had to chuckle at the little man. He was a funny little guy.

### Mid Afternoon

Joy and I were walking into the hospital to see Betsy. We had dropped Noah off at Shay and Bobby's house. They were always willing to help with Noah when we needed them. Shay hugged Joy and told her to tell Betsy she was thinking of her. Shay had given birth to their second son Shawn three months ago. Another easy birth for her. I hoped Joy's was just as easy.

I held the door open for Joy to enter first not really sure what to expect. Adam still hadn't told Betsy about the hysterectomy. Betsy looked really good. She was sitting up in bed. Joy told her the color was coming back to her face. She and Adam exchanged uncomfortable glances. I knew what they were thinking. Soon they needed to tell her. Declan was sleeping in his crib. I just wanted to get my hands on the little or not so little guy. I walked over to the crib and peeked in after giving Betsy and hug and kiss. I touched his cheek. Took off his cap so I could see his thick dark hair. Yep, he was Adam's kid all right.

"Joey, you can hold him," Betsy told me.

I smiled at her. She knew me. I was itching to get a hold of this kid. I scooped him out of the crib into my arms. He didn't like this hold squirming against me. So I laid him against my chest. Declan kept trying to hold his head up. I looked at Betsy in amazement. Newborns just didn't do this did they? Declan did. His determined eyes met mine. I loved this kid instantly.

I could see the stubbornness. The determination. He was a fighter. Bigger than his brother had been at birth. Jamie had always been bigger than me. A bit tougher. A determination in his eyes that I could see in Declan's newborn eyes. It brought tears to my eyes. I sat down in a chair with him. I held him close. Something in this child touched my heart. Tears slowly ran down my face.

"Joey are you all right?" Joy asked me.

I couldn't respond. The words would not come out of my mouth. It was like God had given me a second chance with my brother through Declan. My hand rested firmly on Declan's back. I knew that I would protect him with my life just as I would Noah. I nodded. Adam looked at me oddly. He didn't understand my reaction. None of them would. I wasn't sure I understood it myself. Maybe it was losing my son and gaining another. I didn't know. I didn't question it. I felt peace for the first time in a very long time. I kissed the baby's head.

Adam walked over to the chair where I was holding his son. He patted my shoulder. Maybe he did get it after all.

I held the Declan for a long time. They let me. No one wanted to take him from him because of my reaction to him. I held him close and rocked him. When he was hungry I gave him a bottle. When he needed changed I changed him. I had bonded with the little guy in a very short time. When I laid him in his crib my hands trembled. I really didn't want to lay him down. I didn't want to release him just yet but I knew I had a lifetime of holding him of loving him. Something I wouldn't have with my own son.

Betsy was napping. Adam, Joy and I stepped out into the hallway. He knew he had to tell her. He just didn't know how. When she woke from her nap. Joy told him he had to explain what had happened. They were releasing Betsy tomorrow. She was coming home with Declan. We offered to stay with him while he told her. He nodded his head. He needed us.

### Adam

Joy was holding Declan now. She rocked him gently cooing softly to him. I didn't think Joey was going to let her hold him at first. He rested on the slight mound of her growing belly. Just as Joey was always touching Betsy I got to touch Joy. It was a weird relationship the four of us had to anyone looking on the outside in. Joey always talking to my wife's stomach. Touching her. He loved her I knew. He just didn't love her the way that I loved his wife. He didn't feel the way I felt when I was touching his wife's belly. We were a fucked up bunch but we needed each other. Now more so than ever. We were just waiting with dread for Betsy to wake so I could tell her about the hysterectomy.

When she finally woke she stretched awkwardly trying not to hurt her incision. I helped her to sit up. Joy handed Declan to Joey who took her seat in the rocker with my son. Joy climbed on the bed next to Betsy and put her arms around her.

"What?" Betsy asked.

"We need to talk to you," Joy said quietly. She wasn't going to let me out of it this time. I had chickened out too many times.

"What's wrong? Something with Declan?"

"No sweetie. He's perfect."

"Then what is it?" She asked beginning to get teary.

I sat on the edge of the bed near her legs. I took her hand in mine. I knew this was going to devastate her. I didn't know how much. She was young. Too young for this to happen to. Women in their early twenties didn't have hysterectomies unless they were dying. Betsy would have died without it. I had to make her understand that.

"Betsy when they took Declan during the C-Section you were bleeding heavily," I began.

"I remember," she said uncertainly.

"They couldn't stop the bleeding," I told her.

She looked at me then at Joy. I couldn't go on. I couldn't tell her. Joy sighed heavily.

"Bets," Joy said sadly. "They had to do a hysterectomy to save you." Her voice got quieter as she said the words.

"What?" Betsy's one word was filled with so much pain. I squeezed her hand harder. Joy held her tighter. "No."

"Betsy I'm sorry baby. It was the only way to save you. You had lost so much blood. You would have died otherwise."

"Adam, how could you let them do that to me?"

Joy's eyes met mine. I knew Betsy would be angry. Hurt. To blame me? Had never crossed my mind.

"Adam, I can't have any more babies." She turned her head into Joy's neck and sobbed. Her hand slipped from mine. She spurned my touch.

Joy looked at me sympathetically. Her eyes told me to be patient. My heart felt like it had been cut into two. It was my fault. I had signed the paperwork giving permission. I dropped my head. I rose from the bed and walked to the window staring into the distance. I had taken what Betsy wanted more than anything to fill our house with children.

Joey rose from the rocker and placed Declan into the crib. He walked over to me and put his hand on my shoulder. "Hey let's go to the cafeteria."

I nodded. I followed Joey out of the room and down the hallway to the elevators. In the elevator he pressed the button for the first floor. As we rode the elevator down I felt myself coming undone. My shoulders began to shake. I lowered my head and covered my eyes with my hand. Joey grabbed me and pulled me to him. He held me tight in his arm.

"Man she didn't mean it. She's hurting."

"It is my fault though. I am the one that signed those papers letting them do this to her."

Joey shook his head sadly. "You don't really believe that do you? Betsy would have died otherwise. Adam, man don't do this to yourself."

I wiped the tears from my face when the bell dinged letting us know the elevator doors were about to open. I kept my head low. Joey guided me through the hallways to the cafeteria. He sat me at a table.

"Have you eaten anything?" He asked.

I shook my head no.

"I will be back."

Joey brought back coffee and a cheeseburger and fries that looked somewhat edible for hospital food. He had a coffee for himself. He shoved the plate in front of me.

"If you need more let me know," he said.

I nodded taking the burger in my trembling hands I took the first bite.

"I'm going to have a son," he told me.

"You and Joy?" I asked with food in my mouth. "I thought your ultrasound was next week."

He snorted in a disgusted way. I looked at him puzzled. He looked away. Unable to meet my gaze. I grew uncomfortable in that moment waiting for him to say more.

"No. His mother's name is Ria. You were right about your hunch. She's a little further along than Joy."

Jesus Christ. What had he done?

"She told me she was on the pill." His eyes met mine now. They were despondent. "She's leaving town soon. Told me she would let me know when he was born."

"That explains your reaction to Declan."

"There was more with Declan. I just can't explain."

"Jamie?" I asked him. I had seen it in Joey's eyes. The connection. The surprise. I wasn't sure at first but then I got it. It made sense. Something about Declan reminded Joey of Jamie.

"Yeah something like that."

"So a son," I said.

"I don't know what to do Adam," I replied.

I whistled between my teeth softly. "Joey I can't imagine not seeing one of my boys ever but I can't imagine how Joy is going to take that news if you decide to tell her."

"This thing with Ria only lasted two weeks. As soon as Joy started wanting to have a baby I broke it off."

"You know you don't deserve her," I said honestly meeting Joey's eyes across the table.

"Yeah, I know."

We walked back to the elevators carrying the coffee cups with us not speaking to each other. I had given up Joy for him. She had given up me. Suddenly I was pissed off about it too. I wouldn't have my boys I reminded myself if this hadn't happened. I couldn't imagine not having them. We rode the elevator back to the maternity wing. Outside Betsy's room Joey took my arm.

"You won't tell Betsy or Joy will you?" I asked. "I had to tell somebody Adam. It was eating me alive."

"God no. I won't tell either of them." If I told Betsy she would be pissed enough to tell Joy. I wouldn't be the one to break her heart.

I opened the door and walked back into Betsy's room. The mood hadn't changed. Declan had been taken to the nursery. Betsy wanted us to leave. She wanted to be alone. I really didn't think it was a good idea. The nurses convinced us to leave though. I could call later and see how she was.

Joey drove us home in silence. I sat in the backseat. I kept picturing her face. I wanted to at least kiss her good bye. She wouldn't let me near her. Joy hugged her before we left. Joey hugged her and kissed her temple. She had clung to Joy. Joy had offered to stay with her for the night but she insisted that she wanted to be alone. I didn't know what else to do.

I asked them to drop me at the farm. Noah calling to me. I told him I would be home soon. Pop needed to take care of the animals. He nodded his sweet head. Trusting. My son trusted me. His mother no longer did. I walked to the barn and watched them pull away taking him with them.

### Joy

It was nearly 9:00 PM and Adam hadn't returned to the house. I tucked Noah into bed after reading several books to him. He always hooked Joey and me into reading more than a couple. I kissed his brow several times ruffling his hair I stepped away from the crib and turned off the light. His nightlight kicked on illuminating the room with a soft glow.

Joey was sitting on the front porch when I found him. I had the truck keys in my hand. I told him I was going to the farm to check on Adam.

"Do you want me to go?" He asked.

"I can do this. Check on Noah in a bit if you don't mind."

"I'll go inside so I can hear him," he said.

He kissed my forehead and slipped in the front door. I walked to the truck and climbed behind the wheel. I drove across the yard to the lane and turned right heading towards the farm. I parked the truck in the drive and hopped down. Wearing sneakers and capris and a tight fighting knit shirt over my rounded belly much more comfortable than I had been earlier when we were at the hospital. I walked to the barn. I called Adam's name. No response. I walked back to the house. I opened the door and called to him. He wasn't there. I stepped to the porch and looked in the distance. I knew where he was. I went into the house and grabbed a flashlight. The sky was getting dusky. I didn't want to trip and fall.

I headed across the field toward the woods. I found an entrance where the bushes were less thorny. I flipped on the flashlight and walked through them. I shined the light at the ground and walked down the path towards the water the faint trickling sound greeting my ears already. I called Adam's name. He responded.

I walked into the clearing that surrounded the watering hole surrounded by nature. Beautiful wild flowers. Stones and a hillside where water cascaded into the water below. It was peaceful. I knew this was why he sought this place. He was looking for peace.

"How are you?" I asked him.

"You shouldn't be here. What if you fell?"

"I'm fine," I told him walking directly to him.

I put my arms around him and held him to me. He rested his head on my belly awkwardly. His arms around my waist.

"She didn't mean it. She's hurting."

His big dark eyes turned towards me. He was sitting on our rock. He pulled me into his lap holding me tighter in his embrace.

"She meant it," he said.

"I'm so sorry this happened. I'm so sorry you are hurting. That she is hurting."

"Me too," he said resting his forehead against mine. "Joy it feels so good to hold you in my arms. I just want to feel this and not the pain." His voice broke on the last few words.

I cupped the back of Adam's head. I held him to me. I kissed his jaw. I didn't know what else to do to ease his pain. I loved him so much. I didn't want him to hurt. I wanted to ease his pain.

His hands pressed into my back. Adam pushed back from me. His eyes. His big beautiful dark eyes intense and full of longing met mine. His head tilted towards mine. His lips covered mine tentatively at first. Then the kiss changed to one of passion and hunger. My hands went up to caress his face. Breathless we pulled back. Our foreheads touching again.

"We can't do this Adam," I said.

I wanted to so much. His hands went to my ass holding me to him so I could feel what I was doing to him. He was hard. I closed my eyes.

"Do you know how long it's been?" He asked hoarsely.

"Since you've had sex?" I asked uncertainly.

"No, since I've had you," he replied unsteadily.

"The last time I closed my eyes Adam," I declared with all the pain and longing inside me. "You love me in my dreams every time I close my eyes."

He pressed me tighter to him. Adam kissed my neck. "You're mine Joy," he whispered in my ear.

"Always Adam."

He rose to his feet with me still wrapped around him. He held me for a second before he allowed my feet to drop to the ground gently.

"I will walk back with you. Is Noah tucked into bed?"

"Yes," I replied.

He put his hand on my lower back just above my ass. His fingers intimate on my body protecting me as he guided me back through the woods. The flashlight guiding the way.

*The next day*

*Betsy*

I called the house early and talked with Joey. I asked that Joy come alone to bring me home from the hospital. I knew I was killing Adam. I didn't know how to bring myself out of this funk. Deep down I knew it wasn't his fault but I was hurting and I was angry and he was the one I wanted to hurt because he had signed those damned papers.

The sad part was I didn't even want to hold Declan. I blamed him to some degree too. My innocent little baby was not at fault either. I just hadn't gotten to the point where I was willing to accept who really was at fault or that no one was at fault. Eventually I knew I would have to forgive Adam. I just couldn't do that right now. I was too angry. I couldn't accept that he signed the paperwork granting permission to take my uterus to save my life. He had taken my ability to have more babies. I was too young for this to happen.

The nurse made me climb into the wheelchair. Joy started to hand Declan to me.

"Could you carry him?" I asked her.

"Hospital regulations won't allow that," the nurse replied for Joy.

She looked pained that I had asked her to carry my son. I took him. My eyes were glued to Declan's innocent face. He was an intriguing combination of Adam and me not just Adam like Noah. The crazy hair and full lips were definitely Adam and most likely his eyes were going to be Adam's as well but the rest of him like the shape of his face, the nose, the high cheekbones reminded me of myself. I pressed a kiss to my son's brow.

When we arrived outside I immediately handed him back to Joy. I got out of wheelchair and climbed into the truck leaving her holding the baby. She sighed heavily. Joy buckled Declan into his car seat. She took the other items from the nurse and put them in the back seat behind her side of the seat. She climbed behind the wheel.

We were quiet for a while. She kept looking at me out of the corner of her eye but she didn't say anything.

"Go ahead," I finally said.

"It isn't Adam's fault or Declan's fault for that matter. How long are you going to punish them?"

I felt the tears well in my eyes. It was harsh. True but harsh.

"You don't understand," I snapped.

"Don't I?" She snapped back at me. "I think I can understand to some degree. I've lost two babies. You can't have anymore but you have two healthy beautiful sons. I will be happy to share any I have with you just as you've shared with me."

"I need time." The words were broken and choppy as they came from my mouth.

She shook her head. "You need to be turning to Adam not pushing him away."

I know. I huffed and looked out the window. Later when we pulled into the drive we hadn't spoken to each other anymore. Joey is who met us in the drive practically running out the front door. He took Declan from his car seat after helping me from the truck. I walked in ahead of them leaving them to take my son and my other things into the house.

### Joy

Inside Adam was standing in the kitchen door looking in the direction of the staircase.

"She walked right by me. Didn't acknowledge me," he declared. "Maybe I should move to the farm until she feels better."

"You will do no such thing," I told him forcefully. "Your son needs you. She needs you."

"Joy is right Adam. That is the worst thing you could do," Joey put in his two cents worth.

We had our hands full with two kids and Betsy not wanting to help with either of them. Luckily Joey was nuts about Declan. I still hadn't figured that one out. He never wanted to put him down. The crazy fool was always talking to him and smiling at him. Feeding and changing him. Noah sometimes joined in and the two of them would snuggle with the baby in the recliner talking to Declan like he understood every word that they were saying to him.

Adam and I stood in the kitchen doorway a lot while we were fixing dinner watching the three of them in amazement and awe. It was too cute. Betsy was depressed. She still hadn't forgiven Adam or Declan.

### A few days later

Joey met me at the doctor's office on the day of my ultrasound. We were so excited to see our baby on the screen to see that it had all the required parts. To count the finger and toes. To see if it was a girl or a boy. Adam was still saying girl. He kissed my forehead before I left for work that morning and whispered in my ear that he couldn't wait to see the video and pictures tonight of the little girl who would look just like her momma. God help us all if it was a girl. She would be spoiled rotten by the two grown men in her life Adam and her daddy. She didn't stand a chance.

Joey held my hand and waited while the technician put a glob of gel on my belly. We watched the screen come to life with our baby's image. I gasped at the features that really did seem to resemble my own. I know we were only looking at an ultrasound but she did look a great deal like me.

"She is you," Joey agreed with the thoughts going through my head.

"She?" The technician said.

"Can you tell?" Joey asked. His voice was soft and husky. Joey who was usually loud and booming.

She moved the wand around on my stomach. We saw fingers and toes. A long skinny leg. The curve of her spine. She pushed a little on my belly.

"There she said. He's right. You are having a girl."

Joey smiled at me although there were tears glistening in his eyes.

"A baby girl. Adam was right. One who looks like her beautiful momma." He said lifting my hand to his lips. He pressed a kiss to the top of my hand.

She printed the pictures of the ultrasound for us to take home. She gave me the video too. Everything was perfect with our little girl. Her name was Stevie after Joey's dad. If she had been a boy she would have been called Stephen Luke but since she was a girl Stevie was her name.

After dinner we sat in front of the television with Noah on Adam's lap. Declan in Joey's arms. My ultrasound video on the television screen watching the image of the baby floating around the screen.

"Noah that is Joy's baby that is inside her tummy," Adam told his son. "Her name is Stevie. She will be coming out to live with us in a few months."

"My Joy Joy not having a baby," he said petulantly.

We all laughed. I heard Betsy's laugh too. We turned our heads to see her sitting on the bottom stair watching from a far.

"I had to see it too," she said quietly. "You two can't spoil her," she said specifically to Adam and Joey.

"Like hell I can't," he said. "She's our little princess. Right Adam?"

"And Noah it will be yours and Declan's job to help us protect her and take care of her. Okay?"

"No," he responded. "My Joy Joy not having a baby Stevie."

We all laughed again.

Joey looked at the baby in his arms. "Declan my little buddy. It's all up to you. You will have to protect my little princess cause I don't think Noah will ever get over that his Joy Joy is bringing another baby into the world."

### Chapter Eighteen

*Joy*

As it turned out Noah became very protective of Stevie when we brought her home from the hospital. At her birth her daddy was the first person to hold her after they cleaned her up. Betsy was second. I knew then the healing was in process. Betsy was getting better. It had been a long hard road for her coming to terms with not having more children. Not blaming Adam or Declan any longer.

Noah was concerned when Stevie would cry. He wasn't like this when Declan cried. We all found it funny that little Noah would try to comfort the baby. Soon she became *My Stevie* and I was no longer *My Joy Joy*.

If Noah wasn't fawning over her Daddy was holding both her Declan in his big arms. I thought for sure he was going to drop one of them. At times it looked like Stevie was laying on top of Declan in his arms. I just shook my head at him. He was crazy about the kids. If he wasn't holding her Adam was. She spent very little time in her crib.

The blonde haired beauty with my darker skin and big green eyes had won over the men in the family. Betsy and I just rolled our eyes. We were going to have our hands full with this little girl and these men. It wouldn't be long before Declan was a sucked in by Stevie as well. He just needed to grow up a little.

*Joey*

I pulled my mail from my mailbox at work and walked to my office. Familiar hand writing on an envelope caught my eye. I knew the letter was from Ria. I shut my office door and plopped down at my desk turning towards the window behind my desk. Stevie was a month old so my son was probably six weeks old if not older.

With trembling fingers I opened the envelope. A picture fell into my lap. I picked it up between my thumb and forefinger and held it to closer to my face examining it carefully. The child in the image looked just like me when I was a baby. My son. I turned it over and looked at the back. *Joseph Chance Bonds born September 1st. 10 pounds. Twenty-Two inches long.*

Ria had given him my last name. Tears formed in my eyes but didn't spill over. I held them in check. I took out her letter and began to read.

*Dear Joe,*

*As you can see I gave Chance your last name. I put your name on his birth certificate as well. I never want him to feel like he does not have a father. I hope you are okay with that. Nothing you can really do about it if not. I wanted you to know in case he decided to look you up someday. That is something you need to be prepared for. I can't stop him from finding you when he's an adult.*

*I named him Chance because I took a chance and made a mess of things. I screwed up royally and got this beautiful boy out of the deal. I love him so much. I imagine he looks like you as a baby because he looks like no one in my family. He is gorgeous as you can see from the photo.*

*He was born a week early thank god since he was such a big boy. I could barely breathe during the last few weeks of my pregnancy. Everything turned out fine. He was healthy. He is a sweet baby. A great sleeper.*

*I don't really have anything else to tell you. I promised you a picture. It took me a while to figure out what to tell you. What I wanted to say. I don't know if I will send you more pictures of him. Only time will tell. I think this will be it. Just know that I will love him enough for both of us. I will treasure him.*

*Ria*

The tears that I had been holding back streamed down my face as I folded Ria's letter and slipped it back into the envelope. I held the picture of my son to my chest knowing I could not hold him was breaking my heart. Finally I put the picture in the envelope with the letter and tucked it into my briefcase.

That night I drove straight to the farm to show Adam a picture of my son. He was in the field still. I knew he would be. He and Betsy had moved to the farm house a week ago. The girls missed each other so much. Noah wasn't adjusting so well either so we ate dinner each night at the farm so we could tuck Noah in bed the four of us together.

Adam stopped the tractor seeing me walking towards the field. He climbed down. We were hidden by the barn. I handed him the envelope. He looked at the picture and read the letter. He looked at the picture again. His face was filled with emotion when he grabbed me with one big arm and held me to him.

"I'm sorry man. I know your heart must be breaking."

I sobbed while Adam held me trying to come to terms with the fact that I would never know my son. I didn't even know where they were. I had a postmark, nothing more. With my tears dried our arms around each other. Adam and I started walking towards the house.

"Don't you have more work to do?" I asked.

"Nope, not tonight. My friend needs me," he said.

"Thanks man. I love you Adam."

He stopped walking and looked at me for a second a long and hard look. "I love you too Joey," he declared.

### *Adam*

### *Age 55*

There are times in a man's life that determine his path in life. There are moments that he never forgets. Feeling Joy's stomach with our child growing inside her has been one that has never left my memories. It is forever burned in my brain. I have tried to block out the unhappy memories that surround Joy and losing her. Those moments that have caused me great pain.

Through the years Joy and I continued to meet in the woods usually just to hold each other. Then Joey died. Joy couldn't do it after that for some reason. Usually Joy and I would just talk or hold each other. A couple of times we did make love again. Every time we left the woods I always told her. *You're mine Joy.* She always responded with *Always or I know.*

As the kids grew up I watched them get closer and closer becoming more and more like us. Noah always watching out for Declan and Stevie and the two boys protecting her like I knew they would. I couldn't love that little girl more than if she was of my blood as my father had loved Joy.

So many of my best memories are of the kids growing up. Simple things that stick out in my mind. Stevie her long blonde curls flying about her face as she chased after the tractor across the open fields. Hearing the women screaming at her from the barn yard afraid she would get hurt. I stopped the tractor to catch her up in my arms. She was six I think. I could see both mothers glaring at her from the yard because she hadn't listened. I knew she was in trouble. Maybe if I kept her with me on the tractor long enough they would forget their anger.

She had wrapped her slender arms around my neck and I was lost.

"You're in trouble little girl," I told her.

She looked over her shoulder. "I just wanted to see you Pop and take a ride on the tractor."

"You know they don't like you riding with me."

"You'll protect me," she said having all the faith in the world in me. Stevie kissed my cheek and I knew then and there that those two women no matter how pissed off they were would not touch her. I couldn't let them. It broke my heart when they spanked her little bottom.

I knew the ladies meant well. Stevie was constantly chasing after Declan and Noah. She was a wild child running barefoot through the fields. She didn't listen well. She was stubborn like her mother and her father. She was quiet until she got pissed just like Joy. She stole my heart the first time I held her in my arms with her fuzzy blonde head knowing she was just like her ma. She continued to make my love grow with every minute of her life.

The day Declan and Noah brought her home with the skin of her upper arm taken off Declan crying his eyes out I wanted to knock their heads together. They were always letting her do dangerous things that she shouldn't be doing. She had fallen from a tree. It could have been much worse.

The boys had been trying to get away from her tired of her traipsing after them. The women defending the boys. I just saw that my little Stevie was hurt. I wasn't seeing reason. Later I had apologized to my sons when I realized that they were just as upset that Stevie had gotten hurt as I was.

Seeing the three of them cuddled in one bed asleep. Usually Stevie draped across Declan with Noah and Stevie bottom to bottom. They all had to be touching somehow. They just wanted to be together most of the time. Made my heart swell with pride that we had produced three beautiful children.

Until Joey and I wanted to take the boys fishing. Stevie was supposed to go shopping with the women. She sat on the picnic table pouting. I watched her watch us put the gear in the truck. I had already said something to Joey about taking her. The women said no. He agreed if we could convince them we should take her. He was no more capable of seeing her sad like this than I was. Stevie preferred fishing to shopping. She wanted to be with Declan and Noah than without them. The boys groaned when we told them what we wanted to do.

"Declan look at her," I told my ten year old son. "Do you really want to leave her behind?"

"Yes," he had replied angrily.

Joey and I had struggled to hide our laughter.

We knew part of the problem was she always caught bigger fish than they did.

Then our little Stevie turned thirteen and boy did she grow up. She turned into a beautiful young lady. Unfortunately Declan didn't like the boys in their class pointing that out. Betsy and Joy both made several trips to school to pick him up for fighting because some boy even ones who were friends of his had made a comment about Stevie's newly developed chest.

Declan was uncomfortable with this new side of Stevie. They no longer spent as many nights together we noticed because Declan didn't want to. Poor Stevie didn't understand. She still stayed at the farm but didn't share a bed with the two boys anymore. Probably a good idea we all thought.

Those kids thought I wasn't smart enough to figure out they were skinny dipping in my spot in the woods. I hadn't caught them. I didn't really want to. I just saw them heading that way. I knew what they were doing. I was a kid once. I had been there with Joy more times than they could count. If I wasn't sure about the two younger ones I was sure of Noah. He would keep them out of trouble. As long as the three of them were together I was sure they were safe. Someday I would tell them I knew.

Then the unthinkable happened. Declan and Stevie started dating. They were sixteen years old. I knew. Joey knew that the feelings they had for each other weren't like the feelings that Noah and Stevie had for each other. The ladies were shocked. They didn't spend the time with the kids that me and Joey did. They didn't see the transformation take place from protector to puppy love. I guess that is what you would call it. They thought it was real.

At eighteen when they broke up I saw Stevie falling to pieces just like her mother had when she lost our baby. She lost weight. She stopped eating. I was lost. I didn't know how to help her. She wanted to cut herself off from the rest of us but I wouldn't let her. I made her come to dinner even though I knew her heart was breaking. I held her close when she got there and just as tight when she left.

Declan was going through the same thing. We had to pick him up from jail more times than I cared for drunk and disorderly or fighting. Living in a small town the Sheriff didn't press charges. Joey finally set him down and talked to him. Declan was just as heartbroken about their breakup and not sure what to do with himself.

Betsy was good with Stevie helping her through the heart break. Joy and Stevie had a strained relationship starting when Stevie hit the teenage years. They were too much like each other. Joy loved that little girl with everything in her but also feared her. Feared loving her for losing her. Sometimes she kept Stevie at arms' length letting Betsy do the nurturing. It broke my heart.

Then we got ready to send Stevie to college and for the first time in years Joy started having panic attacks. We were worried about Joy. Worried about Stevie. Worried about Declan. Hiding the panic attacks from the kids became our focus. She didn't want them to know. She didn't want them to see what she considered her weakness. We snuck off to the woods more during that time because she needed me.

Joey received a graduation picture from Ria of their son Chance. Again, I got to see the picture of the son that he had with the short affair he had with Ria Jackson. It was only the second communication he had with Ria about Chance. Chance apparently had talked about contacting Joey. She wanted to make him aware he was thinking about it. It didn't happen.

I wasn't sure how often he thought of the child that was born the month before Stevie. The son he never got to know. The boy looked exactly like Joey at that age. He was attending the University of Cincinnati. If Declan had his way that is where Stevie would have gone where she might have run into her half-brother.

One day out of blue Betsy and Joy showed me and Joey a Facebook picture of Declan handcuffed to Stevie's bed. The kids were twenty-five.

"That is Stevie's bed isn't it?" Joey had asked peering at the picture a little closer.

"Yes," Joy answered uncomfortably.

"Does he have on clothes?" I asked scratching my head.

"I'm not sure Adam," Betsy had answered my question.

"Oh boy. He doesn't look happy. How exactly did she manage that?" I had asked puzzled that she had gotten the best of him.

Noah had gone to Stevie's and turned him loose. Declan was none too happy. That was the start of things. The start of them getting back together. Making Joey a happy man. Just before he fucking died on us.

I looked across the field. I had been sitting on the tractor letting it idle for God knows how long thinking about my life. How things had turned out. Why they turned out the way they did.

Joey had been gone for several years. I missed the son of a bitch. My chest still felt heavy when I thought about him. A stroke took him from us suddenly when he was just fifty years old. Betsy gone for over a year. Brain cancer taking her. It was just me and Joy walking on egg shells around each other trying to figure things out.

I saw Stevie standing in the drive. A set of dark haired twins and her triplets two dark haired like her twins and one silver haired with curls like her surrounding her. She waved to me. I returned the wave happily. My grandsons were the light of my day. Another car pulled into the driveway. My other daughter-in-law Lexi. She got out of the car and removed her baby Tierney or Tie form his car seat propping him on her hip. He was a red head like his mother. A beauty like her too with her big doe eyes. Then Sophia got out of the car. The only granddaughter who looked like Noah's first wife taken from us too soon but then there wouldn't have been Lexi.

Joy liked to say that everything happened for a reason. Maybe she was right. Life without her had been one big fucking heartbreak but I couldn't imagine my life any different because then I wouldn't have Noah, Declan or Stevie or these amazing grandchildren they had given us. My boys were lucky. They were with the loves of their lives.

It was time now. I had waited for a respectable time after Betsy's death. I had the blessing of both of my girls Lexi and Stevie. Noah was indifferent and Declan well he would have to get used to it. After I walked the kids to their cars. Kissed them all goodnight. Dusk was just beginning to fall over the farm. I had left a note on Joy's nightstand asking her to join me in the woods.

I walked to the woods unsure of what to do when I got there. I waited. Then I stripped down and jumped naked into the water and I waited a little while longer until finally I saw the light of her flashlight. Then I saw her. She stopped when she saw my clothes on the ground. She looked at me.

"What are you doing Adam?" She asked softly.

"Waiting for you."

She was afraid. If she could feel the beat of my heart in my chest she would know how terrified I was too.

"You're mine Joy," I told her hoping to ease the tension in the air.

Tears welled in her eyes.

"Always," she finally replied.

"Get your ass in here with me," I told her roughly.

"Adam what about the kids?"

"Declan is all we have to worry about. The others will be fine. We'll get him through this. We deserve this Joy. It is our time," my voice was hoarse. "The girls told me so."

She turned off her flashlight. I could see her smile in the fading light. She laid the flashlight on the ground. It had been years since I had seen her naked. I waited impatiently while she slowly removed her clothes. My breath caught in my chest when she dropped her shirt to the ground. Then her pants followed and Joy stood before me in matching pink bra and panties and time seemed to stand still. She wasn't a fifty something year old woman she was seventeen again. I felt like a kid myself as I licked my dry lips.

"Hurry up woman," I said urgently.

She unclasped her bra let it fall to the ground. Her hands grasped her panties and slid them to the ground with her pants. She stepped out of them and naked she walked towards the pool of water. Joy dove head first. Her head breaking through the water's surface close to me.

She was still as beautiful as she was when she was seventeen. Her face smooth but for the fine lines surrounding her green eyes. Her long dark lashes spikey with water. Her mouth full and luscious. Her lips pink and waiting to be kissed. Her silver blond hair with just a touch of gray in the front slicked back with water.

I cupped her face in my hand and pulled her to me. "I love you Joy," I told her.

She turned her head into my hand. Her eyes closed and I took advantage. I tipped my head towards her and my lips covered hers. Her hands went to my waist pulling me the rest of the way to her. I knew that we would be together now. Nothing could come between us again. Joy was where she finally belonged in my arms.

*The End*

## About the Author

Lee Wardlow has written several books in the Point Royal series about a small Ohio fictional town based loosely on her own experience growing up in small town Ohio.

## Pointe Royal Series Books

*You Were Born for Me- Declan and Stevie story*

*Never Leave Me – Noah and Lexi story*

*I Knew I Love You When – Codi and Jessie's Story*

*For Always – Scarlett and Ben's Story*

*I Will Always Love You – Tegan and Rhett's Story*

*What She Wanted - Part 1 of Joy's Story*

*What She Got- Part 2 – Joy's Story*

More Pointe Royal Books to follow:

*At Last – Shawn Martin's story*

*Title to be Determined – Chance Bonds story*

Her first book was **Welcome to Hell: Rediscovering First Love** about another small town in Michigan known as Hell. It is a very real town with Lee's own special fictional twist.

Lee spent most of her adult life in one form or other being an IT Geek. A career she continues until writing, her passion and obsession can be a full time career. She is artistic as well as having a love of reading other author's Romance novels.

She is the proud mother of one daughter Caitlin with two beautiful grandsons Gavin and Jase. Life is never boring with them in her life. She has been with her husband Bill for eleven years. They have two four legged babies Dixie and Evi the spoiled pups.

*Contact Lee at Lee.Wardlow.12@gmail.com. She would love to hear from anyone reading her novels.*

*Acknowledgments*

*Front Cover Photo @ MAXFX – Fotolia / Dollar Photo Club*

*Read on for excerpts from other books by Lee Wardlow*

*You Were Born for Me*

**Chapter Two**

Reaching the ER, our parents were waiting in the visitor's area. My sneakers squealed as I came to a halt beside them with Noah hot on my heels. Our strides were vastly different in length as he was seven inches taller but even he was having difficulty keeping up with me. Anxious didn't describe my mood at the moment. The word wasn't strong enough. Our mother's looked pale and worn. Our father's looked stern and worn. I would say their usual expressions for the fathers when dealing with the children. I was just plain panicked. They better tell me something quick.

"They're moving him to a room now Stevie. We decided to wait on you and Noah here," Declan's dad Adam (Pop to all of us kids) told me before I could ask any questions. "We've been with him most of the day. We're all exhausted and heading home. He really just wants to see you."

"You aren't coming up?" I asked glancing at the four faces I had loved my whole life like four equal parents. We had backup parents I thought, suppressing a chuckle. Just in case anything happened to one set we still had the other set. It really wasn't that funny.

My ass had been tanned by both mothers for one thing or another but neither father had been able to bring themselves to discipline me. My pseudo siblings had taken the heat for me on more than occasion unable to allow me to accept the punishment for the crime that I had committed. I was the baby. I was the girl. If they could prevent it the men in the family protected me probably to my detriment. Although I could shoot pool and didn't run or fight like a girl. Somebody needed to explain the benefit of that to me? The mothers were always trying to figure that one out as well.

Declan's mom Betsy (Momma to all of us kids) put her hand on my arm. "We are exhausted sweetie. Like Pop said he really wants to see you. Why don't you go? Noah will go with you if you want."

Noah was gazing at me with the same dark lashed eyes that were so like Declan's. They had their father's eyes. Agreeing without words that he would go to see his brother if I needed him. I shook my head no. I just wanted to get to Declan. I needed to see for myself that he was all right. I needed to touch him. To kiss him and know for sure that everything was right with him. Hugs were exchanged and Noah and the parents left the hospital. I didn't wait to see them walk out the front doors.

A nurse, Ella Marks at the ER desk gave me Declan's room number. I knew her well. She was older than me. More like our mother's ages although she treated me like an equal not like a daughter. She smiled with understanding when she gave me Declan's room number and told me she hoped Declan was better soon. I thanked her and was walking the halls to the main elevator. I punched the button and waited. My heart beat furiously in my chest with need to get to Declan's side. To see him to know he was all right. The ding startled me when the doors opened in my face. I climbed aboard the car and pressed the number for the floor to take me to Declan's room. It was a small hospital but it seemed like an eternity before I reached his floor. Another ding of the elevator let me know I was on his level. Then the doors opened.

I took a deep breath and stepped into the open corridor. I walked down the hallway and past the nurse's station towards Declan's room saying hello to the nurses at the station there. Some I had worked with and knew well. Some I had not. They were busy charting so I didn't stop for conversation. With a hospital this small I at least new their names and they knew mine.

I opened Declan's door and slipped into the room quietly. His lights were low. The walls the usual light gray making the room dimmer. Curtains pulled shut. Machines beeped softly letting me know that his heart was not missing a beat.

His hair nearly black against the white pillow was mussed. His face usually dark from working outside was pale. His eyes closed. His long dark lashes lay against his cheek. I had to fight with myself to keep from caressing his cheek. His mouth so tender and relaxed begging me to kiss it was slightly open like he was sleeping soundly. I had seen him like this. I knew the signs. I was going to slip into a chair and wait until he opened his eyes but like he knew I was there his eyes flew open just as my butt was about to hit the seat beside his bed.

"Hi," he said startling me. His voice sounded drained.

"You just don't know how to behave do you?" I asked him. Always joking with him but the words came out on a sob.

"Don't cry Stevie. I'm okay." He grabbed my hand in his holding on tight so I couldn't leave not that I wanted to. I wasn't going anywhere. I thought about telling him he could loosen the grip he had on my hand but the words would not come out.

"You don't look so good."

"Come here," he said indicating for me to come closer. I stepped to the bedside. He scooted over in the bed and lifted the covers. "Get in," he whispered.

"Against regulations, "I told him trying like hell to hold back the tears. Trying like hell to avoid being that close to him even though my heart was saying *crawl into bed with him.* Too intimate. Losing myself in him right now when we were both vulnerable would not be good.

"I don't give a damn. I want to hold you." He sounded so vulnerable. I couldn't deny him. The look on his face desperate and wanting. Needing me close to him. "They told you didn't they? You know what happened?" He asked his voice deep and husky barely above a whisper.

I could only nod. His heart had stopped. The what if's kept playing through my mind as I stared at him still holding the sheets up for me to get into bed with him. What if his heart had not started? The scariest what if of all.

I had been trailing after Declan Moore since we had learned to walk. He had been my first and only lover. He knew me like no one else. I slipped off my shoes and slid into bed beside Declan. His arm wrapped around me instantly holding me tight against the length of his body in the small hospital bed. My cheek rested against the strong wall of his muscled chest.

"You look cute in the hospital nightgown." I teased him.

"Shut up," he said good-naturedly. "Want to see what's underneath?"

"Now I know you're all right." I rolled my eyes.

I could feel the beat of his heart hard where it rested just below my hand in his chest. I moved my body so that my head was resting more to the center of his chest.

"What are you doing?" He asked looking down at me.

"Listening to your heart," I responded, taking comfort in the sound that filled my ears. He was going to be all right. Declan squeezed me tight in his arms. Then his hand was in my hair, tangling in the mass of curls tied back in a ponytail. He understood. He would have had the same reaction.

"I love you Stevie," he said. His hand large and warm was caressing my back again.

"I love you too Declan," I responded in kind thinking we were talking about the kind of love we had for each other before we decided to take it to the love/sex type love we had shared as teenagers. We hadn't whispered these words to each in any way since we were eighteen. I felt relief that we could say them to each other again.

"No Stevie, I mean I love only you always and forever," he clarified determined yet husky. "You are it for me. I guess you always been." His voice was so soft and gravelly causing warmth to spread up my spine. My heart clenched in my chest. "You have been driving me crazy since we were sixteen years old. I never got over you when we broke up. That kind of I love you Stevie."

I couldn't look Declan in the face. I couldn't see what emotions were playing in his eyes. I thought he was confused. I thought he was having a reaction to the events of today. Sure we would probably always have strong feelings for each other but revisiting that time was not a good idea. He had to be frightened. A near death experience brought out all kinds of baggage that he was trying to deal with right now because he was scared but did he really love, love me? Like a forever kind of man and woman love?

"Declan, we tried that once," I finally said. "We nearly destroyed each other and our family." He was quiet not responding to my statement so I continued. "I think you are confused. Maybe scared because of today?" He squeezed my body tighter mashing my breasts into his chest. His bandaged hand came around to encircle my body with his other hand to hold me so that I couldn't possibly break away. I wouldn't leave him. Not now. Not when he needed me.

"I don't think so Stevie. I know how I've been feeling before today. I just didn't know how to tell you. I didn't know what you would say. I didn't know how you felt anymore."

*The same way you feel but it's crazy. It will never work.*

"I would say that you are a crazy boy. No more talking tonight. TV? Holding each other? I can do either."

Any option but this conversation would be better. This conversation scared me. Right this minute after the fear of possibly losing him forever, I couldn't deal with this discussion. I was perfectly content if he wanted to just hold me. We were gathering comfort from holding each other. Declan and I had always been that way even as small children. You would find us snuggled together with a blanket thrown over us as tight as we could be wrapped in each other's arms with Noah sometimes on the other side of me butt to butt offering his protection to both of us as the big brother.

It was different for Declan and me. We were usually clinging to each other for some reason, for comfort? We just weren't good together as lovers.

*God help me.*

I didn't know what to say to him.

"Are you off tomorrow?" He asked.

"You know I am."

"Can I stay with you?"

I raised my head slightly looking into his black eyes. "Sure," I answered uncertainly.

*What the holy fucking hell?*

"The doc advised I not be left alone for forty-eight hours after being discharged. I don't want to go to the folks place," he explained. "Noah and Moanie's place is too small."

I laid my head back against his chest. My foot rubbed absently against his bare leg. Forty-eight hours alone with Declan Moore. Something we hadn't done since we were eighteen years old.

*Oh hell.*

*I hope he knows what we are doing because I sure as hell don't.*

****

The next morning at ten o'clock Declan was released from the hospital. Dressed at eight a.m. sharp. He was more than ready. I wasn't sure I could hold him until the doctor released him he was so anxious to get home. The only thing that kept him there was I had the keys and he had no other way home. For a while I thought he might be considering walking. His pacing was getting on my last ever loving nerve.

Declan and I slept in each other's arms the entire previous evening mushed together in the small hospital bed. Between bouts of sleep we had whispered of good times as kids. I had carefully avoided further conversations about love. We had not been so intimate since our teenage days. To say that I had missed Declan would have been an understatement. In the light of morning I pushed the feelings back into my subconscious where they needed to stay for my sanity.

The ride home in my Jeep was a quiet one. Neither of us saying much. Unsure of what to say. The words of love from yesterday were not repeated. The quiet country landscape passed by in a blur as I steered the vehicle towards my home.

To make Declan's walk shorter, I pulled the Jeep into the garage. Usually I kept the Jeep in the driveway because the one-car garage was tight. Declan hopped out of the car and walked around meeting me at the garage door. I was still unsure of this arrangement but could not have told him no. We stepped into my dining room from the garage.

In Declan's home the garage led into the laundry room then into the kitchen. I liked his layout better. My carpet in the dining room would become worn over time if I continued to use the garage for the entrance.

In my home where he would stay for a few days he made himself at home. Why wouldn't he? It wasn't like we were strangers but still it surprised me at how comfortable he was with me after all these years apart. We had only seen each other at Sunday dinner or hanging out with mutual friends at an occasional party. Family events. We weren't exactly awkward with each other but we weren't as friendly as we once had been. Most importantly, we hadn't been alone like this in years.

To anyone looking at our relationship since I returned from college it appeared we had returned to being friends. Declan teasing me when we were hanging out with mutual friends. Me giving as good as I got. Then there were the pranks. Those seemed to be never ending. But when Noah told me Declan was hurt...all I could think of was getting to him and touching him and ensuring that he was all right. Those weren't friendly feelings I was pushing down into my subconscious mind. Those were intense, physical feelings. Feelings that I kept trying to hide from him, from our family from our friends from everyone.

*Dammit, he was getting under my skin.*

Finished with straightening in the kitchen. I went to the living room to check on Declan. Broad powerful shoulders filled my recliner where he lay back in a settled position of complete relaxation. He looked comfortable. His long dark eyelashes fluttered against his cheeks as he fought to stay awake. He was exhausted. I could see it in his eyes. His white tee shirt stretched across his muscled chest invitingly.

*I could run my hand down his chest to his six pack abs to his....never mind.*

*Mind out of the gutter girl or we aren't going to make it past tonight without jumping each other.*

"I'm going to take a shower," I told him a bit shakily.

*A nice cold shower to cool my libido.*

He had showered at the hospital.

His eyes fluttered open. "Okay," he responded scrutinizing my face.

*Why?*

"Want the remote?"

"Sure."

I handed Declan the remote careful not to let our fingers touch and headed off down the hallway towards my bedroom taking the hair band out of my long silver blonde hair while I walked. I could feel his eyes following me but I refused to turn and look back at him.

*Eyes forward.*

*No looking back.*

*Too much temptation in the other room in the form of one hot sexy male.*

Safely, in my room decorated in neutral colors simple like me I stripped throwing the scrubs I had worn to the hospital the day before into the laundry basket. Buck naked as the day I was born I stepped out of my walk-in closet to the main part of my bedroom. I looked up and saw Declan standing in my doorway gazing at me with a dark longing in his eyes. He no longer looked tired.

However, he did look like he wanted to go to bed. I tried covering myself with my hands.

"What are you doing Dec?" I asked my voice rising several octaves in embarrassment.

"Looking at you," he declared huskily.

I was frozen to the spot. Goose bumps raised on my perpetually tanned looking skin. I wasn't a fair person. My mother was dark skinned too. We had this beautiful café au lait skin tone from her mother who was a product of a black mother and a white father. The generations had left us with lighter skin than my great-grandmother and the silver blonde hair and greenish/hazel eye color of my Nordic looking great–grandfather. It was an odd – exotic combination that had always made me stand out in a crowd.

I was teased as a child for my unusual looks the reason Declan had always been in fights protecting me. Noah always comforting me. Telling me to pay the other kids no attention. Both telling me how beautiful I was. The parents had raised the boys to protect me. Declan had taken it a step further by falling in love with me. Now, well now he was just being damned rude invading my bedroom while I was naked.

"Leave Declan," I finally said finding my voice, still unable to move though. Our eyes locked on each other.

"Make me," he challenged me.

His broad frame filled my doorway. If I found that I could move where would I go? He was blocking my exit. The hand that wasn't injured rested above the doorway. The injured hand was draped casually across his abdomen. Feet crossed at the ankles. He looked cocky and sure not tired like he had sitting in my recliner only minutes ago.

"Dec, I'm too tired to play games."

"I'm not playing anymore. This is for keeps. I meant what I said last night Stevie. I'm all in forever. I want only you."

I rolled my eyes at him. One hand covered my crotch. One arm covered my breasts not covering much at all really. What the hell was I going to do? The fire of desire and anger filled my belly. He wasn't going to beat me. He wasn't going to win this round. I wouldn't give in to him but I wouldn't make it easy on him either.

8

I dropped my hands to my sides. A sharp gasp escaped him. His arms dropped to his sides as he anticipated my next move. I marched over to him and tried to shove him out of the way, stark naked while he towered over me.

*Talk about intimidating.*

"Get out of my way. I'm taking a shower," I snapped angrily.

He yanked me roughly into his big arms. Our faces just inches apart. "Tell me you don't feel this too," his words a whispered breath against my cheek. "Look me in the eyes and tell me you don't."

"I said I'm taking a shower," I replied as coolly as I possibly could even though my body's response to him was a dead giveaway. He just had to look closely for the signs. I was shoving against his chest with my hands trying desperately to get him to let me go.

Reluctantly he released me.

I walked naked down the hall to the bathroom. My round bare ass swaying with more swagger than I felt. I heard his muttered *fuc*k beneath his breath whether he meant me to or not. I slammed the bathroom door behind me with more force than I had intended. My hands were trembling. I could not let another us situation like before destroy what we had rebuilt. It was too important to me to our family as a whole unit.

And dammit, I didn't think I could survive Declan Moore again. He damned near tore my heart out of my chest the first time. There had been times during that period crying on Moanie's shoulder that I wasn't sure that I would endure after what had happened between us. I had lost weight dropping two sizes until my collarbone and ribs were visible. I couldn't sleep. I couldn't eat. It wasn't until I left for college that I started to bounce back. I knew Moanie had been worried about me. Our parents were worried about me. Hell, I was worried about me. I couldn't do this again with him. I just couldn't.

I turned on the water and let the temperature adjust before I flipped the knob that switched the flow to the shower head. My brow was wrinkled in concentration not really seeing with my eyes what my fingers were doing of their own volition running back and forth through the spray of water while I waited to be sure the temperature didn't change. I pushed the shower curtain slightly aside and stepped into the tub.

My knees joined my hands in the trembling department. Tears hanging on the edges of my eyelashes waiting to flow over if I would let go. If I allowed myself to cry I might not stop. The stress of yesterday and the feelings he was reviving in me that I couldn't seem to push back into oblivion were taking their toll. The water poured over my head drowning all thoughts away. All thoughts but Declan. He wasn't going to go away. He was stubborn. I knew this. I knew him. Did I really want him to? The words kept tumbling through my brain. My heart. Last night asleep in his arms had felt so right.

Hands resting against the shower wall in front of me my head beneath the spray of water the tears finally let loose. They flowed freely down my face. I didn't hear Declan enter the bathroom. So absorbed in my misery of loving him losing him and almost losing him forever my body shook with the sobs that I didn't notice the flutter of the shower curtain when he pulled it back and climbed in behind me. He turned me around and pulled me into his arms. Declan just held me tight against his naked body. The water now making both our bodies' slick.

"Don't cry," he told me roughly in my ear.

I couldn't stop. Dec held me while I sobbed out my pain. I had remained strong yesterday because I had no choice. Today the overwhelming need to break down to finally let the realization that Declan could have died sunk into my system nearly brought me to my knees. I loved him still. Did he know this?

"I'm okay Stevie," he said drawing me tight against his warmth and his strength comforting me. Kissing the top of my head.

With his good hand, Declan took the loofah off the rack in the corner. Gently he nudged me. I grabbed the soap bottle from the same rack and squirted it for him onto the loofah. He rubbed the loofah down the front of my body whispering words of comfort while his hand cleaned me. I stood there like a child taking comfort as much in his soft touch as I had in his embrace.

"Turn," he said.

I did as I was told. Giving Declan my back he began rubbing the loofah in slow sensual circles around my spine then down over the curve of my ass. I gasped feeling his fingers brush against the tenderness between my legs where only Declan had known me. Declan and my vibrator. My purple dream. That is what I called my vibrator. Only they knew how to satisfy me. Warm tingles filled me. Then his hand trailed down the backs of my legs.

"Rinse," he ordered.

I stepped under the shower head and let the water rinse the soap bubbles from my squeaky clean skin. I felt him reach around me. I heard noises but didn't know or care what he was doing until I felt the shampoo hit my scalp, a gentle tug on my arm pulling me away from the water then Declan massaging my scalp working the soap into a lather.

"This isn't easy with one hand," he chuckled. "Especially with all the hair you have."

"I can help." I started to raise my arms and he shoved them away.

"No fucking way," he barked teasingly.

I almost moaned out loud as his fingers caressed my head in slow circles working the soap through my thick, long hair.

"Fuck Stevie. You moaning like that…rinse before I throw you up against the shower wall and fuck you so hard you can't stand up or walk for a week." His voice was hoarse and breathy igniting a fire between my legs.

I opened my eyes just a slit and glanced down at Declan's body. His cock long and thick was hard and ready. I knew. I ached for him too but couldn't make the first move. It would be a mistake. Our families wouldn't survive another Declan and me, love fest. Hell, we wouldn't. We were too volatile. I couldn't take the heartbreak afterwards. I stepped under the shower to rinse my hair. Maybe just sex, one night of pure, hot lust and lovemaking?

I had missed him. I had missed his touch. I was dying inside without him. I knew this from spending last night in his arms. I also knew that one night would never be enough and more than one we would start to fight then we would destroy each other just like before.

Declan reached around me and turned off the water. He shoved the shower curtain aside cold air touched my skin causing goose bumps. Dec grabbed the towels that were hanging on the hooks on the wall. He wrapped one around me and the other around his waist. The towel didn't hide the fact that Dec still had a raging hard-on. Standing on the cold tile in my bathroom, we were facing each other. He took the towel I was wearing and released it baring my body to his eyes. With the towel in his hand he began rubbing across my body drying me.

"Glutton for punishment?" I asked him in a soft teasing tone.

His dark eyes twinkling when he gazed back at me he said, "Gives me an excuse to touch your body."

Then he was really touching me. My most intimate spot with the towel but still touching me. Rubbing the towel against me with the pretext of drying me but watching my reaction none the less. My face became flushed. My breathing tortured short gasps of air begging my lungs to expand but couldn't.

*Dammit Declan, I haven't been with a man since you. Since I was eighteen.*

I wanted to tell him.

*You're making me nuts. You always could though.*

My eyes never left his face. I didn't say what was running through my mind. The need to feel him inside me, to confirm that yesterday was just a bad dream put behind us was crushing me from the inside out.

Declan dropped the towel at my feet and his fingers slipped so gently into the soft folds of my body touching my center causing me to gasp all before I knew what was happening. I shivered and would have dropped to my knees had he not caught me in his arms.

"Whoa," he whispered against my cheek. "Get this thing off me Stevie," he said referring to the bag covering his bandaged hand. "I have fingers on this hand I can use to touch you with too." Referring to the fact that his entire hand was covered with bandages except for the tips of his fingers.

I did as he asked removing the bag from his injured hand with my own trembling fingers letting it drop to the bathroom floor. The fingers of his injured hand were suddenly trailing up my back leaving tingles of pleasure in their wake. While his other fingers were sliding in and out of my body. Then his mouth covered mine. His tongue slipped between my lips exploring and hungry. I sucked on his tongue and bit his lower lip causing him to growl deep in his chest.

"Bed," he whispered against my mouth.

I nodded in agreement. Declan scooped me into his arms with an urgency that told me he wanted me as much as I wanted him. He had broken through my fears and reservations for now. Later I would have to put those walls back up. Later I would keep him at arm's length again. As if that was even a possibility my heart was insisting as he laid me softly on the bed covering me with his big strong body.

Oh god, the warmth of him pressed into me. Every inch of his slick body was rubbing against me as his mouth took mine in a possessive hot kiss. His hair tickled my face as he leaned into me. Tongues tasting each other. Lips splendid and excellent pressed against each other's lips getting hotter by the second. His fingers were twisting my nipple and caressing my breasts until I gasped into his mouth making him chuckle.

"Fuck I want you so damned much," I told him my nails raking his back leaving marks on his otherwise smooth skin. "Inside me now Dec," I ordered in a raspy harsh voice so filled with desire that it sounded unnatural to my ears.

Declan centered himself over me. I could feel the tip of his cock teasing my body. Then he slammed home filling me with a powerful thrust that caused me to gasp his name out loud. I was so tight and he knew it.

"Damn Stevie, you feel good, so fucking good," he said breathlessly stroking in and out of my body with his. He stopped moving.

*No. No. No. No. No.*

"Are you on the pill? I don't have a condom?"

"Remind you of another time?" I asked softly into the skin of his neck. I nipped him there making him growl in frustration.

"Yeah," he whispered huskily against my temple. He still hadn't moved within me.

"Yes I'm on the pill."

He began moving inside me again. The sensations of him sliding in and out of me were like something out of a dream. Too good to be believed. My eyes closed to take in all the feelings engulfing me. He was balanced on one forearm his good hand was holding my leg opening me further to his forceful thrusts.

"Open your eyes Stevie," he ordered. "I want you to see who is making you feel this way."

"I know Declan," I answered.

*There has never been anyone else but you.*

I wanted to keep my eyes closed. I didn't want to see the power or the depth of passion and emotion in his dark eyes but I couldn't help myself. I opened my eyes as he commanded and found myself drowning, hitting rock bottom and bouncing back with an explosion that started in my clit then the walls of my vagina joined the party tightening around Dec with spasms of ecstasy until my whole body seemed to shiver to completion.

"That's my girl," he groaned against my mouth. "I'm right behind you."

He thrust several more times into me until his body went rigid and shook with the force of his own orgasm. His body ejaculating into mine with an energy that left me wet and weary. Sweat covered his torso dripping onto mine. Declan collapsed onto me crushing me into the mattress but I didn't mind. His lips were pressed into my neck while he whispered words of love following our lovemaking.

No my mind was saying. Not love. Only sex. I was already putting the walls in place. This could not happen again no matter how good it felt. He felt, I corrected myself. We couldn't do this to each other again.

Declan rolled over onto his back. His thick black hair was mussed in all the right ways making him sexy as hell. I wanted to run my fingers through it. His chest still rose and fell a little heavier with the exertion of our lovemaking but was slowly returning to normal. His eyes were staring at the ceiling. His mouth tight. He had something on his mind......

*Available at Amazon*

*Welcome to Hell: Rediscovering First Love*

Chapter Twenty

Labor Day came and went with cooler weather, thank you Jesus because I still had no baby. My due date September 4th passed without event. Guess what? A baby? *Oh. Hell. No.* I was starting to think the child was never coming out. He liked it inside his mommy. He liked torturing me. Two days past my due date on Saturday a familiar band of tightness around my stomach started in the early morning hours. Oh yeah, I remember that feeling.

Eighteen years had passed since I had given birth but I was fairly sure the pains were contractions and not the Braxton Hicks kind either. These contractions were keeping me awake. They were hard gripping pains in my belly and back like a steel belt was constricting my body making it difficult to breathe but they weren't consistent.

Glancing at the clock I saw that it was one o'clock in the morning. I crawled from the bed trying not to disturb Kerry in the process. He remained sleeping. So peaceful, hair across one eye. Arm flung behind his head. Gosh, I loved this beautiful man. I tip toed like an elephant (large, pregnant woman) out of the room and down the hall to the staircase leaving him to rest.

On my way down the steps I heard the bedroom door open where Adin and Brad were sleeping. We both peeked at each other through the alcove me above and her below until we saw each other. Then Adin's footsteps resumed lightly as she padded barefoot on the wooden steps. I waited in the stairwell for her to catch up to me. Adin was wearing Brad's boxers and a tank top. Briefly, I wondered what Brad was wearing?

Without make-up and her hair pulled back in a loose ponytail she looked as young as Keegan which disgusted me. I felt like a big hot pink whale in my hot pink nightgown, hair a mass of wavy black curls uncombed flying about in different directions. Damned unruly hair. So very unattractive. So very large.

"What's wrong?" She whispered when she reached me.

"I think I'm in labor," I told her resuming my descent down the stairs expecting Adin to follow.

"What do you mean you think?" She asked trying to stifle a yawn. She did follow. "Don't you know?"

"It has been eighteen years," I told her grumpily.

"How far apart are your contractions?" She asked.

"Seven or eight minutes. Ten minutes," I responded. "Not close enough."

"Where are you going?"

"Walking."

At the front door I slipped on my sandals awkwardly. Remember large belly, me not so graceful? I had left the sandals there earlier this evening and grabbed my hooded sweatshirt from the hook. In Michigan, evenings in summer anytime could be cool and we were having a cold snap right now. The low was fifty five tonight. It was September after all.

"Do you know what time it is?" Adin asked incredulously.

"Of course I do."

She followed me outside, down the porch steps to the sidewalk. "Why are you going for a walk?" Adin sounded more than exasperated with me while she slipped on a sweatshirt and flip flops trying to keep up with me while dressing on the move.

"Because walking is supposed to speed up your labor. I've been very uncomfortable for hours…hell I've been uncomfortable for weeks Adin. I'm ready."

She followed me down the sidewalk to the gate, which led to the sidewalk that paralleled the street in front of our house. Adin held the gate for me. I stepped through.

"Uh Gab don't you think you should wake Kerry?" She asked uncomfortably.

Trying to dissuade me was not going to work. I glanced at her and growled. "Either walk with me or go back inside. I want to let him sleep as long as possible. God knows when I'll need to go to the hospital. There is no sense in both of us being awake now."

I was a woman with a mission. This child was coming out soon come hell or high water. My pace was quick for a woman with my belly girth.

"I'm not letting you go alone." I was a fast walker normally. The pregnancy hadn't slowed me much. Adin was a slow walker and was having difficulty keeping up with me. "Hey, you walk pretty fast for someone your size. Could we slow the pace just a bit? It is one o'clock in the morning."

As if she had read my thoughts. Adin was getting winded. Hell, I was getting winded. Stopping in my tracks, I turned and glared at my sister who nearly crashed into my back. You know it was okay for me to think this but not okay for anyone else to think or say the words out loud.

"What?" She asked shrugging her skinny-assed shoulders. She really didn't know why I was so upset with her. Usually stupid comments came from Gemma.

"Someone my size," I groused.

"Sorry. I didn't realize pregnant women were so sensitive."

"You sound like Gemma." *That got her! Point Gabby.*

"God please don't compare me to our little sister."

Adin followed me to the corner where we turned right putting greater distance between myself and my parent's home. My mind was focused on walking. Our footsteps echoed in the emptiness of the street. There were few streetlights here so the darkness was eerie making me jumpy as was my sister at every little noise.

"Do you know where you're going or are you just fucking winging this? What if they wake up in the house and we aren't there?"

Stopping again, with a glare at Adin, I replied, "Go back so they will know where I am or shut the fuck up and keep walking."

Potty mouth remember? Pain making it worse.

Her hand was on my back. Comforting me? No, she had placed it there again to keep from crashing into me. "Why are you so crabby?" Adin asked with disgust.

"What the fuck Adin!" Fists clinched in frustration. Anger evident on my face. She had no clue what it felt like to be this big with a baby. Being so uncomfortable you can't sleep. Indigestion. Heartburn. Needing to pee constantly. I just want to hold my baby. I felt myself tearing up. "Because I am enormous. This child doesn't seem to want to come out. He kicks and I pee myself a little." *Gross, I know.*

"I can't sleep. I can't get comfortable. He has his own Cirque De Soleil performance going on my belly and if there is anything I can do to help it along believe me I will be fucking helping it along." The last few words were punctuated and forceful. "When you and Brad have a child you will understand."

"I can't wait."

I glanced at her quickly. Adin wanted a child. Were they trying already? Her head bowed. She was watching the ground while we trudged along.

We walked to the next corner where we turned right again. My plan was to make a complete circle around the block, which was exactly two point three miles. That should take a good forty minutes I estimated. I had walked this block many times with either a sister or Issy.

Then I thought I would sit on the porch for a while to see how my labor progressed. I was restless. I wanted the baby to come and come quickly. I was tired of being exhausted. I was tired of being uncomfortable. Getting up two to three times a night to pee was testing my patience. I was out of fucking patience. I was emotional. I was a crazy woman ready for this to be over.

I was ready for the sleepless nights because my baby was waking me to eat or have its diaper changed not because I couldn't breathe or couldn't find a comfortable position.

"Gabrielle?"

"What?" I asked huffing at the exertion of carrying around extra weight that I wasn't accustomed to, all of it in front of me no less. My steps were slowing down. The physical exertion was taking its toll. *Maybe this wasn't such a good idea. Holy hell.* I slowed so I could catch my breath. Adin appreciated it. I could tell from the expression on her face but I wouldn't give Adin the satisfaction of letting her know I had slowed for myself

"Thank you," she said in a voice that expressed her gratefulness.

I nodded. Let her think I slowed for her. Secretly I smiled to myself. At the next corner, so close I could see it. We were half way around the block.

"Are you afraid?" She asked. Her voice sounded small and uncertain.

"No. Just eager."

I tripped on a crack in the sidewalk, not watching where I was going. It was pretty dark. No moon. A little cloudy with just a few twinkling stars.

"Careful," my sister told me grabbing my arm to steady me. "I wasn't talking about giving birth. I was talking about Yancy dying."

"Oh." I really didn't want to talk about our mother's impending death. I looked intently at my sister's face. Difficult to see in the darkness but I could see enough and I could hear plenty. She needed to talk. Sigh. Dammit.

"Well."

"Yes, I'm scared. I can't imagine...Oh" I stopped and grabbed my stomach cradling it in my hands. That contraction was intense, harder than any others that I had experienced so far. When it passed I started walking again then I replied, "I can't imagine not being able to call her on the phone or walk into her bedroom...see her propped up in bed, smiling. She still smiles even when the pain is so excruciating, even so sick. I can't believe her strength," I marveled. My heart clenched at the thought of losing her.

Adin agreed.

We walked further. Further from our parent's home. Just a few more feet, a few more steps and I had to stop again. Another contraction gripped my body forcing me to take deep breaths until it passed. *What the hell?* I kept my panic to myself not wanting to alarm my sister. The warm wetness of my water breaking with another very hard contraction startled the hell out of me.

"Ah shit," I was holding my sister's hand while the water continued to gush from me. At least it felt like it was gushing. A waterworks of amniotic fluid pooling at my feet soaking my sandals. *I love these sandals too.*

"What?" Adin asked unable to see my feet.

"My water broke," I replied softly trying to keep calm. I looked at her. She looked back at me and we both looked scared out of our minds.

"You can't have the baby here," Adin said panicking.

I laughed out loud imagining me lying on the sidewalk, feet in the air, vagina bared for all of Hell to see and Adin telling me to push and then another contraction nearly brought me to my knees. A gasp of pain escaped me and I was no longer laughing. I grabbed her hand holding on for dear life.

"You're hurting my hand," Adin squeaked. I was grasping her hand so tightly in mine while I breathed through the pain.

"Let's walk," I told my sister in a less than calm voice, when the pain eased guiding my sister back towards the direction we had come closer to our parent's home. Closer to help.

We had gone more than half way around the block. We were a little over a mile from home and I didn't want to waste any time getting back. I could feel pressure building in the region of my pelvis. Pressure telling my body to push this baby out now. Another contraction stopped our forward progression.

"I want to push," I told her.

"Don't you dare," Adin squealed. "Walk faster." She was trying to push me then she was trying to pull me as I resisted against the pain in my belly and pelvis.

"I can't walk faster," I shouted at her nervously. I breathed through the pain.

In this part of Hell only Pop and Yancy's house was close and it was still a good mile away. The next house was a mile in the other direction. Adin held my hand with one hand and had her other arm wrapped around my waist guiding me trying to push me, pull me along while I had a pretty damned hard contraction.

"Stop that," I yelled at her shoving her away from me.

"Breathe," she said. "Why the hell didn't you stay home?"

"I am breathing dammit. I'm sorry I didn't stay home. How the hell was I supposed to know that walking a mile would cause the labor to really speed up?"

"Your contractions were probably more regular that you realized dumbass."

"Adin, I'm not fucking stupid," I shouted. "I think I know how far apart they were."

Maybe I really didn't. I was so exhausted. *Hang on little one. You can't come out now.*

"Didn't Keegan come quickly?" We started walking again. My sister was concentrating on each step that we took that would ultimately bring us closer to home. Pushing me. Pulling me closer to someone who could help us. We weren't really getting far. We looked like we were playing tug of war with me as the rope. It was like an episode of *I Love Lucy.*

"Yes she did but not this quick. God, we have to stop." I gasped for air trying to take as much as I could into my lungs. I wanted to squat down and pop this kid out onto the sidewalk the pressure was so great in my pelvis. I was biting on my lip, gritting my teeth. Trying anything to get through the pain.

"Why?"

"Because I'm having another contraction," I nearly screamed. Bent over at the waist. Hands on hips, legs spread apart, panting. I waited for the pain to pass then I said, "Keegan came within two hours once the contractions started. The doctor was surprised at how quickly she arrived considering she was my first baby." Babbling was a nervous habit of mine. "I can't go any further."

"Gabby, don't do this to me." My sister sounded terrified. "I can't deliver your baby here on the sidewalk."

I really couldn't go any further. I wasn't kidding when I said I wanted nothing more than to push.

"You better leave me here and go get Kerry and the car." I was scared now because I really, really wanted to push. It was taking all my strength to not push.

"I'm not leaving you here alone." I could tell she thought I had lost my mind from the look of total shock on her face.

"Who the hell do you think will bother me? We live in Hell. Run," I told Adin fighting the urge to push while I tried to take another step. One more step closer to home between contractions but not nearly close enough. I could only manage baby steps. "Or you," I emphasized poking her shoulder, "will be delivering this baby on this very street."

All alone on the darkened street, I watched my sister run to the corner lose a flip flop, stop to get it and then thought better of it.

She proceeded to kick off the other flip flop before she picked up speed and disappeared into the darkness. I hadn't had to repeat myself. There was no way she was going to deliver my child on the street corner in Hell. I tried to take small steps but the pressure was intense. I cursed myself for taking this walk. I cursed Kerry for making me pregnant. I cursed God at that moment for making women have babies instead of men. I gritted my teeth against the pain.

The contractions were so far apart weren't they? I hadn't been concerned about taking the walk when I finally got out of bed too frustrated to sleep. Or so I had thought. Now I wasn't so sure. Maybe they were closer than I had realized? Maybe Adin was right. *Damn, I hope she's faster than she was in high school or I will be delivering this baby myself.* Breathing deeply I kept taking small steps. Minute, little, tiny baby steps. It was something but not much.

At the corner where Adin had turned I held onto the stop sign for dear life and breathed deeply struggling against the intense pain and the urge to push the baby out. The pain almost taking me to my knees. I struggled against it. I wouldn't allow it to get the best of me. *Hold on, baby boy. You cannot come out to play just yet. Mommy isn't ready. I'm all alone.*

The pain ended and I took another small step. The car, Adin's SUV screeched to a halt beside me and I was grateful to see Brad and Kerry hop out of the car as the tires barely stopped rolling. Adin was behind the wheel and Keegan was getting out of the front seat.

"Are you insane?" Kerry yelled at me wearing nothing but jeans, no shoes, no shirt.

"I wanted the labor to speed up," I said in my defense trying not to cry.

"Well you did that," he said helping me to the car, his strong arm wrapped around my waist guiding me. Hell who was I kidding? He was holding me up.

*Available at Amazon.*

8

Made in the USA
San Bernardino, CA
07 April 2015